# SUSAN ARDEN

Author of *Collared for a Night*
and *Tempted by Trouble*

# DRAGON HEART

# CRIMSON ROMANCE

F+W Media, Inc.

Published by
Crimson Romance
an imprint of F+W Media, Inc.
10151 Carver Road, Suite 200
Blue Ash, OH 45242. U.S.A.
*www.crimsonromance.com*

ISBN 10: 1-4405-8697-7
ISBN 13: 978-1-4405-8697-2
eISBN 10: 1-4405-8698-5
eISBN 13: 978-1-4405-8698-9



Cover art © 123RF/Linda Bucklin and iStock/CURAphotography

This book is dedicated to Crimson Romance, for in giving me a start to writing series romance, you opened a door in my imagination and a place to pour out my heart. Each step, you have helped me become a better writer…a more adept feeler of feelings. *Namaste*, Tara and CR team.

A special thanks to Julie Sturgeon. For giving more than a polish. You worked your magick. Superstar editing!

"Matilda said, 'Never do anything by halves if you want to get away with it. Be outrageous. Go the whole hog. Make sure everything you do is so completely crazy it's unbelievable'…"
—Roald Dahl, *Matilda*

# CHAPTER 1

Shay paced along the terrace railing of her family's villa, her anger churning, and gazed across the shimmering bay of *Rio Tejo*. Since she wasn't about to drown herself in the bay below, a bucket of alcohol would have to do the trick of deadening her desire to scream bloody murder.

She poured two fingers of cognac into a tumbler and downed the amber liquid fire, burning her tongue and throat as she swallowed.

"Holy goddess!" She slammed her glass down on the marble-topped wet bar and sucked in a breath.

The scorch to her senses didn't equal the fire racing along her nerve endings. Her calf muscles and hamstrings twitched as she reeled in her rage. She was on the verge of shifting into a roaring hot mess. As an unmated leopardess, she was hell-bent to be free—remain free—and roam the untamed Lisbon countryside far, far away from the lecherous stare of a man old enough to be her grandfather.

She raised her eyes to the starless sky, awash in pearlescent light. The nearly full moon lit up the horizon, creating a craggy silhouette of the mountain range off in the distance. The jagged cliffs and a baying wolf reminded her of home. Her heart lurched. In a few days, the moon would be full. The red moon. Her twenty-second.

"What are you doing out here and alone?" Drake asked, coming up behind her in the noiseless fashion he'd perfected as her bodyguard over the past few months. His tone was rough and she flinched at the gravelly voice that triggered a shiver deep in her belly—the type of arousal that made her skin prickle.

Dammit! She hated when he did that—appeared out of nowhere. How long had he been standing there? Swiftly, she straightened and stripped her face of all emotions.

"Are you here to read me the riot act because I forgot to check in with your team of jailers?" Shay poured another liberal serving of cognac into her glass.

"Tempting as that is, it's not the reason I'm here," Drake replied from the shadows. He must have stopped behind her.

What the crap? Fine. She wasn't going to seek Drake out and ask his help…or could she? Jesus Freaking Christ, if anyone might have an answer it would be him—with his all worldly experience. The man marched to his own drum doing as he damn well pleased. He most likely already knew her dismal future. As her parents' chief security advisor, Drake O'Connor was privy to everything— why not this monstrosity? But surely, if that were true he would have mentioned something. Done something to prevent her from being forced into a marriage with Dimitri Necrodemas, a decrepit leopard shifter who required heart pills, a blood pressure cuff, and a nurse. God, she'd never seen so many prescription bottles before. Forget Viagra—he'd keel over. God, what if the ancient shifter actually did take some sort of sex stimulant? *Gag. Me.*

Dimitri spent his days as Chief Justice for the Council of Mediterranean Shifters, and she'd spent the last four hours in his insufferable company, listening to him drone on about what he owned and whom he controlled.

It was all dubious, self-inflating drivel in her opinion, considering the recent unchecked bands of uncontrolled shifters ravaging the area and one in particular: the Unruled, a violent gang who tagged their black spray-painted symbols on surfaces all over the city here and across Europe. The violence roused fear in shifters and humans—yet humans were taking action. They were indiscriminately locking up shifters—innocent and guilty alike— in detention centers from which there was no return.

"I just came back from Dimitri's dinner party. And since we're playing twenty questions, I didn't see you there. Were you playing hooky?" she asked, fighting to focus on the waves lapping at the stone pilings below, and put aside the bomb Dimitri had dropped. A marriage proposal that sounded more like a business deal and he'd assured her once, if not fifty times, how much power she'd wield as his wife. *Who the heck cared?* She'd be a glorified nursemaid and a political pawn if she were lucky. The other possible choices were unthinkable.

"I was outside patrolling his grounds. Necrodemas has his own security pack working the interior of his home." Drake remained directly behind her when he answered—which unnerved the bejesus out of her. She felt the heat from his body permeate the space around her, inciting her leopardess instincts—so much so, her skin began to tingle as racing darts of arousal hijacked her intelligence.

"Home? More like mausoleum," she muttered, on edge for Drake to do something besides talk to the back of her head. Hell and high water would come before she turned around to face him.

"His art collection is impressive," he retorted. "Did you see the relics Necrodemas claims to have acquired?"

"Questionable pieces of art. I'm not impressed by Dimitri's prowess in black market finds."

"You weren't there to debate fair trade. These upper echelon shifters are your people, are they not? Better get used to rubbing elbows with his kind," Drake replied.

"How can you say that?" she hissed and would have stared daggers at him if he were standing next to her. Dammit, she shouldn't be peeved at Drake...it was her parents who set this roulette wheel in motion.

"Not my opinion. I go by your family's directives, and how they acquire support isn't part of my job duties."

"Support? Is that what this is called?" She'd been introduced to Dimitri years ago and met him again earlier this summer in Monaco. Only then, he'd been categorized as a business acquaintance of her father's—not even a true friend. Dimitri came from new money and ceaselessly flaunted his power and privilege. Yachts, a vineyard, homes—he referred to himself as a successful entrepreneur. Hah! That was rich. He used charities as tax shelters to appear magnanimous. On paper, she supposed he was some woman's dream. In person, he was her nightmare—and she was her family's pawn in a political power grab.

On the surface, of course, they sent her on this trip as an envoy from the States to jockey a continental union between Europe and North America. She was supposed to show the people back home how much *fun* it was to vacation abroad. This was nothing short of propaganda to leverage shifter support, a joke that ran counter with her apolitical aspirations.

"The Barclay team has set its sights on acquiring Necrodemas's support for the upcoming election as you well know."

"Dimitri is not on any team of mine," she snapped and rolled her eyes. "Or should I have that tattooed on my forehead? Haven't you heard anything I said this week? I feel like I've been talking to the walls." Heaven help her. Did Drake also take her for some trophy wife to be bartered off? Anger rocketed through her body, a cutting force she tasted on her tongue, bitter and razor sharp. Now with her emotions bubbling upward, she was no more than a hairsbreadth away from shifting. A low rasping snarl crept up her throat.

"Could have fooled me," he retorted.

"You are so not amusing, Mr. O'Connor!" She fought to keep watching the waves instead of releasing the brunt of her frustration on Drake.

"Careful, your claws are showing, kitten."

*Did he just call me "kitten"?*

"And you might get scratched, if that's your best comeback." She chugged her cognac, and then chucked her crystal brandy snifter onto the rocks below.

"Don't make promises you can't keep." He chuckled, the sound of his voice a sensual whisper that glided over her skin like satin and aged whiskey. "Is that some far-fetched challenge? 'Cause if I recall correctly, I won the last one. I'm so sick of not being taken seriously," she said.

The sound of Drake's rumbling laughter crystallized her anger and the butterflies in her stomach swarmed. And yes, her actual leopard claws did feel uncomfortably close to the surface for all the wrong reasons whenever she was around him.

Unlike earlier tonight, when she sat alongside Dimitri and ice water flowed in her veins. All evening Dimitri had licked his lipless mouth like a hungry toad while gazing at her chest, her mouth, her legs…the man was beyond revolting. Her skin didn't just crawl, it shrank. *Never, ever,* she vowed silently, gripping the metal rail so tightly her knuckles hurt.

How was this possible in the twenty-first century? She'd graduated early from high school, gone to Duke, double majoring in business and accounting, and graduated *summa cum laude.* At her parents' insistence, she toured the south of Europe as a graduation gift and fully expected to return home and begin her career as an audit specialist in financial due diligence for Sternberg and Fink, the largest accounting firm in Colorado. So far she'd snagged a large investment company as a client. According to her plan, the custom-built furniture she'd ordered had been delivered to her Denver office suite. A cocktail party was scheduled for next month, when she'd officially accept new clients for the firm.

Instead her mother was excited about throwing an elaborate engagement party. Numb, she'd listened to Mother's ideas for hand-engraved invitations, wedding dates, and going to New York for fittings for her *trousseau*. More like a set of straightjackets in varying pastel shades of discontent and dissatisfaction.

Drake broke apart her mental rumbling when he picked up and corked her bottle of cognac.

"Why so upset? This isn't like you, Shannon. Everything went according to plan. Did something happen tonight?" he asked in a voice that rubbed her the right way. "Necrodemas's driver brought you back without a problem. Correct?"

He better not think for a second that she was onboard with this marriage plan. Holy hell! Was everyone bonkers? But he was correct—she was close to losing it. Badly.

She inhaled, trying to siphon her outrage. "You mean that black Hummer caravan. I rode in some version of a tank that smelled of stale liquor, cigars, and only God knows what else." *Unlike Drake's motorcycle.*

"From my vantage point, I don't have a complaint. You're safe." He came up next to her at the railing, and his arm brushed against hers, unleashing a high-powered zing that tore through her and made her fingertips tingle. "His team delivered you back here on schedule, without a hitch."

"That's not how you travel," she lowered her voice, "is it?" A strange spiraling in her belly expanded as their arms continued to touch. She slanted him a glance, encountering his chiseled profile as he gazed outward through his ever-present wraparound sunglasses. Even at night he had them on, preventing anyone from tracking his gaze. Probably part of his Navy SEAL training; whatever it was, he appeared ready to rock the world on go.

"*Mea maxima culpa.* I never should have let you know about my ride." Drake didn't look over at her, saving her from encountering his panty-melting smile that accompanied his arrogance. It was a wonder he'd ever unbent enough to let her ride on the back of his motorcycle, even if it had taken a bet she could escape his security crew to force the moment.

"Don't be sorry. It was the high point of this so-called journey. I won't tell…if you don't."

"You know my lips are sealed where you're concerned. I've got your back." Abruptly, he faced her, holding up his fist, and of course, his full lips were quirked, displaying his customary and very irritating smirk. Stubble littered his square jaw, and tonight like every night, he wore a black shirt, stretched snug over his broad shoulders. He looked good enough to eat.

*Not helping, Shay!*

Bumping her fist to his, she swallowed and nodded. "I hope that's not just talk. I have heard enough cheesy promises to last a freaking lifetime or two."

"Shay, I've always been here for you. Ever since we were kids."

She sighed and nodded. Yep, they did go far, far back; so much so that Drake always seemed to be lurking in the shadows of her mind. He was her older brother Shawn's good friend who then had the audacity to serve under her father. A freaking Navy SEAL on some covert mission in the Persian Gulf that neither he nor Dad talked about except in whispers and winks. What would Drake do with the information of her pending marriage—did it mean nothing to him?

Abruptly she stopped her mental wrestling match and spoke her mind, letting go of the railing. "My parents have called me home," she began, testing the waters of what lay between them.

"I'm aware of that plan. High priority as of twenty minutes ago. So far, I spoke with your father at length. Even your mom personally telephoned me." His voice came out sounding hoarse… strained. "They expect you by Friday."

"Arrangements all made for my return? How very professional of you—are you counting down the seconds?" She bracketed her hands on her hips, jutting her chin as he lifted his sunglasses. Whoa! She was unprepared for the sizzling jolt that raced through her when she encountered his jade-colored eyes—eyes that few men possessed.

The key word being *men*—Drake's dragon ancestry shone through every one of his nuances, delivering a marked difference in her reaction. Really, it was like her brain short-circuited. That one distinction set him apart from anyone she'd ever encountered, including her all-powerful father Richard Barclay and Shawn, her only sibling. She could debate any issue with them—jointly or separately—until the cows came home and win. Not with Drake. He reduced to her a dithering, melting mess.

Standing inches away, he gazed down at her, and she felt the jagged edge of a connection that rippled through her each time their eyes met. She fluttered her lashes, the pit of her stomach knotting from his power. The roiling sensation swirled lower, making her yearn for fiery friction—something so decadent, she failed to conceptualize the specifics, only that this craving involved him.

Was he aware that he did this to her? She bit her lip, curling her fingers tighter against her hips to keep from reaching out to him. It was like she wanted to fight him and at the same time, fuse her lips to his.

"Not as of yet," he said, oddly reticent. Usually, he had plenty to say…on her behavior, way of dressing, her friends—endless volumes he shared without being asked.

She whispered hoarsely, "It's less than a month before my upcoming…marriage."

"I thought—" His head snapped upright and his eyes flashed brightly before he wiped all traces of emotion from his face. Now, he returned her stare, stoic as ever. "So you decided to accept Necrodemas's proposal. That surprises me."

"Not yet. I mean I haven't formally. That depends. Will you take me…home to finalize the arrangements? Apparently, this is more than a wedding." She sought an affirmation from him.

Leaning in his direction, she inhaled his smoky scent with her overwrought leopardess senses. *Stop, Shay. Don't be a fool…OK, don't be an even a bigger fool.*

"The jet has an engine being overhauled. It's grounded for the time being." He frowned at her from behind hooded eyes. "We need to talk."

No. They needed to kiss. Or better yet, get naked.

"Technical mumbo jumbo? Please, don't bother."

"Little girl, I'm sure you of all women can keep up with whatever comes out of my mouth."

If that included his tongue, she'd love to try.

"I'm game."

"Always rising to every challenge. Why am I not surprised?" Drake murmured.

"Well?" she inquired. "Is this about the travel arrangements or more chaperone nagging nonsense?"

Was he playing her? Surreptitiously, she sniffed the air and her mouth watered from Drake's pervasive alpha male scent working her senses. Her canines were ready to pierce her gums—a sign she was ready to mate. How awkward!

Unless she put this moment to good use.

For instance, a way out from a stifling engagement. The kind that would force the groom-to-be to break off his marriage proposal.

Her mother would have a cow if she knew the thoughts tumbling around Shay's head. According to Amelia Barclay's rulebook, a leopardess of good breeding didn't dilute the line. Her parents had talked incessantly since before she'd gone off to college about the importance of finding an *appropriate* mate. She didn't have to ask Mom to define appropriate—she could recite the laundry list of requirements in her sleep, and all of them designed to actualize her potential as an alpha leopardess so the Barclay clan would be that much stronger. Totally warped thinking on their part.

Drake was the opposite of perfect in her parents' playbook, but so far that minor detail didn't derail her from a secret and growing attraction.

At the moment, her heartbeat hammered, vibrating over her skin from the energy Drake's dragon shifter body radiated. Being this close to him was far too raw. Factor in the full moon, and both of them became the components of a chemical equation about to combust.

"Well?" she inquired.

"Never mind," he replied.

"Don't you dare *never mind* me. You're thinking something. Tell me." She held her breath, meeting his glittering stare and noting the muscle ticking along his jaw that she longed to trace, lick, and suck. His angular features could have been carved out of granite the way the dark stubble rose along his cheek, beckoning her to run her fingers over his skin.

"Just be prepared to leave. Thursday. Midnight. We'll take the latest departure, or if need be, we'll fly commercial. You and me."

"You'd do that? Deliver me and then what? Dammit, Drake! Every second of my life, you ride me about making the right decision. How is *this* the right decision? There's a freaking elephant in the room and like, what? You're just going to stand there and pretend it doesn't exist."

"You're wrong there," he retorted, his pupils transforming into entrancing elliptical versions. "From what I can tell—whenever it's just you and me, alone—it's more like a parade of pachyderms!"

She pressed up to him, proving him all shades wrong, licking her lips and watching his eyes trace her mouth. "Then don't try and play this off like it's just flirting that's going on between us.

"In case you haven't noticed, little princesses aren't on my menu."

"My, my." She laughed—not the pleasant-sounding kind. "I never took you for a man who backed away from a challenge." She wanted to take hold of his fingers and bite them. Hard.

"Don't flatter yourself. I'm not scared of you. *You* aren't my type."

She looked down at the boner in his jeans, then met his eyes. Right!

Controlling her desire to get him to own up to their mutual fascination, she spoke slowly, "Yes. I. Am. Or would you care to divulge exactly what kind of six-shooter you're packing down the front of your pants. Cowboy, sooner or later, we're going to do more than *talk*. I'm going to climb and ride you like I'm a cowgirl, breaking a bucking bronco. And you, dragon boy, are going to like it." She ended up jabbing him in the chest while panting heavily.

Drake caught her wrist and yanked her to him. His hot breath caressed her skin and her nipples peaked into points, aching for his mouth. Their gazes locked together, their mouths were inches apart, and she felt her ability to maintain control dissolve as he leaned into her. He growled, the vibration of his voice spreading fire over her skin. "Sweetheart, you're more than mistaken. That's not going to happen. It can't happen. Do you understand?" He released her hand and stared at her, both of their chests heaving.

"Says who? I'm right here. We're standing in a private villa." She undid the sash to her robe. Desperate times required desperate measures…more than desperate when he wanted the same damn thing she did: hot, screaming sex with no strings. "Look at me, Drake. I'm a woman, not a child. I grew up, in case you haven't noticed. I'm not looking for a fairy tale or a prince. I'm looking for a man who can take care of my needs."

"Get that crazy idea out of your beautiful head," he said, staring down at her with flames slipping from his mouth. "You have no idea what you're doing." His muscles flexed and clenched when he took a step closer in a move that fully enflamed her leopardess cravings. He reached for her fingers, brushing his own across her belly and she snarled in response to a sharp jolt of hunger, rocketing inside her body and landing between her legs. She needed him, ached for him to give her release.

In utter disbelief, she watched as he stopped her from yanking open her robe. Drake covered her hands with his large, warm palms and squeezed her fingers, his face a shimmering mask of lust and power. One she saw right through.

"Yes. I. Do. I want you. Don't stop this," she replied, unwilling to put aside her wanting him. The overpowering feel of his capable hands pressing down made sane thinking next to impossible

The skin of his palms sizzled over her hands as riotous sensations swirled deep in her belly, demanding relief. Her primal hunger swam in her veins and her leopardess nature crouched near the surface—lying in wait for a sign. Come on, one silly sign.

This close to the full moon, she was a click away from doing something courageous…or incredibly stupid.

The next ten seconds would tell.

Maybe he didn't realize what she wanted. "I'm offering myself to you. No strings attached."

"Fuck," he said, closing his eyes and rubbing his thumbs across her fingers, a soft fluttering caress that pulled her nerves taut.

Bingo! Jerking her hands out of his grasp, she called out his name. "Drake, please."

He flashed open his eyes—emerald swirls within his irises glinted. She fully undid her robe, exposing her completely naked body underneath, and relished the slow hiss he released. A solitary wisp of smoke spilled from his lips, curling around his head like a hazy halo.

His gaze roved down her body as a muscle twitched along his sculpted jaw. "Shannon, you're gorgeous. The most beautiful woman I've ever seen." Sparks escaped from his mouth with each word and his gaze raked her over with erotic flames. He had the power to unlock her deepest desire, setting her fantasies free.

Between her legs, her flesh pulsated to feel his touch. More…to feel him sink into her.

Talk about a scalding turn-on. Is this what it would be like to fuck a dragon shifter? Holy hell, she felt her canines scrape across her lips and a growl rise from her chest.

"Drake, touch me. All over." She licked her lips, her body trembling, waiting for him to make a move.

"Your skin is golden perfection. I could spend the night with you and never get tired." He actually stepped back. "And there's a reason why that's not gonna happen."

Her pulse skyrocketed at his refusal. "How can you deny us? Just try to tell me I'm wrong. Tell me you don't feel this pull. Tell me you're fine with me marrying another man."

"You're playing with fire. Literally and figuratively. You're a leopardess and haven't a single, solitary clue about dragon heat. This type of flame burns until you have no choice but to cross the line. Cover yourself. Now, Shannon." The swirling green in his eyes leapt outward like scorching sparks, licking down her body, and ensnaring her with a white-hot craving for sex and sin.

"No. First touch me. One time, Drake. You know you want to."

The muscles along Drake's arms turned to granite. "Shay, I only have so much willpower."

She fought to keep from roaring a mating call—not that Drake hadn't already seen her in leopardess form, just as she'd seen him as a dragon when he'd flown overhead, a silhouette against a starry sky. It was his job to protect her, and he'd been the one to accompany her on her nighttime runs. She'd already rubbed up against him, nudged her cheek along his shoulder and then they'd almost kissed—almost but not actually—the night he'd given her a ride on his motorcycle. As a full-blooded leopardess, she'd basically marked him as her territory. This crazy idea made more and more sense.

*Except for one hard-headed roadblock!*

"I'm not afraid to go after what I want. You said you weren't either. Prove it." She traced her fingertips along her belly, her gaze grazing over his dark, winged brows. His eyes were glowing now. From head to foot, his alpha masculinity qualified him as man fucking candy. She rubbed her fingers over her breasts, plucking her nipples and sucking on her bottom lip. "Wouldn't you like to taste me?"

"You can't imagine how much, but no way am I crossing this line." Even as his clearly visible erection strained the front of his jeans, Drake held himself in check.

He was off limits. To her, Drake was like a piece of broken glass she held onto, piercing her deeper and deeper until she no longer noticed the risk—only the torture of being near to him.

He was part of a draconian dragon dynasty. Good God, everyone knew they were only into other dragons. So it didn't matter how many nuclear fusion stares they traded. Didn't matter if he was the last in an ancient line almost extinct. Or so she liked to pretend to no one but herself. Ludicrous to think he'd act on their attraction freely.

"Drake," she groaned in exasperation. He was so close, yet so freaking far away.

"This isn't the type of fling either of us can walk away from."

"Oh no? Just watch me. I know you're not innocent. All those women who flock to you and your Harley Shadow. Don't you think I know what you do when you're not chewing my ass? I'm not asking to bear your children. Jesus H. Christ, Drake. One. Night." She couldn't believe she was reduced to begging. But, she reminded herself, he was her only doorway to freedom, and she was prepared to do whatever it took to break down his ridiculous resistance.

Whatever absurd scruples he had that prevented him from giving into her didn't matter. She needed his help and he was too hot to walk away from if one night meant her freedom. Even if it was one time, he had the means to unchain her from Necrodemas. Sullied goods were not acceptable to a man of Dimitri's standing. All of his wives had been untarnished. And he'd outlived all of them. She wasn't about to be the next stepping stone in that lascivious old leopard's lineup. Some unspoken and overpowering dynamic attraction lay between her and Drake. Tonight was the night to uncover why he made her feel alive like no one else did. He was her ticket to freedom. She needed him to bend.

*Maybe this type of truth will set me free in more ways than one.*

"Please, Drake, I need your help. Do me this favor. I'll never ask for another thing," she whispered, leaning closer, tingling from the way his eyes feasted on her breasts. "You could be here. Right now." She touched her nipple, then ran her fingers down, across her belly, all the way to the apex of her sex. "Inside me." Without an ounce of shame she rubbed her finger between her lips. She moaned his name, watching him watch her.

His pupils that were once slivers dilated into full black. "This isn't something you want any part of. I don't fuck like other men."

"One night," she said in a low, low whisper. "I'll ride you the way we both want and then disappear. Gone. You know I can't marry Necrodemas ... "

Why didn't Drake just cave? She wasn't asking for his help indefinitely.

"One night?" He grimaced like he was in pain. "That's not likely to happen. If I fucked you, we'd both need more. We're so close to the full moon. You know, I didn't stumble upon a leopard clan last week. Whoever mounts you would have to dish to get you through your heat cycle. You up for that kind of action?"

He cupped her breast, rolling her nipple between his fingers, and her knees wobbled from the shivering pleasure that shot through her. He bent his head and licked across her peak with his now forked tongue. Her nipples hardened as the sharp tips tantalized her to the point of snarling and she arched, forcing her peak into his hot mouth. He sucked and she felt herself melt. Christ, what would a forked tongue feel like on her clit?

She dug her fingers into Drake's shoulder. *Think, dammit. Say something convincing.*

"We could use protection."

Like her, he was on a mission to avoid a forced union, one he didn't discuss. All she'd gotten out of Shawn was that Drake was ex-communicated from his family in Oregon after he'd joined the military. His clan occupied some massive compound in the Cascade Mountains and some private castle in Spain. All hush-hush. Of all the people she knew, he'd understand her plight.

"Unless you're on the pill, dragon body temperature doesn't permit me many options, to be blunt. Condoms are a no-go."

She stiffened, her mind reeling.

"We come from different species. The chances are infinitesimal. I've never heard of leopard and dragon mixed children."

His fingers traced down her ribcage and lingered at her navel as his gaze flicked down the front of her robe. He cracked a smile and nodded. "Right as always. There aren't any dragon-leopardess offspring."

"Case settled. Get undressed and let me fuck your brains out."

He exhaled a serrated breath, gripping her hips and drawing her forward to him before he stopped and held her aloft, not an inch separating their hips. "Shannon, you're breaking me."

"I'm going to. I promise, if it means we'll be naked." To see him tempted, almost torn made her want him even more…as though her hunger had nothing to do with seeking a solution. He was a decadent doorway. One she wanted to cross, if not possess extemporaneously.

His breath came out hot and made her nipples tighten. She sniffed the air and licked at the scent of endorphins coming from his body. She glanced down and flashed her eyes back to his face. What did he have housed inside his jeans?

"Do you have the slightest inkling of what you're asking for… I'm an alpha dragon, Shay."

Even if her experience was nil, sex was sex. Sure Drake was frickin' hot. Sex with him was probably off the charts…but still sex. Wasn't it?

She stammered, "We're not mating. So you're wrong about lasting out the full moon. We can do it once. We're hardly two shifters falling head over heart hard. No one said anything about you claiming me as your mate. As long as you keep your fangs clear of my neck, we're kosher. Okay?"

He stared back at her like she'd just announced she had the power to walk through walls. "Shannon, there are still irrefutable issues. This is a no-win situation for both of us," he whispered, closing his eyes as though that might sever the bond between them.

"Why?" she demanded. "Because you served under my dad a million years ago. So what? And now, who gives a rat's ass if you work for my parents? I'm not looking for forever, just once."

He opened his eyes; fire and heat swirled in their depths. "Is that what you're telling yourself or trying to get me to believe? What would you have me do? You don't understand the gravity of us in bed. We'd be on the run. Penniless."

"I get that this is going to torrentially rain on some plans. I don't care about the money. I've got my own destiny."

"Kitten, with your Prada purses, designer lattes, and chauffeur driven Bentley, how far do you think you'll get without your daddy's credit card? Ever made your own bed, fixed your own meal…shot a gun?"

Her eyes widened. "Stuff. Details. I'm not afraid."

"Your parents—hell, the justice councils on two continents would hunt us down. Not to mention Shawn and Richard. Collectively your brother and father will go ballistic."

What Drake said had a sliver of truth, but eventually Mom and Dad would get over her not marrying Dimitri. And the justice councils didn't matter diddly-swat. She and Drake weren't breaking any laws. In six months, this would blow over and la-de-da, everyone would forget about this idiot idea of using her as leverage to join forces with the Mediterranean Council. Let them find another leopardess to broker—someone who actually had political aspirations. She would be happy, single, and have her accounting career. And Shawn, he'd understand. They were close as siblings—felt each other's life force.

No way she'd marry Dimitri. This was her life—her way. A one night fling and *voilà*. That was her *happy ever after*, minus the lovey-dovey goo. Getting hitched—in love or not—was so not her plan. Leave that to the other leopardess shifters in her family.

"I'll learn to take care of myself. You can teach me."

"Big talk for a little girl who goes around with a security team. Sweetheart, wake up and smell the Folgers. Why do you think I'm here with you?"

"Because you don't have the balls to deal with your own family," she flung back without mercy. "It's too much fun dealing with mine."

Drake's eyes widened and his face hardened. "Off base. We're not from the same world. You have no idea how far apart our lives are."

"Probably true but irrelevant. I need *your* assistance. Tonight, Drake. What you do tomorrow is your business." She inhaled and reached out to him, touching his chest. "I know about dragons. I have money and you could go your own way. Start your own pack."

"For your information, we're called a *rage*…not a pack and for good reason." His muscles tensed under her fingertips, growing hotter, and she moaned from the burn.

For a second, they stared at each other and he shook his head. "I sidestepped a forced marriage. You willing to do the extreme? Like me…I'm nothing but a hired gun. It's not like you're in love—this is some rebellious phase. You'll wake up one day and remember where you belong, but I wholly doubt your parents, Necrodemas, and the justice councils will forget."

"You walked away from your family. Something or someone must have prompted you to. Was it for love?" she asked, holding her breath and searching his eyes. If he was in love with another woman, this might not work.

"Romantic notion and no. That's hardly my story." He plucked her fingers, lifted her hand, and kissed her knuckles. She felt weak in the knees but stiffened when he set her hand back on the railing, and avoided lowering his gaze to her opened robe. He took a step backward, resuming the role of the perfect gentleman, and that pissed her off more than anything he'd ever pulled.

"Then what is your so-called story? I want to know. You owe me." She gathered the edges of her robe together, covering herself. She felt so stupid.

Pressing his full lips into a line, Drake darted his eyes down to her now covered body. He clenched his jaw harder and appeared pissed, on the verge of going off. "Doesn't matter," he said.

"Really. 'Cause each time I wanted to let loose and have some fun on the beaches and boardwalk, you're frowning, arms crossed, and yeah I heard your muttering a mile off—let's not even get started on the bars and dance clubs you won't let me visit. You're the official buzzkill on this trip. You won't let me ad lib anything. If I'm supposed to be innocently sowing my PG-rated oats for the PR machine back home, why did I get saddled with the all-time party pooper? You're like some form of dragon chastity belt I'm forced to endure."

"In case you'd like to remember, I was recruited for this job as a favor to your father. So I agreed, thank you not very much!"

"You could have said 'no.' But why? You'd miss out on torturing me," she said and reached out, this time poking him in the chest. "You're not having any fun and I sure as hell am not!"

She must have done something right. Drake came at her, his heat undeniable and only a couple of inches from touching her. "Well maybe, just maybe it's because you're spoiled to the core, Miss Barclay. You push people's buttons without regard for the toll or repercussions. I'm warning you, don't push me."

"That's a lie. Name one person's buttons I push." She leaned closer to him. Another inch and she'd be near to rubbing up against him. "Besides yours, Mr. Navy SEAL."

"Bull's eye." He raked his fingers through his hair, his gaze roaming down her body, then springing upward. "Got that one dead center. During three tours of duty, I didn't encounter anyone like you."

"And what are you going to do about it? I'm curious. You want me and I want you. Will you stand by and let another man take me to his bed, put his hands on me?"

"Never." His nostrils flared.

"Then put up or shut up," she said.

"Dammit. You really are something." Without further warning, he had her back against the railing. He pressed his body to hers as he ripped open her robe. "This body is mine. Only mine. Say please. Nicely."

"Saying please. Very, very nicely," she repeated, biting her lip as he pushed her robe off her shoulders. He didn't stop until the sleeves were down her arms and the robe lay in a heap at her feet. His fingers set off a chain reaction, fusing the scorching heat from his touch with the fire in her blood. A billion prickling pins shot over her skin, demanding she shift and allow him to mount her in the most intimate of ways. But that would mean she was claimed—owned by Drake if she submitted to him primitively. To preserve her independence, she fought the instinct of her leopardess nature and remained in her human form. And yeah, what he did was a rush. He trailed his hands over naked her flesh, taking possession of her breasts by spanning his long fingers over her curves.

"How about this for starters?" He thumbed her peaks that hardened under his scalding touch.

"So very nice. Keep going," she whispered, pushing forward into his palms and hooking her fingers in his belt loops. Oh she'd heard talk about dragon speed but nothing like this.

"Do you realize what you risk?" Drake's hard body held her pinned in place as his gaze swept over her face, blazing a trail that ignited her leopardess senses. He palmed her breasts, rubbing his length against her thigh then moving over an inch or two as his fully erect cock nudged her belly.

"I risk going insane if we don't do more than talk," she hissed, the scent of their mutual arousal unleashing a swarm of goose bumps over her arms as the space between her legs throbbed. Unbearable heat swam within her along with something she'd never acted on, an escalating urge to be wildly mounted and claimed under the moonlight.

He backed up and began to unbuckle his belt. "Got to hear it from your lips. Do you want me to fuck you?"

"Please. Yes. All night. Hard. Rough. Fuck me, Drake, until I scream. But only in human form. Can you do that?" The words spilled from her lips, blistering and bubbling as a fire raced through her and left her drenched and ready for him.

Without breaking eye-contact with her, he unzipped his jeans, and growled, "Perfect answer, kitten."

# CHAPTER 2

Shannon's silky skin was softer than he'd envisioned in the million fantasies he entertained of her over the years. He ran his fingers across her shoulders, releasing a sparkling essence that glowed like magical moonlight. Dammit, if he wasn't the perfect mark. He thundered from his own internal combustion, craving more than the phantom feel of her body. Everything about her teased and tormented him to distraction. She had his scruples by the balls. *Back, say hello to the wall.*

"Baby," he said, pulling her into his arms and giving into the wild ride they both were about to embark on. "I might not make you roar, but I'm going to make you scream my name."

"Pretty cocky. That line work with your other conquests around here?" Shannon wasn't shy. She gripped his cock and squeezed him hard.

Holy fuck! His nerve endings burst into flame, spreading a wildfire from his dick throughout his body. His dragon nature savored being touched by a woman who knew what she wanted. When he screwed, he did so with an unrelenting force. He imbued *fucking like an animal* with a whole new shade of savage.

He laughed at her spunk, pumping his cock within her curled fingers, and whispered into her ear, "Sorry to disappoint you. I don't make it a habit of seducing the locals. Been busy twenty… four…seven…keeping track of you." He made his hips piston, rocking his cock as he spoke. "That's it, Shay. Let me fuck your hand."

She stroked him in her warm palm and he pressed his lips to hers, unable to keep from thrusting his tongue deep into her mouth and showing her how he'd enjoy eating her pussy.

Her lips were petal soft, unlike her barbed commentary, and when she opened to him, he devoured her mouth. Without letting go of him, she reached up her other hand and raked her nails across his scalp, tangling her fingers in his hair.

Sweet Lord, he was going to spew flames and come all over her lovely fingers if she kept up her hand mudras on his hard-on. He wrapped his forearms around her waist, hauling her closer to him, and rubbed his crown up and down against her fingers. Shit. Her hands felt so fucking good.

"Better stop stroking my cock or I'm not going to last in round one. Open your thighs for me," he growled. "Wider. I'm going to go down on you under the stars."

"Like this?" Arching a brow, she lifted her lovely leg, giving him access to thrust into her balls deep. A girl like Shannon had him wild, reckless and skating the edge, doing things he hadn't done in months.

He held back—had to for a beat to gather his self-control. "Do you realize what you're doing to me?"

Her husky laugh was answer enough—a challenge he refused to back away from. His grip on her tightened and he slammed his hips into her, connected his cock with her mound, and for a second he saw shooting stars. The urge to drive himself into her jetted. Without thinking, he pumped his hips, making her glide over his fully erect shaft without entering her. This teasing boosted his dragon hunger as she whimpered against his mouth.

"That's it. Pleasure yourself. I could thrust into you right now and fuck us mindless." He had a choice: either he take her to her bedroom, or hoist her upward, wrap her legs around his waist and make her ride him rough.

Naw. Their first time, he wanted her beneath him as he controlled her every move. He needed that type of action with her.

"Drake," she moaned in the sexiest voice that commanded all of his senses. He had to thrust into her—own her—right now or he'd blow a gasket.

"Wrap your legs around me. Don't make me ask again." He lifted her, wrapping her slender legs around his hips and walked into her bedroom. He only paused to kick her bedroom door closed. Hell, he'd been ready to take her up against the wall at the word go, but now he'd own her on top of a bed as she spread her legs. His cock throbbed and felt harder than forged steel. He breathed out a lungful of smoke, careful to refrain from expelling fire. He lowered them and hovered over her, making the mattress springs squeak. "You ever had your wrists and ankles bound?"

"Come again?" Shannon asked in a hoarse voice as he laid her down on the bed.

"Ever had a dragon lover?" he asked, not really wanting to hear her talk about past partners. But his ability to breathe fire necessitated some precautions to keep her from getting blistered, and limiting her movement would help.

"Not one," she whispered, a cloud of color suffusing her cheeks.

He liked that response and smirked. "So I'm the first dragon to share your bed."

She blushed deeper and closed her eyes. "You're the first man to share my bed. Period." Then she opened her amber-colored eyes and stared back at him, unblinking, and for several long seconds he was speechless.

He dropped his gaze to her spread thighs, her pink swollen lips, and his throbbing cock actually got harder at the thought of being her first. "This is the first time—ever?"

Shannon bit her lip and nodded.

For months, he'd sported a hard-on keeping his distance from Shannon. She was his Navy commander's kid, his friend's sister, and he'd sworn to her family that he'd watch over her with his life. He'd imagined that she'd acquired some experience in college. If he took her virginity, how much would his life be worth? Zero. Nil. Nada.

Richard Barclay would gather a hit team composed of hardcore SEALs. Shawn would castrate him first—torture second. Kill third. And he'd deserve everything his friend dished out.

He channeled his fingers through his hair. "By *first*, do you mean that you haven't ever had sex before?"

"Yeah and don't look at me like I just announced the world is about to end."

"It might…" He reached down and ran his hand over her waist, tormenting himself. His dick throbbed mercilessly. Conversely, instead of actually being put off at the thought of the shit hitting the fan, he wanted to thrust so deep into her on so many levels and make Shannon his—that was friggin' ludicrous. Had to be his dick talking.

*She belongs to me.*

The thought burst into his brain and tore through him.

Horrible way to pay back the Barclays. When he'd been down on his luck and walked away from his family's archaic polygamous mating rituals, his old commander had taken him in, a recently discharged SEAL without a mission, a.k.a. useless. According to Drake's family, it was time to take the helm in a dwindling draconian dragon line after his tours of duty were over. But it was not his thing to marry his cousins, the three women who waited for him so he could procreate the bloodline, then step into a cushy corporate career at O'Connor Tech, play golf on Sunday, and attend family reunions annually in Hawaii. Of course, a major part of the time would involve downing Viagra as his brothers did in trying to fuck their wives nine different ways to Sunday.

Begetting a live dragon birth was near impossible these days, and all males under the age of fifty spent most of their time in bed with an icepack on their balls. Three, four, five wives with thermometers, logbooks, and daily doctor visits. Huge sums were awarded to a live dragon birth—last time a truckload of cash went to his brother and his fourth wife. Before that a third cousin, but that was two decades ago.

He'd never fall in line and left his family's rage, refusing dragon dynasty bribes and threats.

As the head of security at Barclay Enterprises in Denver, he'd been happy knowing nothing about little princesses... until Shannon had returned from college. His first encounter with the girl who'd grown into a woman stalled him in his tracks. Gone was the skinny teenager with braces and in her place, a jaw-dropping beauty. The sight of her endless curves had hit him square between the eyes, not to mention had his dick standing up and taking extreme notice. Then she opened her mouth...oh yeah. He remembered her quick comebacks that never quit and sent his motor into overdrive.

Active tours of duty overseas during full-on scrambles, and his military training hadn't prepared him for this earth shattering news. This level of intel hit him in the gut. Now, Shannon leaned upward, giving him a challenging look, and took hold of his cock again. "Stop overthinking this. Where's all that fire? Drake, I know this is what you want. So, let's just do it."

He stared down at her, then lowered his eyes to her incredible pussy: her pink lips parted and her tiny nub of a clit peeked out. His cock juddered and he tore his gaze away, but focusing on her mouth was equally torturous.

"You're just going to give yourself...away."

"Silly. Between us, this isn't arbitrary. I choose you. If I wanted to give *it* away, I'd have let some random guy at the beach...or Dimitri. He's the problem. He expects a pure wife. If you do me this favor, he won't want to marry me. I get what I want, and you get what I want, which also happens to be something you desire." She spread her legs wider and swiped herself with her fingertips. "How can you turn down a woman in need?"

Holy. Holy. Holy fuck! His cock went harder than rebar and took extra special notice of her wet pussy displayed and offered to him. His dragon sense roared in frustration and greedy need. His dick seconded the motion to shut the fuck up and thrust into her, claim her, and do it all again, over and over for the next week.

"Playing dirty pool," he snarled.

"If you don't help me out, I'll find someone who will. I'm not going to marry that poor excuse for a leopard. Not him…or anyone who isn't my choosing. Ever."

"Just this once? Is that what you think? Shay, we won't be able to stop." The muscles all over his body constricted until he spewed a flame from his internal strife to hold back from claiming her. She didn't get it—he had to get her to understand.

"How about one night? The whole night," she asked, her eyes glowing golden and shredding every last one of his good intensions.

He inhaled. Did she have any idea what she was asking for? "I wasn't lying about riding between those beautiful legs hard. Rough. Wild…and you're a virgin. Us having sex will hurt."

"Good. I want to remember tonight. Remember what I had to go through to garner my freedom so that I never forget."

"Listen to me. If we do this, you'll be mine. All mine. This isn't the usual run-of-the-mill shifter screwing…I'm a dragon, for fuck's sake, and dragons don't just hump. Shay, I swear you'd better get this memo: I'm going to supremely fuck you. This isn't just sex. It's more. Deeper if it's up to the male—"

"Shush. Don't go all dragon domination on me." She winked and splayed her pussy for him. "I've got a plan. No more excuses. Touch me, Drake."

He couldn't hold back. He reached down, stroked his finger between her lips, and fuck him backward, his rod throbbed so hard his cock jetted pre cum. Every dragon cell in his body hummed as though attuned to an ancient verse that strangled all volition except one: he had to fuck her, sink so deep inside her they became one. He stared down at Shay, this mind-wrecking carnal urge breaking him. For years he'd turned away, suppressed his dragon nature. Now logic turned to primitive lust and his dragon nature demanded he take her. Claim her. This female was his and every atom in his body demanded he mark her. Nothing else mattered. Not his past. Not his family…not even hers. Dragon mating was singular and once the instinct was unlocked, there was no stopping him.

"Baby," he growled, circling her wetness and holding back, not wanting to hurt her.

Drake lowered his head and kissed her on the mouth as he rubbed her pussy—*his pussy*. She tasted so sweet—irresistible to his dragon—the perfect fuel to enflame his feral instinct. He clenched his jaw, shaking off the drowning feeling of coming apart by focusing on what needed to be done. Like right the fuck now! "I'll secure your wrists and ankles until you know what to do when I make you come."

"So you'll do it more than once?" Shay transfixed him with the glow of her feline eyes.

Shit. He'd stay hard all night the way he felt. Hell, by morning Shannon would be fully aware she'd been fucked by a dragon.

• • •

Drake climbed between her legs, his cock rigid and outstretched, but instead of thrusting into her, he removed two pillows from up against the headboard. "Lift your hips."

"What are you doing?"

"I'm going to make certain you don't get burned. This is serious and your skin needs to be protected, kitten."

"And what about you? You'll need protection from me," she huffed and showed him her leopardess claws.

He chuckled, running the tips of his fingers across her nails. Why did the deep timbre of his laughter stop her breathing… pierce her chest? Nerves. *My leopardess self is highly strung. Nothing more.*

"Teeth. Claws. Those don't work against a dragon even in human form. Our skin is virtually impenetrable. Tougher than leather." He cupped her bottom and positioned her hips on the pillows. He knelt between her legs, his erection brushing up against her sex and she jerked, gliding along his length. Excitement raced through her, and he didn't fare much better. His mouth tensed and his whole body rippled, muscles undulating in a wave.

"Shannon," he groaned deep, low, and the forceful sound shook the bed. They moved against each other in a step beyond dry humping.

She cried out his name. "Drake! Please, don't tease me."

"You like that?"

She bit her lip, sucking in a shaking breath. "Very much."

"Beautiful temptress." He grunted, then leaned over her stomach and took hold of one wrist, flicking his thumb along the sensitive underside, surprising Shay by lifting her hand and kissing her palm. His lips were sweet. Tender. And yes, searing as though she'd touched an open flame.

She could hardly speak and when she did, her voice came out husky. "You mentioned binding my wrists."

"Ah, yes. Speaking of leather. We'll need a belt. Several." He still held her hand and frowned, staring down at her arm. "Too fragile. Silk for your lovely skin. The sash of your robe will do, but we'll need more."

"Silk scarves. They'd work," she offered, hypnotized by his fingertips. When his shimmering eyes met hers, she forgot her thought and the blistering burn of his body. "You're the beautiful one," she murmured.

He returned her unblinking stare. "I don't know if this will work. I've never been with a leopardess. Your skin is so sensitive."

She roused herself with his sobering words. "You must."

"There is a way," he murmured.

"Magick?"

"Not the type you might be accustomed to."

"Is it true about dragons?"

"Oh brother," he said, giving her *the look* that indicated she'd said something off-the-wall in his book. "Which myth shall I debunk?"

"I heard that when a dragon desires a woman, his mystical eyes can bend her will. But first he has to mate with the girl and then he owns her mind…body…soul."

"That's more fairy tale than truth—first a dragon must connect physically to form deep mind link. I was referring about binding you to maintain my concentration instead of shooting out scorching fire."

"Fire? As in flames that could burn my skin?"

"Trust me, Shay. I have no intention of injuring you…the opposite in fact. If I can concentrate for more than two seconds in your company. I have the ability to release a cool flame. They're highly erotic. Pleasurable to human and non-dragon shifters."

"Oh," she said, studying his full lips.

"Oh…I need more of a reply than that." He scowled darkly down at her before he rose off the bed, crossing to her closet. "Scarves?" he called out.

"What about the women, emphasis on the plural?" she asked, not wanting to imagine him with another woman and his cool-flame-throwing ability.

"That's not my style," he retorted wryly. "Now, how about giving it up on the location of the scarves, Shannon."

"Inside. The center island. The top set of drawers." She tried to rise but felt lightheaded from staring into Drake's eyes as he watched her from the closet doorway.

It was the dragon's way and since he was a draconian lord by birth, he had the power to possess—fairy tale or not. Every shifter knew shifter facts. A dragon by his very nature had to procreate with several women…draconian women from his own clan—no, *rage*. Who didn't know that…but it was true, Drake wasn't like anyone in his ability to live a life on his own terms.

"Jesus. How many clothes do you own?" he asked from inside her closet.

She rolled her eyes and instead of answering, she called out, "Promise not to steal my will. I'm giving you something that is worth a bundle. I don't understand why men's egos are so incredibly vast and fragile, but all I can say is *thank you*. Come tomorrow, I'm a free woman."

Silence, except for a few harsh mumbles as she heard drawers opening and slamming shut. He suddenly appeared at the threshold of her closet, and she gasped, captivated by the countless shadows crisscrossing his body, marking the contours of his flexing sinew, and her eyes widened. Widened a whole lot more when her gaze lowered to his swollen shaft.

From across the room, his hard-on appeared long, thick and perfectly formed but there was no getting around one painful fact: Drake was built in huge dimensions.

"Kitten, before tonight neither one of us was looking for long-term, but you do realize that this might get much more complicated than just sex. If we do this, I can promise we'll both be leaving. Your idea of getting far away from here may mean traveling farther away from Denver."

What was he talking about? She intended on returning to Denver and getting her own apartment and living on her own terms.

"Surely, you can return home and explain that I left. I'll leave tomorrow night. Won't be the first time I've gotten away from my keepers."

"The last time, I gave you room to roam, but I was well aware of your whereabouts," he said. "I won't return to Denver and act as though nothing occurred."

Oh. Shit. What was she asking of him? This would cost him and yet he made no excuses and didn't throw the truth in her face: after tonight, he would be the man who'd fucked the daughter of his boss. The sister of his friend. None of that should matter—it didn't in her book if she'd stop being a flippin' worrywart. The facts: his body, her body. Sex. She refocused on his cock, which swayed as he walked toward the side of the bed.

"You're letting your principles color your vision. You're giving me my freedom. One day, my parents will understand."

Drake set the scarves down next to her and captured her hands. The tantalizing feel of his fingers encircling her wrists as he lifted her hands made her stop talking. He placed her palms in a prayer position upon her chest. She watched him loop the silk, each swipe of his fingers making something inside her chest flicker like the wings of a caged bird about to be set free.

"Your freedom," he murmured, knotting one of the scarves. "I wish I could as so noble, but baby, it's not your freedom that has me grinding my teeth."

"Drake, whatever your reason, know this. You are helping me maintain my absolute independence. I want to forge my own destiny."

"The irony that to do so I must bind you hand and foot, notwithstanding ravishing your body, isn't lost on me." His chest rose and fell as he moved off the bed and gingerly repositioned her ankles, then secured her legs, spread-eagle to the footboard of her bed.

Fully exposed to him, she didn't feel ashamed; instead she bowed her body, anticipation making her tremble and moan. "Please, come to me."

Drake climbed in between her legs, his body a rippling work of muscular art as he knelt in front of her, lowering his shoulders between her legs.

"Your pussy is so pretty."

"What are you—" Oh. My. God. The first lick of his forked tongue across her sex made her cry out. He spread her and returned again with his tongue, the twining tips trailing up her lips, dipping into her opening, and she fought to keep from shattering. "Please. Yes!" she begged before he made her lose all sense of reason.

Tonguing and sucking on her, he pressed his face against her as heat danced across her folds. Swirling jolts of pleasure and arousal swam in her body and she opened her legs wider as he plunged his tongue into her faster and deeper. When he sucked on her flesh without mercy, she moaned his name. The ends of his tongue wrapped around her clit and stroked her, intimately. He fucked her with his mouth at full throttle—she cried out until she thought she'd burst apart. The feeling of falling coupled with a glowing pleasure filled every corner of her being, and she tugged on her restrained wrists, wanting to wrap her arms around him. Drake swiped her pussy then drove his tongue into her as she bucked against his mouth. "Oh God. What's happening?"

"So sweet. You're coming," he said before he returned to licking her. He stopped and slid his finger inside her, pumping his hand, and she matched his tempo with her hips. Riding his finger, she felt the coil of tension and pleasure unravel and flow through her body, leaving her floating on a river of bliss.

"Drake. So good," she moaned, clawing her own palms with her leopard nails.

"That's it. Come for me," he groaned, plunging his finger into her harder. He lifted his head and roared. Several blue-tipped flames exited his mouth.

A blast of heat shot past her thigh and in seconds, Drake was up and over the side of her bed. "Don't move," he snarled. He grabbed a blanket and covered the charred linens. He wasn't joking about the need to keep out of the line of fire.

"Flailing arms surely could get scalded."

"That's why yours are tied," he said and returned to the bed. This time he rose and knelt between her legs without bowing down. He moved, positioning one of his hands by her shoulder as he swiped the head of his cock over her sex, and throughout her body a storm of tingling jolts erupted.

"Drake, more," she whispered, rubbing against him. They moved in harmony as he grazed his crown to her opening and pushed forward. He was hard. Hot. Huge.

Leaning down, he brushed his lips over hers. "Kitten, there's no way to stop the discomfort."

"Just do it," she whispered, wishing she could reach out to him and wrap her arms around his neck.

"I want to…but you're so tight," he said, changing position, cupping one of her hips and drawing her closer. "Relax for me."

He flexed upward. The muscles over his shoulders clenched, and arduously he slid inside her, incrementally at first, and then he surged forward a few more inches. The slice of pain expanded and shot through her when he plunged inside. She cried out as he pumped his hips, thrusting into her all the way, and groaning her name. Drake fused his body to hers in a jolt of stinging pain.

Red-hot tears fell from her eyes; she roared, bucking her hips, but he pinned her body underneath him. He held onto her and she fought to stifle a sob by biting her lip until she drew blood.

"Ssshhh. Baby, no more pain." He covered her lips softly with his finger.

She inhaled as he traced her mouth, murmuring soothing sounds for long seconds.

"Better?" he asked, meeting her gaze.

She faltered, staring into his incredible eyes. In that second, she felt lost. This was just supposed to be sex, yet the flickering twinge in her chest felt foreign…No. *This was just sex.* Only sex and if she didn't act like her brain cells were working he might stop.

"Yes," she exhaled, completely conscious of his cock deeply imbedded inside her body and how much she longed to ride him. Her leopardess nature demanded to be mounted, and now that the stinging pain had passed, she purred, rubbing her cheek against his chin.

He chuckled, tipping her face and brushing his mouth over hers. "Is that a hint you're ready for more?"

"Yes. Please."

Drake held her chin up to his face, plunging his tongue into her mouth, and kissing her deeply until she whimpered. He moved his hips, sliding out of her, and simultaneously groaning. Was he going to stop?

"Drake," she moaned, blinking up at him, a pang in her chest pinching. "Are you leaving?"

"No one could get me to leave you now. It's time for your pleasure." He shifted his hips and drove his cock back into her. Over and over, Drake gyrated his hips forward and back, powerful pumps that plunged his cock farther and harder into her.

Unrelenting.

Purposeful.

Pinned under him and to the bed, she arched to meet his thrusts. Rippling pleasure drizzled through her. He stopped moving, stared down at her and smiled. "Can you take more?"

"Yes. Don't stop." She reached for him, encumbered by her bound wrists, but still she managed to trace her fingers over the rippling muscle bunched along his chest.

Gracefully, he pushed upward, planting his palms next to her shoulders and pushed his length inside her. Oh. Holy. Holy. His cock stretched her folds tight and she groaned, squeezing her muscles around him.

"Kitten," he growled above her and she met his jade eyes. "When you do that, I'm ready to burst."

"Is that a bad thing?" she asked, her brows drawn together. Shifting onto one hand, he held himself aloft and wiped his fingers across her forehead. He leaned down and kissed her. "Do it again." The raw heat emanating from his body skyrocketed, but she didn't feel the burn. Hot, yes. Insurmountable pleasure. "Sooo, so good," she whispered.

Grunting, he took hold of the headboard, leveraging his body, and when he slammed his cock, he ground himself against her, burying his length inside her body, forcing her to cry out his name. The headboard shook and the bedsprings squeaked in harmony, an erotic rhythm, punctuated by their breaths, their groans, their murmured words. "I'm close," she said.

"Fuck. You feel incredible around me. Get to the edge, baby."

"Drake, I'm there. Don't hold back."

They were so close to the brink of shattering and coming undone, yet with skin-on-skin contact, she held back, relishing the moment. His heartbeat was so loud, so forceful, she felt the echo threading in her veins, her breath, her very soul. Mesmerized, she watched his shimmering eyes, full of dragon magick, drawn to his power.

"I'm going to explode. Take me all the way, Shay. Now."

Holy goddess! She threw back her head, clenching around him, arching and giving him access to pump his cock deep into her body. "Oh…" she whimpered as he drove his length full force into her.

"Perfect. Unbelievable," he grunted, droplets of sweat dripping down the sides of his face, his muscles contracting into rock-hard ripples as a spasm overtook him and he bellowed, snapping his head upward and releasing a stream of fire that charred the wall black behind her bed.

Drake hoisted her hips to him and she couldn't hold back, releasing a feline roar mixed with the cry of his name as she came hard in a splintering surge of fiery pleasure.

He lowered her hips to the bed, leaned down and kissed her belly. Drake undid her ankles and pulled her to him, enfolding her in his arms. He expelled hot puffs of air as he kissed the side of her head, so tender in how he held her and murmured her name against her neck. Far from what she'd imagined having sex with him would be like…well the sizzling part, yes. But this side of him, the snuggling, made her breath hitch, and she played with the idea of how he'd be beyond one night. *No. Don't go there.*

When their heart rates subsided enough to stop gasping, Drake traced the edge of her jaw, nuzzling her neck. "How would you rate your first experience?" He shifted her on top of him, holding her to his chest as he stared up at her.

"Yummy," she replied, wishing she could reach out and entwine her arms around his neck. She settled for lowering her head and kissing his chin.

"Ride me, baby," he said, suddenly sitting upward and arranging her legs around his waist. He hoisted her hips, aligning the head of his cock with her and easing her downward along his length. Inch by delicious inch, until she stretched around him. He thrust hard, pumped fully into her, making her ride his cock.

"Faster. Please, Drake."

"You feel so fucking incredible." He flipped her onto her back as he returned to wedging his hips between her legs. "Gotta take us to the edge. Again."

When he began flexing his torso, their skin slapped together hard and loud; she felt her eyes roll back in her head. Glittering pleasure, dark, swirling, and decadent as the heat in his magickal eyes swam through her. Rocking her hips, she met him thrust for thrust and savored the rumbling groans spilling from his beautiful mouth. He pushed upward, capturing her shoulders, hauling her to his body and moving farther into her, owning her completely.

He pumped his hips, slamming his body against her, ramming his cock into her in a pounding rhythm. A primal tempo. Raw. Rough. And perfect. Shannon arched her neck, her body simmered as if searing, and between her legs, she contracted tight around him.

"Drake," she cried out uncontrollably. Oh. Soooo deep. *This is what it means to multi orgasm!*

"That's it. Come all over my cock. Now, Shannon." All of his muscles went rock hard. A spasm thundered through him and he roared, filling her with a sensation of fiery wet warmth. The effect of his release was like glowing embers that blazed through her body, bathing her senses from the inside out.

Again, he pummeled her hips with his own, his cock plunging deeper, and he filled her by cupping her bottom and hauling her up to meet him. He ground his dick into her, bowing his body over hers, and burying his face into her neck.

"Fuuckk!" He shuddered and came again. More this time. Hotter. And the cresting wave of pleasure that accompanied their mutual orgasm blew her mind.

Droplets of sweat dripped from his face as he lowered his hips between her legs and lifted up to meet her gaze.

"Baby, you've just been fucked by a dragon."

"Twice," she added and he flashed a sexy-as-hell smile that reached up to his jade green eyes. His expression had the power to set off fireworks within her bloodstream.

"I stand corrected. Twice. Care to do it again, spitfire?" He crushed his mouth down on hers before she had the chance to answer, alternating soft sucks on her top and bottom lips. He whispered over her mouth, "I have plenty of positions in my arsenal."

"You drive a hard bargain." So powerful, she couldn't deny him. She blinked, swallowing. Was she succumbing to dragon magick?

"May I have my hands untied this time?"

# CHAPTER 3

"Miss Barclay." Shay's maid rapped softly at her bedroom door. He exchanged a quizzical look with Shay.

Gathering her robe off the side of the bed, Shay motioned to him remain silent while she cracked opened the door. "Yes?"

"Mr. Necrodemas is downstairs," the young woman announced.

Dammit. What the heck was Dimitri doing here? He rose from the bed, looking for his shirt.

"I'll be down in a few minutes. See that he's offered something by the pool," she replied to the maid.

Shutting the door, she swung around to him, her face ashen. He crossed the room and came up next to her, curling his fingers around her arms. "Forget it. You don't need to speak with him," he snarled. "I'll go down and deal with him."

"And what will you say?" she whispered, searching his face with her golden eyes.

He lowered his gaze down her incredible body and frowned. "More than you could by wearing a robe and nothing underneath."

"Fine. Just don't pick a fight with him," she suggested, cinching her sash tighter.

"I suggest if you don't want me to get into an argument, then you'd better be waiting for me in bed. And naked when I return." He swatted her bottom before he slipped on his shoes. He'd be lucky if he didn't lose it completely in Necrodemas's presence.

Once outside Shay's bedroom, he crossed the corridor and went inside his own room. Not this side of hell would he meet Necrodemas dressed as though he were on vacation. He changed in to his customary all-black work attire that included a Glock .40.

He descended the backstairs noiselessly as he reviewed the streaming video feed of the closed-circuit cameras from his cell screen. Necrodemas had arrived in a private Hummer accompanied by another man, one Drake didn't recognize. He typed in a message to his team about the identity of Necrodemas's companion and immediately received a response as "unidentified." *Fuck!* He walked soundlessly through the small sitting area overlooking the patio, his attention focused on the pair out by the pool. He observed the two men through with the wall of French doors, perturbed by their odd behavior. He sent a text, alerting his security team to take their marks, and remain stationed near the patio area until further word.

Drake exited behind the bar, making eye contact with the guard who served as the bartender, and grimacing quickly. The bartender nodded his understanding, and tapped the handgun under the counter. Already one snafu and he'd have someone's ass for admitting a guest without a proper ID check.

Dimitri sat lounging by the pool, enjoying a glass of Scotch he'd obviously taken from an open bottle on the tiki bar. His companion, a younger man with skin so white it glowed blue stood by the edge of the pool. The dude's back was to the old leopard and he nodded, as though conversing absent-mindedly.

"How many I help you?" Drake asked so abruptly that Dimitri's companion snapped his head around less than gracefully. The man no longer appeared ash-gray in color. Had it been his imagination? Drake turned his focus on his target. Necrodemas had spilled his drink mid-sip. Ah, one of the perks of being a noiseless dragon, Drake thought. He used it to his advantage.

"Dammit, Drake," Necrodemas swore softly, sitting up and dabbing his shirt with a napkin.

As Drake got closer to Necrodemas, the other man—his bodyguard or whatever he was—switched his focus first to him and then the doorway from which he'd come. He noted impatience and a flicker of annoyance on Necrodemas' face while the other man didn't move a muscle. Not a blink beyond tracking him.

Drake sniffed the air and scanned his infrared vision over the pale man. So, he was a werewolf. But not just any werewolf: he was an alpha and, oddly, he smelled of diesel fuel—more than a trace but that shit didn't compute unless he was some kind of mechanic. Drake scanned the shifter's hands which didn't resemble the likes of any grease monkey he'd ever come across. For a summer day, the wolf's dressing in a leather jacket was equally out of place. It had to be almost ninety degrees in the shade even in the early evening. He kept his focus on Necrodemas but remained cognizant of the wolf's presence.

"I wasn't aware that the head of Barclay security was now playing host," the old leopard replied, clearly pissed that Shannon was not with him.

"Miss Barclay is indisposed," Drake offered through clenched teeth, and not another morsel of information, preferring to watch Necrodemas's reaction.

"I still want to see Miss Barclay. Just a word and I'll leave." Necrodemas stood and straightened his shirt, tossing down the napkin onto the table.

"That won't be possible. Not today."

Necrodemas narrowed his already beady eyes and shook his head. "I'm not leaving until I have the chance to speak with Miss Barclay. Alone." He bared his teeth and Drake felt himself instinctively rise to the challenge.

He kept himself impassive. Any trace of heat flares resulting in him exhaling puffs of smoke would get noticed. His ability to spew fire was less than conventional among shifters and the thermal powering up in his body would clearly signal his anger, a dangerous Achilles heel for someone in Drake's position. For all that he desired to wipe the floor with Necrodemas, for Shay's safety and their plan to escape he had to remain emotionless. He nodded as though thoughtful.

Drake signaled to his team stationed at the corner of the pool house as well as the one playing bartender and the two other guards off the patio, observing from the interior of the villa. "Mr. Necrodemas, as I said, that won't be possible. These are Miss Barclay's instructions. If you would be so good as to follow her security. Thank you."

His security crew came forward, two of them holding onto trained guard dogs. The pair of Dobermans growled as they walked by Necrodemas who ignored them. Each security guard was equipped with a semi-automatic rifle, not unheard of with the Unruled causing havoc, and the unspoken message was evident: it was time for Dimitri to take his leave.

Drake flicked his gaze over to the werewolf, Necrodemas's companion, who cocked his head and smirked. The wolf mock-saluted him and arched his brow as he walked by but Drake didn't return the nod. The werewolf stopped in front of the Dobermans and stared down at each. In turn, the dogs pawed the ground, lowering their muzzles, and fuck him if they didn't tuck their tails between their legs. If his crew had not had the hounds held tightly on short leashes, these *highly trained* dogs would have rolled over and presented their bellies to the werewolf. Drake didn't require a neon sign to fully understand that this motherfucker was the person to watch. The pompous duffer with the Italian loafers and Scotch stained-shirt was nothing but a front for the werewolf. Drake considered the leather-clad man who walked behind Necrodemas and out the front door of the villa. Fuck, he'd see more of that son of a bitch. He felt that the unshakable assurance deep in his bones.

• • •

Closing the bedroom door, Drake padded across the floor toward Shay. "Kiss me," he said hoarsely, as a niggling itch expanded within him, provoking a sense of unrest and a need to protect Shay to the point of claiming her right here and now. All it would take was to sink his fangs into her flesh and infuse her with his serpent magick, linking them together as his dragon demanded. If she were his eternal mate, he'd have the means to secure her safety and that instinct flared in his dragon. His craving spiked for another taste of Shay's sweet mouth and the softest texture of heaven he'd experienced between her legs.

He lowered himself to the bed alongside her, savoring the way she ran her fingers along his skin, gifting him with a seductive smile. "Come here," he commanded.

He unwound the tendrils of his mind prompted by dragon instinct—one he didn't fight. Since first fucking Shay, his desire to connect on a deeper level with her took over his mind and body in a driving urge impossible to contain. He wrestled with the idea of linking their minds together—a step he could take in setting a course to fully claim her as his mate.

Not that she was looking for a mate…but dammit, being a dominating dragon didn't always rely upon democratic decisions. Shay was his, and she was unlike anyone else he'd ever encountered. On paper, she was a purebred leopardess who easily could rise to the rank of alpha. She was a million degrees different—and he'd had centuries to sample his share of every type of female—yet some essence of hers was achingly familiar to him.

In a split decision, he linked their minds together, but he couldn't effortlessly delve into her deep thoughts to uncover her secrets as his dragon nature desired. Linking minds usually required only that he breach the walls of her consciousness by way of mutual physical contact and then plunder the recesses of her thoughts. It was the reason why dragons grew disenchanted. There were few mysteries after sex—so much that for years he'd not even wasted time with mind-linking. He fucked mindlessly. Not with Shay. For whatever reason, her mind wasn't the usual type with lackluster corridors and passages. To uncover her mystery was as easy as following the path of a butterfly within the Amazon jungle.

"Don't you ever get tired?" she asked, beckoning him to lower his face to hers.

He stopped Shannon, held himself aloft and stared back at her. "Not where you're concerned. Wherever you go, I'll find you, kitten. For another one of your kisses."

"Really? Is that so? Mighty confident."

"Yep. Bank on it! Now kiss me and show me how much you enjoy me fucking you."

He picked her up and rolled over with her on top of his chest, but he held her from him, curling his fingers around her forearms. Her eyes widened, sparkling golden rays he didn't want to resist much longer.

"It's a good thing your dragon dick is as big as your ego." She smiled and he lowered her to his chest, cupping her chin. Shay stroked her tongue across his, and he let her take the lead for the first part of this tryst.

He dueled his tongue with hers, going for broke. He reached down, squeezing the curve of each of her ass cheeks in his palms, rubbing his cock between his temptress's legs.

"Mmm," he groaned. "I need more of you."

"Greedy." She giggled, squirming and brushing her hips against his straining cock.

"Guilty," he replied, almost to the point of asking her…*Shit.* He'd better get his head screwed back on before it rolled across the floor.

A buzzing on the night table and she cocked a brow. "You gonna get that?"

He reached for his phone, leery that it might be one of the Barclay clan.

"Are you hungry?" he asked, looking for an excuse to think about something other than hurling his phone across the room.

"I can't very well order up food. I told my maid I was ill with food poisoning."

"Point taken." His kitten had a foolproof set of excuses for remaining inside her bedroom unable to visit that asswad Necrodemas. The more he'd found out about that motherfucker, the more he wanted to get Shannon secured so he could effectively go and settle a number of scores with that idiot, say when he took his walk on his estate at eight sharp each goddamn morning. Until he had Shay ensconced in his castle, he'd keep his spitfire laying low in Lisbon, naked and under him.

*Buzz. Buzz. Buzz.*

"Dammit," he swore. The phone call was from Noah, one of his oldest friends, a phoenix shifter and a Navy buddy. Noah was part of the small circle Drake had contacted to help set up the means to leave the villa and take Shay with him. Besides Noah, Drake's crew consisted of Grant and Evan. They'd been tight during several tours of duty, dispersing since being discharged but they stayed in touch. He'd kicked around the idea of starting a private security company with the SEALS…well, fuck. It was time. If anyone could procure info to material goods, Noah was Drake's go-to.

"Alley-oop," Noah yodeled.

"You got my attention. News?" After a few sentences from Noah on the state of acquiring suitable aircraft, Drake met Shay's inquisitive eyes, clenching his jaw as his gaze roamed over her naked body.

Cradling his phone between his shoulder and chin, he wedged her legs open wider and he knelt between her thighs, and ran his thumb up her pussy, then sucked in a breath at how wet she was. Every single muscle on his body constricted in blistering need. His cock stood at attention—he thrust his finger into her. So close and all he had to do was click his phone off and slam into her. She lifted her legs, squeezing the mouth of her pussy around his pumping finger. He faltered, beads of sweat erupting along his shoulders.

"Are you listening?" Noah's voice came out louder. This was the second time he'd asked that same question and Drake silently swore, releasing his hold on Shay.

"Better focus," she whispered and pushed away from him, shaking her head.

Her husky laugh didn't help Drake's mood when he crawled from her bed, silently cursing, and trying to focus on the conversation.

"Yeah man. I'm right here."

"Oh no, you're not!" Noah laughed. "Whatever you got going on must be something."

"Seriously, it's no big deal." Great, Drake was surrounded by people who thought this was funny. His cock was not amused. It needed to fuck. Hard. Rough. Shannon.

"Bullshit."

"Talk to me," he grunted, biting his lip and casting a long excruciating glance back at Shay's body draped over her comforter as she twirled her ankle and foot, biting the end of a stylus while she looked over her digital planner. Christ almighty, if he stayed within striking distance of her, he'd chuck his cell over the terrace railing, but Noah had info he needed to deal with this shit storm about to happen.

He rose and walked out to the terrace, where it was easier to focus and hopefully get his dragon side to relent for a few minutes. In the early evening, there wouldn't be anyone about the grounds except for his security crew and he'd already heard them pass by with the Dobermans two minutes and forty-two seconds ago according to his watch. "So things are serious?" Noah asked.

He almost choked, unwilling to admit aloud the direction of his out of control dragon intentions where Shay was concerned. "What are you talking about? I'm helping Shannon out.

Serious—far the fuck from it. She's gonna stay at my place in the mountains and we're back to rocking and rolling. I'm done with the corporate route. Way too mundane. What's the news on your side?"

"Ah, fuck that noise you're spewing about the girl, but okay. I'm game if you're finally ready to start your own company. The plan is you're going to have to fly up the coast."

"Noah, I got that. I just need a plane. What have you found out?" He spoke low, careful to keep his voice from carrying out to the grounds below. Things would be even worse if Shay got wind of his plan to do whatever it took to keep her safe.

"Not good. Everything is on lockdown with the recent shifter gang attacks on high profile targets, making headlines all over the stinking globe. This is some fucked up shit and it ain't pretty."

Immediately, Drake lurched up and off the railing. He gritted his teeth and silently swore with several curse words in rapid succession as he computed the distance they needed to travel just north of Navarre to his mother's family estate that lay hidden in a concealed valley. Castle Herensuge—he'd only been once. Years ago when he'd come of dragon age and it had been time for him to claim his heritage as the youngest son of his father and the only son of his mother who'd died in childbirth. He doubted Shay would much appreciate traveling to his home on the back of an ass. He glanced over as she tapped a text on her iPhone. Double hell no! "Noah, find something. A refurbished chopper."

Noah snorted. "Dude. You're not listening to me. It's a no-go if you want to make tracks and not leave a trace. I'm talking... *you* have to fly her. As in dragon wings, talons, and paws. Up. Up. And away."

"When I get back to the States, remind me that I owe you a round in the ring. Just you, me, and your messed up sense of humor." He grimaced, leveling his shoulders, and gazed at the wide swath of rippling moonlit water.

After several seconds of silence, he heard Noah clear his throat. "Did you ask her?" His crewmate's voice came out low.

He closed his eyes and did a few neck rolls, combating the trouble he had articulating his thoughts. Easier to remain closed-mouth than divulging to Shay what his dragon side demanded he do—claim her as his one and only mate. She was the type of woman he could get lost with and never regret giving up a life, living on the edge. She was so unnerving—she kept him hopping, not knowing what the hell to expect. Being near her was adventure enough and shit, the way she fought him—he'd have to hone his countermoves left and right for years to come.

When he didn't answer, Noah spoke up. "I take it that's a negative."

"For now. I'm working up to it."

"This isn't a freaking triathlon. You don't go and pace yourself. Hell. If anything, this is like parachuting from a plane. You got your pack. On three. Dive, man. And don't look back. Just jump. I mean if she's the one."

After excelling in free fall parachuting in the military, dealing with his dragon instinct about Shay felt ten times as dangerous. Drake could feel his face tighten. "Excuse me, but since when did you become so knowledgeable? Exactly how many women have you…ya know, claimed?"

"I got sisters, okay? And I know plenty about what makes a woman tick. Just because I haven't found the right one doesn't mean dick. I'm right on this matter. Do it!"

"Fuck off!"

"Are you scared? Shit, you are. Aren't you?" Noah barked out a loud cocksucking laugh. "Damn you to hell. You got it bad. Bro, you got it so fucking bad."

"Are you finished?" Every fiber of every muscle in Drake's body knotted at that moment.

"Fine, Obi-wan Kenobi. I won't say another word."

"Just find me something that can be flown."

"I'll put the squeeze on some contacts. But it'll cost ya."

"I don't care about the money. Get me some wings and I'll take care of your contact and you. And another thing, I'm serious about being ready to open up a private security firm. Assemble the team. We'll meet and talk."

"If you're serious."

"I am. Like a fucking heart attack? You in?"

"Hell yeah! Give me a few and I'll ring you back."

Drake clicked off his phone and turned around. Shay was leaning against the patio doors with a glass in her hand. "It's margarita time, and I have a friend I'd like you to meet."

Flashing a glance at her reddened mouth, he exhaled sharply. *Got plans for those lips.* "Is this your new friend?"

"Yes. And she's delicious. Care for a sample?"

"Only if happy hour is being served splattered all over your incredible breasts."

• • •

Shay held out the glass to him and prayed he wouldn't notice her hand was shaking. She could feel his fiery presence in her mind. Over the last three days, he'd had an uncanny ability to—God, she knew it sounded ludicrous—but it felt like they could read each other's thoughts. At first she'd felt she was coming unglued, but she'd gotten out her cell phone and Googled the term *alpha dragon male.* Not the fairy tale myths but the studies conducted in hospitals and universities. Over and over she read about the phenomena of dragon mind linking ability that included crawling through a target's brain and even erasing memories. Totally screwed up mind-warping stuff that only got more serious. After an initial touch, a male alpha dragon didn't require a physical connection to do a mind warp—confirmed in a research project where dragons possessed the ability to mind link at frickin' will!

And she was oh so sure Drake was doing that to her. Did he intend to take her to some secluded place and do what? She wasn't a plaything for him or Dimitri. If he took her for a fool, then he'd be the *fool*.

With Drake's precision hearing, he'd zone in on her heartbeat unless she did something so ungodly attention-grabbing that she rocked his whole boat. "What do you think about anal?" she asked suddenly.

Drake choked all right. He tried to keep from coughing, but his face turned seventeen shades of red and his glowing eyes turned bloodshot.

Bingo! Now when he heard her heartbeat it would be entwined with his own, ramped up and attributed to explicable nerves, and his choking episode. As if on cue his formidable dick was back to standing straight at attention.

"Are you okay?" She came forward and clapped him on the back—his muscles rippled like moving speed bumps under her fingers. She fought to blank her mind just in case he was reading her thoughts.

"Here. Take this," he said, then suddenly seemed to notice her get-up. "Hold on. How much tequila have you had to drink?"

"This isn't the alcohol talking," she murmured, holding his gaze. "But I had a cocktail. This one's for you. Drink up, cowboy! We'll do a finger of tequila afterward, and maybe you'll answer my question concerning decadent sex."

She swung around, giving him a money shot of her derriere. She'd changed into a black thong, black lace garters, heels, and with one of the scarves he'd used to bind her wrists tied in her hair. He was burning a hole in her ass cheeks right this moment… on that she was sure. His macho, over-the-top dragon desire was ready to launch and just the thought of him taking possession of her sent a swarm of goose bumps over her skin.

Yet he told his buddy on the phone she was "no big deal." Funny—when she'd said it, it made perfect sense, but to hear him talk about what they had as casual made her want to rake her nails down his back. Hard.

She got that he wasn't sold on her, that he just enjoyed taking her body for a test drive. She wasn't a dragon and therefore he'd never fully mate and claim her. Never in a gazillion years. But if she offered her ass on a silver platter, no doubt Mr. O'Connor would acquiesce on his way out the door. Her rational mind was fine with the idea of hard, dirty, and yeah, casual—but her leopardess nature silently snarled as if caught in a snare. Something foreign shifted in her feline mind, but no way was she about to be ruled by carnal instinct. Stamp a big fat "no" on that one!

All she needed was distance and time away from one alpha dragon who made her toes curl. Then her feline self would simmer the hell down. She wasn't going to sidestep one old geezer for a younger virile version who happened to make her heart thump—loud and way too fast. She needed to walk away with her sanity intact. Not teeter on the edge of some ludicrous infatuation with a dragon.

Shay bit her lip. How soon would her life settle down? Being on her own was going to be an altogether novel experience. If she got going.

She peered over to Drake's reflection in her bedroom mirror, praying he'd focus on her and down the drink. It contained a little sleeping powder her maid had given her last week, to help her sleep when she'd tossed and turned at night. It would come in handy now.

"If you don't finish that drink, I'll be forced to make another batch and that'll take time." She turned, bit the center of her lip provocatively, and watched as Drake tossed back the drink.

His eyes flashed over the rim, then he grinned as he set the glass down and was over across the room, pressing her up against the wall before she could blink. "Now, what where you saying about…anal?" he asked.

• • •

Drake slept next to her, his arm thrown possessively over her waist. At first, she remained still, gazing out the terrace doors, searching for the moon, and noted its position in the sky. From what she'd learned over the years in shifting, running, and using her leopardess senses when in feline form, the hour had to be near to eleven. In Lisbon, a city of nightlife found in bars, clubs, restaurants, and shows of all kinds, she'd easily hail a taxi. She had to keep her mind busy, think about the steps required to put her plan in play. If she began to contemplate the man next to her—how he made her feel—she'd be on a helicopter and flying up the coast tomorrow into impassible mountains with sheer drops, Drake had assured her. That was God-knew-where exactly in Navarre and there wasn't a departure date from his castle. That wasn't going to happen. No way.

She lifted Drake's large hand, strong and dark, and heavy in sleep. She laced her fingers over his, and for just a second, she allowed herself to absorb the shape of his fingers that had touched her intimately. The first man to do so. She'd remember him forever. Her chest squeezed, squeezed so tightly she felt a piercing deep inside. Setting his hand down next to his face on the pillow, she slowly curled upward all the while watching to see if he stirred.

The sleeping powder must have worked. Hard to believe. He was after all a dragon and these shifters were prone to be insusceptible to many medicines, spells, and incantations.

Luckily, not this time. She dressed quickly, picked up her satchel, and stood at the doorway of the bedroom, staring at

Drake's sleeping form. For a solitary second, her chest heaved and her heart was torn. *Shay, no rethinking! He'd hold you back. Now, buck up. Time to split.*

Under the cover of darkness, she slipped out the basement door. She walked out the service entrance to the wrought-iron gate. A few streets over were busier at night with traffic, which would increase her odds of catching a cab to the airport. She'd take the first flight available to get back to the States. She didn't care as long as she headed west, across the Atlantic.

Skittering over the sidewalk, she power-walked in the shadows for two streets, and when she rounded the corner, she held up her hand to shield her eyes from the glaring bright lights. She waved her arm at an approaching taxi. The cab rushed by without breaking speed. She repeated waving her arm and again, a second cab flew by. Damn. She planted her feet wide when another bright yellow cab came barreling down the street. But this time, she stuck her fingers into her mouth, releasing an ear-splitting whistle. Well all-righty. The cab slowed and stopped right in front of her.

"*Aonde você vai?*" the driver yelled.

Oh jeez, she needed to do more than stare at the man and sprinted to the taxi. This was the first time she'd hailed a cab. Normally, she just rang a servant and a private car took her where she wanted to go.

"The airport…*aeroporto*," she hollered back when a car behind the cab began honking.

"*Belas.*" He nodded, waving her inside.

"Awesome," she said, then scrunched her brows. "*Incríveis?*"

From watching movies, she vaguely knew that when he threw the meter handle down, he'd accepted her as his next fare. She opened the door and climbed into the cramped back seat of the Prius. He picked up his cell and spoke in rapid slices, writing on a clipboard. He smiled at her from the rearview mirror.

"Do you have flight leaving in a little while?" He spoke in English. "You look like you're in a hurry."

"No. Well. Not like I'm late or anything." Could she sound any more unsure of herself? She inhaled and smiled. "Your English is good."

"I went to school in New Jersey."

"And now?"

"Now, I need to eat," he replied and laughed. "I'm an exchange student. University of Lisbon."

"What are you studying?"

"Architecture."

"I graduated from Duke. Accounting. Business." The excitement she'd held onto through the summer didn't inspire her as she spoke. Her insides twisted as they drove away from the villa. Away from Drake. Oh God, what had she done leaving him? She glanced out the window, unsure if she wanted to tell the cabbie to turn around or if she should suck it up and stick to her plan. A little while longer and she'd be free. Wasn't that what she'd worked for?

What mattered in the end?

# CHAPTER 4

*Five months later.*

Shay tugged back on the handle, holding a frosty mug under the tap, and half-watched the stream of beer filling the glass, until the amber liquid changed into pure foam. The bubbles overran the rim and spilled over her fingers. "Son of a beach ball!" She dumped the foam and set the mug in the sink, then wiped her hands on a bar towel.

"We're tapped out," she called out…to no one. "Dammit," she muttered to herself. *Where is Solomon?*

"Want me to change out the keg?" Damien asked. He was one of her regulars at Mony Mony, the bar where she'd worked for months. The werewolf came in every night. He didn't say much other than a greeting and to order a microbrew—whatever beer she recommended. But boy could he tip. Every buck she earned went to purchase supplies on a forever growing shopping list.

"Nope," she huffed, her brows drawn tight. "That's not your job."

"Psst." Mara, another bar regular, used finger signals to remind Shay to *make eye contact and smile.* Mara was a behavior coach for supernaturals and when Shay agreed to accept some advice, she'd gotten an earful that now meant nightly helpful pointers. Relating to others openly came hard for Shay. Especially since she felt numb, as though her leopardess self were caged. Even after months of being on the run, her natural reaction was to close down, box in her emotions, and silently stare at the world around her.

Hard to believe she'd gotten a top-notch university business education. What a waste.

Shay nodded, and tacked on, "Damien, sit tight. If anyone comes in, tell 'em I'll be right back." She plastered on a smile directed at him then cast a snarky glance toward Mara who returned an equally snarky thumbs up.

She unscrewed the tap connectors. When would Solomon bite the bullet and invest in modern metal beer kegs instead of these old-fashioned casks? Walking around the counter with the empty wooden barrel, she headed for the kitchen and walk-in refrigerator unit. Before she could get more than five steps from the counter, the front door opened, admitting the swirling wind inward, carrying bits of dried leaves, dust, and a heart-stopping scent.

Shay's leopard senses pricked then changed to a full-on-alert as her hair stood on end. Her nostrils flared, the skin tightened over her body—her claws under her fingertips threatened to pierce through her skin.

This overreaction had to be her imagination.

A sensory mirage.

No way in hell had *he* found her.

The moonlight backlit and outlined the man who stepped through the doorway. No mistaking the spiraling smoke that swirled around his head. He sure wasn't smoking a cigar, but he was smokin' all right.

Dragon. Fire.

Serpent. Smoke.

She remembered all too well the depth of Drake's nuclear fusion heat.

The purposefully dim lighting cast shadows along the room of the small hole-in-the-wall bar, assisting the regulars' desire for anonymity. Inside a few tables were scattered alongside a postage-stamp stage and equally small dance floor. It was too late to backtrack and reach for the pistol under the counter. The carved oak bar took up a great part of the space, curving and covering two walls in an L-shape, and she seriously doubted, in human form, she could clear the bar in the time he could clear the door. Besides there were customers seated at the bar.

Mony Mony was the place the locals from Harmony came to hang. Although not far from New Orleans, Harmony remained off the grid—a haven for supernaturals who didn't want the crowds coming through like it was bake-day in one of the Amish parishes. The paranormals around Harmony sucked at putting up with an ounce of crap from human tourists who lacked the gray cells to keep from snapping photographs or the sense to refrain from asking asinine questions.

Down here in Harmony, the code was shut your piehole. No trash talk. No finger pointing. And especially, no snitching.

So how in the heck had he found her?

She dropped the cask and it thudded to the floor as she studied his shadowy silhouette filling the doorway.

"Hello, Shay." Drake's low masculine voice cut through her thoughts with steel blade ferocity. "It's been awhile."

Holy goddess! She backed up a step, her knees suddenly weak, and her brain a malfunctioning sieve, unable to piece together how…why the man who'd turned her life upside down had found her.

"What the hell do you want?" she snarled, her leopardess on the verge of shifting.

"Kitten, that's no way to welcome an old…friend," Drake said, coming through the doorway dressed in motorcycle leathers. Same dragon bronzed skin. Still built like a Mack truck.

But it was his green eyes that held her captive once their gazes connected—more like locked. She fought against the unmistakable and very familiar tug on her body, a simultaneous thunderbolt and hooking that dove deep into her awareness. With a word…a look…now Drake had found her and her tenuous inner sanctum. The secret place within herself she'd kept locked. Untouched. Untapped. Ever since she last saw him five months ago.

She glanced away, refusing to give him the power to wipe her mind. Her regular patrons had turned around. Damien was off his seat, his silver eyes glowing red and his canines already visible. Two others, Carl and Keegen—twin Viking vampires—stood as well…tense, silent, and sneering, weighing the emotional tension as only vampires could. She flailed her arm when they bared their fangs.

"Jesus. Joseph. And Mary! Guys, sit down," she scoffed. "This isn't your concern."

"What do you want Níðhöggr?" Keegan snapped, staring at Drake. His fangs caught his bottom lip and he grimaced, reaching up and wiping a dribble of blood off his chin.

"Not here to hurt the little lady," Drake returned. "So no one needs to worry."

"We'll be the judge of that *drage shadown*," Carl said, his icy arctic eyes narrowed and he hissed a vampire warning.

Drake only sneered at the Viking brothers. "*Lindworm, wyrm, snake.* Best you got? For the record it's *Herensuge* or *Drac*. Don't try to insult me, boys. I'd hate to knock those precious fangs down your Swedish throats by accident."

Shay curled her thumb and index finger between her lips and blew a shrill whistle. "Geez. All of you. Fold it and hold it. This isn't some preternatural pissing match."

The vampire brothers muttered something about mouthy bartenders, but they took their seats, unlike Damien. "What's going on, Shay?" he asked, still standing.

"*No big deal.*" She shook her head. "Really not a thing. This is less than nothing. Now, I really need you to tend the bar until I get back. I'll text Solomon. He was—"

"Don't get your drawers knotted, I'm here." Solomon appeared, rubbing his arm over his face. He was a grizzly shifter with a hankering for sweets and in denial over his recently diagnosed type 2 diabetes.

"Were you eating honey, Solomon Breaux?" she asked incredulously. "I swear I'll call up Trish and let her know." Trish was Sol's wife and the Harmony shifter doctor who treated the residents for general medical stuff—cuts, sickness, vaccinations.

"Looks like you got your own issues to deal with…wouldn't you say?" Solomon cocked his head toward Drake. "Who's your friend?"

"Nobody." Shay's whole body trembled from unspent energy. Either she shifted and kicked the shit out of someone or she needed to get outside and walk off this desire to roar. "I'll have this dealt with lickety-split. Give me a minute."

Solomon cut a glance toward Drake, then paused his focus, flicking his eyes up and down over their unwelcome visitor. "That's a whole lot of nobody."

"I'll be fine," she bit out.

"Maybe it's not you I'm worried about," Solomon snorted, then lifted the empty cask. "Take all the time you need. In fact, your shift is done and none of us are going anywhere soon."

Should she warn them to refrain from coming into contact with him and looking into Drake's eyes? That wasn't necessary. Only she'd been stupid enough to give him the power to mind-bend her to his will. No matter how far she ran, her inability to stop thinking about him *ad infinitum* was all the evidence she needed that he'd employed some dragon mind-warp to her brain. And to think, she'd been dumb enough to trust him.

Still, it had spurred her to act on her refusal to marry Dimitri Necrodemas. Not that she'd thrown it into her parents' faces—but they knew she'd been *touched*. All leopards could ferret out scents—lucky for her Drake's dragon scent was so difficult to identify, but she couldn't believe no one put two and two together.

By giving away her virginity, she'd tainted herself, at least in the eyes of a man of Necrodemas's status. Shut the door on any marriage proposals with her act of rebellion—and she was glad.

Except for one minor detail. It wasn't an act and she'd ended up in Drake's bed. For days. Little did she understand what it meant to be fucked mindless by a dragon who'd decided, without telling her, that she was his.

But it was Necrodemas who'd made the ultimate stink with his emails and threatening calls to her parents. Accused her of being a tramp and trying to rook him into marriage. What a fucking farce. Who would believe some old alpha leopard who'd been chosen for her by her parents to unite the shifter regions would end up causing such a rift? This was the freaking United States, not a village in the foothills of the Himalayas.

Her brother gave her his grudging approval at sidestepping Necrodemas, but he didn't approve her running away from the family or Denver. Easy for him to say, considering he was the shining star for Mom and Dad and the entire shifter populace in the Southwest…and where did that place her? Black sheep, selfish, not doing her duty—the list was endless. She'd received enough ugly anonymous emails and phone calls, and then was let go from her job at Sternberg and Fink. It was too much to bear the fall from grace. Still, Shawn had offered her money when her parents shut down her trust fund, tangling it in legal knots trying to sway her to reconsider staying, but she refused. At least she walked away with her head held up.

Unfortunately, the freak fest didn't blow over—she'd recently gotten information that Necrodemas was looking for her. That part she didn't understand, but she'd still flown under the radar, unwilling to test whether or not the old alpha actually possessed all the power he'd boasted.

Score one for Drake in being the first to find her.

But she'd die before admitting that he was right and she was wrong about her being free to just walk away unscathed.

Didn't matter, since that their little sex affair was a total snafu. She didn't just jump from the skillet into the flames, she'd started a firestorm. And she didn't settle for a tiny flicker of heat, Oh no! She'd thrown gallons and gallons of combustible fuel on the backdraft by harnessing herself to all-powerful dragon in wild, messy hair, screaming sex. In retrospect, their blistering affair had ended all too quickly before she'd left the villa and had the chance to recoup her sanity—turn the tables on him and his mind-warping ability.

It was the last time she'd seen Drake. The last time she'd talked civilly with her parents before they'd angrily disowned her. The last time she'd lived without looking over her shoulder.

Now, her body clenched at the potent scent of him this close. Achingly familiar—bone deep—and in seconds she longed to strip off her clothes and meld against his warm skin and hard body. The way his scent torqued her self-control made liquid fire run free in her blood and fill her from the inside out. Lust roiled in her veins as all her thoughts dissolved save one: fucking him.

*No. Goddamn. Way.*

"Come with me," she said between gritted teeth, curling her fingers into fists, and marching past him. This dragon mind game was going to end and it was going to end right now.

"With pleasure," he whispered in a gravelly voice that massaged her in places she'd forgotten about and by rights should have exorcised out of her system. "Speaking of past experiences, it was perfect being in back of you."

She swung around, her nostrils flaring, and her canines bared. "Don't push your luck."

"I believe I was the one who said don't push," he growled as his eyes glowed green, flashing her with a fire she remembered oh-so-well.

"Is this about settling a score?" she asked before she resumed walking. Over her shoulder, she tacked on, "Better get in line."

Once outside, she noticed his motorcycle. The man hadn't changed. Had she really ridden with him once? Her arms wrapped around his waist, burning up the mountain roads outside Lisbon?

"Kitten," he said. "Put away your claws."

She spun toward Drake, without gazing up into his face, and unfortunately found the contoured pecs that strained his T-shirt right in front of her nose. "What in the name of all that's holy are you doing here?"

Oops! She'd forgotten. With lightning fast reflexes that only a dragon was capable of, he had her up against the side of the building, in the shadows, his body pressed to hers. "Didn't I say I'd come find you?" Then his glimmering eyes widened and he looked downward as though noticing her protruding belly for the first time.

She was dressed in a loose fitting shirt and apron that so far had hid her condition. But his speed was never a match for her ferocity and she pivoted him a full one hundred and eighty degrees and slammed him against the brick wall. Besides picking up some social skills training, she'd studied martial arts these last five months and twenty-six days.

But who was counting?

She did better barefoot, where she was unencumbered by shoes like the heavy work boots she wore or these jeans. But with her forearm pressed against Drake's throat, she was pretty sure he got the message. Then he moved his hand to her rounded belly, spread his fingers over the front of her jeans, and pressed.

"My baby?" he whispered, his warm palm cupping her abdomen. "Shit. Why didn't you contact me?"

"Don't mess with me," she hissed, trying to back away, but he held her steady with his iron grip on her arm and his palm still tenderly squeezing her. His green eyes focused on her and her gaze collided with his. "Why are you here?"

"Apparently a lot has changed between us." He frowned. "First you'd better answer my question."

"What was the point?" she scoffed. "I can take care of myself. I'm not some wilting daisy. Pregnant or not, I can kick ass."

"We're talking about my baby," he growled. "You're not going to kick anyone's ass. Hell, I have a good mind to lay you over my lap and spank your bottom."

She released him and smirked, then backed up a step and waved him forward. "C'mon. Why don't you give it try? Give me your best shot. I'll have you laid out. Promise."

He took hold of her. Again. Not lightning fast and she easily could have avoided him. But she didn't want to—this had to be more dragon mental wrangling.

"Little girl, we gonna do this dance? 'Cause if memory serves me correct, you liked it rough, but in the end it was with your wrists and ankles tied to my bed. We never tried mine…unless you've developed a taste for doing the tying. If that's what it takes to get you to talk to me, I might acquiesce to your whims."

"Drake, stop playing with my mind! Don't you dare go there," she warned and turned from him, only to hear his scurrilous chuckle fill the air. Oh Jesus. Her skin was seared from his touch—worse from his words and stare.

"If I could, I would. In a city second. I'm here on business so put away your claws and canines unless you want me to mount you. And darling, I'm a click away from reminding you how good we are in bed."

"Is that what this is? You want to make me remember? I have enough, way more than enough, to never forget the nights you spent in my bed."

He arched a brow. "That's not why I came. But now, our little reunion has taken a turn for the serious."

"Whose business?"

He leveled her with a look, setting his jaw with just the right amount of displeasure to come off as badass sexy. "Shawn needs you," he said, his tone turning solemn. "Damn, I can't believe if he hadn't contacted me I never would have found out about my baby. What are you thinking? You shouldn't be alone. All this time and I could have helped you."

She snapped her head upward, risking her wellbeing, and searched Drake's eyes for clues as to what he had yet to divulge. Her heart squeezed. "What's wrong? Is Shawn all right?"

"Your brother is fine. He's in charge of the council."

"And you came here to tell me that instead of him. What of my father?"

"Quick as ever, kitten. I'm here on council business. Things are heating up in Denver. All over the country. The Western council needs to harness the power of other sectors, other continents." Flickering green sparks, tendrils of heat flared from his gaze… and she felt herself begin to fall under his spell. Dragon magick. Intoxicating to only one: the mate to an alpha male dragon and he'd branded her without her consent. Marked her to every other male—not that she was in the market for another over-the-top dragon…or any other guy.

"Don't start that serpent mental shit with me, Drake," she whispered, tearing her gaze away from his by closing her eyes and drawing in a deep cleansing breath. The muscles in her extremities trembled and the spiraling sensation deep in her belly pulsated—only one way to stop the coiling and he damned well knew the effect he was having on her. She glanced down to avoid looking into his eyes. But seriously! The sight of his bulge—clearly erect behind his leathers—was of zero help.

"So Shawn is fine? Swear it!"

"Yes. I swear. It's strictly the council. A meeting is planned and requires all heirs to appear. There. I've done my due diligence."

Drake said, then paused, his breath caressing her cheek. "Do you have a reply?"

"I don't owe you reply."

"On that, you're wrong. We can stay out here all night, and if that's what you need, I'll accommodate you. But we could be naked right now and on our way to a more fitting reunion. One that I promise won't disappoint you."

"How the hell do you get a helmet on that ego of yours?"

"Darling, that's not the head you should be concentrating on right this second."

"You're insufferable. Really, Drake," she said.

"I meant yours, not mine," he replied.

# CHAPTER 5

Seeing Shannon again and pregnant with his baby rocked his entire world. But hell would freeze over twice before that slipped from his tongue. Sure, he'd had a jackass plan coming down here. Originally, he would have given his left nut to fuck her. Then maybe, just maybe, he'd stop incessantly carrying this torch he'd rooked himself into ever since she ran out on him. His plan on hooking up with Shannon ran pretty linear: he'd find her, fuck her, leave her…forget her.

In that grand order.

With one minor issue: she was his mate and forgetting her was as easy as forgetting to breathe. Every goddamn night she haunted his dreams. His dragon ego had demanded that he let her go when she'd hauled ass away from Lisbon. When she'd left him, only his blasted pride enabled him to build a wall around his dragon instinct to claim her, when rightfully she was his. He would have gone solo through eternity rather than let her see how deeply she'd crawled under his skin—but that was before he'd discovered she carried his child.

She paused in front of him now, and flipped him off. "My head is just fine. I'm here. Employed. And so far, I'm not married to some old geezer or shacked up with some control freak who spews fire."

"You aren't anywhere near living fine and dandy. Dammit, you're on the run. Holy hell," he muttered, reeling and fighting the urge to encircle her in his arms. According to his grand plan, sometime soon, he'd have to divulge that she was due back in Denver on the private jet her family was sending. Except encountering Shay with her rounded belly filled with his baby dissolved all plans. He wasn't ever going to leave her alone and certainly wasn't about to let her go back to Denver to face Shawn by herself.

"How would you know anything about me?" she asked, crossing her arms over her chest.

He tried not to stare at her tits, but looking at her rounded belly did things to him. Off the charts things like want to protect her and at the same time, strip her naked and explore her body.

"I know plenty. What's important and from now on, I won't be fucking ignored or cut off from you. You're carrying my child and I will be a father...an involved father, Shay. Better get used to it." Glancing around the parking lot, he sucked in a breath that tasted like smoke and lust.

"How magnanimous of you. Don't I have any say?"

He flashed his focus over to her, itching to kiss her quiet, but the chance of that happening: zilch. Well, not yet, and he looked for an angle so she'd put away her claws. "At least things are laid back down here."

"Things were laid back. Until you showed up...you could have called," she retorted.

"And risk you running again? I'm not just a pretty face for your pleasure, *my lady*." He winked at her, then let his gaze roam down to her chest and lower to her curvy figure.

Apparently, she still wanted nothing to do with him. The way her tits were rising and falling, tempted him to do more than stare, but most definitely, she was breathing air if not fire where he was concerned. Well that stunk for her. He wasn't going anywhere until she gave birth.

The question was how to get her to stop fighting him. For sure, he could use his dragon mind linking. Mind read and wipe. Even mind warp, but he wouldn't do that to her and had fought linking his mind to Shay all these months just in case she was sensitive enough to realize. Some shifters knew exactly when a mind link occurred, and he bet Shay was one of those sorts. Underneath all the bullshit swirling around his own brain and lashing his chest in barbed wire, he craved that she meld to him of her own accord. Maybe this was all a challenge, and heaven only knew too well, he'd be up for scaling his personal Kilimanjaro in the form of a golden-eyed feline with a smart mouth.

No, he needed to get to know her…on her terms. Show her he could be trusted and then maybe she might put aside fighting him tooth and nail. "So you tend bar now?"

"Idle chit-chat?" she commented, arching a brow. "Should I ask you over for tea and we can catch up?"

He scrubbed a hand down his face. "So I suck at small talk, but we still need to talk. I'm the father of your baby and do you seriously think I'm going anywhere?"

"We have nothing to discuss—"

Without thinking, he reacted, eating up the distance between them until he had her in his arms, so close from thigh to chest it was impossible to distinguish where their bodies began and ended. "You're carrying my seed. Do you know what the statistical relevance of you becoming pregnant is? So low I didn't even worry about protection because it's near impossible to impregnate another dragon…forget about a leopardess. And yet here you are pregnant with my son or daughter."

"Is this some type of cold analysis of offspring reproduction rates on your part? Are you saying you're going to take your progeny back to your dragon family? I'll fight you with everything I have at my disposal."

"If I wanted to whisk you away from here, do you think there's anyone or anything that would get in my way? I warned you once, don't push me." He moved his hands to her hips, spreading his fingers over the curve of each of her ass cheeks and cupped her bottom, hiking up her hips and pressing into her. "You're mine. I tried to warn you, but you refused to listen."

"Please, don't use what we did a few nights so long ago, I can't recall the actual details…just the effect."

Fuck. Did everything she say have to come out like chewed glass from her beautiful mouth? "You said you'd never forget," he murmured, savoring the feel of her heat spreading over his erection. Yeah, his baby was inside her. He absorbed the energy wavelengths that were stronger than usual for an infant dragon. "We need to get you checked out by a doctor familiar with dragon pregnancies."

"I'm aware of what happens to dragons, Drake. I'll never agree to go to your family's compound."

The back of his neck tightened. "So am I and that's not what I'm suggesting."

"Then you're also aware that I'll never subject my children to those archaic traditions. If I didn't do that to myself, I sure as hell won't do that to my babies." She untied the apron and lifted the neck strap over her head.

"Babies?"

She glanced downward, uncertainty flashing through her expression. "Twins. A boy and a girl, and they're strong. Growing and as I understand, I'll give birth in April."

"Twins?" he repeated and his knees weakened. He'd witnessed all sorts of war atrocities without flinching, yet hearing that Shay was not only pregnant but with two babies stunned him; he stared with his mouth wide open.

"I was a twin, but my sister died. Fraternal and identical twins are common for leopards."

"Do you know anything about giving birth to a dragon…let alone two?" he asked. "I don't know if April is correct."

"What do you take me for? I'm not some idiot. Just because you saw me the summer after graduating, trying to let off some steam, doesn't mean I'm an airhead. Besides, who says our babies are dragons?"

"My children are dragons," he snorted. "And yes, I'm well aware of your level of intellect and creativity…you slipped by my team enough times to have made that point."

"I can slip by you again." She notched her chin up and his chest tightened. This was not the time to push one wayward leopardess.

In truth, she'd slipped by him and out the door of the villa. For months he failed to track her down. Without resorting to mind linking, and without the monetary backing of the Barclay Enterprises, he'd relied on his navy buddies' connections and he'd gotten a handle on where Shay had ended up. Louisiana of all places. She was smart all right. Down here was one of the few places on earth where the supernatural community didn't sell out to outsiders. Harmony had some hardcore eyes and ears as evidenced by the glowing red eyes yards away, observing him and Shay. He imagined if those same eyes perceived Shay was truly in danger, they'd try to subdue him. "Try" being the operative word.

He needed to make her feel safe. Secure. It would be her natural shifter instinct when pregnant to secure a place for herself. Since he couldn't handcuff her to his bed, he needed to do whatever he could to make sure she didn't give him the slip. "You have friends here. Several who protect and watch over you. I don't want to inadvertently harm an overzealous buddy or two."

"This is a safe place and why I settled here," she said. "Isn't that what you preached?"

He nodded. "Glad you listened to something. Can we find a place to talk? I promise not to try anything you don't want."

"No mind tricks? Promise me."

"I don't need to use mental kink to get a woman to spread her legs."

"*That's what he said*," Shay scoffed, then she shrugged. "I guess I always knew this day would get here. C'mon. I live above Mony."

"After you." He motioned that he'd follow her and he did, far enough away to keep from overshadowing Shay. He took advantage of bringing up rear by admiring the gentle sway of her hips and recalling the times he'd spent in back of her, making them both dive for the edge of ecstasy.

Below the staircase, he noted a bike and a set of skates on a hook. He took her elbow as they scaled the steps, casually glancing around from the small porch and observing the dark shadows scurrying from behind trees, threading between cars, then a bleep as something darted behind a wooden fence. A wind chime clinked above his head as the breeze swept across the deck. A set of chairs and a table were off to the side, and a pair of running shoes were propped up on one of the seats.

Shay unlocked the door and pushed it open, but he reached out for her. His whole body tensed and he stalled, unable to move as he grabbed for her arm. His pulse raced, a byproduct of watching the shadows below and wondering if they were all friends…or not. The scales below the surface of his skin began to rise, and he breathed out, shooting a cloud of smoke from his lungs. All of a sudden, he felt a sense of needing to protect Shay rise from his core.

"Wait," he growled, his dorsal fin rising along his spine as his cranial horn pierced the skin at his forehead. Wings would follow if he didn't reel in this overzealous craving to shield Shay.

"Okay, really. There's such a thing as secondhand smoke and it's not good for babies. Either you learn to moderate or we can't have a conversation inside. Rule number one: no smoking inside my place."

He clenched his jaw. "Makes sense. I'll turn down the heat."

Fuck! That wasn't possible. If anything, he was powered up, ready to either fuck like a dragon—who hadn't had a woman since this one—or succumb to the pressure of safeguarding the perimeter.

"Rule number two: I don't want to fuck you. It could hurt our babies. Do you understand that concept, Drake?"

Inhaling and staring down into her eyes, he knew he'd never do anything to purposefully harm her or his unborn infants. For as much as he needed to talk and then assuage his hunger to claim her as his mate, he heard the twining messages in her words. Loud and louder. Twins. His. She could be in danger if he was too rough. Dragon sex. Always rough.

"Got them. Two rules. No smoking. No rough riding."

Her eyes widened, then the blush overtaking her cheeks made him temporarily forget everything—except the razor sharp instinct to make her his. Whatever it took.

"Good. You're thinking with your brain this time," she said.

"I promise. You'll be safe with me."

• • •

Backed up to a wall inside her apartment, Shay met his stare. "Then why the hell do I feel like I have just brooked the worst idea in history by inviting you inside my place?" Holy shit, she'd meant to just think that…not say it out loud.

Drake's lips thinned and sealed shut. In Lisbon, he would have been all over her for a comeback like that one. With his clenched jaw and arched brow, she remembered all too well what he was like then. And talk wasn't what came to mind as she glanced down his body when he closed the door and locked it. *Big words, Shay, with those rules.* All she could think about was smoking hot sex. Was she mental?

She wasn't about to tell her him what Dr. Sosa, the obstetrician had pronounced: leopardess mothers were hardcore. She could bench press probably as much as her brother. A hell of a lot more than the guys at the gym. Dr. Trish confirmed what the obstetrician had said and delved further into her dragon pregnancy, as was Trish's nature. She plied Shay with loads of materials to read about dragon babies and badgered her about nutrition.

So Shay understood this wasn't like any regular shifter pregnancy. There was some sort of anomaly in how her body had changed to accommodate her developing infants. Every day she had to expend her energy, Dr. Sosa said, or she'd hurt from muscle atrophy. At first her martial arts training gave her an outlet, but more and more she required the burn—or release of the burn—from too much lactic acid build-up in her muscles. If she didn't exercise, her muscles ached and hurt like she'd overtrained. Weird. But she got with the program and ran ten miles daily. Or cycled, covering miles and miles through the flat country back roads. She'd recently taken up skating.

Faced with Drake, her potential mate, she needed distance immediately and it would be far easier if he believed his way of wild sex was off-limits. Bogus, but let him put on the brakes.

"Care for something to drink? I have juice, milk, water, and herbal tea."

"I'm good," he said, his back to the door; he'd yet to cross the tiny foyer.

Oh yeah. He was good…in bed, between her legs, and especially in making her scream his name.

"Are you going to come in or stay posted at the door all night?"

"Just waiting for you to show me the way. It's customary to invite your guests to where you'd like to sit. Am I right?"

Goodness. Where were her manners? She was struggling to act normal with him staring holes into her body—not that his overpowering gaze wasn't enjoyable once she got used to it. "This way," she choked, still uneasy in his presence as she led the way to her makeshift living room.

The apartment was a hob-cob matrix of small rooms that were still part storage for the bar, but the rest Solomon said she could do with whatever she desired. For free rent, she couldn't complain. From her tips, she bought food and the fire retardant supplies required for everything from cribs to sheets to material to make dragon baby clothes.

"Thanks," he said, looking around her place.

"Okay, you said you wanted to talk," she said, watching him walk toward her with his alpha male demeanor and his eyes glowing green in the low lighting. "I'm all ears."

"Should I just say what's on my mind or do you want me to organize my thoughts in some sort of order?"

"I'm fine with random."

"First item," he said, stopping in front her. "You're my mate. Nothing in this universe will change that. No shifter will touch you without first challenging me to claim you and I'll never release you, Shay. We're bound."

"*Bound?* Like to your bed?" She couldn't encounter silk scarves without shivering, and the memory made her heartbeat race.

"Sweetheart, not that kind of bound. We're linked by DNA now."

She was determined not to flinch or drop her gaze, but it was damn hard to stand under his livewire perusal and remain unaffected. "There must be something that can be done. Can't we find a physician, a shaman—dammit, what about a witch doctor?"

"Didn't I warn you?" He hooked his finger gently under her chin, and the draw to give into him filled her. Ache and need swirled in her body and his babies fluttered within her abdomen. "You are mine," he told her in a deep voice.

"I wasn't myself last summer. I would have agreed to selling my soul that night."

The corners of his lips curled and he raised a brow. "I thought you didn't remember a thing. Apparently, you recall a few details. Tell me the truth, don't you want me inside you? Right now?"

"You already are. I'm carrying your children."

"Thank you for clarifying that point, but you know that's not what I'm referring to. I'll be gentle with you. Just the tip of my cock and we can enjoy each other. Or my mouth, fingers, and nothing more. As dragon and mate, we need skin-on-skin contact and we won't be able to refrain from each other—to do so would put us at risk, unable to think logically when our primal instincts become fully roused. From the way I feel right now, it's only a matter of a few hours. If you know so much about dragons, then surely you realize what I'm saying is true. Don't try and run, once we encounter each other, this instinct can only be abated one way."

"I didn't study mating rituals. So no, I'm ignorant to dragon mates."

He laughed. "Not that ignorant to mates." He placed his hand over her abdomen and the twins kicked. "Our children are strong."

"Please," she said, wanting to move back. She'd been so stubborn, refusing to read about dragon mates even when Trish forewarned her that she might find those tidbits more than trivial. But oh no! She'd held on staunchly to the idea that mating was irrelevant to her pregnancy. She'd been a fool. Now she actually leaned into his hand on her belly. The feeling was so relaxing to her ragged senses, a deep moan bubbled up her throat.

"You'd feel better naked. Let me massage your skin. I promise, nothing will happen that you don't want and skin-on-skin is what you need. Didn't your doctor relay anything about dragons?"

There weren't any dragons that she knew of in Harmony until now. "Dr. Sosa sticks to the care and treatment of me and the babies."

"Lie down on your bed and let me make you feel good. I'll massage your back and shoulders."

"I don't believe that's a *good* idea." In the few short minutes of being alone with Drake in an enclosed space, she learned she needed more than a few paltry rules to keep them from ripping both their clothes off.

He brushed a few strands of hair behind her ears. "This color looks pretty on you."

"Another product of my pregnancy. Not my choice," she said, shivering under his touch. Her hair was no longer blue-black but had changed to a fiery copper. Even the fine hairs on her arms were reddish, as were her eyebrows…and other places.

"Yeah, I remember you were all about choices in Lisbon. I would never stop you from doing what you desired. I'm not like Necrodemas."

"Night and day." She nodded. "No joke. He made some threats before I left Denver," she added.

"And now?" he asked, his pupils elongated rapidly.

"He…hasn't contacted me but he's out there. And I know he's dirty. Or at least he was last August in how he acquired art as a Chief Justice."

"Your brother should be reminded of that. He's well informed by Tristen and Fin. They're on his team, helping him manage his businesses around Denver. Those two hardcore beta wolves have his back. But in case he doesn't have a line on Dimitri's dealings, it might help if they know your thoughts on the other justice councils across the world, especially when humans are pitted against shifters like what occurred in China and Syria," he commented, the heat from him radiating over her skin. Unlike last summer when she felt a burning connection with Drake, this sizzle was perfect. So magnetic and aching that her nipples hardened.

"Why don't you tell him?"

"I'm not close to Shawn as we once were."

"Because of me?" she asked, her voice pitching upward as she instinctively leaned nearer to him, and his breath swept over her face.

"Don't be ridiculous. Because of me," he countered. "I take responsibility for what occurred."

"Then you told them…how much?" She bit her lip, wondering how her family took the news coming from him.

"I took responsibility for what occurred. I wasn't going to lie to them. They fired me and it was tense. At first."

She wrapped her arms around her middle as her stomach twisted. She closed her eyes, shaking her head for a second. Hard to believe they'd both lost their jobs—worse, they'd both been fired. Swallowing her guilt at being so headstrong, she trained her focus on him. "Drake, I'm so sorry I got you caught in the crossfire."

"You didn't. Don't you remember? I was more than a willing partner. I can take care of myself and our children."

"I still can't believe my parents would have made me marry that bag of wind. I don't understand why they sided with him."

"Don't think of them harshly." His features tensed and she recognized his shuttering facade. Enough to track the glow fading from his eyes as his pupils stretched into slivers. The dragon sign for suppressed emotions.

"Wait. What aren't you telling me? Out with it, Drake."

"Your parents," he said softly, "aren't the same."

# CHAPTER 6

His pupils elongated into slits. He felt the change as his vision sharpened. In response to the tension of being this close to his mate, his whole body incrementally transformed into a minor shape shift, bringing him nearer to his dragon nature. Shay unclaimed or not, his body only knew one thing: she was his. The physical changes in her confirmed they needed to take the last step in a mutual claiming and she'd be his forever. Easier to protect her since they'd share an undeniable lifeline as mated and claimed *dragons*.

How to relay that fact? Did she realize where her future lay? She'd fought like hell when another shifter had wanted her, for all the wrong reasons.

Would she fight tooth and nail when he sought to claim her? There was no way he'd let her go or go on without him.

Pregnant with twin dragons—what a spitfire. The feisty mother of his children. Of course, the mate he'd sought out would have to be this headstrong woman—a woman who hated the idea of him. She had always fought him at every turn and more than likely, always would. No wonder he couldn't put her out of his mind. Couldn't bed another in her place. His whole mind, body, even soul had been in chaos over the last five months as he fought to ignore the driving force to find her.

Shit, this trip was turning out to be a regular powder keg.

"I haven't been in touch with my parents since the summer. What are you talking about?" Shay asked.

He slid his hands onto her shoulders. She needed honesty, but how to make it less brutal? "They were in a car accident. No one knows if it was just an accident and I'm not part of the inner circle where your family is concerned. What was released to the press isn't the whole story. Another reason you need to get in contact with Shawn."

Inches apart from Shay, he absorbed the heat of her body, speaking to him in an ancient message that demanded he do more than tease his instincts. His stiff cock rode up the back of his zipper, going granite hard. Her exotic leopardess scent mixed with a haunting fragrance overpowered his ability to think straight. He'd heard what happened to alpha dragons in the presence of their mate. He hadn't accurately envisioned the depth of the allure she'd possess over him. The draw to her ran bone deep. Ah hell, this was cell deep.

His response to her was more like some reptilian response where the primal impulse was to eat and mate when they were next to one another. Strike that. Only "mate" remained as the blaring operational message commanding him and infiltrating his bloodstream. She was his and pregnant with his children. Those two factors made him all the more ready to drag her to bed and plunge his dick into her, filling her up with his release while sinking his fangs into her and marking her intimately. She'd have the power to use her canines and mark him as well. Together they'd be joined, sharing emotions and having the power to telepathically communicate. Empathic. Dragon nature.

He imagined he wouldn't be able to leave her side for the next week or two. His body would demand that they mate over and over again. Generally, once a female was impregnated, her mate would then be a regular fucking machine until he was physically worn out. Probably the law of survival acknowledged the odds if he could do it once, then he'd do it again. But hell, he wasn't about to look for another bedmate even if the dragon nature was to acquire several at once.

"God. This has something to do with shifter politics. Doesn't it?" Her chin quivered as she looked to him for an answer.

"There's a lot of violence in cities. Shifter on human and shifter on shifter."

"My parents worked for justice and shifter equality, and I ran away because of what? A few instances of name-calling. What have I done?" Shay slumped forward, and leaned onto his chest. The silky texture of her hair brushed against his chin and it was too easy to draw her next to him.

"What you had to…" he murmured, savoring her scent. He withheld from running his hands down her body and reacquainting himself with a hundred reasons why she tormented him.

She pressed her forehead into his shoulder. "Please. How bad do you think they are? Tell me what you know that's fact."

This time he wound several silky strands of her hair around his fingers and deeply inhaled her fragrance, the mysterious lingering scent that haunted him, leaving him on edge as though he were back on a search-and-find covert mission. The familiar essence in her glowed like magical moonlight, but he'd didn't understand why she'd glow cool warmth if she were filled with his babies. In his encyclopedic knowledge, he couldn't find anything related. Not that he had much on the subject of spitfire leopardess shifters. On that chapter he had next to nothing and it left him feeling more and more like a clumsy idiot in Shay's presence.

"I'll tell you what I know, but you must promise to remain calm." He was grateful to concentrate on something other than his overzealous hunger to sample her mouth. Relaying the dismal facts squelched his primal urges…at least for the moment.

Lifting her face to him, he saw her slender brows drew together as she nodded. "I don't fly off the handle. Not as easily as when you knew me last."

He searched her face, unwilling to admit her untamed nature wasn't a real problem in his book, except when she thwarted his authority. He captured her hands in his and squeezed gently. "Your dad was hurt but he'll recover. According to the specialist's diagnosis and the trauma Richard's suffered. Your father's doctor said the induced coma will reset his pain threshold."

"Coma! My dad is in a coma?" She jerked her head upward.

"It's a medical procedure to help alleviate pain."

Shay gripped his hands. "Don't stop until you tell me every damn detail. I'm serious, Drake!"

"There's not a lot of detail beyond what I've already told you. Your parents were in an auto accident. But from what I understand your father is on the mend, and I'm not sure about your mother."

"My mom is all right…isn't she?" She bit her lush lip in her signature move that failed to hide she was torn.

"Yes. From what I have heard. Your mom is at home and safe. Your dad will be back home in a day or two. This is exactly what Shawn said and why he seeks you out. He's your blood as they are—it's not hard to understand why they want to repair the rift." That was the truth and his chest tightened when he felt her shoulders begin to shake, and her jagged inhalation as though she couldn't breathe.

"And you promise, this isn't some trap. Not from them…or you."

"Shannon," he whispered, tipping up her face, and whipping away her tears. "There's no trap being set. Trust me. I wouldn't lie to the mother of my children."

Her golden eyes held his, flashing green fire in the dim light, forging an electrical connection that ripped through him, and he couldn't step back, not in a million years. Sweet Jesus—she was changing into a dragon mistress right before his eyes. He lowered his mouth to hers, fusing their lips. He had to withstand his hunger to do more than kiss her and ran his hands down her body, holding her aloft by squeezing his fingers around her hips. Difficult when she opened her mouth and pressed her tongue across his. So sweet, she had the power to dissolve all his anger, rage…and even his hurt over the fact that she'd disappeared and left him.

"Drake, I do believe you," she moaned, reaching her arms up and around his neck.

"I respect your need for rules, but you're living by a few that are difficult, if not impossible to ignore. Let me know what you need, I'll get it for you. Anything. Just tell me." He didn't want to come right out and say he had needs. A very hard one at the moment.

"Please, stop talking," she murmured against his mouth, then nipped his lip, drawing it between her teeth before flicking her tongue back into his mouth, teasing all of his senses. She threaded her fingers into his hair, crushing her breasts to his chest, eroding his last vestige of self-control.

A roar worked his throat muscles and holding back from Shay became impossible. He promised himself one pump of his hips against her softness, just to relieve the mounting pressure in his cock. He rubbed his hands down her lush ass cheeks, plump and round and begging for him to do more.

She melded to him, the temptress of his dreams materializing when she arched her body to fit perfectly to his. "That's it," he said, overtaken by a bone-shattering urge, and he hauled her hips up to his, nudging her mound with his aching crown.

Without warning, she reached down and gripped his cock through his leathers and squeezed him. "Like this?"

"For the love of all that's holy," he groaned. "Perfect."

"Cowboy," she replied, stroking her fingers against his fully aroused shaft. "There is something you can do for me."

He lifted his head and stared down in the golden pools of her shimmering eyes, framed by long lashes spiky from crying. "Anything. What do you want to do?"

"To get in touch with my parents and let them know I'll travel back." Looking down at his zipper, she squeezed his cock within her palm. So fucking amazing, but then she stopped, releasing her grip on him.

"Baby." He gritted his teeth now that his balls were beyond blue.

"Listen to me." She tapped her fingers along his belt, so close to where he needed her fingers to be. "But only for a couple of days and I don't want them to know where I'm at—not yet. I should have known something happened. I phoned and my dad's cell went to voicemail. But I'd thought…" She shook her head, her chin quivered and she blinked rapidly. "I thought he didn't want to take my call."

"No one knows you're here. Did you leave a number? From here?" he asked alarmed.

"I wasn't born yesterday," she replied, steeling her expression after she clearly had decided to veil her features—powering back up into smarty-pants mode. Was she trying to hide something from him? "I called when I had to make a run to gather some supplies. Up in Chicago."

His brow tightened. "What on earth did you need to get up there?"

"Does it matter?" she asked, too flippant for his taste.

"Very much. Now tell me or I'll get the truth from you one way or another." Christ almighty—he'd read the reports of shifters being killed left and fucking right in Flint, Detroit, and Chicago.

She narrowed her eyes. "No. Don't you dare try to dive into my mind!"

He stared at her and shook his head. "I wouldn't. I haven't…is that what you think?"

"Don't try and act like you haven't—"

"Shay, on all that's sacred. Fuck, yeah—I did. Once at the villa but not afterward. Not once afterward. Now before I lose what little cool I still possess, tell me why you were all the way up in Chicago? Shit, did you at least have an escort?"

"I've learned how to take care of myself. So no. Just me, myself, and I went up north." She stared back at him, her eyes wide as if in shock. "Don't jump down my throat 'cause I did what I had to do."

"Which was?"

"Come with me."

"Where?"

"Follow me." She pulled away from him—or tried to—before he hauled her back.

"How far are we going?"

"Now who's lagging behind?" She rolled her eyes. "Silly dragon boy. Come with me *down the hall*. I went there to pick up stuff. What'd you think I was doing?"

"There are delivery companies. I don't understand why you'd risk traveling to Chicago of all places in your condition—" He stopped talking.

She led him down the hall and paused by the last doorway. "Take a look."

At the threshold, a pastel green and yellow room beckoned him. "A nursery," he said.

"Not just any. Fire retardant."

"Ah. Chicago. The Fire Safety Board capital."

"Bingo. I attended the conference on safe fire retardants that don't impair health. Everything in this room was tested, approved, and is dragon baby safety rated." She picked up a blanket and held it out to him.

The blanket was downy between his fingers. A small giraffe had been embroidered near the edge. The built-in shelving held another folded blanket, exactly the same but with a duck, next to sheets and towels. Another shelf held tiny articles of baby clothing. These were his children's possessions. *Correction.* He shook his head. Things that she'd acquired under the radar for *their* children.

"I guess I haven't thought much about fire safety. I just blow my stack and deal with the fallout."

"Oh brother. What does your bedroom look like?" she blurted out and then he enjoyed the pink blush that stole across her cheeks before she spun on her heel, and approached the slates of wood propped up against the wall. "I need to assemble the cribs. That's my next project. Little by little. But I think their nursery is coming along."

He watched her pat her stomach and then rub a hand down the curve of her belly, giving him the first real glimpse of her pregnant profile. She stopped his heart. Gripping the blanket, he reminded himself to not overreact. He set it back on the shelf and shoved his hands into his pockets. "I can do that," he murmured.

"So you'll do as I asked? Relay to my parents I'm returning, without blabbering to them my whereabouts. I mean besides telling me that Shawn needs me, you don't need to hang here. Don't you have a job somewhere?"

"Shit, Shay, I've got my own business," he replied, not seeing how he'd be able to take her back to Denver and let her face Shawn on her own unless he wrangled an agreement out of her to let him protect her—night and day. He trusted Shawn; he just didn't trust any of the other shifters who were currently seated on the justice council. Namely Dimitri Necrodemas and two of his grown children who were spoiled and acted like the whole idea of a justice council was beneath them. According to Drake's underground intel, they were in league with dark forces, but there was no evidence in which to have them removed from their positions—only gossip. "I'll do as you ask on one condition."

"As if," she scoffed. "I still have connections in Denver. I don't need to agree to anything."

He reacted without meaning to fly off the handle. He crossed the room and stood inches from her, staring down into her open mouth and wide eyes. Gently, he took the tip of his forefinger and closed her mouth. "Kitten, listen closely to me. I once tied you to my bed, and I have no problem doing it again if it means keeping you safe."

He allowed her a moment to digest his level of seriousness. His muscles contracted as he kept himself in check from drawing her to him.

"Oh I bet you'd like to do that again. Wouldn't you?" She jutted out her chin defiantly.

His cock twitched at her spirited rebuttal. Inhaling her scent deep into his lungs, he fought to remain levelheaded. Fuck. He clenched his jaw. "So much, you have no idea. But that isn't the exact point I was driving home."

She arched her brow but remained silent, her chest heaving. He allowed his gaze to trace her body and fondle the curves since he had to keep his hands to himself.

"Well, exactly what is the point you're trying to drive home? Besides the one straining your zipper."

"Darling, things have gone haywire in Denver. No joke, Shay. It's not the same city as when you lived there. Down here, in this tiny town, things aren't changing as rapidly. But surely you have kept up with the news in the larger cities."

"Actually, I haven't," she said. "Easier to accept this as my new life. Why torture myself with what isn't going to happen in my future? Shawn's the family star, starts and runs several businesses… what am I? Fired from my first job."

He winced. God, how incredibly stupid he'd been to have turned his back on her out of pride. She believed it shameful to have been let go from some asswipe firm that kowtowed to the political forces that be. She could have been Warren Buffett and they'd still have kicked her to the curb. In leaving Denver, she'd actually saved herself. But she'd given up a lucrative career in which she could have literally and figuratively remolded her life if the shifter violence hadn't reached epic proportions. Now she had to remain off the grid in hiding, and it would be still harder since she had to find a safe refuge while pregnant.

"All of what you've said isn't necessarily true."

"Oh really?" She pursed her pink lips.

"Yeah, really. Here's a fact, you're as stubborn as the day is long," he muttered.

"No. I just decided to prioritize. Isn't that what you do to deal with stress and energy expenditures?"

"So you have read up on dragons to some degree," he replied. Hell, he'd need to broach birthing, child rearing, and dealing with wayward mates himself soon. "But that isn't what I'm referring to. Denver is dangerous. The justice councils, for the moment, have joined forces."

She gasped. "How?"

"Not by marriage, I can assure you. A vote to rewrite the by-laws and I don't know the minutiae involved. You can quiz your brother, if it interests you. All I know is in order to permanently affect an international justice council, all the heirs must appear and cast their vote in a quorum."

"Why? That makes no sense. I'm not political. Never have been. I haven't kept up with the issues. Does any of this have to do with my parents and what happened to them?"

He exhaled, gritting his teeth at having agreed to be the sole bearer of bad news. "As I've said, I'm not sure of the facts. From what I understand, your dad didn't leave specific instructions as to his wishes in the event he was incapacitated. Now, you and Shawn must cast a vote."

"And if my vote runs counter to my brother's?"

"My guess…sure they're counted with equal weight, but they cancel each other out insofar as impact."

She didn't say anything, only stared at a small silver frame that contained a photograph of her family. "I never thought this is how my life would end up. Not that it's good or bad. Just vastly, vastly different."

"Who says that you and Shawn don't see eye to eye?" he asked. If he weren't careful, he'd relay how Necrodemas was being less than gracious in asserting his Machiavellian quest for dominance. This was the reason why, Drake suspected, that Shawn stood on the precipice from which the shifter and human worlds were poised for disaster in Denver. A cagey situation that fed into Necrodemas' psychotic desires. That fucker had quite the underground reputation for a taste of destruction and mayhem, which he used to divide and conquer his opponents. Not the most sophisticated of tactics, but Drake could attest to others in history who'd used similar madman methods and brokered results.

Shay looked up abruptly, a blush creeping over her cheeks, and she exhaled. "What else do you know? Don't go and spill dribs and drabs. Man up. I sure as hell can take the news."

He'd had about all he could take with her sass. "If you want to know anything else, it's going to cost you, little girl." And with that he hoisted her to him, crashing his mouth down on hers to squelch the rolling barbs she was all too capable of flinging. He walked her back to the wall, planting his hands beside her head and caging her within his arms. Her pillow-soft lips opened to him with a breathy moan as she danced her tongue into his mouth. He held back from tongue fucking her, enjoying this tantalizing kiss that rocked every one of his sense. His fingers crept to her head, skimming along her luxurious hair that he wrapped around his hand. He yanked a handful, hiking up the sensation between them and giving her a taste of what he had in store. Just in case she was interested. The teasing feel of her body under his control tempted every dragon male instinct he possessed. All she had to do was give him a sign.

*Come on, Shay. One blasted sign.* He'd have her riding his cock, even if it meant he could only thrust into her sweet pussy part way. Fuck, he'd use only his crown in ways that would drive them both berserk.

She lifted her leg, rubbing her calf along his, and he clenched his jaw, bringing his other hand down to her hip, farther down, hooking his hand under her raised thigh. "Baby, what do you want?"

"Oh I think you know," she retorted. "You have got to promise to be careful."

"Promising to be extra, extra careful," he grunted out. His cock throbbed and he fought to remain sane in his desire to get her naked and on her back, legs spread, and screaming. "Where's your bedroom?"

She reached up and feathered her fingers along his cheeks. "No smoke. No fire. Or we're gonna have a big, big problem, *muchacho*."

"*Entiendo, mi vida*," he said.

Her brows rose. "You speak Spanish. High school?"

"My mother. She was from Spain and I spent summers in Barcelona. Why do you think I opted for the European tour?"

"Navy SEAL training," She scrunched her face. "Hold on. You're mother's name is Katherine."

He shook his head, tracing his fingers along her jaw. "Katherine is my stepmother. One of my father's mates. My mother died in childbirth. *Paloma O'Connor de la familia Draco Herensuge*."

"I'm sorry. How come I don't know that about you?"

"Until now there was no reason to share that detail. I took my mother's family's name," he replied. "But now, you're carrying my children."

"Are you saying your life is an open book, Lord Herensuge?"

"That would have to go both ways." He held her unblinking stare. Didn't she realize that's exactly where they were headed if they claimed one another?

"Really now." When she lowered her gaze and bit her lip, softly sliding one solitary finger down his chest, he sucked in his gut at the jagged piercing pleasure she unleashed in his body.

"Shay," he hissed out a warning, catching her hand. His pulse kicked up like he'd gone ten rounds in a boxing match, but that did little to curb his appetite for her. If anything, his dick throbbed mercilessly in need of relief. A serious workout that only she could provide.

"Come with me." She tugged on his hand. "That is, if you want to stay with me."

"In a word, yes," he choked and his cock swelled, getting stiffer by the second.

Wordlessly, she pushed her palms on his chest, causing his pulse to race if that were fucking possible. He had to get his head together and stepped aside, following her out of their babies' nursery, stopping only to turn off the lamp. She walked to the next doorway down the hall and paused. "This is my bedroom and not anywhere near the type of room I had when we first…you know." She glanced down, breaking eye contact with him.

"I'm not here to compare thread counts. I can't recall what your other bedroom looked like except for you being naked and under me. Ask me the color of your eyes or the way your voice hitched when I fucked you, and I can go on and on. But the shade of the walls, the floors, or the furniture? I have no idea." He cupped and lifted her chin. "Shay, only you've filled my memory, tormenting me for five solid months. Only. You."

"You don't have to say that," she replied, her voice soft, sexy, and breathy to his ears.

"Those aren't just words." He reached for her, lifting her upward into his arms, and flinging open the door. He clasped her against his chest and wandered inside the dim room. "Where's the lights?"

"There's a small lamp on the table. By the mattress."

*Mattress?* Shit. He could make out a mattress with a quilt covering it and a rickety table that stood next to the single mattress. A collapsible chair with a neatly folded pile of clothing and that was it. The hardwood floors were bare and from what he could tell so were the walls. Austere came to mind. Fuck, he'd get to the bottom of what her needs were. Entirely. Tonight her body. And tomorrow, he'd sit her down and they'd sure as shit would have a come-to-Jesus talk. This girl was going to accept his help. Come hell or high-the-fuck water! The mother of his children was not going to bed down on a mattress on the floor. Or in the very least, not beyond tonight since he realized he couldn't very well haul her out the door to a hotel.

# CHAPTER 7

Within Drake's arms, Shay drank from his power that flowed like the pink champagne she'd once sipped along the Rivera when they traveled down the Mediterranean coast last summer. His arms tensed around her as he walked into her immaculate but sparsely furnished room. She chanced a glance upward from beneath her lashes and her stomach muscles twisted.

"What wrong?" Drake paused and clasped her even tighter in twin bands of steel as he looked about her room.

"It's nothing," she tried to assure him, but she was more than certain with his dragon perception, he undoubtedly heard her heart clattering furiously as though she'd run a race.

Her whole face heated as he trained his focus on her without blinking, like a bird of prey. He suspended taking a breath as he watched her every move. She fought to let go of this stupid sense of pride she wore as if it were a robe that might protect her. In his presence, her sense of right and wrong—the things she'd held onto—were in flux.

He'd accused her of engaging in flighty, fun activities last summer, but really she'd spent a majority of that trip convinced she had no idea who she was in relation to her family and had needed a break after four grueling years of college. In the end, he'd proven himself correct in many of the assertions he'd tossed around like soap bubbles on the breeze…until every last one had burst and left her flailing to find her footing.

"Shay," he murmured, kneeling by her single-mattress bed and with one hand, pulled back the quilt and laid her down with the epitome of dragon grace. He ran his hands down her body, all the way to her shoes, and began untying her laces.

Oh dear God, his fingers were magick on her skin. A hedonistic shiver wracked her body, and she rolled her lip between her teeth to prevent the small moan that followed. No, this couldn't be happening.

"What are you doing?" she asked, lifting up onto her elbows and trying to wrench her foot out of his fingers.

"Taking off your shoes." Gifting her with an arched brow, he held onto her ankle without relenting. "You need to get some rest."

"Oh. Is that what you call what we're going to do? The last time we tumbled into my bed, there wasn't much sleeping or resting. Not when we were naked." Holy shit. She didn't just say that!

"Ah, yes. I do recall." He laughed easily, stroking his fingers along her ankle. The low provocative rumble of his voice was a heady reminder of the things they'd once done in bed, surprisingly a balm to her senses. "All right, after the shoes, I'll undress you completely. If that's what you're saying."

Good thing her room was poorly lit—he might not notice her face had turned fire-engine red. Or felt like it. "I'm not in my right mind. Obviously," she muttered.

Drake set her foot down and regarded her with a serious expression, cocking his chin slightly. "I don't want you to be unnerved by me. I want you so bad I can taste the essence of your leopardess self. The fragrance at the back of your wrists, the texture of your lips, how you moan when you come all haunt me. But you must give yourself to me, Shay. You're my mate and I will have you. Entirely. There are things I uncovered about Necrodemas which are troubling. Like a fool I believed I could come here and see you once and that would be the end."

"What do you mean?" She swallowed hard.

"You're mine to protect. If I find out that Necrodemas even suspects this is where you are…I'll move you. With or without your permission."

She bolted upright. "How can you make unilateral decisions for me? I'm a grown woman, Drake!"

"Are you now?" He remained poised by her ankle, at the foot of the mattress, but he might as well be made out of granite in how he tensed all over. She sniffed and what radiated off Drake made her heart race. The scent of rage permeated the air—like the smell of an electrical fire.

She licked her lips that had gone dry and nodded her head. "Why does he care so much? I'm only a leopardess and not a very good one."

He stared back at her, his dragon gaze powered up, and if his eyes had held heat-seeking missiles before, his emerald orbs now torpedoed her. "I wish it were as simple as Necrodemas' pride but that's not all that is at stake. Your lineage is of use to him. Apparently he had some genome studies conducted and you're more than a suitable mate. The offspring you would give him would result in unusual versions of leopard shifters."

She rubbed a hand over her belly. "My babies aren't unusual. Well, aside from the fact that they're half-dragon."

"Necrodemas isn't a purebred leopard as he'd like the world to believe. The truth is problematic for him in his ability to broker unions with other clans by offering up his offspring in arranged matings as far away as Russia, and recently Serbia. A daughter just last week."

"How horrid and calculating!" She abhorred the treatment of women as chattel. "What exactly is he, besides a monster?"

"A Heinz 57 shifter type. Enough that he can't refute being a hybrid if pressed. His children are on the board of the justice council, making all sorts of ridiculous rulings that go against the shifters they're supposed to help. Necrodemas can't control his progeny, and in turn, the gangs are rising up against anyone who opposes them. It's bordering on a crucible ready to combust. There's an undercurrent of anarchy, and if something doesn't change, fast, our communities are in jeopardy. The humans will disband the councils and issue martial law to deal with the insurrections."

"Including Necrodemas? I'd venture to lay odds he'd be the first to garner special treatment," she scoffed. No doubt the tyrant owned a half-dozen politicians, if not more.

"Exactly. He, more than anyone, has a parachute ready. He's slipperier than a goddamn eel and I say that from experience. I'd take him out yesterday, but he's not the one who concerns me. He's easy to track and has become a necessary evil."

"I don't like the sounds of that." *Necessary evil?* How much did Drake stay involved in geopolitics?

"Then let's stop talking about him." Drake set her boots to the side and rolled down her socks, tucking them into her shoes.

"But I still have questions."

"Of that, I'm sure. You are the most curious and confounding woman I've ever met." He walked on his knees to her and stopped next to her waist.

"Big talk, coming from you. Still travel with all the technology?" She swallowed, stiffening in anticipation, not knowing how he'd react to her blossoming tummy.

She watched Drake's fingers pop the button at her waistband and lower the zipper of her jeans. "Lift those beautiful hips," he murmured. "Or I can rip these off your body. No problem."

"Don't!"

"Then you better comply before my heated brain goes on autopilot. I won't be responsible for what I do if that happens."

"Oh *reeallly*," she snorted, trying to act like this was nothing but routine for her while the pulse along her neck jangled frantically.

"Yeah. Really, baby." In Drake's usual quicksilver impulses, he shifted up to her, too fast to keep tabs on, and pressed his mouth to her neck, kissing a line down the side of throat, and imbuing her blood with a dose of decadent desire that swam all too fast in her veins.

Her heart beat an SOS tempo against his tongue as he traced the tip along her skin. Oh God! Did someone set her skin on fire? She moaned as the sensation of his mouth shot an electrical jolt all the way down her body and landed between her legs. It was as though no time had passed since the days she'd spent with Drake in bed. She was flabbergasted at her over-the-top response to him.

He more than blindsided her. Drake, in his dragon take-all and ask-no-questions assault on her senses, employed the subtlest of enticements in his arsenal. She'd demanded that he not seduce her. Specifically, she'd made him promise not to fuck her and here she lay with her thighs open. Wide, wide open. Surreptitiously, she slid her knees together—or tried to until his hands shot out and locked onto her legs.

"Stop." Drake lifted his head and gazed down at her.

"Is that all this is? Hot, screaming sex?"

"Naw. We've talked. A little." He wrapped his forearms along the sides of her chest, pinning her arms to her body as he held onto her shoulders. He shook his head and stared at her, his eyes wide and unblinking. "I'm not accustomed to having to talk much about emotions. But that doesn't mean I haven't got any. Especially where you're concerned."

She was so floored, she didn't have a comeback. Drake normally wore arrogance like the pair of wrap-around glasses he constantly sported. Except now. In her bedroom, both in Lisbon and Harmony, he faced her with his mind-bending gaze and something else. Seeing him waver…a sort of tender vulnerability came over him that was equally intoxicating. He, furtively sharing his Achilles heel, got to her.

Unless this was all a huge act. He was a player on an extreme level, being a sensuous shifter. Dragons were born knowing just what to say and do when it came to scoring.

Great, she was at the edge of a cliff with a choice. She could luxuriate in his consummate strength, power, and ability to drive her insane in bed. Enjoy herself as she'd done for days last summer. *I mean hey, officially I can't get any more pregnant than I already am.*

Or conversely, she could dive into a sea of mental torture. Sludge through the cold, tumultuous waters where self-analysis, doubt, and second guessing his motives swirled, all too ready to drown her. If she basked in this moment, without trying to read the future or trying to formulate a set of ridiculous expectations, she might have a chance of not driving herself crazy.

Okay, fine, she'd ask for his honesty and if he stepped up to the plate, she'd meet him. Trust or game playing—she'd lay the choice in his court.

"More specifically, what do you feel? About me, I mean."

He took a deep breath, seeming to sense this was a flipping fulcrum, and exhaled. "That you are complicated. So much more than anyone or any situation I've come across. Ever!" He smiled though, and the white of his teeth against his bronze face, even if it was a flash, made her chest tighten. She liked making him smile.

"No more than you ever were," she returned, but far less caustic than she'd been throughout the last hour. He continued smiling down at her, and dipped his head, bringing his nose an inch or two above hers and sniffed.

"You smell so incredible. Like fresh green grass and something baked. Something delicious." He waited, hovering above her face, but he moved over an inch, directly above her mouth now.

She stared into his mercurial green eyes with the power to bend her mind into a pretzel on so many levels. Oh jeez! She felt herself melt. "What should we do?" she whispered.

Without knowing why, the worry that she'd held onto vanished from her traitorous body. She actually shivered uncontrollably and would have sighed if she weren't horrified to admit he still had the goods in getting her aroused.

"We can do this." He must have felt her body relax and lowered his head, fusing their lips.

Oh. My. Lord! This wasn't like before where their mouths, hands, and bodies needed hard, demanding, total fire. His lips were warm and inviting, and so unbelievably sensual, barely skimming hers. She liquefied under his seductive dragon kiss that was methodical and captivating. Dear God, the feel of his male hardness surrounding her, his glowing heat, his deep voice rumbling in his chest…it was all complete sin in the making.

Pleasure flash burned across her body, just beneath her skin. She moaned his name against his lips while running her fingers freely over the curving muscle along his arms.

Drake sucked her bottom lip between his teeth; his breathing deepened as he curled an arm under her waist. As she arched her body, melding to him, her fingers continued their mad trip up the contours of his arms, over his shoulders, up his corded neck, until she touched his chiseled jaw. He nibbled her lips until she opened her mouth to him, and plunged into her with his tongue. The power in that kiss made her simultaneously weak yet left her wanting so much more as her pleasure soared higher, sharper.

"Let me in. Trust me." He moved over her, pushing her down but without holding her imprisoned under his weight.

"Oh, God," she said. "You tempt me."

"That's what I want to hear." He tipped her face, giving him better access to drive the sharp tines of his forked tongue across her lips, his beard scraping her chin. He cupped her ass cheek and rocked against the space where he'd owned her once before.

She was so wet and in need as coiling pleasure deep in her core pulsed for him. She groaned in frustration—a mixture of a feline growl and a womanly sigh as she sucked his tongue. He grunted and rubbed harder with his thigh, going deeper with his tongue. Hoisting her hips, he rocked his erection perfectly against her clothing encased clit, hard enough to make her jerk and then shudder, calling out his name as she flexed against him. She snaked her arms around his neck and he pulled her closer. He kissed her deeper, dissolving the thoughts right out of her head. Employing a sinful tempo, he teased her with his cock and tongue, rubbing his crown against her mound, and she opened her legs wider, needing him inside her. Right now!

"Please. Stop," she hissed.

He reared back, gazing down at her with his brows drawn, the angles in his face chiseled sharper in worry. "Have I been too rough?"

"Oh. No," she panted in a hoarse whisper. "Please, take off your shirt. I want to feel your skin."

"Definitely a good call." Drake barely lifted. The tension in his granite body became tauter when he grabbed the collar from behind his head and pulled his shirt off his body in one lithe gesture before he sent the shirt sailing to her solitary chair. When he leaned back down, adjusting his weight onto one of his elbows so he wouldn't lie on her pelvis, she palmed his pecs and gasped in pleasure. His dazzling dragon gaze was as warm as his skin and he smiled. The brown discs around his nipples puckered when she swiped her fingernails across each tip. He sucked in his stomach, giving her an eyeful of what an eight-pack looked like up close. *My. My. Someone has been working out.*

"Tit for tat," he whispered, kissing her lips. "Your turn, gorgeous."

•••

"Then you'll have to get up so I can disrobe, Mr. O'Connor." She stroked her palm along the side of his face and his whole body felt on fire. Allowing her room to move farther away from him? Not going to happen.

He raised his hands to her neckline and in one fell swoop, rent the front of her shirt in tattered halves. "Or we could just do it my way."

His kitten stared wide-eyed back at him. Silent, but not for long and he moved with one mission in mind before she stormed. He knelt between her legs, reached under her lush bottom, and pulled her jeans off her hips. Without stopping, he removed her already unfastened pants as if he were a magician and she was wearing nothing but a checkerboard tablecloth. He unsnapped her bra, meeting her gaze.

"Uh…" she said, holding onto the straps.

"Let go," he replied, tugging them out of her hands. "Your tits are mind-blowing." She placed her palms across her exposed breasts. He moved, covering her mouth in a caressing sweep of his lips, kissing her back into silence, and refused to stop until her body relaxed against him.

"Drake," she murmured against his lips as he removed her panties.

He spread his palm over her rounded belly and inhaled deeply. *Holy hell!* Running his fingers over Shay's skin—he was dumbfounded. Partially in awe and Christ, his hands actually trembled. He stared down at her, spreading out his palms on her belly until only his thumbs touched and she lay before him. *My mate. The mother of my children.*

His cock throbbed. He needed to join their bodies and mark her. He lifted upright and rubbed his hands up her thighs. "You're so unbelievably beautiful. Impossible to imagine you could be lovelier than you were during the summer…but you are."

Shay spread her legs further apart as he moved in between. His cock was rock hard and he felt like a god the moment he aligned his crown with her pussy. He juddered and planted his palm next to her ribcage on the mattress. "I'll be gentle with you, baby."

Wet silk surrounded his crown as he drove into her warmth. She was tight, so tight his balls throbbed and he arched upward, sliding his tip into her. He pumped his hips, sinking his cock deeper into Shay's pussy. He watched her expression for suggestive nuances, and paid attention to what made her lips part and moan his name. This wasn't fast and easy screwing—not that anything with Shay could be construed as fast or easy or simple. But this, oh yeah—this was making love to his mate. He found his rhythm, using his whole body to maneuver his cock and rub against her clit, then hit her G-spot, and she clenched around his dick.

Foreign territory if there ever was some, and not in any Special Forces field guide. Prickling sweat erupted along his shoulders as he held himself aloft over her, guarded against his consuming craving to mount her and fully claim her as his. Fuck!

"You feel so amazing. Shay, I could fuck you for hours."

"Come closer to me."

His senses were on fire from her pliable body under him, surrounding him, and his babies in her belly—this woman was his mate. *His mate.* The words echoed inside him. Over and over, he pumped his cock into her, getting his girl off. Threading pleasure tore through him and he fought to subdue the flames creeping up his throat as he held back from yelling her name. God, he was right there. Fuck, he felt himself on the verge of exploding and held back, holding her hips as he worked his crown at the mouth of her pussy.

"Tell me how this feels."

"Drake, so so so so good!"

That's all he needed to hear and he sped up his thrusts, not fully inside her for fear of hurting her or their children when he was this close to coming. "Shay," he rasped as he emptied himself into her. Again, he came hard, spraying his release inside her.

Leaning over her body, he pressed his lips to hers, tasting the sweetness that had haunted him for five months and three weeks and two days. A lifetime. And he wanted more. So much more. He wanted all of her.

"Not too rough?" He stroked his fingers along her cheek, clenching internally at wanting more from her.

She shook her head.

He fought asking if he was still the only man she'd let into her bed—that would go down as the ultimate dickhead move. He'd not sought out other females and wasn't about to broadcast that she had him by the nuts, craving her completely.

How could he get her to do more than occupy a slot in his brain as his ultimate fantasy girl?

Shay turned on her side and ran her hand over his chest. He threaded their fingers together and lifted her hand to his lips, and kissed her palm, inhaling the delicious scent wafting off her skin. He wrapped his arm around her waist and gently scooped her to him until they were melded together and he nuzzled her neck, searching for the spot that made her laugh. He kissed a path up to her ear and sucked harder at the place where her vein pulsed. She pushed her palms against his shoulders at first, then wrapped her arms around his neck and threw back her head, giggling his name as she tried to wriggle free from his grasp. While she was laughing and gasping, he stopped tormenting her, and gazed at her. The breath caught in his throat at the fire in her eyes, and the color rising on her cheeks.

# CHAPTER 8

Drake carried two mismatched mugs into her bedroom. She sat upright, the sheet slipping away from her upper body, and the way his eyes darted down from her face made her conscious that she was naked under his scorching perusal.

"Herbal tea," he murmured, handing her a mug. "With honey."

"Thanks. Observant as ever and up early." She wrapped her fingers around the outside of the mug, enjoying the feel of something solid between her fingers as the world seemed to shift around her.

"Old habits die hard," he said, wearing a pair of low-slung jeans. "What are your plans today?"

"I imagine you didn't come to Harmony to sightsee." With the early morning sunlight streaming into her room, she realized they had to talk, now that they'd gotten past sparring. "What's your timeline?"

She sipped her tea and watched him over the rim. He settled next to her on the mattress, tugging his hands through his thick hair, and meeting her gaze. The effect was the proverbial arrow to her heart, and she gulped a mouthful of tea, praying the tickle at the back of her throat didn't mean she was about to start hacking and coughing. She swallowed—more like drowned—and let fly a burst of air, a judder outward from her lips. So not smooth. Drake leaned closer, so seamlessly she felt him before her lust-soaked brain recognized the searing hard body was his, not a tank in her bed. He lifted the mug from her fingers and had her back to the mattress, and him over her, pinning her down.

"You. You're my timeline," he said. "Better get used to it."

"But you said—"

"A bunch of meaningless horseshit. This is real. This is where I belong. I'm not leaving here. Not that I'm taking you anywhere either. Not until we have a plan." He skimmed his hand over her belly. His large, calloused fingers spread out, squeezing lightly, cradling her abdomen right above the spot where she felt twin pairs of feisty little feet kicking her at the moment. Drake partially clothed and next to her made her want to lie still and listen to him tell her how to repair her out of control life. But this wasn't a fairy tale.

She blinked rapidly, not about to believe one badass dragon would solve all her problems. If anything, his showing up here had piled her plate high with volumes of new dilemmas—the ones she'd locked away. Well, the shit was about to hit the fan.

For a couple of minutes—just a few more—she'd enjoy life without the hassle of her version of a snarky reality. Snuggling up with Drake, she inhaled his all-male scent, the one she'd tried to forget but couldn't, and she softly moaned.

"Yeah. I guess we need a plan. That's step number one." Even if she wanted to tell a bold-faced lie, she couldn't deny that even with a mountain of crap about to rain down, being next to Drake—his familiar presence—calmed her down. She tried to remain logical in thinking about her parents—her family that had all but deserted her. She had to go back to Denver even if she didn't totally trust what she was hearing. "I have a shift down at Mony tonight."

"Like hell you do."

"I can't run out on Solomon. Not when he's been so good to me."

"Define good," he snarled, moving his hands between her legs. "You're mine."

"Jealous much?"

"Kitten, where you're concerned, fuck yeah." He captured her hand, examining her palm, tracing the scar that ran from one side to the other.

"Dial that down, cowboy. Solomon's wife and mate is my doctor. Trish doesn't put up with any nonsense down in the bar. She's like the big sister I never had. You'll like her."

"Perhaps. I'll find out tonight."

She tugged her hand but stopped when it dawned on her exactly what he said. "Why? What are you doing tonight?"

"From what I know about you, you won't welch on your commitments. I'll cover your shift. You can sit at the bar and make more baby clothes or blankets."

"Uhh, no you're not."

"Yes. I. Am."

"Have you ever made a Blow Job or a dirty martini?" She added, "Lately."

"That's why you can keep me company while I keep you out of trouble."

"Solomon won't like it." She shook her head, trying to dislodge the visual of her boss chewing her ass on why a dragon of all possible shifters was now in residence in Harmony. After she'd made a few friends, found a job, and a place to live, the way she'd repay their kindness was in the form of inviting into their midst an overarching badass. The very same one who felt it was his right to decide the course of her life and more than likely theirs, if they stepped out of line according to his rulebook. "I don't like it!"

"You and I are going to be hanging out together for a long, long time. Better get used to me. Same as I'll have to get used to you."

"Jesus, that's an understatement—wait a second. How exactly is your coming down here and upsetting the balance of things any way the same me upsetting your well-ordered life?" Without meaning to, she ended up jabbing her finger against his granite wall of a chest.

His eyebrow rose, letting her know the act wasn't lost on him. It just didn't mean a whole lot either. He grunted his displeasure. "Would you rather debate the details that, up to now, aren't fact? Just BS that has gotten in our way since day one. We could enjoy an early morning quickie, kitten. Or I could go slow…using my tongue, teeth, and lips to get you to scream. Lady's choice."

All the conjecture he'd previously referred to evaporated and in its place, he wedged his hard body between her legs and took up every last millimeter of space in her mind. "Not my fault," she managed, not sounding as relaxed as she'd like. But then again, with his hard-on nudging her clit, biting down on her lip came as second nature, followed by a deep moan. She ran her fingers up the rippling contours of his abs and hooked her fingers on his forearms as he lifted her knees, hoisting her naked hips. "Let me fuck you."

"How can I stop you?"

"Trust me. Baby, you can." He lowered her and unzipped his jeans, freeing his cock. Without stopping, he took hold of his erection, and met her gaze. "Say the words, Shay. Or I'll prove that you hold the power for our mutual pleasure."

She rubbed up against his crown and splintering bliss shredded her focus. "Please. Fuck. Me."

"Love when you talk dirty to me," he groaned, sinking the head of his dick into her. "How much of me can you take?"

"All of you. Please." She was at the point of pleading, she was so in need of him inside her.

He pumped his hips. Slow and sure, until he was seated fully inside her. By planting his palms on either side of her body, he kept his upper torso aloft, his muscles bulging in his arms and shoulders as he remained poised above her, grinding his hips deliciously between her legs. *He's watching me.* Suddenly, she felt shy and reached for him.

"Dammit, come closer. You won't break me."

"Don't want to risk hurting you," he said tightly.

She wrapped her calves around his waist and bumped her hips against his, enjoying the feel of him between her legs. She gripped his shoulders and gasped as he rubbed his cock against her clit, the perfect pressure, and she shuddered through the erotic ride. "Give me what you've got," she replied in a voice she hoped didn't sound as breathy to him as it did to her own ears.

He unleashed one of his smoldering grins, his emerald eyes sparkling with sexual excitement. Under his flagrant perusal, she felt herself grow so aroused, she met his pumping hips with her own special swaying rhythm. Ah, he brought to her the brink and her whole body glowed in ecstasy.

"Baby, how's that? You're tight and hot. I'm going to come so fucking hard."

"Then do!" She lay under him, trapped beneath his cock, and loved every second. She didn't explode, she shattered completely apart. Growling both in feline and some wholly erotic moan, she half-screamed, "Drake more!" She bit her lip to stop from tripping over her own tongue in the rush of emotions that tangled in her mouth.

"That's it, Shay." He pulled her to him, overpowering and volatile in his possession, and so tantalizing to her senses when he jostled their hips with a maddening friction, until she couldn't get any closer. Could she? In less than a day and a powerful dragon later, her once lonely little abode rocked her leopardess world.

• • •

The sweet scent of her arousal engulfed him. If he came hard, she came soft and all the more powerful in how she enticed him. Oh hell, if he were talking truth, Shay sent him over the edge. He pressed up against her, careful of her lower half, and didn't stop until his pecs brushed against her tits. "Give yourself to me. Completely, Shay!"

He came again, arching upward and his need to exhale fire overarching. He held his breath through the firestorm expanding within his body, threatening to overtake him as he filled Shay with his release. Fuck! He saw a flash of white lightning and the top of his head felt ready to rip apart. He panted, leaning a palm against the wall above her bed. Shit. He'd almost spewed fire. In his mate, a fragile leopardess's, presence. "We need some precautions."

"We need to talk. Dragon subject matter. But for now, keep moving and don't you dare stop until you're done." Again she clenched around him, milking his dick.

"Baby! Play nice." Sliding his fingers into the silk of her hair, he tugged her head back, unable to resist melding them together in every possible way. All he had to do was bite down on her neck, infuse her with his dragon essence—but fuck him backward. He wanted to hear her say the words—more than that—he hungered for her to feel and relish their bond…not take from her when she lay open and yielding beneath him. But Christ—would she ever willingly submit to him? Locking his gaze to hers, he whispered a bittersweet promise his dragon bellowed against, "Come to me… when you're ready."

She lifted her arms, moaning out his name, and he hauled her upright, then up and down his length until she cried out his name. Again and again, his name spilled from her beautiful mouth.

He leaned over, setting her against the pillows, still embedded in her pussy, seeking her out. His lips had to be scorching against her mouth, this near to releasing. But Shay didn't flinch when he brushed his mouth over hers. God, he needed to lick across her pillow-soft lips and absorb her moans. All of them. She moaned, urging him to sample, borrow, steal…whatever she dangled in front of him, until little by little she was his. If he wasn't careful, she'd break him and his vow to give her time.

Without hesitation, his little leopardess joined him onboard the crazy train where their tongues danced, dueled, twirled as though they'd not just fucked each other silly. Shay's hands rubbed up his arms, hooking over the tops of his shoulders as she squeezed his cock, plundering his breath. She also pillaged the next thought in his brain while she was at it. If she kept going, she'd own him lock, stock, and smoking barrel if he didn't get control of his temptress and soon.

• • •

"I'm certain there are other houses on the market we can agree upon," Drake offered, and spread out his hands.

"Just to avoid a war, I acquiesced to exploring housing options, but I don't know if we could ever agree on a place. Besides, I already have a spot. Right here."

He laughed, giving her *the look* over the top of his sunglasses. "We can build. From the ground up. Anything you desire, but not so many stairs unless I retrofit the place and installed an elevator. We'll need a perimeter stone wall. No swimming pools, unless it's filled with less than eighteen inches. A safe room. Guard tower, security upgrades—I'll take care of those. So yeah, we just need to define the parameters a little better the next time we go house hunting." He leaned over and kissed her forehead.

Seated behind the wheel of her Civic and ready to pull her hair out by the roots, Shay exhaled. "Ya think?"

"Yup. I do."

She'd spent the day trying to get Drake to accept she wasn't made of spun sugar, and was no way ready to shatter apart if a strong wind came through Harmony. Her phone rang the moment they'd entered Mony's parking lot. She was prepared to answer her cell with a quip for Solomon. He always had the propensity to phone her up whenever she popped up on his radar. But no, this wasn't her boss inquiring if she was bringing in a fresh batch of baked goods as he was wont to do after Trish cut him off sweets.

She stared at the screen then at Drake's face. "It's Shawn," she whispered.

Pushing up his sunglasses, he nodded. "Yeah. He mentioned he was going to call."

"You talked to him. Today," she replied so matter-of-factly she surprised herself. She wanted to return to Denver, yet she couldn't push aside her fear that somehow things weren't going to be any different than they were several months ago. Sure, her dad's accident sucked it. Big time, now that he was undergoing some risky medical procedure. But how would she bridge the larger issue that her father and brother now worked alongside Dimitri or had at some point?

"How about some privacy?" Drake asked and rubbed the pad of his thumb along her cheek. "I'll be right outside if you need me."

"Okay," she said, her voice suddenly husky. She lifted her phone to her cheek and watched as Drake opened the passenger door and climbed out.

"Hello?" She sounded less than confident and inhaled, reeling in her massive attack of confusion and self-doubt.

"Shay," Shawn's voice rumbled through her phone. "Christ, I knew Drake was the only one who could find you."

"Well, he does operate as a team of one, as in one avalanche. But knowing you and your hankering for to-do lists, you can mark off finding me. I'm not running away from him screaming," she replied. "Now, tell me about Dad. And don't put any sugar-coating on the truth."

"Sis, it's not good. And we probably shouldn't discuss anything in depth on the phone."

"That sounds like you've gone over to the conspiracy-theory-paranoid side of the street," she replied. "I want to know about Mom and Dad. Nothing to do with business or politics. Just cut the crap and tell me. How are they?"

"Suffice to say, you need to get back here soon. Mom is okay, not great. It's more emotional with her from the stress of what's gone down. And Dad will be back in two days. Can you get here to welcome him home?"

"So our mom is stable?" Her heart battered against her chest.

"No lie. Yes."

She inhaled a shaky breath. "So why can't I go see Dad wherever he is? Doesn't he need visitors to help when the nurses and doctors are busy?" An uncomfortably long silence ensued. "Hello?" she said, gritting her teeth.

"How much do you know?"

"Apparently, not enough." She snapped her gaze outward, canvassing the parking lot, zeroing in on Drake and her chest squeezed. She sat upright and inhaled, focusing her attention on her dragon man as he knelt by Trish's toddler, Teddy, in his stroller. Obviously, Trish was amused as she smiled at whatever Drake discussed.

"I don't think this was an accident," her brother said softly. "I need Drake to come back here and deal with security, especially while you're in residence."

"Does he know that?"

*So all is seriously not well.* The question was, how off the charts was it if Shawn and her mom were willing to readmit a man with Special Forces experience back into the fold—and where in the world did that place her? Would they welcome her and her children? "What should it matter if I come home or not? Don't you have Fin and Tristen as backup?"

She sniffed the air and perceived the scent of fuel. Not gasoline…maybe diesel fuel. A headache bloomed behind her eyes; she pressed her fingers on her temple and rubbed three tiny non-stop circles.

"Sure. They stepped up and I can't add another job to their already growing list of responsibilities. They're on the move, but stuff is happening all over Denver. Tristen is covering the business end and Fin is dealing with the home front. Together, they're a team and getting used to running the show."

"You mean since you fired Drake. Your right hand. The dude who handled it all—even from Europe. And then *smack!* Done." She drummed her fingers on top of her steering wheel, observing the charismatic power Drake exuded. Solomon had joined them, and Drake appeared to be the epitome of nonchalant, leaning against the fender of a car, arms crossed over his chest. But underneath his black T-shirt and jeans, she relished his sculpted body. A body of an untamed dragon poised to strike, all tense sinew and killer instinct.

"Don't go defensive. You two should have come clean and come together as a couple to talk to Mom and Dad. How was I to know that you and he…that you both—"

"Both what?" She scrambled, ready to go ballistic on her brother.

"Sis, last summer—

"I'm pregnant." There she said it. And again another dead silence. Inside the car it got uncomfortably hot.

"Holy fuck!"

"Does that mean you're happy or not?" she inquired.

"How in God's name did you get an education from Duke and end up living in the swamps of Louisiana? Unmarried. Unmated. Unclaimed. Fuck me flying, I can't even begin to figure out where the hell your life derailed, Shannon Marie Barclay!"

"Technically I'm not unmated. If I were, you wouldn't be a raging bull."

She shook her head and wanted to laugh. At that second Drake glanced over and their gazes locked. Tears pricked the back of her eyes and she flashed him a peace sign. No wonder he'd wanted to escape and never show his face around Denver again. For all her brother's worldly ways, he was a born-again provincial ogre. No way she wanted to relive the nightmare of driving away from

Denver in a used car she'd managed by the skin of teeth to finagle after her parents had shut down her trust fund. Not that she'd wanted a penny. Now she was glad she was making it on her own. Of course in the Barclay world, her living above a bar in a storage area wasn't caviar dreams and champagne wishes.

"Don't act belligerent. Not with me. Either you're claimed or unclaimed. Which is it?"

"Un," she huffed as a clogging sensation rose in her throat and tears filled her eyes. She closed her lids rather than let go projectile tears.

"Shit. I knew something was up with you and I should have acted sooner. I'm going to kill Drake when I see him. As a matter of fact, I'm considering coming to you. Where the fuck are you?"

That did it! She flashed open her eyes. "Oh yeah. That's a plan. Take off and what? You're going to fly down here? How many private jets do you own? Or are you going to borrow one from Necrodemas? Heard you were getting cozy with him on the board of the council."

Drake motioned to her with a chopping sign in front of his throat. The universal shut-the-fuck-up hand signal for anyone with an iota of common sense. She, on the other hand, couldn't get hold of her runaway mouth. She'd kept silent for months—years really. She should have spoken up in Lisbon and laid out her refusal to be a political pawn, and maybe her narrow-minded, old-fashioned family would have listened and not gotten involved with that dumbbell Dimitri.

She grimaced and shook her head, watching Drake's eyebrows shoot upward. He must have inhaled deeply since his shoulders rose and fell before he walked to her side of the car. She watched him rather than focus on actually speaking, so she had time to mash the button on the armrest and lock the doors.

"Shay," he said, knocking his knuckle on the window. "Open the door before you say something you'll be sorry for."

Oh God. She wanted to laugh so freaking hard. And it was so inappropriate. Like succumbing to a fit of uncontrollable laughter at a funeral. She clapped her hand over her mouth. Didn't help. She snorted and tears sprang into her eyes. Hot, fat, sloppy tears that refused to stay put behind her eyelids as she scrunched her eyes closed.

Shawn hollered, "Shay. I can get a plane ticket and be there by tonight. Or I can drive and be there by the morning. Where are you?"

First one snort, then another until rippling laughter broke free from within her, and she couldn't hold back. "Ha-ha-ha—"

Not to be deterred, Drake walked around the car and tore the door from the passenger side, quickly setting it down, and leaned inside. "Give me that before you hurt yourself!"

"Excuse me. That's my door. Thank you not very much." She hiccuped and watched him lift her cell from her fingers and rub his knuckle along her jaw.

Drake switched on the speaker. "Shawn, I take it Shay told you we're expecting. If you're going to upset her, I damn well won't bring her back to Denver. I'll take her to Herensuge Castle for the rest of her pregnancy. And you, your father, and Amelia will be on your own. But mark my words, no one is going to make Shay feel less than perfect carrying my children. So wish her the best and help me help her."

"Drake, this is a torrential screw up!" Shawn yelled loud enough for the whole Mony parking lot to hear if anyone else had been around. Solomon and Trish—thank God—had gone inside.

"Yeah. Shit happens, dude. I got years on you. Don't make the mistake of thinking the last time I let you take out your frustration was the best I had. I didn't raise a finger against you out of respect. There won't be a next time if it involves another word against Shay."

She bit her lip when Drake finished and he smiled. For a beat, she forgot about Shawn's tirade until he spoke up again. "Ah hell, you both deserve each other," her brother replied and Drake held the phone outward so she could hear as well. "Put my sister back on."

"You're a good man, Barclay," Drake held out her cell. "Obviously, your brother has something to say. Can you handle it from here?"

# CHAPTER 9

As Drake reached for a beer mug, she held court a few seats away as she explained, "Simmer the heck down. Damien, I was going to tell you when the time was right but I just knew you'd react like this!"

From the other side of the bar, she watched Drake pour a microbrew for Damien, following her strict instructions on how to pour a beer—not too much foam. Don't slop it. *Make eye contact and smile.* Damn, these shifters would be lucky if he gave them the time of day—except she'd wheedled a promise from him that he'd behave. For her, he'd suck it in and play bartender. She hoped.

Damien threw up his hands. "For shit's sake, Shay! All this time." The beta wolf picked up a blanket and then set it down like it was about to bust apart.

"Not exactly. At first, I didn't know for sure and then, it got away from me. So there."

"Baby, can we move this blanket?" Drake asked. "Or are you going to have everyone who knows you react the same way?"

"How do you mean?"

"Seeing you and a baby blanket is pretty no frills in letting them in on our secret. Why not tell people little by little? Give them a chance to accept the idea that you're—"

"Knocked up?" she interrupted just to get a rise out of Damien.

"Christ!" Damien screeched, and tufts along the side of his face erupted. "You're not—what you said. I can't believe I watched you lift and haul barrels and boxes night after flipping night. You could have said something sooner."

"Like what?" Shay asked, cocking her head.

"Oh, maybe you were expecting," Mara supplied, slipping on to one of the barstools. "I just knew it."

"Did you also know we're having twins?" Shay asked, clapping her hands and delighted to finally let the cat, or rather dragons, out of the bag. She glanced over to Drake and winked. "Chablis. No more than two glasses for this one. Mara Feinstein, Drake O'Connor. My…friend."

A deep rumbled snort of dissatisfaction shot out of his mouth. "Watch it, kitten." He held out his hand. "Pleasure, Mara."

"Likewise, Drake. I can't tell you how nice it is to meet you. Kinda fills in a lot of blanks."

"Drake." Shay tapped his arm. "Mara is the one who helped me learn to act sane again when I arrived and didn't know which way was up. She's a wonderful behavior coach. Maybe she can help you with your possessive side."

"Thanks, doll, but with you, I do believe your man is gonna need every trick in the book." Mara patted her arm. "Let's talk names?"

Shay shook her head. Drake hadn't even asked that question. As he uncorked the wine bottle, he flashed Shay a glance and their gazes snapped together. She shrugged a shoulder. "Haven't gotten that far. This is monumental, just sharing the news."

Solomon lumbered in carrying a barrel from the back of the bar. "It's not only monumental. It's a travesty. I'm with Damien. All this time and you carried these barrels back and forth. I've effectively paid my way well into hell. Thanks a lot."

"You didn't know. And besides, I can out-press you any day of the week, Sol. Just because I'm expecting doesn't mean I'm frail. Seriously, it's the opposite. Tell him, Drake."

Slanting her a 'you're own your own' glance and shaking his head, Drake picked up the bar towel and wiped a spot, feigning a "no comment."

"Drake O'Connor Herensuge, stand up for me!"

"I'm taking the fifth on that one." He held up his palms. "Don't even start with batting your eyes at me, little girl."

The front door to the bar swung open and a frantic looking shifter ambled inside, making a beeline to Solomon. "Keegan sent me with some news. He said you'd know what to do."

"Get hold of yourself. What's the message, Roger?" Solomon clapped the guy on the shoulder.

"Kee and Carl found two scouts not from around here. Said they've been lurking about but so far haven't done anything but stay put. Nothing unusual. Then tonight a whole mess of leather wearing riders rolled in from the south. Wolves on all new bikes, like they robbed a showroom. Leastways that's what Kee suspected."

"Oh really. Keegan thinks they're cycle thieves."

"Not that they are—just ya know…they're outlaws."

"Hold on. I'm not following the problem." Solomon and everyone at the bar watched the slender man.

"They're for real. Black vests, tats, and patches, but so are their Harleys. And every last one is brand spanking new."

"Well dammit, Roger. Maybe it's a cycle club, this is their vacation, and they're into Harleys." Solomon grinned and winked at Drake. "Wouldn't be the first time someone rolled in on a Harley this week."

• • •

Drake's focus pricked. It would be easy to trace and find out exactly who the hell these "outlaws" were. But since this wasn't his gig and no one asked for his help, he'd have to investigate the riders covertly. Last thing he needed to do was step on the toes of the people who'd helped Shay. He nodded to a woman at the end of the bar.

"What'll you have?" he asked, half-listening to the other conversation in back of him.

"Bud Light," she said and pushed some bills across the bar counter. "You Shay's guy?"

"Affirmative. Drake O'Connor." He nodded just as Shay leaned over and laughed.

"He's mine. Disagreeable but I'll take him."

"You'd better. Since he's yours…he's hands off." Ignoring the jibe, he set her beer down and the woman smiled. "I'm Keira. Nice to meet you, Drake."

"See," Shay whispered. "Everyone adores you."

"I'm concerned with only one person," he replied. "What's going on with the bikers?"

"Don't know. Everyone takes a turn on the neighborhood watch. But Kee and Carl are militant. They were in the marines."

"They sure as hell act like jarheads." He turned his attention back to Solomon.

Roger slapped his hand on the bar in protest to something the owner had said and Drake had missed. "It's not like that. Kee and Carl got suspicious after what they've seen so far. They pulled one of their invisible acts and are hanging out over there, listening in on what those hounds are up to. Seems like they're looking for trouble with humans."

Solomon shook his head. "Crap. Wouldn't be the first motorcycle club wanting to feel badass. Who better to pick on than humans, 'cept they're in the wrong place. We ain't got but a few and they're married to shifters. Loyal to us all. I better make some phone calls and send out an alert."

"Maybe we should we call the state troopers," Damien suggested.

"And what, have them come arrest us all?" Solomon shot back. "You remember the last time we called in a problem to the troopers. Unless we got a real honest-to-goodness situation—and I'm talking life or death—I veto it. We could all get hauled away and those who can't make like a banana and split will have hell to pay."

For the smaller shifters and those who were aged, escaping from humans by shifting into primal form was problematic. Arthritic joints, whether human or animal, still sucked and made it difficult to walk—forget running or flying.

"When was the last time a crisis—or rather a dilemma—like this happened?" Drake asked. Being near the Gulf and New Orleans, they had to have their share of bikers in these parts. Quite a few outlaw clubs roamed down south in the winter, but not the type with spanking new rides. That part didn't correlate. After his shift, he'd touch base with Noah and find out if there was any information about a gang of...hell what could they be classified as except hipster bikers? Shit, he needed to lay eyes on them, but couldn't until his shift ended. "How did they dress?"

"All black," Roger replied. "Ya know, like regular bikers."

"Hard to distinguish nowadays," Damien said.

"And that's why *us* sounding the siren might get us all in a heap of trouble with the troopers. Shifters don't cause problems in Harmony. It's why this place exists. If them guys are still here tomorrow, we'll round up our watch group and take a ride over. Won't be the first time we've had to *explain* how things work here. Don't suspect they're looking to broker a mess of conflict any more than we are."

There was truth in what Solomon said. And there was always the possibility of warrants being issued. He reached out and rubbed his hand over Shay's arm, wanting to feel her skin under his.

"Turn the frown upside down, mister," she said.

"Baby," he grunted. She flinched and he felt the whole bar around them fade. "What's wrong?"

"Nothing." She smiled, pressing her hand behind her hip. "Just my back. It's not easy sitting on a barstool for an hour."

"Try an hour or two," Mara said.

"Hasn't he asked you out yet?" Shay bumped her shoulder against the woman's next to her while still squeezing his fingers.

"If he had, we wouldn't be sitting here. Let me tell you," Mara muttered loud enough for Drake to pick up. He glanced over to the wolf shifter in question, and yep—the dude was clueless. He let go of Shay's fingers and went to work, pouring a glass of Chablis and then a shot of Jack.

"From a secret admirer," he said, sliding the glass of wine in front of Mara.

"Seriously?" Her owl eyes went plate-sized and Shay snickered.

Drake shrugged. "Hey, I'm doing what I was told."

"You're pulling my leg," Mara said.

"Hush." Shay picked up the glass and pushed it into her friend's hand. "Drink up. And smile. Isn't that what you always told me?"

"Funny," Mara replied.

He refilled two empty beer mugs from another customer, then walked over to Damien and set the shot down next to his half-full beer mug.

"What's this?" Damien asked.

"From an anonymous fan." He winked. There weren't many people inside the bar, but considering it was a Tuesday night, the place kept him busy and would keep the beta wolf guessing. "Drink up," he said, drumming his fingers on the smooth oak surface of the bar.

He turned and met Shay's sparkling stare. She wore a secretive smile and crooked her finger at him. He leaned over the bar and brushed his chin up against her cheek. "Play matchmaker much?" she asked.

"That depends. Are you pleased?"

He heard her draw in a small gasp of air and then exhale. "Yes."

Suddenly, he felt her stiffen and her face went cool against his. Way too cool and he held her by the shoulders. "What's wrong?"

"Noooothing. It's just growing pains. Happens all the time," she said. Which would have been just dandy except her lower lip quivered. He didn't like seeing her in pain. Not one bit.

"You need to rest. Lie down." He looked around. "I'll take you back to your apartment."

Today when they'd gone house hunting and she refuted several acceptable choices, he'd acquiesced instead of demanding that she move to a suitable home. In short order, she'd have him wrapped around her little finger if he caved to her every whim. "I'm not joking. If I have to carry you up there, we're going." He began to unknot the ties of his apron.

Shay shook her head. "No. You're covering my shift. You can't ditch Mony because I'm having cramps. Absolutely not. Otherwise, I won't leave."

"Lord have mercy on me, woman!"

"Do you need to leave?" Damien asked.

"No!" Shay semi-shouted.

"For a minute or two," Drake replied. "No buts."

"I'm on it." Damien was already out of his seat, shouting over to Solomon, "I'm just covering. Shay's not feeling well."

"What the dickens? Should I call Trish?" Sol bellowed.

"Do you see what you've done?" Shay muttered.

He clapped Damien on the back. "I owe you."

"Naw. I enjoy helping out and she never lets anyone. Glad to see someone finally has got her to…bend a little. It's been a chore these last few months."

"What does that mean?" Shay snapped.

"Everybody walks a line around here. Not that it's a bad thing," Damien retorted.

"We have fun. Don't we have fun, Mara?"

"Sure, hun. When you get off and go home."

Shay picked up the baby blanket and stashed it in the bag. "I can't believe you guys. Someone has to keep order over you roughnecks."

"Here." Drake scooped up a skein of thread that had fallen onto the barstool. "Is this yours? Might be mine."

"Hardy, har har. I'll take that thank you very much."

He looked up and met Solomon's stare and nod, which he returned. "Be right back," he said over his shoulder to Damien.

"Nothing is going on tonight so take your time," Damien returned, grabbing some peanuts out of the bowl and tossing one up into the air and catching it in his mouth.

He held the door for Shay and breathed in her fragrance as she walked in front of him. The soft sway of her hips mesmerized him for a beat, then he blinked at the darkness surrounding them and realized almost in shock that it was evening. "It's like a time warp inside the bar. Didn't think it would be dark already," he said, wanting to go up to her apartment and just hold her. But damn, he had to do the chivalrous thing and contend with three more hours of a bartending gig. Another item on his fast-growing list of what he needed to rectify. He kicked a rock and watched it fly across the parking lot, barely missing one customer's car.

"Did you mean to do that?" she asked.

"No…yes," he muttered, taking hold of her hand. "Shay, we need to talk. When I get off tonight. Can you wait up for me?"

"You're covering my shift. Of course I'll be up." She slowed and faced him. "Everything okay?"

Staring down into her glimmering eyes, his mouth went uncharacteristically dry. Shay made whatever he wanted to say suddenly catch in his throat and he coughed. Damn. He could bark out orders to a hardcore platoon, and this woman had him fumbling. Badly. He raked his fingers through his hair, then scrubbed his hand down his cheek, wanting to slap his own face. *Snap out of it.*

A bleep went by, barely noticeable except to his ultra-perceptive senses. Maybe that's why having a conversation around here was next to impossible. So many nosy neighbors always homing in.

Christ. He'd lived in a close community but had forgotten about how everyone was in everyone else's business. "Ya know there's something called cable television," he snapped, loud enough for whomever was careening about to hear.

"What are you talking about?" Shay asked, shaking her head.

"It's like Grand Central Station around here. Hard to believe you don't get a little pissed at how other folks are nosier than hell."

"Oh that," she said and squeezed his hand. "You get used to it. I guess."

"Standard operating procedure could use some tweaking here in Harmony," he grumbled, pulling her against him. "I don't need a chaperone where you're concerned.

"Maybe you don't, but I like having my own personal escort. Sometimes."

"Don't you trust me?"

"You? I'm learning. But for months it's been me and me alone. And late at night, it gets kinda lonely out here solo."

He glanced around the parking lot, his chest tightening. Fuck, he'd had his head up his ass these last months while Shay had been here. *Alone.* He'd been lonely, too, but he wasn't a woman who had to worry about being overpowered. His damn pride had choked the sense out of him. He should have come for her sooner, instead stewing and sulking. The softness of Shay's body compounded his guilt a million times over, especially when she leaned into him and he felt her rounded belly. "I'm sorry."

"I didn't say that to make you feel bad. Coming here was my choice. Everything I've done since the summer has been my choice. Because I had the freedom to decide, I'm not sorry where I ended up. Not one bit. I would have been miserable if I'd stayed in Denver, and who knows what would have happened? That SOB Dimitri really pulled a number on my family. What I can't believe is how my father could have fallen for the load of crap that Dimitri was slinging."

He stiffened and wrapped his arm around her shoulder as he glanced around the parking lot. Yeah, he didn't get the sense that these nosy Nellies were up to harming anyone—lurking to keep the peace. But what he wanted to share wasn't their business. "Let's go upstairs."

After she closed her apartment door, he picked her up and carried her into her bedroom and laid her on the mattress. "Baby," he grunted, kneeling next to her. "I don't think your dad has been himself for the past year. Richard was—is under an incantation. Not unheard of, especially for someone like Necrodemas with his connections in the black market. They sell all sorts of shit there."

Shay's brows drew together. "Why didn't I think of it?"

"It's not the first conclusion to draw since your father wasn't acting outrageous in his council duties. The idea crossed my mind in how strange your parents were behaving with regards to bartering you off in marriage."

She tried to sit up but he climbed over her body and pinned her beneath him. "Does Shawn realize? We've got to tell him."

"Ssshhh," he whispered, seeking to undo her worry. "I have and he had your parents submit to an evaluation, confirming it's a strange spell. Explains why your mom agreed to you marrying Necrodemas and that was that fucker's mistake. He was greedy in the degree he exerted his influence over your parents, swaying them away from what was in your best interest. It threw up all sorts of red flags. When your brother asked me, I provided a contact. I only wish it had been sooner."

"Why didn't Necrodemas put a spell on me?"

"Don't know. Just be glad he didn't."

"And you're sure my mother is going to be fine?"

He grimaced under the weight of the uncertainty. "I hope so. It's the reason your mom is in recovery. Breaking a spell is dicey and laborious. Last I heard, Shawn hired my contact. A woman from England. Sherry Delacroix. She lives just outside Denver. Have you ever met her?"

"No. I don't know any witches."

"She came highly recommended from Noah, a guy on my security team, and she seems competent. Spell breaking takes time."

"Is that the same guy you were talking to? The night I drugged you?"

He cocked his head. "Yep. That was pretty underhanded. Woke up the next morning in a state. My head felt amazingly awful. I'll have to spank your ass for that as well. You deserve it."

"You're acquiring some list there."

"Possibly." A bolt of possessiveness flared within him. "Marry me, Shay. I'll protect you and you'll never be alone again." The timing felt synchronous and he didn't overthink, didn't fight.

"But you're a dragon," she said, her voice twisted with pain and no longer husky and calm. "You don't want me. What we have is *no big deal*. I heard you say exactly that on the phone to Noah. One day all this playing at adventure will get old. What is it that you want from me? I can't be a plaything for you, Lord Herensuge." She tried to wrench free of him.

"Just what do think you I'm saying?"

"Words. Easy to say."

"Not for me," he snarled.

"I get what you're offering me. You think I need your name for our children. That's so old-fashioned. Maybe a hundred years ago when you were a boy, it was semi-required. But not now. Unmarried women have children all the time."

"Not my mate. And not my children. You are going to marry me and I'm going to be by your side." He felt his whole body heat and his heartbeat accelerated. Goddammit! He wasn't going to have a meltdown over the fact that when he finally popped the question, she reacted exactly as he'd expected. He inhaled a ragged breath and rolled off her. He stood, staring down at Shay, and scrubbed his hand over his jaw. "You're mine. That won't ever fucking change. I know you feel what I feel. We're linked."

She sat up without breaking eye contact. "Well, maybe Mr. Over The Top, that's one of the problems. I'm not your anything. I'm my own person!"

# CHAPTER 10

She sat on the mattress for several long minutes after Drake had left or rather stormed out. Suffocated is how Shay felt. Abso-the-hell-lutely, she couldn't breathe. He'd proposed and instead of discussing it like a normal person, she'd heard only one message and met his possessive fire and with her own brand of flame. Her heart's staccato rhythm beat a loud, blaring run for the hills. Now, with adrenaline spiking her bloodstream, her whole body was a churning mess of confusion mixed with frustration and doused with liberal amounts of anger. She didn't know if she was more upset with Drake or herself.

She was overdue to let off some steam.

She headed for the front door. Yeah, she noticed the flickering bursts of energy that Drake had mentioned. Snap! If she left on a run, those jokers would probably go blabbering to Solomon and Drake, and she'd have an escort just like in Lisbon. She snorted silently. And just like in Lisbon, she'd ditch her chaperones. She grabbed her sneakers off the chair and glided back inside. One of the ways she'd learned to outmaneuver her security team was to do things that weren't expected. Not once had she used the back door to her apartment. That entrance was stockpiled with used barrels that one day Solomon intended on making into some sort of outdoor seating area for the spring and summer.

Tonight she'd do a jog to the edge of town, stow her clothes and then she'd head to the deserted state park and out to the swamps in leopardess form. No one would bother her out there. It had been ages since she'd run unrestricted. Since becoming pregnant, she didn't want to risk being naked in her human figure but tonight, she needed to be free. Being in her primal form would renew her and might also help calm her enough to act rationally and explain to Drake her confusion at having gone from college student to heiress to runaway—and now on the brink of motherhood. So many hats, but none helped provide her with a heads up on who she was as an individual.

*Would the real Shay Marie Barclay like to stand up? How can I now leap into becoming the wife of a man—excuse me, a dragon? Talk about doing the full monty.*

She changed into leggings and a sweatshirt, socks and sneakers. Softly she opened the back door, which overlooked an open field. There were no bleeps of light and she slunk down and descended the stairs, hoping that the Viking vampire town criers were off doing something important like sharpening their fangs for Halloween in nine months. Keeping watch over her was most assuredly a waste of their time.

Ah, hell. Why take a chance? On the last step, she picked up a large rock, then another and another. She crept to the corner of the building and low and behold. There were Kee and Carl, leaning against the redwood fence and smoking. They spoke in what sounded like a mixture of English and Danish but could have just as easily been Swedish or Norwegian. She heaved the rocks across the parking lot and aimed for the trash dumpster. The rocks hit the target and came down, sounding like gunshots. She watched Kee and Carl vanish into thin air, presumably now over at the dumpster.

*And that's how a girl outsmarts a pair of guys.* Worked like a charm every time. She wanted to congratulate herself further but she'd better go while the going was good.

She hightailed it across the field, not even breaking a sweat when she reached the road, sprinting past a stand of cypress, past a gnarled massive live oak, and the shadows of the swaying moss. The brisk evening breeze made running that much more enjoyable and the few stars dusting the sky looked like bits of glittery eye shadow she'd once spilled on a black lacquer bureau in her room back home in her parents' house. She ran over the flat terrain—this was nothing like the muscle pumping runs she'd traversed up in the Rockies.

What if what Drake said was true? That her parents were under some sick spell and they'd be better soon. She prayed that she'd return home and find her parents were back to normal, recovered, and wanted her happiness? It would have been a horrible injustice if she'd married Dimitri and his less than stellar lineage under these circumstances?

She jogged onward and flinched at a muffled yip. She glanced in the direction of the sound and noticed the twinkling red glare of several pairs of eyes that blinked and stared back at her from the darkness. Out here, on the edge of town, there wasn't much except for farmland and a large cluster of cypress trees up ahead. Where were those bikers located? Perhaps this was where they were camped out.

She edged away from the stand of trees and turned to follow the path leading toward the fields. On the other side of the open land lay the edge of the state park and a swamp. She could outdistance most animals if she could get into her primal form. She'd have to strip off her clothes, and she glanced around, sniffing the air. *Better not think too much on that one.*

Over there were several trees! Shay cut back toward the cypress rather than risk being surrounded in an open field. *That one.* She spotted a tree with low-lying branches. Sure as hell, glowing eyes flickered closer, following in her wake. Dammit! She wasn't going to stand there and chart distance-to-object ratios. Picking up her pace, she sprinted to the cypress. At the base of the trunk, she stretched but the branches were beyond her reach. Jumping, she grasped a branch and kicked her feet against the trunk, hauling herself upward, using her upper body strength.

Again she grabbed the next branch then another as she scrambled up into the tree. When she was high enough to feel safe, she perched on a branch and pulled off her sweatshirt and kicked off her shoes. The baying of a wolf from below sent chills over her skin and she felt the rumble of a roar materialize from her chest and throat. The leopardess inside her did not take kindly to being threatened. Long two-inch claws erupted from her fingertips and her canines broke free from her gums. Off came her socks and then she heard a man's voice.

A man wearing leather from neck to foot had his face upturned and stood staring at her. His skin was so pale he glowed like skim milk. Unblinking, his cold bluish-white eyes resembled liquid nitrogen, freeze burning a path across her body. Every hair on her body stood up. The shock of seeing him made her jerk and hug the tree.

"Miss Barclay," he said. "You're outside the protection of Harmony once you left the town borders. All the way out here with no warding and no one to help you. Come on down. Don't make me come up there and get you. I will, you know, and it won't be like the last time met."

She didn't recall ever meeting him. "Who the hell are you?"

He laughed. "Mr. Necrodemas sent me to retrieve you. He doesn't care if you're harmed in the bargain. So please, why not make this easy on both of us?"

*Dimitri was behind this gang coming to Louisiana?* She sniffed the air and perceived a rank odor that made her nose twitch. She shivered at the recognition—he was that driver who'd stared at her nonstop during one of Dimitri's parties; and then again she'd sniffed this scent in the Mony parking lot. The neighborhood watch had gotten it wrong. He was only part wolf. This was Dark Fae stench. A gypsy, not the usual type, but that was going off her limited knowledge of the Light and Dark Courts. No one she knew had much experience with either since Fae were unpredictable. Capricious during good times, but could just as quickly become savage, lacking any and all emotional depth.

Several headlights glowed from the road. Bikers. Why weren't they in wolf form?

*Shit*. No time to waste wondering about that mystery. She steadied herself, standing up on the branch, and using her toes to grip the limb, she peeled her leggings down her hips and off one leg at a time. The gypsy Fae directly below her whistled a slow catcall. Laughter erupted and she noticed the flickering of more red glaring eyes around the base of the tree trunk. She didn't care that she was almost naked as she felt her whole body began to transform. Her shoulders and hips broadened and her spine elongated; she cradled her belly, worried that her babies might get squished. Rapidly, her legs and arms shortened, and she easily balanced on the bough. Then the final change as her pelt of spotted fur broke free: her skull altered shape with her jaw now more than pronounced as she roared a warning to the gypsy Fae.

As a leopard, leaping thirty feet was simple, but where to land to give her the best advantage? Shay lifted her head and peered outward, flattening her eyes and using her night vision. With her keen leopard sight, she memorized the shape of the horizon and points along the terrain. She panted, to further tease out the nighttime swamp scents and confirm the view. She wasn't worried about the bikers nor the wolves if she could get a head start. It was the gypsy Fae she was leery of. No way in hell could he touch her, sap her life force—he'd kill her children.

She crouched and burst from the cypress tree, landing on her forepaws and then coming down onto her hind legs without breaking stride. A black wolf leapt in her path and she snarled, lifting her paw and raking her claws across his muzzle. He whined, and she barreled forward with her two hundred pounds of feline force and trounced him. Would have crushed his windpipe if he'd tried to stall her progress. Luckily for him, he ended up in an irrigation ditch, and she heard the sound of the bikers, gunning their engines, and the growl of wolves behind her. She burst through the field of swaying cordgrass and leapt into the air, spanning a long arc over several fallen logs, and dove into a canal. With her center of gravity a bit off, she ended up doing a semi belly flop. Still as a leopardess, swimming and running were as natural as breathing and eating and she paddled, ever watchful for gators. A head of one bobbed to the surface, a shifter she thought she recognized from the bar, but she couldn't be sure. The gator didn't track her, just stared and blinked…or winked. She noticed several other gators appear and form a line then recede beneath the surface where a few air bubbles floated.

A pack of gray wolves howled and she clambered out of the canal, onto the opposite bank and shook her coat, shaking water droplets in all directions. She glanced over her shoulder and caught sight of the gypsy Fae pointing and the wolves diving into the black murky canal water. Stupid Fae, she snarled, and heard the first yip of a wolf. Then another and another down in the swirling black water. The gators weren't as nice to the wolves as they'd been to her. That's what good bartending skills could get a chick. She gave one more shake and tore off, bounding up an embankment toward drier terrain, away from the marsh and prickly grass. A cell tower with twinkling lights was the only thing noticeable on the horizon besides the mangrove marshes that reminded Shay of fingers pointing up out of the dirt. If she stayed on the high ground, it would be a heck of lot easier to navigate. She swung around, hunkered down, and prepared to leap until she stared at the bright spotlights on top of a Jeep swamp buggy, hauling ass toward her.

• • •

Drake closed out the register, counting the bills and rubber banding them together before placing them and the receipts in the bank bag. "Here you go," he said to Solomon.

"Smooth sailing," the bear shifter replied, turning off the interior lights and lumbering next to him down the back hallway.

He nodded, removing his apron and tossing it into the bar laundry bag at the back door. "So far, so good."

"Guess I should be looking for a replacement. Don't suspect you need a job?"

"Nice of you to ask, but I have something I kick around. Keeps me busy."

"Yeah. Guys like you always do." Solomon flipped the light switch.

"Good night," Drake said. "Thanks, by the way."

"For?"

"Watching out for Shay. She's been safe here and I won't ever forget that."

"Shay's a special girl."

He inhaled. "Yep. I keep hearing that."

Sol clapped him on the shoulder. "She's been waiting for you. Glad you finally got here. I was wondering if I'd have to hire a detective to find you."

He felt his brows shoot up. "If I had known sooner, I would have come immediately."

"Hey. We've all been on the receiving end of a hardheaded woman. You're here now."

Drake laughed. "Sometimes I don't know which way is up." He shoved his hands into his pockets and walked around toward the staircase. Mounting the stairs two at a time, he twirled the doorknob in his hand and frowned. Dammit. How hard was it for one leopardess to remember to keep the door locked? He entered the apartment and reminded himself to stay low key. Barreling back inside after storming out wasn't going to help his situation of getting Shay to plainly see how good they were as a couple. He'd been a fool in how he'd demanded she marry him. *What a jackass!*

An independent woman didn't acquiesce to diktats. If he wanted Shay, it was going to be a partnership or nothing. He totally got that, or at least he understood after Mara and half the bar—the female half—had laid into him for the last three hours. He'd gotten an earful and an education on what it meant to have a mate, or more specifically, a pregnant mate. And equally important, according to the brouhaha downstairs, how the hell to be sensitive, masculine, the perfect gentleman and the perfect whatever for Shay. His head spun from all the advice.

"Hey, you still up?" he called out as he approached her bedroom door, vowing he'd not link with her. He'd come clean and admit he was an overbearing brute and if she wanted her independence, he'd honor her wishes…as much as he could being an alpha obstinate dragon.

Inside the room was dim from what he could tell of the cracked door and he wondered if she'd fallen asleep. Pregnant women had to need more rest. Didn't they? He pushed open the door and stood there. With his dragon vision, he perceived the thermal temperatures within the bedroom, scanning the bed specifically. Shay wasn't inside. He stepped to the nursery and opened the door. No Shay. His heartbeat started to throttle in his throat.

He backtracked and passed the kitchen and the living room. Zilch. He scanned the walls and the various thermal prints with his infrared vision; Shay's faded thermal handprints were hours old. He followed her footprints on the floor, almost too faded to perceive, all the way to the back door. What the shit? On the back porch his gaze trailed Shay's footprints up and over the barrels, and down the stairs. When the footprints went in one direction— into the deserted field—his heart clawed its way up his throat. He roared in frustration, tearing off his shirt as his cranial horn burst through his skin. Forget the idea of not linking their minds.

*Where are you? Shay, for the love of all that's holy, answer me! Baby, tell me where are you!*

Fuck. Fuck! Silence permeated the corridors of his mind. His wings unfurled and he felt his body begin to shift. His fingers turned into claws with sharp as fuck talons. The seams of his jeans burst as did his motorcycle boots until the tattered remnants of his clothing fell away from his body as he leapt over the side of the railing, landing on the ground below as his wings broke through the skin below his shoulder blades.

"What in the world are you raising Cain about?" Carl stood a few steps in front of him. Kee cleared the corner of the building, still hovering in the air and looking downward. Both the vampires had blood on their lips, smeared on their mouths, and running down their chins; obviously they'd come during feeding.

It was a little after midnight and Drake sniffed the air, dissecting the scents and picking up the faint residue of that diesel odor that intermingled with the other gasoline scents lingering in the parking lot. "Fuck! How could I be so imperially stupid?"

"You're a dragon," Carl offered.

"Shut the fuck up, bloodsucker. Shay is gone. And not in a good way as you'd like…away from me." He snapped his wings, hovering above the ground. *Shay! Answer me, sweetheart. Where in the fuck are you?*

Carl wiped the smile off his face. "Where?"

Kee landed next to Carl. "What happened? Where is she?"

"That way." He pointed and simultaneously stabbed the air with his forked tail. "Those biker wolves. Where are they located?" He growled, flames shooting out from his mouth. If the vampires had been any other creatures, Carl and Kee would have a pair of singed faces, with third degree burns.

"Near the swamps. What does that have to do with you breathing fucking fire left and right?"

Drake roared, "Shay's out there and has run headlong into the Unruled all by herself!"

# CHAPTER 11

"It's a hell of a thing," the gypsy Fae said loudly. "Would hate to take a piece out of you by accident. No time to get a doctor to repair the damage. Come on, Miss Barclay. I can stay out here all night and all tomorrow. It's gonna be a sunny day. You'll need water eventually. Little leopardess, where are you hiding?" His sing-song voice made her fur stand on end.

Shay was certain…nearly certain that he had no idea where she was hiding. A swatch of light swept over the ground and she hunkered lower, pressing her belly to the damp, mushy soil. Oh God! Under her, she felt something slither along her ribcage and prayed the cold coiling was a non-venomous snake seeking her body heat. She flattened her ears and sniffed. The *crunch-crunch-crunch* of the gypsy Fae's boot steps were getting closer. Shay poked her head up and then dunked her chin onto her front paws to avoid the beam the spotlight cast in her direction. That shithead was wielding a machete back and forth through the cordgrass.

She crawled backward, past clumps of wiregrass, clenching her jaws all the while. *Note to self: running out the door, toward a swamp is not a beneficial way to blow off steam.* Instead of sequestered at the town gym, safe and sound and deciding which machine and how many reps, she had to slink into one of the smelly canals that crisscrossed the salt marsh. Slowly, she scooted—not flipping easy with her belly bulging on either side. *I'm gonna be fine, my babies are safely cushioned inside my body.* She kept that on repeat; but still, she gritted her jaw, her canines stabbing her lip with each sharp rock that jabbed her underside. Her coat was wet and smelled fetid from the brackish water. Probably why the Fae was having trouble locating her. Just as she could sniff out his rank Fae odor, he was equally perceptive of her leopardess scent. Or in the very least, his wolves were keen. If he'd only shift into his werewolf form, she'd show him a thing or two about what it meant to mess with a mama leopardess. But that moron wasn't a complete idiot.

She stuck her back paw out and wiggled her toes into thin air. Holy Jesus, she was on the edge of steep embankment. This must be some sort of irrigation canal behind her. Manmade, judging from the sharp cut in the ground, and she scooted her body parallel to the edge to see what lay below. Keeping one eye peeled on the Fae, she adjusted her position just as he shouted an order. Shay clung to the edge, peering downward. The drop was at least fifteen feet, maybe more, going by how the moon reflected on the rippling surface of the fast-moving water. Geez, it smelled horrible. She didn't know what was down in that water but as she peeked over the edge she heard a voice. *Shay! Answer me, sweetheart. Where in the fuck are you?*

Her claws shot out as she instinctively flinched and squinted, using every last rod and cone of her nighttime vision to scan the brackish water below. Was Drake down in that god-awful water?

The Fae wasn't more than ten or so yards off to the side. If she snarled, he'd hear her. She couldn't give up her location. *Shannon Barclay!* Wait—that shouting was inside her head. What the flock was happening?

Again she heard Drake's voice crystal clear. *Baby, talk to me. A word. One word, Shay. Now!*

Inhaling, she closed her eyes and focused on linking her mind with Drake's. For all her bitching and moaning about having him infiltrate her mind, this was some awesome skill he had and she'd apologize later.

"Point the lights over there," the Fae hollered. "Get those fucking wolves out here. Now! I don't care if they were bit and are bleeding. They'd better do their job and sniff out where the Barclay bitch is hiding or it'll be their hides I nail to the wall."

*Drake? Can you hear me?* She felt Drake's presence inside her mind, but she couldn't seem to form the words so he could hear them. Even in her mind it sounded more like leopard growls and snarls.

She clung to the muck as a warm glow filled her with a calming sensation. *He must be doing something.* The golden serpentine essence expanded, a relay racing across her nerve endings as if he were one with her.

*We're coming to you.* His deep voice radiated through her as a beacon, a shimmering energy. His dragon heat filled the deepest and darkest corner of her soul.

If she wanted to converse with him, she needed her human brain in command. In leopard form, she could understand when Drake spoke, but she wasn't articulate in English or any other human spoken language and he didn't speak feline. Not yet.

*Okay. Here goes nothing.* It was one thing to be a wet leopard stooped over the spongy swamp ground. It was quite another thing to be a woman with sensitive skin, lying prone in a salt marsh. Holy goddess! She shivered, her tummy pressed against mud and cordgrass, as she laid her forehead against the back of her interlaced hands. She disengaged her fingers and quickly reached down her thigh, scooting the snake away from her leg. The tiny hairs all over her human body rose from the chilly night air and her damp skin. But more than the cool temperature, she felt the sensation of Drake's powerful magick washing over. She didn't fight him linking minds with her and the feeling was exquisite, even lying in the muck and aside from being the target of a psycho gypsy Fae jackass.

*Drake? Can you hear me?* She tapped her forehead and waited for a return message. Please, let him hear me. Plea—

His voice boomed inside her mind.

Shay, we're coming to you.

*You can actually hear me!* She dug her fingers into the soggy dirt; a jolt of adrenaline shot through her body.

Yeah. About mind linking, look, there wasn't a choice.

*Drake, please shut up. So not a problem. Come find me. I'm in the swamp—but I don't know where.* She looked up, and dammit she couldn't find one point in which to reference.

Find some landmark. Anything.

*Err…there's a swamp buggy and it's got a bright search light. Oh, about a half a mile back there was a cell tower. But nothing else is out here except the Fae and his crew.*

Nothing. Silence. *Drake?* She tapped on her forehead, trying to improve the reception, then realized it more than likely didn't work that way.

Yep. That's the Sprint cell tower. Got it.

*Drake, I'm in human form. I need to change back.*

"Well, well. Look what we found here. Won't be so pretty when I get hold of you now, and then that dragon lover of yours. He's the real prize I'm after. What an incredibly simple trap to lure a dragon out here, past the warded borders of Harmony. Fucking child's play." At the sound of the Fae's voice so near, panic took hold of her. She swung her face around and locked gazes with the Dark Fae. He was less than three feet away and the skin all over her body shrank. He lunged for her, leaving her no options. Scrambling, she rolled over the edge of the embankment, willing to do anything to escape that creature's touch. *Oh my God. I've got to shift back into my leopardess. I'm going down.*

"Motherfucker!" the Fae yelled at her. Lights flickered from above and illuminated the canal. The water was the color of café au lait, and a water moccasin sped by her.

Shay, what just happened?

*Drake, I had to jump into the water.* By the time she'd kicked her legs twice, she'd shifted back into a frantically paddling leopardess, moving in league with the water current away from the spot where the Fae stood.

She blew the water from her nostrils and blinked as water droplets ran down her face and into her eyes, partially blinding her. Did Drake realize she could still hear him but couldn't send a message back? The water moved with greater force and she bumped into the sides of the canal. Roughhewn sections, they more than likely connected the swamp basin and led out to the Gulf of Mexico, not that she was planning on riding the current that far.

He won't jump. Dark Fae and water don't mix. Nor can he roll around in the mud. Earth elements will send him back to the realm from where he came.

Drake continued talking to her and with his voice in her head, she felt a sense of calm in the midst of a total calamity.

Good to know. The choppy water current carried her along the high-cut walls and the canal widened. More like the walls gave away and she saw why. This wasn't just a canal, it was some sort of dike with several waterwheels spinning, lashed together. She paddled in earnest instead of being carried along and began swimming in the opposite direction, away from the wheels, churning up the water into white thrashing bubbles. Where in the freaking world was she? Some sort of water treatment plant but how could she get the message to Drake? She'd have to shift back again. She'd never shifted this rapidly in succession. She fought every instinct that told her to remain in primal form. As a leopardess she was stronger. A capable swimmer. A lithe feline force to reckon with. In human form, she could do a respectable breast stroke and tread water. That was it.

She tasted the tang of metal—a brittle sour taste on her tongue. Was it fear or the electricity being produced by the water wheels? Shay glanced around at the fencing designed to keep people out and trapped her inside a watery conveyer belt.

She shifted again, kicking her legs and dove underneath the water.

• • •

Drake circled around the cell tower. He'd called Mara for her ability to sweep into small spaces and her in-depth knowledge of the swamp. She flew next to him in owl form and the vampires zipped by like rockets. They had little control over how to glide on air currents and he gritted his teeth. If the Fae noticed them, that fucker would step up his game in attempting to trap and capture Shay.

Baby, give me a sign.

*Drake!* She sounded as if she were choking. Or coughing. *I'm in some sort of water treatment place.*

He swooped down to the cell tower, using his ability to be noiseless. Stealth. "Where's a water treatment place around here?" he asked Kee.

"Fuck. I don't know. Hold on." The vampire removed his iPhone from his pocket and tapped the screen. "That way. According to my navigation application it's one point two miles."

Mara perched on one of the metal rungs of the tower, softly screeching and blinked, flapping her wings and nodding. Apparently, she was aware of the place. She took to the air waves and he followed, until he locked in on Shay's life force. Squinting, he identified the waterwheels lashed together across the canal. Some joker's attempt to harness solar power and remain off the grid. Shit!

He swooped down.

*Shay. I'm here. If you're below the surface, can you come up for air?*

*Oh Drake.* One slender hand, then another surfaced, followed by the top of Shay's head.

He torpedoed her location, rocketing downward. Gingerly, he curled his talons over her body, unsure how to hold her. This was the first time he'd touched her while in dragon form and her delicate skin concerned him. She was so much smaller than him. She curled her fingers around his foreleg, and stepped up into his paw that he held out, wrapping her arms around his knee. He felt as though every nerve he possessed was suddenly exposed and simultaneously amped with energy into a state of hyperawareness. She felt incredibly soft against his tough skin—like sensuous silk to his senses. When she hoisted herself completely out of the water, he was unprepared for her sleek, wet, and very naked body to break the surface. Her rounded belly and bouncing breasts spoke to every possessive atom composing his body—his soul went on red-alert status.

Holy shit, did he just turn into a creature with all thumbs? His dexterity all but disappeared. He beat his wings and rose up into the air, focused on shielding Shay while vainly trying to enfold her in his paw. *Christ almighty! Those dipstick vampires better keep their bloodsucking eyes to themselves. Fuck, I'm not going to be able to deal with this Fae until I get Shay situated.*

"Hey. I can hear you," she said aloud and squeezed his foreleg, shivering. "Would you rather I shift back into a leopardess?"

Don't. I don't want to chance you losing your footing. I'll have you back at your apartment shortly. Mara will need to stay with you. I'm going to track down that Fae fucker and deal with him. One-on-one.

*No. Please. He has a mob with him. We'll come up with a plan and then deal with him. Not like this. Drake, you can't risk something happening to you. I'm asking for our babies. Don't come back to the swamp...for me, do this one thing.*

He roared in frustration, shooting a plume of fire upward into the darkened night sky. The ground rumbled underneath them and from a languid flight, he tore through the air in anger. She could feel his rage and stroked a hand against the rough hide covering his chest. He was large, the size of Greyhound bus, but she didn't fear him in this roaring, untamed state.

His chest rumbled and after having flown a mile, he snorted, shifting his emerald eyes and regarded her. She felt him mind link and purred in response to the exquisite sensation of warm tendrils filling her body.

We're leaving tonight. No ifs, ands, or buts. I'm taking you away from here. Understand?

She hung her head. *"Oh really. And just where are we going?"*

That's up to you, baby. We'll talk face to face as soon as we get back.

Shay's head snapped upward and she met his gaze. *"As in person to person?"*

He winked and flapped his wings harder, flying higher to reach her apartment, where he gently set Shay down and shifted into human form. "Before you run up those stairs, I won't lay into you about running off, but that shit won't ever fly again. Now, I get what you were upset about earlier. I have had my head up my ass for months. Then I came here with guns blazing and made another fucked up mistake. You and me—it's hardcore because we're hardheads. You have your own style, but running out a door isn't cool. Either you learn a lesson or one day, you're not going to recover. Do you hear what I'm saying, Shay?"

She leveled him with a wide-eyed look that went off like a bomb inside his head and landed full-force in his gut, but no way was he going to show any impact. This was so fucking serious—that douchebag Fae was still out there and this sick business wasn't finished.

For once, she wasn't coming at him with everything she had and when she bit her plump lip, his knees were ready to buckle. "Thanks for coming for me. Just like you said."

"Baby, don't thank me. It's what I have to do. You're mine. And what's mine, I protect."

# CHAPTER 12

Drake paced while Shay packed a bag. He'd dressed in jeans and a black T-shirt but was barefoot, not having packed an extra pair of boots. His anger rocketed through him, fire in his veins that demanded retribution, but he couldn't leave Shay. No matter how much he wanted to tear that Fae SOB apart, he couldn't risk leaving her alone. Trust was a commodity he was running low on at the moment. He sure as fuck wasn't going to airport, a wide open place with too many opportunities to run amuck. That made that decision easier.

"We're driving your car back to Denver."

"Instead of flying?"

"I repaired the door. If we leave now, I'll get us to Denver by tomorrow."

A knock reverberated on the front door, which he unlocked and swung wide, ready to kick ass. He stared into the faces of Trish and Solomon. Mara was behind them scaling the stairs, calling out, "Wait for me."

"Here," Solomon said gruffly, holding out a pair of hiking boots. "Might be a tad large, but at least you'll have something on your feet."

"Hey, girl," Trish said on her way down the hall.

"I'm in here." Shay poked her head out from the nursery. "Did you bring tape?"

Drake sat on the sofa, pulling on a pair of socks and then the boots. "Thanks," he said to Solomon.

The bear shifter bent down and picked up a box. "All packed and ready?"

"Hardly. We'll be back when things settle."

Sol slanted him a look, bordering on total disbelief. "Why?"

"For more reasons than not. And mostly because Shay wants to come back."

"That girl is stubborn," Sol replied. "What else you got going?"

"A few boxes in the nursery. Just in case."

Shay, Mara, and Trish appeared in the hall, their heads tilted together, and whispering. Even from the living room and in the dim lighting, he noticed the shadows under Shay's eyes. She was tired but refused to sit down and let him pack up what she wanted to take. If he had an inkling that he could easily trespass into their female conversation he would have, but instead he picked up the suitcase and opened the door. "I'm gonna take this down. Give them a few minutes alone."

"Good idea." Sol ducked out ahead of him. On the landing he paused, sniffing the air. "Kee and Carl, where the hell you two at?"

Carl materialized from the shadows below, alongside Kee and Damien, who had his hands shoved down into his pockets. Drake was unable to resist making a wisecrack. "You finally found the courage to find yourself a date?"

"Apparently. Never knew dragons moonlighted as matchmakers," Damien flung back. "Anything you need?

"Besides a woman who is pushing each and every one of my buttons? Naw."

"She'll keep you real," Damien volunteered.

"More than that," Carl said. "She's got your back."

Drake arched a brow. "And how the hell would you know that?"

"It's the truth," Kee retorted. "Vampire. Dragon. Fae. We don't trust each other because we're empath parasites to some extent."

"How can you tell what she's feeling?" he asked, aware that he as a dragon possessed the skill, and yeah, Fae did too. But those creatures touched to leach a life force. His in-depth knowledge of vampires amounted to urban myths and he didn't know how much was truth from not. Vampires—the undead—weren't on his radar. They didn't like his kind and what Kee extolled was true. He wasn't partial to them either.

"Shay saved me."

He snorted, not liking the way this was coming out. He wasn't in the mood for kicking some vampire asses. "Then know and accept, *I'm* here to safeguard her and I don't need any backup. Thanks for what you did tonight, but I've got a handle on what to do from here on out."

Kee held up his hand and mock saluted. "No one is going to overstep your plans Navy SEAL dragon, sir."

"Oh you're a riot." He bumped Kee's outstretched fist and said, "A regular bloodsucking wiseass."

Carl held out his hand but he did so to shake, not rib him further. "God knows it's hard to trust someone with horns and wings, but since we don't have a choice and, apparently Shay sees something in you, good luck."

He met the Viking's violet colored eyes and nodded, taking hold of Carl's cold as fuck hand. "Back at you."

Shay appeared at the top of the stairs. Her voice and that of Mara and Trish's floated in the air and everyone turned and stared. Shay's skin was luminescent and had that same fiery glow he'd seen the other nights. After showering off the muck of the swamps, her hair lay in soft damp waves, cascading over her shoulders and his breath hitched like a bubble expanding painfully in his chest. He let go of Carl's hand and fist bumped Damien.

He faced Solomon, and both men eyed one another. "Take care of her and call. Day or night if you need our help. We can deal with mountains, if we have to. It's been awhile, but what's a little less oxygen. Right?"

"Absolutely. We'll be in touch," he said, opening his arm for grizzly man-hug and slap to the back.

Shay joined them and she was swept into Sol's embrace. She raised her hands in surrender and laughed. "Don't think you can get rid of me this easy. We'll be back and you'd better be sticking to your diet. Deal?"

"What do you have to throw into the pot insofar as making concessions?"

"How about moderating the flying by the seat of my pants. And that's a whopper. So there. If I can make a few concessions, then so can you, Solomon. So c'mon, shake!"

"All right, I give you my word. I'll stick to my diet, if you stick to thinking before acting." Sol laughed along with Shay, but Drake noticed her liquid eyes peering over to him as she blinked rapidly. He drew her next to him, steering her to the passenger side of the Civic.

"Oh Damien?" he called out.

"What's up?"

"Can you take care of my bike?" He tossed his keys to Damien, who caught them in his palm, wearing a smile that split his face.

"I'm on it. Literally and figuratively."

"Oh dear God! Me too, I guess," Mara said.

"Count on it." Damien waved.

Drake settled Shay into the front seat, then walked around the hood, and climbed inside. "You ready?"

"I made this trip five months ago and yep, it's time to go back."

• • •

She felt the tension begin to build in her body as they crossed the Colorado state line and stopped for gas in Trinidad, a small town. She rubbed the knotting muscles in her shoulders and neck. "Want me to drive?" she asked, wishing to do something—anything besides sitting there and fretting.

"Sounds like you're on edge," Drake said in a low husky voice.

"After seventeen hours, a little." She hadn't slept for more than a few minutes and had spoken with Shawn briefly. Since they were going to get into Denver during the middle of the night, her brother suggested that they stay at his condo in the city but then he called back a few hours ago. Tristen reported someone broke into the apartment. Now, they were going to some business her brother owned that had guards. A club she'd never heard of but apparently Drake was acquainted with the place. "What do you know about this place, the Downtown Den?"

He held the steering wheel so tightly he made a funny scrunching sound with the grip. "Uh…you'll be safe."

She slanted her gaze over to him. "I didn't ask about whether or not I had to worry about being pursued. What exactly do you know, Mr. O'Connor?"

Drake inhaled and she watched the familiar rise and fall of his chest. Holy crap, something was up. "This place isn't like a regular club. It's for shifters. Only."

She blinked. "Why is that so unusual? There's most definitely something you're not saying. What the heck is it?"

"Shit, you're going to find out. Just don't lose your cool. Okay?"

"Mmm-k, I promise."

"The Den is a sex club," he said in a low, raspy voice, so soft she stared at him in disbelief until he nodded and his eyebrows rose.

"Hold on a minute." She laughed so hard she couldn't speak for a second. "My old-fashioned stick-in-the-mud brother not only has me put up in a sex club, but he owns the damn thing. I don't freaking believe it!"

"Believe," he muttered. "But trust me. This isn't like any sex club you might have heard of before. The Den has a five-star restaurant and a jazz club."

"But it's a sex club. Don't you see how this is gonna play out? All this time I thought I was the black sheep of the family and *all along*, my brother has been tap dancing around a pretty hot subject. Sex clubs are the rage." She wrapped her fingers over his forearm. "I don't mean like a dragon group kinda thing."

He lowered his palm to her knee and squeezed. "Don't give your brother shit about this. He and his friend opened this place to help the shifter community. Scads of shifters are arrested left and right if they turn up inside city limits in primal form."

"Oh I get the reasons why. It's just so flippin' perfect for making my own case. Fine and dandy when it's a stranger having sex. And speaking of strangers, exactly *how* do you know of this place?"

"Baby, don't go there." He exhaled and rolled his eyes at her. "I haven't been back since before I first fucked you."

"Seriously. Not entered the place."

"Okay, let me state for the record, your honor, I haven't used the upstairs. The bar, yeah I went there with Shawn and I might have run the security setup. Does that please the court?" he mocked.

"Holy shit! That's it. I've got it."

"Dear sweet Lord. What have you got?"

"We need to get Dimitri thrown off the council!" she volleyed back to him, folding her arms over her chest and nodding.

"Hold on. You do realize Dimitri and his kids sit on the council?"

"But he can't if he's in league with Dark Fae. It's not allowed—forbidden and better yet, he can't hear a case that involves himself," she snipped. "I'll have him recused and then removed. Booted all the way back to whatever rock he crawled out of. As a matter of fact, I'll have Dimitri and his family recused…anyone remotely affiliated with him, and I want a ruling. If I have to study night and day, I'm going to know those ordinances so I can recite them in my sleep. If you don't want to help that's okay. I can go after Dimitri single-handed."

"Not to rain on your parade, but he plays dirty pool. Guys like him aren't going to roll over belly up, and admit they've done wrong. Fuck, Shay, there's a word and it's retaliation."

"So what, we should just take this lying down? We know he's in bed with Dark Fae. Who knows how low Dimitri has sunk?"

"This isn't just a 'What if the council rules against us for bringing up charges' situation. That shithead will want retribution worse than he already does. We'll need to get our ducks in a row before an epic and dangerous mudslinging ensues where he blindsides us."

"He won't. No one is going to trust him for enlisting the services of a Dark Fae against a shifter. Dimitri is a council executive. Some role model for mediating shifter justice. When the truth comes out, shifters will crucify him for being a hypocrite and a liar. Anyone with a brain is aware of the consequences of consorting with Fae. It's so against the law. Human and shifter. I read some of those justice council ordinances. I wasn't just sunbathing on the Mediterranean last summer. And maybe, just maybe, my parents will see this as something positive. Something I've accomplished besides and beyond my infamous act of running away. It might even get them to give me back my trust fund. That money is from my grandmother and it's mine."

"You don't need the money," he said in a hard tone.

She swallowed, not wanting to insult Drake, but they needed some serious cash to deal with this psycho Fae. "Drake, our babies are going to need protection around the clock, and from what I saw, that Fae isn't going away."

"Sweetheart, I have the means to protect you and our children. I'm not operating with blinders on where you're concerned."

She felt sparks of frustration erupt along her shoulders. What to do about this dragon's ego and possessive nature? First things first. "Will you stand in my way if I go after Dimitri about that gypsy Fae?"

"Of course not, I'll help you in any way I can. Christ, that admission goes against my better judgment." He paused, exhaling as a muscle along his jaw pulsed. "You might as well know, my team texted me that the Fae's name is Gustov Pestrolii. He not only worked with Necrodemas as his right hand man, he's the marauding force behind the Unruled. He's the one who's directly responsible for the savagery. The brutal attacks on humans and shifters."

"I remembered him from one of Dimitri's parties. He said that Dimitri had sent him and he couldn't wait to face you."

"What the ...! See what I mean?" he snarled. "No way are you going to go blazing into Denver and after Necrodemas. Promise me, Shannon Barclay. Right this second, or I swear I'll turn this car the fuck around."

"Uh, *Dad,* that won't be necessary—"

Before she could finish, Drake slammed on the brakes and pulled off the highway, driving over the rumble strips and making her whole body vibrate. He stopped, flipping on her flashers. A vein in his neck pulsed rapidly as his pupils elongated. He leaned over, a click away from losing it, and hooked a finger under her chin, tipping her face upward. She stared back at him, clasping her hands in her lap, and felt their babies kick.

"Listen to me, young lady. I swear on all that's sacred that I'll go to the extreme to make certain *you* remain safe. I didn't go back and deal with that Dark Fae piece of shit because you specifically asked me not to." Instead of yelling, Drake spoke in a near whisper, so tight and cutting, she flinched. "Don't push me, or I'll be forced to take steps you, sweetheart, might not like, to keep that SOB and Necrodemas from harming you. If forced, I will operate unilaterally if that's how you're gonna play. Decide right now. Are we a team or not?"

She surreptitiously crossed her fingers, her mind spiraling on what to do, and more importantly how to get him off this subject before he extracted all sorts of vows from her. "Fine. I promise. We're a team. You and me. Please, stop worrying so much."

He crashed his mouth down on hers, kissing her hard, and thrusting his tongue across hers with the aplomb of a very pissed off dragon. When he lifted his face, he inhaled deeply and nodded. "Okay then."

"Yep." Licking her lips, she gripped the door handle unsteadily. Damn, the man could kiss her silly. He put the car into gear and sped forward, rejoining the highway traffic. "So, do my parents know about the Den?" she asked innocently, changing the subject.

"I don't suspect. But who knows? It's one of those things where shifters don't have hang-ups about their sexuality until they start to try and meld with humans. Then there's all sorts of pseudo-religious issues on morality and everything—"

"Goes to hell in a handbasket. I believe that's the saying." She smirked and traced the edge of his thigh. "Are we staying upstairs at the Den?"

"Oh count on it, baby."

# CHAPTER 13

He gassed the engine, flying down the highway for miles until they hit the LoDo section of Denver. They didn't even drive a mile beyond the interstate before they were idling at the wrought-iron gate of the Den as two security guards approached. Their eyes glowed shifter red. Beta wolves, and with their buzzed haircuts, he recognized a pair of jarheads when he was confronted with their Semper Fi seriousness.

"May we help you?"

"Drake O'Connor and guest. We have an appointment."

The guards didn't miss a beat and stoically asked for their identification. The first guard pressed the button on his mic connected to a headpiece, advising the front office of their arrival. Whatever was relayed, the guard reacted by straightening as he trained his eyes on them, nodding. "Roger that."

The other guard advised him, "Just need a print from both you and the young lady." The guard held out a scanner with a blinking red dot on the screen. He wanted to laugh. This was his idea and he'd set up the security program. Glad to see Shawn still believed it was worthwhile. He pressed his thump onto the screen and waited for the red to change to green. It did and he passed the scanner to Shay, holding it as she followed suit.

He handed the scanner back. "We good?"

"A-ok. The doorman will take care of parking your car. Enjoy your evening, sir."

He drove onto the grounds, recalling the manicured lawns now white with fresh falling snow, and how he'd once been part of the team that set this place up months before Shay had graduated college.

"My, seems like my brother sure knows how to play both sides of the street. This looks high-end. From the outside. Bet the human community has lots to say, and if he's all for shifter good, then he should be happy about us."

"Everything isn't always black and white." He wasn't about to start bitching just yet and calling anyone a pot or a kettle, not with a plan starting to crystalize on how to breach the great divide of his own family. If he knew anything about Shay, it was that she was intractable if she got an idea into her beautiful head—like justice against that cocksucker Necrodemas—and for her sake, he had to figure a way to reach out to his own family.

"Yep. I see the duality of do as I say, not as I do, but not from Shawn. He should get that about me. He made a mistake and he needs to man up about it."

"Just give him the opportunity without getting on your soapbox," he murmured.

"I am…"

The club came into view and Shay stopped talking. From what he remembered, the club was perpetually booked and there was a wait list. The fact that they had a room on the spur of the moment was no small feat. Someone had done some down and dirty rescheduling. At the front door, there were several sentinels dressed in all black. The guards at the gate wore khaki, but in the club he'd advised for melting into the background they stick to one color: black.

Would Quinn be here tonight? If Shawn wasn't, then his partner was in residence. Another requirement Drake had discussed with them given the off-the-charts testosterone shifter alpha males possessed, and God help them if that male just happened to encounter his primal mate. Things could get dangerous in a hurry. Only Den sentinels were permitted inside with a weapon and he was concerned on that one facet. He had to meet with Shawn or Quinn and get leeway on that rule. No fucking way was he going to be hanging out without some firepower and that included the customary anti-Fae weaponry of mineral infused bullets. It was the only type that had worked in the past. Fae had the ability to spontaneously heal and he didn't know if they'd crafted any new shields that worked against what the military had perfected. So much for staying outside his U.S. military underground.

He parked and opened the door. He recognized that he might enjoy the brisk Denver temperatures, but Shay was still part leopardess and human, and she was dressed for weather in New Orleans. He gazed up into the overcast sky—perhaps more snow was on the way. Tomorrow he'd have to secure clothing for her that included snow gear.

The front door opened to the Den and he met the grinning face he remembered all too well. Quinnlan Rothschild, IV, a midnight Lycan, and Shawn's partner. "It's been far too long," Drake said, opening Shay's door. He shifted his focus on his mate as he reached inside and drew her up and out. "Kitten, look who's here."

"Hello, Quinn." She nodded with her golden eyes wide, gazing up at the polished brass light fixtures, adorning the exterior walls and columns. Shay smiled over at the doorman who dipped his cap, scurrying by in a starched crimson uniform. "Pretty swanky," she said at the general over-the-top atmosphere.

That had been a primary goal Shawn had sought for this place—no matter how good the restaurant or how renowned the jazz club, he feared it would always get slammed as just a sex club. "Classiest place around," Drake replied, taking her elbow and guiding her over the spots of frozen water on the ground.

"As I live and breathe. Where have you been hiding these last months?" Quinn cocked his head.

"Man, it's nice to see you again. I owe you a game of pool."

"Ah yes. If you're around later this week, we can settle an old score. There's a tourney planned, if you're up for some competition." Quinn turned to Shay and his expression became serious. "Shay, how are you besides all grown up and more beautiful than any girl has a right to be?"

She blushed but grinned back. "You don't have to try so hard on my account. Thanks for giving up a place to stay on short notice."

Quinn threw back his head and chuckled. "Still sharp as a tack. Good. Your brother can use some reality. Come inside. Care for a drink or some food?"

Drake glanced at Shay and she shook her head, saying to him, "I'm fine. Do you?"

"We're tired," he replied to Quinn for them.

"Give me a second to find out about your rooms. Warm yourself in front of the fire. There's wine or cognac, coffee or tea." Once inside Quinn excused himself and walked over to the front desk.

"A cup of tea?' he asked, steering Shay over to the cozy sitting area.

"Tea please." The gleaming mahogany paneled walls and polished floors reflected the fire blazing in the glass-fronted fireplace and he felt Shay's body relax. Blood-red leather sofas and deep-tufted cushioned chairs flanked the reception area.

He made a cup of tea for her and poured a glass of cognac for himself. "Cheers," he murmured, handing her the steaming cup.

She tapped her cup against his glass and sipped, still wide-eyed as she leaned against him. "Everything is so elegant. I never would have imagined. For all my big talk, I owe my brother an apology for what I'd initially thought about the Den. How long has Shawn had this place?"

"A while. After the Matrix, he got serious when he opened a few restaurants in the city and tapped into the vein of discontent that flows around Denver. Hard to ignore with shifters being arrested left and right."

"I guess I was really out of touch. Here I thought my brother owned a graphic design firm and a few small businesses. Now it turns out that Matrix is one of many businesses he's in charge of plus the Council. I could have helped him. What a fool I was, living the easy life on a college campus, safe and secure in my nice, comfortable ivory tower."

"You didn't know. Why would you? Not many people do. Things are hushed up and the news stations don't report the injustices confronting shifters. Human news channels are slanted. *That's not news.*" He didn't want to get up on a soapbox and start spewing about what it had been like in the military with their segregation codes and no-tell rules. To this day, shifters were still being forced into platoons comprised of only supernaturals and housed separately from humans.

She exhaled. "Maybe not to you. I have been way too naïve for far too long."

"Well, it's never too late," he said.

"To be part of the problem or the solution?" She arched a brow and he drained his two fingers of brandy.

"Good evening," a woman said in a crisp British accent, entering the reception area. She had unusual topaz-colored eyes that flickered to Shay's waist, and her smile deepened. She extended her hand and clasped Shay's. "I'm Sherry Delacroix. We've been expecting you."

"Generally, Sher isn't here late at night but she stayed to help settle you in and ward the place," Quinn said. "The entire inside of the Den is protected to some degree, but not outside, so be careful when you leave. Be on the watch for Fae—or any flickering lights. I have to keep an eye on things down here, but you're both in brilliant hands with Sher."

"Thank you," Shay said and her smile faltered as her gaze flickered to his. *She's the spellcaster. Right?*

Are you conversing with me on our private channel?

*Yes. Am I a jackass? Look, I'll figure out the where and when we can go this mental route but for now just answer me. 'K?*

Yes. Sherry's the person working with your mom and dad. You can trust her.

"Your rooms are ready." Sherry motioned for them to follow her. "Do you have any special requests? All services are available at night. We close during the day with the cleaning crews and groundskeeper taking over. The chef is here as well with his prep team in the morning, so you can order pretty much anything you'd like off the menu or even something commonplace. The food from the restaurant is rich and sometimes people just want scrambled eggs and toast. Don't be afraid to tell Marcel what you'd like. He's accommodating, especially if the request is for Shawn's sister."

On their way to the elevator, Sherry explained more about what to expect on the second floor. Their rooms were part of a private wing that required a special code to access. He smirked to himself. Again, more of his security measures were still in place. But even with the impact he'd made here at the Den, beyond stroking his ego it did little to disrupt the words Shay had articulated.

They needed funds.

Not the type to blow for good times. They needed an absolute fortune to build a fortress in which to safeguard their children.

Dragons—infant dragons—were extremely rare and in a heartbeat he understood that the Fae more than likely had known or now knew that Shay was pregnant. And black market gossip flowed like water. Prior to Shay's abduction, only he, Shay, and their friends in Harmony were aware that she carried twins. How many questionable folks had put two and two together and were tracking the statistics of what type of children a dragon and a leopardess would produce? The thought that someone would use the information of their forthcoming family in a way to harm either Shay or their children knifed him and his gut clenched.

He walked beside Shay, half-paying attention to the girls' conversation as he sunk deep into his thoughts. When the door opened to a private suite and they were shown around, he stopped back at the entrance and held out his hand to Sherry before she exited. "This is excellent. Thank you."

"Shawn will be here bright and early. Before he goes over to Matrix." Sherry reached over and patted Shay on the shoulder. "I'll stop by tomorrow and check on you. We can go shopping later in the week and have a girls' day."

"Sounds wonderful," Shay murmured, smiling and threading her fingers between Drake's.

"Good evening then." Sherry stepped to the door and he opened it for her.

"Goodnight," both he and Shay said in unison.

Closing the door, he pulled her against him and inhaled. "So you're pleased."

"More than you know…except. What's up?" She searched his face with her eyes glowing golden in the shadows.

He wrapped his arms around Shay's soft body and savored feeling her growing belly rub up against him. For hours and hours of searching, finding, driving he'd harnessed his hunger for Shay. Inside this room, his consummate need for her that he'd kept under wraps began to unravel. He felt his blood enflame and in minutes, he'd be in a frenzy to assuage his hunger to join with her. "Time for some truth."

"Oh Jesus. You're not going to tell me you're a VIP card carrying member of this place?"

"Damn, what an imagination." He snorted and shook his head, rolling his eyes. "I'm going to contact my family."

# CHAPTER 14

For the first few seconds, her mind spun. Then she spluttered, "Do you mean that draconian rage of fire-breathing dragons who expects you to marry your cousin? Oh wait. Correction. Cousins. Those people?"

He shook head as he frowned. His emerald eyes went from being seductively alluring to cold. Gone was the heat swirling in his eyes and in its place she met fierce, concentrated power.

"The very same," he growled, still holding her up against him.

She noticed Drake's eyes were bloodshot and then she felt the pit of her stomach give way. "Talk to me," she said softly.

"You are right. Our children will need protection. Fuck a fortress. We're going to need a small army. And if you're willing to fight for your trust fund, I'm not going to stand around when I basically walked away from more than enough to keep you and our children safe. My ego isn't that monstrous that I can't go and get what's mine. My family will be pleased with the news."

"We're unmarried. Your family will want to control—will take away my children. No. You can't mean you'd do that." She planted her palms on his chest and tried like a fool to push off of Drake. Like that was going to work. She swallowed down the urge to fight him fang and nail.

"Woman," he scoffed and picked her up like she was nothing more than an article of clothing and carried her into the bedroom of the ginormous suite. It had been months since she'd been in rooms like these and she felt the confusion of what Drake announced and where they were right at this moment. Coming back home should be a joyous event, but instead the doors had been blown clear off her comfort zone.

She'd walked away from her family and felt guilty…then what about Drake? She was back amongst hers. Didn't he deserve that same chance to make things right with his family? He'd been out of touch from his parents and siblings, like her, and maybe this might be a moment where they both could heal the wounds of the past. But to build a bridge—what did that entail when a rage of dragons was on the other side?

He snarled, looking down at her, and responded, "I'd like the chance. Same as you."

Instead of speaking out loud, she channeled her thoughts, linking to his mind. *Are you listening in on my personal conversation? My you're a very nosy dragon!*

Don't forget domineering, possessive, and very, very horny.

She snickered and he laid her gently onto the bed, coming down right next to her on the mattress. Tracing the edges of his lips, she sighed, "See? I'm not spoiled. I do try and consider both sides. But a rage of dragons? Who stops them if they decide to take away my babies?"

"They're not a bunch of kidnapping shitkickers."

"No. They're not. They're a group of eternal beings who can't reproduce very readily and now we're about to give the world two dragons. I might be wrong, but with my business degree and what I've learned, it's a fair assumption that our children are a very valuable commodity to lots of beings for a variety of reasons. Aren't they?"

"Without question. And it's those folks who aren't related to me that should worry us." He picked up her hand and kissed her palm. "Baby, we can go to my castle in Navarre, but we'll need to retrofit the place and get it outfitted with modern standards of security."

"That's my choice?" she asked, her voice careening in disbelief. "Your castle in the mountains. Does it even have Wi-Fi?"

"I'd be lying if I said I was sure. I don't know. We could start from scratch but we couldn't tell anyone where we are. Not until the children are older. But I know you only just arrived and are trying to reestablish yourself with your family."

"Nothing comes easy to us. Why?"

"Because we're complicated. I have no complaints in that department." He lifted her arms above her head.

Enough talk. I want to make love to you.

She laughed. *Oh you do?*

Or I could just fuck you for old time's sake.

*Give me what I need, Drake. Don't hold back.*

"Never, baby," he growled and crushed his mouth down upon hers. He thrust his tongue across her lips, stealing her breath. She felt herself melting and falling and unraveling. Dear God…*Yankee Doodle went to town riding on a pony, he stuck a feather in his—*

Abruptly, he stopped kissing her. "What on Earth are you doing?"

"Kissing you?"

"You're singing. While I'm kissing you." He stared at her. "You're hiding something. Something you're afraid I'll hear. What is it, kitten?"

Her heartbeat clattered and her thoughts tumbled, leaving her confused. Christ on a cracker, she wasn't about to give one over-bearing dragon a VIP pass into her mind. *Rubber baby buggy bumpers. Sally sells sea shells by the seashore.*

He waved his hands. "Okay. Okay. Stop. I can't take it. I promise, I won't listen to your thoughts. Seriously. I'm tuning you out."

"How can you?"

"Aren't you doing that to me?"

She blinked. "Oh yeah. I am." Then she laughed and clapped a hand over her mouth. "I didn't realize."

"Baby, I promise. I won't listen in on your thoughts unless you ask me to. You do the same with me. Do we have deal?"

She held out her pinky. "Swear."

"All right. I guess this makes it a binding and official agreement." He linked his pinky with hers.

She sat up and slipped off the bed. Drake's gaze followed her as she brought her hand to her waistband and lowered the zipper. Not an inch of space remained and very soon she wouldn't fit in these jeans. She glanced down. "Oh my goodness," she exclaimed.

"You're growing," he remarked. "Good. You're far too thin."

"But how?" She pushed off her jeans and stared down at her now very rounded belly. She rubbed her palms over the curved dome and felt her babies swim and move under her caress. The feeling was magical. "A week ago, I could still hide I was pregnant. Not now."

Drake's eyes gleamed green swirling flames, unmistakable pride, and he moved so swiftly, stealthily next to her, that she gasped in surprise. He spanned his hands over hers and arduously traced the rounded curve as intense pleasure rippled in her core. Her whole being sang in an ethereal joy—near to rapture. She quivered and her nipples tightened into diamond points, tingling and needing to relief his mouth could provide.

He pushed her panties down her hips and knelt in front of her, lifting her ankle. "Dragons grow at different rates than leopards. I don't know if what Trish said was correct about April."

"How soon?" She moaned as he slid his finger in between her legs, teasing her mercilessly. "Please, Drake."

He skimmed his face over her, and flicked his tongue in the cleft at the top of her lips, then splayed her open and speared his tongue in between her labia, targeting her clit. Oh God. So good. Holding onto his head, she dug her fingertips into his hair and pressed up to his wicked tongue and mouth. He licked her, making her body burn.

She reached behind and undid her bra, allowing her breasts, now round and heavy, to be free. Drake rose and pulled off his shirt and she bowed her forehead to his smooth chest.

"From what I know of simple math, you got pregnant on August fifteenth ... Shay, we need to get you checked out. An ultrasound. Tomorrow."

She lifted her head at the note of concern in his voice. "You didn't answer my question. You said back in Harmony that you thought Trish was off. How off?"

He raked both sets of fingers over his scalp until his hair stood up on end. "Next month. But there's different parameters."

"If this were a leopardess shifter pregnancy I'd have four months—maybe five but Trish said based on each baby's growth, she estimated more like a human pregnancy. So you're saying for a dragon...it's six."

"We aren't anything like humans. We develop much faster. Can be less than six months, but don't quote me. It's not like I have called home and asked." He removed his boots and undid his pants. Naked, he stood before her with his cock ramrod straight in front of him. "Baby, bend over."

She bit her lip and God, no argument—not one—resounded in her mind. "Over the bed?"

"Yeah. I'll do all the work. Fuck, Shay. I'm going to need a couple of rounds after all we've been through. Can you take it?" He wedged apart her legs and slowly drove his cock into her inch by inch. *He's driving me wild!* She shuddered from the jolts of mind-blowing pleasure he unleashed in her body and mind. The deeper and slower he thrust, the stronger bliss blossomed into a howling tsunami threatening to overtake her senses. She clawed the bedspread, feeling her body grow hotter and she noticed talons formed on her fingertips.

A pressure mounted in her head, at the center of her forehead, and she growled, "More."

"That's it, Shay. Baby, you're mine. Let me claim you."

She felt him inside her body. Inside her mind. He poured himself into her, but instead of overwhelming her, she felt her being fill with light and she clenched around Drake, drawing him deeper into her body. He shuddered, holding onto her hips, and ground himself into her, filling her with semen and his essence. Together they rode a wild wave, and she bucked, squeezing him and shattering as the pressure built within her head. Not painful, but something was going on and she saw flashing stars and closed her eyes, her knees buckling, and Drake picked her up. He had her in his arms, and then she was lying on cool, clean sheets and he was tugging apart her legs.

"Shay. Oh my God. You're beautiful. Your skin is glowing. It's dragon power. Dragon magick."

She didn't understand. Was he talking about himself? She gazed up at him. The vulnerability she'd once glimpsed in him was back and she opened her arms to him. She swallowed the sizzling words on the tip of her tongue and said instead, "Come to me."

He leaned over, planting his palm next her shoulder, and he plunged his cock back inside her body all the way to the root, and simultaneously he fondled her folds. She arched her back, like a sensuous cat without shame and clenched around him, watching him pause momentarily and shudder. Withdrawing his cock partially, he pinched her erect and sensitive clit and drove his cock back into her. Her whole body clenched, filled with a rush of erotic pleasure. Oh he gave as good as he took. "Please, Drake," she moaned, her craving for more of him spiraling, untamed and out of control.

"Baby, I want you to come apart for me." With a cocky grin, Drake lifted up on her legs to give him better access. He pumped his hips, and she came for him. A second orgasm and he toggled her clit until she screamed his name. "Tell me who does this to you. I want to hear you say it, kitten."

"You. Only you. Please. I—" She met his incandescent eyes and nodded, swallowing back a stream of words. Unsure what she'd almost admitted, she glanced to the side. This emotion had to be his commanding personality and a cocktail of hormones swimming in her blood—surely whatever she felt was a case of potent sex scalding her brain waves. "Uh…nothing."

Undeterred he asked, "What's on your mind, beautiful?"

Her heartbeat thundered in her chest as she clutched the sheets, battling her hyped up urge to escape. *Slow down, Shay!* She trusted him to keep his word about mind linking. Didn't she? "You're pretty amazing when it comes to rocking my boat," she said.

"Shay Barclay, you're so incredibly stubborn, more than amazing. And one other thing…"

She laughed, plucking the sheets between her fingers. "Oh yeah and what's that?"

"You're the woman who means more to me than anything in life. You'll never be alone," he said softly, easing the tip of her chin back until their gazes reconnected. "Don't be afraid to give yourself to me completely."

"I'm not afraid."

Drake lowered her leg and lowered his body—not all the way—caging her between his arms as he brushed his hands over the sides of her face and held her head, not letting her escape his searching dragon eyes. He lowered his mouth to hers and kissed softly. Sweetly. He drew out the caress of his lips with the sweep of his tongue, sucking hers into his mouth. He groaned in a husky voice and the note became a long, echoing vibration he infused in his kiss so that her lips resonated with the sounds he made.

"Mine." He exhaled deeply. "Do you understand that concept? Forever mine." He groaned and began to piston his hips with a newfound urgency.

She felt the pressurized pleasure building and raked her nails down his back—gently, since she had newly sheared dragon-like talons and he roared a sign of his own raw pleasure. The whole bed shook, the headboard knocked against the wall, and at first she tried to brace herself as he slid in and out of her, moving faster and with longer strokes. What Drake did felt so good. His face was ablaze with a savage ferocity as he spoke about claiming her. With his body, he carried her away. Far, far away, and she didn't fight his possession. Together they were carried off with uncontrollable fervor, something ancient and untamed. He didn't stop but sped up, driving himself into her as she matched him in his primal rhythm, and the pleasure so delicious, the walls echoed with carnal sounds she shouted.

He continued until he yelled at the apex of his climax and released, searing her nerve endings while he held onto her hips, hoisting her up to him. He appeared wrecked. He sure wrecked her! She smiled as he pulled her into his arms, murmuring her name, over and over again.

# CHAPTER 15

Drake heaved a heavy sigh. It was mid-morning and he'd been up for hours, contemplating their future.

"Shawn phoned. He's on his way up," Shay announced and smoothed a hand down her dress again.

He stood next to her, absorbing her emotional state of being on edge and knowing he had a pretty big part in her discomfort. Last night they'd been so close and he'd almost spilled the truth, but he'd held back sensing her own emotional upheaval. Didn't matter, there was no way he could hide from the fact he'd fallen in love with her. The question was simple. Was his love for her greater than his pride? In an instant, he committed to the direction he'd travel tomorrow and lengths he'd go for his mate.

"You look beautiful," he said, taking her hand. "If you want to stay here in Denver and start your business, we can do whatever it is you'd like. We just need a security system and I'll work out the details."

Her eyes widened. "But you said we'd have to live where no one knew. Disappear like smoke."

"Even smoke leaves a trace." He laughed and it sounded hollow to his ears. He kissed her hand, inhaling her scent—the one he carried within him. "It's possible to live in a city and no one actually is certain where that same person is staying. Even a small rage of dragons. Trust me, I won't falter. All the plans will be worked out and finely tuned."

"Seems like we've both been doing some thinking." She sighed. "Well, regarding accounting. I can do that anywhere. So I'm still open to possibilities so long as the plans permit you and me to make *all* the decisions about the upbringing of our twins. I won't be secluded within an off-the-charts group of crotchety dragons— all vying for control of our children."

"We're in total agreement on that one," he said, squeezing the tips of her fingers.

A knock on the door startled her, but she quickly wiped any sign of nervousness from her face. If he'd been anyone else, he might have fallen for her outer appearance of tranquility. Dialing her hair behind her ear, smoothing her dress, or the twisting to her lips along with the tiny nibble to the corner of her mouth when she believed no one was looking. Definitely his lovely leopard spoke volumes, telltale enough for him to get the drift.

He opened the door and was immediately reminded of the sibling bond Shay shared with Shawn. They both had the same eye shape and golden gaze, only now Shay's was becoming tinged with an emerald-colored sky burst pattern around her irises. They'd both been born with a unique skin color, light golden. Both had long, lean limbs, although Shay was built more like a runner where her brother had some brawn.

"Dude, mission accomplished," Drake said, holding out his hand.

"Never had a doubt, where you're concerned." Shawn clasped his hand and came forward with a one-arm hug. "You're looking well."

Out of the corner of his eye, he noticed Shay standing off to the side, observing them. Shawn must have noticed his sister for he heard him exhale sharply. "Sis," he said.

"I'm home." She came forward as Shawn went to her.

He engulfed Shay in a hug, lifting her up a few inches from the floor. "Damn. I can't believe it."

"I can't believe you and this place," she replied, patting his back. "So amazing."

Shawn grinned and glanced back at him. "Drake helped with the security features. Many are still in play."

"So I saw. Glad to be of service." Drake walked forward. "Need to address one small issue, but we can do that later."

"What? You found a weakness in our system." Shawn's forehead creased but his eyes narrowed. Ah yeah, he also remembered that his old friend relished perfection. Type-A personality all the way just like Shay.

He smirked back at Shawn. "Hardly. Maybe the opposite. This is personal."

"Oh." Shawn nodded, then he said, "I get where you're coming from. And sure thing. Definitely we need to talk. There's a sentinel outside the door up here and at the elevator. We've beefed up security."

"Excellent news. We were met by Quinn and Sherry last night." He was already aware that Tristen and Fin were onboard. But now, he wanted to get the rooster on recent hires and run a thorough background check. His to-do list was growing by the minute.

"No worries. We all remember your speeches. Trust me. We take security measures seriously around here. We'll discuss specific parameters after we have a chance to chat." He drew his sister out from under his arm. "But how are *you* doing, young lady?"

"Feeling fine," Shay said and blushed. "Come and let's sit down."

Shawn followed his sister into the living room area and sat down in a chair opposite the sofa. Drake joined Shay on the couch, and watched her scoot forward. "Coffee?" she asked her brother.

"Love a cup. I'm beat. Sorry I couldn't stick around this morning but I do rounds all over this city. Tristen has me on a schedule for site visits, thanks to you." Shawn jutted his chin to him.

Drake laughed in response, unfurling his arm along the back of the sofa, behind Shay. He thought about offering his services to help alleviate the burden of what Shawn had to be going through. "He's a good man. Let me know if you need any help. It hasn't been that long since I did a few surprise visits."

"Might take you up on it," Shawn said as he accepted a cup of coffee and gazed back at Shay, his eyes taking on a serious expression. "You probably want to see Mom. I told her you were coming and she's happy."

"Happy," Shay shot back. "Are you being truthful? 'Cause something sounds a little off."

"Mom doesn't do extreme emotions these days. She's highly medicated and with Sherry working with her, hell I don't know. The doctors and Sher keep assuring me, but they also have said over and over that everything takes time. I don't know much about spells and charms. It's all a mystery. The shifter doctors have one theory and Sherry is trying to work in concert with them. Truthfully, I feel out of the loop. Sometimes, I wish she'd be a little more aggressive, but easy for me to say. Right?"

"I bet Mom will improve when Dad gets back. How is he doing?" Shay poured another cup of coffee and handed him the cup. Their fingers touched for a second, her eyes lifted to his and she smiled. Drake fought the instinct to drop his hand positioned on the sofa back onto her shoulder and pull her close to him. "Thanks," he said softly, forcing his focus back to Shawn.

"Not the best. The doctors phoned this morning. Dad came out of the coma and his condition isn't what the doctors had hoped for." Shawn grimaced and shook his head. "He's in Mexico—state-of-the-art facility—and still in some kind of twilight sleep. Per Drake's recommendation the location of his treatment still hasn't been disclosed publically. Only a few of us know the details. Today's the final day and soon he'll be brought out of it. We're all keeping our fingers crossed."

Shay turned to him. "Did you know where my father is? All this time?"

"Not precisely." Drake felt his whole body constrict. He'd been through the fire with Shay's family and still he wasn't treading on terra firma yet.

Shawn interjected, "Sis, we're all trying to figure out how we can work out what we've all been through. Mom. You. Drake. Me. And we have the voting to attend to."

"When is the justice council meeting?" Shay asked, and stirred her cup of tea.

Drake shot Shay a message.

Be sensitive to what Shawn's going through. Maybe now isn't the time.

She flashed him a smile. *I won't do anything to rock the boat. Promise. I can see plain as you that Shawn looks like he's been through hell. I'm not that big of hardass.*

He arched his brow.

Cough—yes you are—cough!

"End of the month. I thought we'd start slow. How about an informal dinner tonight? If you're feeling up to it? Dad might be back by early evening," Shawn said, glancing between them. "Then we can address your concerns. All of them."

"Sure. Are we staying here?" Shay asked. "The suite and club are beautifully appointed."

"Not if you want to stay at the house. It's your call but I'll need time to prepare Mom, especially with our father coming home."

"Of course."

"Not to be insensitive to Amelia and Richard, but there's a bigger issue. What about security?"

Shawn trained his focus over to Drake. "I'm addressing that for Dad, but you must be equally concerned. Mind explaining why you think Necrodemas has it bad for my sister?"

"Now is as good a time as ever. You okay with that?" Drake set his cup down and squeezed Shay's hand. "We need to lay down a few cards. I trust your brother."

Shall I tell him about our children or do you want to? He is your brother.

"I'm carrying twins," Shay said without missing beat number one.

"Like you and our sister?" Shawn's face darkened with concern.

Shay blurted out, "Don't worry. The babies are doing fine. Strong."

"Man, that's something. Twins run in families." Shawn nodded, shifting his gaze between Shay and him. "I bet yours are going to be dynamos."

Her face turned bright red. "They are, but the babies aren't like us. Not exactly."

Shawn's head snapped upward. "What do you mean? Are you all right?"

"Our children are dragons. Same as me," Drake said, squeezing his mate's hand.

"Oh. Christ," Shawn said. "As in size and temperament?"

"Shawn," Shay hissed.

"It's all right," he said with a laugh. "Shawn has a point. And to be fair, your guess is as good as anyone's. I'm not like my family, not where my temperament is concerned."

"One of our children is a girl," Shay said softly. "And of course the other is a boy. I'm going to give birth soon."

He leaned forward, still clasping Shay's delicate hand. "The problem that we're faced with is dragon infants are extremely rare. And a few individuals who dabble in the black market would go the distance to kidnap our children."

"But wouldn't abduct you? A full-blooded dragon," Shawn articulated the obvious question: why wasn't Drake walking around with a security team?

"Apparently they don't want to bother. As you already mentioned there's my lovely personality to contend with."

Shawn's eyebrows flexed upward in agreement, then he swung his focus across the sofa to Shay, his eyes locking onto his sister. "And you're in extreme danger then."

*Should I tell him I was almost kidnapped?*

I would. We need to spread the word without arousing the wrong people.

"You need to hear what I'm about to say and not lose it. All right?" Shay asked.

Her brother flexed his jaw and nodded curtly. "What happened?"

"I was chased and almost kidnapped," she said. "But I'm fine."

"Holy fucking damn!" Shawn features hardened. His eyes glowed more leopard than human.

"The reason we came here in the middle of the night is because one of Necrodemas's marauding associates tried to abduct Shay." Drake clenched his jaw, the muscle along his neck tightening. "I met this SOB and confirmed he's not anyone that Necrodemas can control, but they work together. Confirmed, as in Deutsche Bank accounts and wire transfers. He goes by Gustov Pestrolii and he's underhanded. Stealth."

"I've met the man. Aloof as shit, and yeah, he's a bit out there in how he stands around, staring without saying a single word. Fucker is cold."

"He's Dark Fae and masquerades as a werewolf. And his glamour is good. Seamless, even obscuring his scent. That Fae doesn't show his hand."

"Makes perfect sense. Get me the proof and we'll move on him and Necrodemas. As you know, he's working the justice council members along with his kids. Wining and dining… elaborate parties. Deep pocket spending. The whole nine yards to affect his influence. Probably has more than a few officials all over the world on his payroll. He flew several board members down to Vegas a few days ago. No news. But what is news is that the members like me who want to effect real change aren't happy about Necrodemas's agenda or with the direction he and his clan are headed. We have convened an investigation team, looking for proof that he's dirty. If you've got the goods on him, we'll take care of the rest in filing a lawsuit within the human judicial system. Hell, Quinn has connections in the District Attorney's office. But you know shifters are held to a higher standard, unless we all want to be brought in on questioning."

"No, I thought we agreed to being restrained. Not to storm forward," Shay said, her voice rising.

"We won't." He squeezed her hand, forcing his face to appear like a brick wall of no affect, not a clue to the thundering anger rocking through him except that the muscles along his eyes had tightened, making his eyes appear flatter. But maybe she wouldn't notice. "Your brother isn't going haywire."

"So far we don't have enough to even get warrants issued. Any backdoor inquiries would have to be legit or the evidence will get tossed out," Shawn said.

*Christ! Figures that fucker operated as slippery as an eel.* "Let me work my channels. We know he's dirty. I'll get the proof you need but it'll take time since it has to be above board."

"Well above or the authorities will haul you and me in," Shawn asserted. They don't like their systems disturbed by outsiders."

"Oh is that what we're being called nowadays?" he retorted. "The human race has forgotten that a millennia ago, it was a far different world."

Shay added, "Things have a way of swinging back around. History repeats itself kinda of thing."

"Well, not soon enough," Shawn replied. "Guess I should be going. So, we'll see you tonight and for now, you should stay here. I'll work on tightening the security at our parents', but there's still lots of open space around the house. Don't ever forget the Unruled are on the loose. They're not a bunch of guys running helter-skelter. So far they're pretty political if you follow their pattern of what they do and who they borrow."

"What do you mean *borrow*?" Shay asked.

Shawn leaned forward in his chair. "The group has gone from outright random bombing and acts of violence to being highly structured. They only kidnap high-profile victims who have the means to bring about one of their goals and they're ruthless if they're thwarted. Doesn't matter if it's human or preternatural forces."

"Jesus, sucks to be someone in their way," Shay muttered.

"Exactly," he agreed with her.

"Hard to believe they were roughnecks running all over Europe with cans of spray paint a few months ago. What's their mission up here? Anything?" she asked her brother, the color over her cheeks deepening.

Shawn and Drake exchanged a look but it was Drake who spoke, "They want rights. Total civil rights and they're garnering attention all over."

"Well they're going at it in a backassward manner," she scoffed. "I ought to know."

"Baby, they're willing to cut off their own legs if they thought it would further their cause. If they weren't so savage, they'd have a huge following. But they're doomed. And unfortunately, their militant brutality makes everyone seek an eye-for-an-eye."

"Until when…we're all blind?"

Shawn got to his feet and stretched. "Not if we can get the evidence to put away Necrodemas and cut off their funding."

"Ready?" he asked Shay.

"I need your help."

"On three." He rose, encircling her with his arm, holding her possessively. Finally he could bring her soft body into contact with his. She canted against him and he wrapped his arm around her, and noticed that Shawn's gaze fell to his sister's waist. For a second it looked as if the leopard shifter's expression softened, then Shay moaned, and both he and Shawn reacted in alpha male uselessness around a pregnant woman. "What's going on?" he asked. "Tell me."

"Yeah. What was that all about?" Shawn asked.

"Oh my." She patted her stomach and chuckled. "Two very energetic pairs of feet kicking against my ribcage. Nothing to get worked up about. We still have at least another month and lots more kicks."

"Okay. Got the message to calm the hell down. Fine," Shawn said, leaning over and kissing Shay on her check. "See you both later. I'll send a car for you around six? Unmarked but you'll appreciate the driver."

"Sounds good," she replied.

"Fin?" Drake asked.

"None other," Shawn answered and squeezed Shay's arm.

# CHAPTER 16

"I'd better put the wheels in motion." Drake had his cell phone in hand and sat on the edge of the sofa cushion. "Better alert my family that I'm headed their way."

"Definitely. Arriving unannounced would be kinda awkward. I have a few things to do before we leave." Shay set the cups and carafe on the tray and lifted it.

"Hold on. Let me," he said, rising and trying to take the tray out of her hands.

"Just stop," she said, not letting go of the tray. "I can handle this. Stop avoiding the inevitable or do you want me to phone your folks?"

He acquiesced, tapped on the screen of his cell and held the phone to his ear. "This should be short."

She forced a smile and turned on her heel, her breath twisting in her lungs as she walked toward the kitchenette. What would his family say to this surprise of surprises? She imagined him letting loose a cavalier announcement. *Hey, guys—guess what? Me and this chick shacked up and she's pregnant with my kids.* But that wasn't his way. Everything in the hotel suite went still as Drake spoke in clipped sentences for several long minutes.

Without warning, his voice went from measured and controlled to rolling laughter but she couldn't actually hear what he said. He mentioned something about being up and ready for a dragon challenge, but dammit, eavesdropping was so unproductive and uncool…wasn't it? After setting the cups in the dishwasher and rinsing out the coffee carafe, she leaned closer to the doorway, but seriously, the man spoke in guttural half-words. Some form of dragon slang she didn't understand. Figures.

"Okay, it's set," he announced from the doorway and she jumped, grabbing hold of the counter, a guilty blush suffusing her cheeks.

"When were you thinking of leaving?" she asked, pretending as if she hadn't been dying to listen in on his conversation.

"Tomorrow." He came up to her and wrapped his arms around her waist.

"You mean the day after today? What about my doctor's appointment?"

"Don't be silly. I'm going with you to the doctor. Come with me to Oregon. I told my father and mother all about you. We wouldn't be gone long."

"You know I can't. Why does it have to be so soon?" She shook her head, and crossed her arms over her chest. That move got her a growl of dissatisfaction from Drake and he immediately unwound her arms off her body, lifting them above her head.

"Don't force me to convince you this is the right decision. We need a place to live. Pronto. I need the funds to build a fortress. You decide where. There's no wiggle room on security—sophisticated high tech. We don't have a choice. It could take months for you to access whatever funds you might have in a trust account."

"I hear what you're saying…I just don't like that you're leaving." She didn't like that the Unruled were targeting high profile victims. Even though Drake wasn't directly involved in his family's high tech company, they'd pay plenty if he were kidnapped.

"I'll only be gone for a few days at most," Drake said as he rewrapped her arms around his shoulders. "Should I take it personally that you won't accompany me and meet my family?"

She tightened her grip, pressing herself fully into his warm body. *So very warm.* "Don't, because it's not. You know that I can't disappear when my father is coming home and needs my help."

He backed her up to the counter. "Only a hard-ass would argue that point." Then he nudged the proof of his arousal against her mound and ground his hardness into her until they both groaned loudly.

She dug her fingers into the muscular ridges along his shoulders as he sucked on a sensitive point on her neck. God, this was the proverbial moment of being torn down the middle. The chance to finally meet Drake's family was right before her, but she couldn't leave Denver. Not with Dad returning tonight and in what state? Her brother forwarded a copy of the doctor's report, confirming her father had come out of the coma, but there might be trauma thanks to either the Unruled or Necrodemas, and here Drake was headed out the door. On one hand, what he said made sense. With his hard pecs pressed against her, Drake felt so all-encompassing, like he could protect her from whatever might seek to do her or their children harm. But what of him? For all his Navy SEAL training, he'd need backup. Dammit, this was so messed up.

Drake scraped his cheek against hers as he wound her hair between his fingers. "Baby, trust me."

There was a tender note in his voice that pricked her ears and unleashed the stinging that hit her eyes. She scrunched her eyes closed rather than risk him seeing her come undone. What was happening to her? In about three seconds her body threatened to dissolve into a crying mess. This had to be another hormone storm.

"Go easy on me," she whispered, licking the ridge of his jaw before she murmured, "unless you're willing to play the hard-ass to make a point."

"Don't tease me." He used his feet to separate her legs so he could press the crown of his cock along the seam of her pussy. "Ah, that's it. Sweet Jesus, you feel so good."

He rubbed his cock harder with more friction, making her clit start to pulse and her panties dampen. Seriously sexy stuff going on and she would have moaned if she wasn't on the verge of losing it. She sniffed and opened her eyes, snarling, "*Don't tease*, said the black pot! In the category of tormenting, you are the master, Mr. O'Connor."

"Then give it up to me. Let me have you squeezing around me. Baby, Shawn already called and gave you a heads up that Richard's arrival might be delayed by another day."

Each time he stroked his cock across her slit, he set off a slew of electrical charges that sparked her core. Her whole body felt ready to be dominated by one commanding dragon, but first she needed to set the ground rules on this trip. She couldn't bail on her parents, regardless of what they'd done. "I need to spend time with Mom and see for myself her condition. Maybe I can help. I want to try."

"I *need* you." He grunted in greater dissatisfaction and buried his face at the juncture of where her neck met her shoulder. Talk about being a guru of getting his way.

"Look at me." She watched Drake lift his head and take a deep breath, feeling the tingling effect of his chest expanding against her boobs and making her nipples harden. "Besides, this is the first time you've been back home. It might be a good thing if you go solo."

"Solo? But I won't. I'll have you." He took her hand and spread wide her fingers, then placed her palm over his heart.

"Err…" she started to formulate a comeback and blinked. "You go put out fires with your dragon rage and I'll rebuild a bridge with my parents. We'll tag our clans so to speak. And then when the babies are born, we'll be one big family. Hopefully happy."

"I'll be back before you know it," he said. "I'm only going home to lay claim to my inheritance. It's not exactly the most orthodox of activities." His body tensed and she locked her gaze to his. Under her fingertips, the muscles along his arms went rock solid.

"Lay claim? You've said that a couple of times. Sounds more than serious."

"I walked away. Cut all ties. I'm willing to go back for the sake of my children."

For the sake of *his* children. Was that a Freudian slip or semantics? From what she knew, dragons weren't known to be the easiest creatures to get along with. What if his draconian family said one thing, and did another? Wouldn't be the first time an overzealous dragon came calling on her doorstep. Next time it might be an O'Connor unconcerned about her opinion.

She wanted to break her rule about mind linking, but held off. "Tell me right this second what the heck you're talking about." She craned her neck, waiting and watching him. Did this have something to do with the dragon challenge he mentioned?

Under her palm, his heartbeat ramped up and she slipped into his mind without looking for answers. *Trust me.* Then she slipped out again.

*I do.*

His brow creased in concern, or was it worry? He linked with her mind, and the feeling was exquisite, but he didn't enter her thoughts. There were no words to describe what he did.

"I'll take the final step in becoming a dragon lord. There won't be any going back."

"I don't understand."

"Aren't there similar rituals for male leopards?"

"Yes. For all shifters. But dragons aren't the run of the mill shifters."

"Sorry to disappoint but other shifters aren't completely different than my race. Until now, I had no reason without a pregnant mate. I'll return home and meet with the family and it entails some male bonding bullshit. But enough talk of that. Let me inside you. On all levels. You are mine. I'll be open to you as well," he said, giving her a look that struck deep inside her core.

His words echoed across her thoughts. *'No reason without a pregnant mate.'* "Can your family force you to remain there? You won't be a fully mated dragon."

"Put that thought out of your mind. My family isn't going to hold me prisoner."

"But they could…"

"Shay, I wouldn't let them or anyone get in the way of coming back to you."

**Now answer me.**

*Yes. I want you inside me…all the way. Eventually.*

"Eventually?" he repeated aloud.

"I need time. You do understand the concept of not rushing headfirst. Isn't that what you preached?" She was using his very own argument. Her body—most of it—clenched in excitement, ready to strip naked there and then, eager to join with him on the intimate level he proposed. But dammit, her brain got into the act, and reminded her, tapping a cerebral foot in exasperation, once that dragon doorway was breached there was no going back. In between her head, heart, and her nether regions, her stomach knotted with anxiety.

"Can't believe, the tables have turned. *Time*," he groaned.

"Please, can't we take baby steps? Just know, I'm not into sharing you. Ever," she said. Her chest felt cordoned off. This was as upfront as she could be about what lay between them without shutting down.

He stared back at her, his mesmerizing eyes glowing. "Happy to hear since I have no intention of sharing you. What's mine is mine and I fully intend keeping my promise to you. Forever. We're eternals and I won't be put off. Eventually you're going to be all mine on all levels."

Now it was her turn to be confused. Or more confused. "Leopard shifters mate for life."

"Ah, a life that's measured in years. This is beyond the visceral." He searched her eyes, and she was aware he was trying to find answers without climbing into her mind.

"What do you mean, Drake?"

"Dragons are as old as the fire in the first star in the first galaxy. It's where we were created and where we return when we're through here. You'll exist with me long after this planetary system burns out."

"Okay, if that doesn't make me nervous, nothing will." She shuddered and simultaneously shivered, feeling the shadow of a chill.

His piercing eyes snapped to hers and he nodded. "You're more than just leopard now. What went through you?"

"It felt like a premonition mixed with déjà vu but different. Not from the past, but I don't know. It sounds ridiculous to describe."

"Try me."

"Like a cold wind blowing through me followed by fire. A billowing wave of heat. Are you responsible for that?"

"I'll never hurt you. Do you believe me?" He brushed his fingers over her shoulders. "Your skin is on fire.

"I do. Always…I've felt this connection with you."

"Then it's *time* to decide. I'm not pressuring you, but reminding you that time marches forward as it expands all around us. That's all I'm saying. Let me give you a sample of what being mine is like in the realm beyond this world. A taste and then you can decide. But decide you must, Shay. I can't go on like this—in a perpetual state of insanity. You're my mate and I *have* to claim you." He led her out of the kitchenette and toward the sofa. "Bend over," he said, positioning her at the sofa.

She hiked up her dress over her hips as the sound of his zipper filled the room. He brushed up behind her, his body an inferno.

Drake hoisted her hips, kicking his foot gingerly between her feet and separating her legs. He wiped his cock across the seam of her now swollen pussy, swiping his crown against her clit and then in one semi forceful thrust, he slid inside her, rocking her gently along his length.

"Oh…so good," she moaned the words. "You feel amazing. Are *you sure* you can *take me* like this?"

He buried himself inside her, cupping her breasts in his palms, and biting her earlobe between his teeth. Drake groaned, "Fuck my cock, little leopardess."

She clawed the cushions on the couch. A low rumbling roar that sounded more dragon than leopard crept up her throat and spilled from her mouth. She arched and roared, unable to hold back, "Like this? Or harder?"

"That's it. God, I want to take you over the edge."

"Please. Just a taste."

"Fuck yeah! Feel what I feel when I'm buried inside you." She felt the shift between leopard to dragon as soon as he nipped her neck, infusing her body with a tinge of dragon magick. The walls of the suite dissolved and they were hurled into a timeless chasm as Drake pounded his cock into her, linking their souls together. The tiny flickering spark of their children wove a tendril of light into their now joined energy source and Shay was filled with unimaginable ecstasy. All at once they returned to the material world and it was Drake's commanding voice that filled her. "Eventually, you will give yourself to me and we'll be united."

He slipped out of her and carried her around to the front of the sofa, laid her down, and positioned her with her legs wedged wide open. He looked huge—all parts of him—and she stared in awe at his engorged cock. Definitely he was under the influence of dragon magick when he lowered and thrust back into her.

She moaned, opening her arms, and she felt a different set of canines erupt from her gums. Sharper and longer and when Drake presented his neck to her, by instinct she knew exactly what to do, but held back. To give into him meant he'd possess her from now until kingdom come. "No. I'm not ready," she groaned in frustration.

"Shhh. It's okay. I want you to come to me of your own accord. One day, we'll take the final step, baby," he murmured and she stared up into his endless eyes, darkened to the color of deep emeralds, swirling fire in their depths.

"God," she clenched around him, heeding the pull on her core.

He pounded into her, forcing her to the edge of a cliff where she longed to leap. But that would mean linking with him on all levels and what about her independence? She clawed her talons down his back as he pumped his cock into her, over and over, and she was so near to diving.

"Fuck, Shay, come for me."

"Please," she moaned, her body filled with a golden light and she released as Drake tensed, his body going granite hard, bands of rippling muscle corded above her as he shuddered, roaring out a breath hot as fire without the flame.

He lowered himself next to her on the sofa, and pulled her close to him. "Well? Will you let me claim what's mine? Don't be scared."

"I trust you. I-I—" she stuttered against his lips, unable to free the words she longed to say. What was wrong with her?

"That sounds perfect," he replied and then devoured her mouth, and she kissed him with all that she felt but couldn't relay in sensible words.

They snuggled, and then as Shay stretched her muscles she caught sight of the clock on the mantel. "It's nearly three in the afternoon. We were making love for hours."

"Mind rush, wasn't it?" he questioned her.

She flashed him a look. "Have you ever done that before?"

"Why, are you jealous?"

"Answer the question and I'll let you know."

"That experience is part of claiming, so no. Of course not. But it's not like a dragon doesn't know it's out there waiting. And you, kitten, were worth the wait."

"Is that why dragons have more than one wife?"

"It might make the prospect easier to swallow, but I wasn't pulling your leg. That's all male dragons of mating age do from sun up to sun down during their wives' mating cycles and I bet when it's business as usual, that type of sex isn't as mind-blowing for my brothers. Unlike you and me. This is a secret doorway, baby." He enfolded her with his muscular arms. "I love you and I've never wanted to do this with anyone else."

Her heartbeat thundered. *He loves me?* He just said the 'L' word. Her mouth went dry and she gaped as if frozen. Don't just stare at him. *Shay, say something!*

"Never?" she asked.

"Never!" He laughed and arched a brow. "Now give me a date."

"I will when you return from your family and I'm assured they aren't going to hold me hostage," she replied, her heart tripping wildly. "Soon enough?"

"Baby steps." He snorted before a smile curled his full lips. "We're making headway. No argument."

•••

He ordered their lunch from the restaurant below, going downstairs to personally speak to Marcel as well as scope out the security while Shay made some phone calls. He found Quinn on his way out and stopped him.

"Dude, I need to clear something with you."

"Walk with me," Quinn said, slipping on a jacket. "I'm on my way to court."

"Weapons. I need to have my own. Problem?" He wore his gun in his waistband and wasn't going to stop. Hopefully, this wasn't going to be a snafu.

Quinn fixed him with a look and nodded. "I'll take care of it. Sure. But this goes both ways. Understand that if you think for a second that someone is here who shouldn't be, don't go all Navy SEAL and think you're a one-man team. Agreed?"

"I've got no problem in that regard. I'm fully willing to check my ego. Not my Glock .40."

"Anything else?" They were standing at the side-entrance of the club.

"Yeah. Where can I get a ring?" He scratched his fingers along his neck. "A really good one."

"Holy shit," Quinn replied and punched his arm. "Boy. Tiffany's. Ask for Anastasia. She'll take real good care of you if you tell her I sent you."

They fist bumped and he returned upstairs, nodding to the two sentinels and accompanying the wait staff with the tray of food. He tipped the waiter and carried the tray inside. "Where do you want to eat?" he asked, not seeing Shay in the living room.

"In here…if you don't care." Her voice rang out from the bedroom. "We can have a picnic on the bed."

Walking into the room, he whistled at the show of her long legs, displayed on the bed. She capped her bottle of nail polish and wiggled her toes.

"In bed it is," he agreed.

After eating a leisurely lunch composed of an herb-roasted chicken, a Greek salad, milk—he insisted that Shay drink it—and an assortment of fruit, she agreed to shower with him.

He undressed her, nearly groaning, unable to wait as his cock got harder and harder with each layer of clothing he removed. "I need skin on skin with you. Now as much as possible, to get us through being apart. Same for you."

"What will happen?"

Rapidly he disrobed and pushed open her legs, wiping a solitary finger between her lips as he dripped pre cum from his dick. "It feels like an itch you can't scratch. An echo in your ears and it makes concentrating difficult." He glanced down her naked body. Her tits were full and pink-tipped, her belly rounded with his babies, and her pussy tormenting him to sink slow and deep inside her.

"Like what I feel right now?" she replied, holding his cock and stroking up his length.

Fuck. His eyes rolled back in his head and he channeled all his lust, aware he was at the point of no return and he'd have her legs over his shoulders in a second flat if they didn't move toward the shower. "Come on, or I'm going to fuck you here on the bed."

They walked into the bathroom and he turned on the double-shower heads, enjoying the steam that filled the bath, swirling the scent of their mutual arousal, and coloring her skin a rose-golden.

Once inside the shower, he wrapped her legs around his waist and pumped his cock into her, their skin slapping and echoing off the tiled-walls until she screamed his name and on the next breath, he jetted hard and fast into her pussy. He could fuck her for hours…days…in this state. He'd make sure his business with his family was concluded and he'd be back as soon as possible. By then he'd be a wreck. He slowed his breathing, setting her down carefully, and backing her up against the tile wall, and burying his head in her shoulder, sucking a point in her skin. He kissed up her neck, stealing a final kiss from her lips. "Let me bathe you."

He took the bath gel and soaped her back and bottom, running his palms over her smooth skin, over her taut belly, and firm breasts. The mother of his children, and instinctively he released a possessive dragon growl. In turn, she lathered his body with her soapy palms; the feel of her touch soothed him. When they finished, he wrapped her in a fluffy towel, convinced he'd never get enough of Shay.

"Yowza. Pretty impressive," she remarked as they stood at the sink and his cock was still as hard as steel.

"I'll probably have to jerk off if I'm near you and you're naked. It's my natural state."

"Let me help you *deal* with your natural state. C'mon cowboy," she said, removing her towel and dropping it onto the stone floor, then sinking down onto it.

Shay wrapped her lips around his cock and gripped him at his base. She kept her lips tight as she worked her moist mouth up and down his rod. He dug his fingers into her hair and cupped her head as he pummeled into her mouth. When she sucked him hard, every muscle in his body reacted and constricted. His balls hiked up toward his body and that was it. Electrical darts flared along his spine as he watched Shay suck his crown into her beautiful rose-colored mouth. "Baby, I'm there."

She nodded and sucked him harder, sucked him faster and held onto him, taking him farther down her throat. He hammered between her lips, chasing the skittering pleasure that raced in his veins like a voodoo chant…held him until it ripped through him as a torrid blast of need and bliss, and barreled out of him along with an excruciating roar. He held onto to Shay's face, relishing how she swallowed his release, sucking the head of his cock, and licking a lingering drop.

"Mmm," she hummed and he lifted her upward, covering her mouth with his and sucking her tongue still slick with his orgasm.

"Mine," he grunted, squeezing her ass cheeks, and recapturing her mouth for one more kiss.

# CHAPTER 17

Together, she and Drake were seated in a corner of the bar, listening to soft jazz music and they held hands, his gaze lingering on hers. Except now, the intensity in his eyes jolted her. What the dickens was he thinking? She could always mind link and find out, but then he'd have that freedom with her. Bad, bad idea!

A waiter appeared at the table. "The front desk called. Your car is waiting out front."

"Thanks," Drake nodded, standing up. "Ready?"

Mercy, when the man put on a tailored suit, he looked good enough to drool over. Not that she'd ever admit that pricy bit of ego kibble. She picked up her purse, and wasn't prepared for the masculine swoop of her body up and out of the seat.

"Okay. I think I heard you. Not fast enough?" she gasped, breathless this close to him and his good looks.

"Just an excuse to get close to you before I'm forced to keep my distance," he whispered, feigning helping her on with her wrap.

Gone was the rough and ready badass and in his place was a man who appeared at ease in a dark suit and silk tie. Earlier he'd gone out to where she had no idea and returned dressed and ready to escort her to any number of upscale possibilities. Obviously he remembered how her mom served dinner and she wondered to what degree things had changed in that regard.

"You know, it might be sandwiches and sodas. Or maybe just water…I don't know what to expect." She tried to pull away but he kept their fingers interlaced, slowly tracing his thumb against her palm.

"Relax. I'm prepared to lose this tie," he replied. "But not just yet."

"Drake, don't," she rapidly shot back, then countered. "Okay fine. You look gorgeous. Are you happy? Now don't trip all over your ego."

He laughed, his eyes glinting. "You had me wondering. It's been a while since I wore one of these."

"Why'd you ever stop?" she asked, searching his face. "Christ, it's easy to forget, you're the real deal when it comes to names and titles. All this time! I must be bonkers."

"I would have been if I'd kept up this charade. But every now and then, I'm up for going the distance. Like tonight."

"This isn't the first time you've sat at Mom's dinner table," she scoffed, arching her brow. "Are you trying to win her good graces?"

"Not exactly," he said, and all the arrogance vanished from his face. Boyish uncertainty replaced the hard lines he normally wore, and he held out his hand. "I wanted to give you something. Try a different tack and maybe going this route won't be so over the top. I took your advice. Baby steps."

She glanced down to his outstretched palm and her heart leapt into her throat. "Is that what this is about?"

"Yep. A very special occasion."

She tried to lift the box from his palm but her hand shook terribly. "I'm all thumbs. It's not that I don't want to, but I'm so nervous. Can you help with the box?" The aqua box had a white silk ribbon and she watched him untie the ribbon and remove a smaller velvet box.

He set the outer box down on the table as her knees wobbled. "Guess I should have done this while you were seated," he said.

"I guess I need to remember you follow your own drummer."

He got down on one knee and took her hand, "Shannon Marie Barclay, marry me. Be my wife. You have my heart and let's take this step to form our own little family."

"Drake, you sure know how to sweep a girl off her feet." She stroked her fingers along her jaw and when tears threatened her eyes, she no longer tried to hide them from him. She trusted him completely but still she couldn't let go of the words on the tip of her tongue.

"Is that a yes or a no?" he asked.

"A yes. Definitely, yes."

"Baby, you had me sweating bullets." He rose and opened the box, displaying an emerald-cut diamond that captured the lighting and shone brilliantly as an array of tiny rainbows burst from the stone and off the platinum setting. "Do you like it?"

His brows knitted together as if anyone in their right mind could possibly say this wasn't the most gorgeous engagement ring. "It's so beautiful," she replied.

"Not even close to your beauty." Drake kissed her cheek, gliding his warm lips over her skin. He was incredibly handsome when he shared this side of him and she threw her arms around his shoulders, hugging him with all her might. A round of applause rose in the bar. People tapped the sides of their glasses and whistled.

"Thanks," he replied, squeezing her waist. "You can't imagine the chase this one put up."

More whistles and applause and she felt her face blush hotter. She waved and someone called out, "Put the ring on."

She laughed and looked at him. "Let's see if it fits," he said.

As Drake slipped the ring on her finger, the novel weight expanded in her awareness, and her smile stretched her cheek muscles. She met his gaze and a flame ignited inside her chest setting fire to her heart. The words she longed to tell him remained fixed within her.

All she could get out was a hoarse, "Drake…" Shay stared up into his eyes, absorbing the radiant energy rippling off him in undulating waves. Reaching up and feathering her fingers on either sides of his face, she finally replied, "The ring fits like a dream."

"You're mine. To have and to hold, and especially to cherish and fuck," whispering the last part, he wrapped her in his arms and she melted in his embrace, savoring each of his words.

She felt his back being pounded and rose on her tippy toes to look over his shoulder. "Hey, Mr. Zimmer," she gulped. "Guess who just got engaged?"

Fin chuckled and shook his head, making his dread locks shimmy. "Don't tell me, you accepted this SEAL's offer."

Drake laughed. "Why are all jarheads jealous? Never a good word."

The guys shook and Fin leaned over and gave her a quick hug. "How you doing?" he asked. "We were all worried about you. Don't you do that again!"

"Get engaged or disappearing?" she retorted.

"Funny. I know you won't be getting engaged again, so that leaves disappearing. Shawn wasn't a happy camper." Fin rolled his silvery mercurial eyes that changed color. He was a beta wolf, same as his partner Tristen Morrison, her brother's official backup.

The drive took less than forty minutes and during that time, she watched as Drake took call after call. Apparently once his family had been informed that he was on his way back, everyone was calling him to welcome him back into the fold…or rage. What would he have to do to claim his inheritance besides male bonding? She'd seen it before. The runs up the Rockies. Then they'd gather, smoke cigars, talk about the good ole days. And the endless paperwork, and more so for Drake with his titles and land all over the world. Family talk and meeting with attorneys.

Dreadfully boring things and maybe it was better that she remain here. Her balance was off now that her center of gravity had shifted and she didn't feel as light on her toes as she'd been just a week ago. As it was this dress wouldn't fit her next week and she desperately needed some clothes. While Drake was out of town, she'd treat herself to some things that were comfortable, feminine and a little sexy. Since she didn't need to hide her pregnancy, she could even investigate some of the maternity shops. She rubbed a hand over her belly and smiled while gazing out the passenger window on her side of the car.

"What goes through the beautiful mind of yours?" Drake said, pulling her to him and kissing the side of her head.

"I might do some shopping next week. Visit a maternity store or two…I've never been to one yet."

"Well, you'd better hurry or you'll be giving birth and have to wait until the next time." He stiffened. "If there is going to be a next time."

"Are you asking or suggesting it might not happen?"

"It's your body, your choice."

"I'm happy we both agree on that point, Mr. O'Connor," she quipped, her heart steadily beating.

"I may be old as time, but I'm not stuck in the Middle Ages. Not where you're concerned."

The car turned onto a driveway and went through automatic gates that rolled open. Trees lay on either side of the car, and up ahead her old home came into view. Her heartbeat quickened, and she sunk in deeper next to Drake when the car turned along the circular drive. They pulled up to the expansive front porch complete with stately colonial columns where she'd played as a child. Topiaries sat in huge terra-cotta pots flanking the massive oak doors and a gray-haired woman stepped outside, waving down to them.

"Ah, Mrs. Wells," she murmured, a smile unfolding on Shay's face as she fondly recalled her parents' housekeeper.

Fin opened the door on Drake's side and he climbed out, turned and held his hand out to her. When she placed her palm flush to his, he pulled her up and she expected to meet her mother's gaze, standing at the top of the steps, but the doorway remained manned by a solitary Mrs. Wells, and her stomach sank. Her mother had always been one to wait at the door when she'd arrived home from college. She'd grown up with Mom meeting Dad each night come rain, snow, or sleet. *Something must be terribly wrong. Mom's not at the doorway.*

Wait, before sounding the alarm.

Drake took her hand and placed it in the crook of his arm. He guided her up the front steps and she smiled at Mrs. Wells. "Welcome home, Shannon."

"It's so good to be back," she replied and hugged the housekeeper she'd known since she was a baby. They followed Mrs. Wells inside and Drake helped her off with her coat.

"You're looking lovely, dear," Mrs. Wells remarked, fluttering about and then she leaned over, whispering to Drake. "And you, Mr. O'Connor. Proud as a peacock I suspect with two wee ones on the way."

"How did you…" Shay replied.

"Your brother, of course. Told your mama and me as soon as he came home. I know we're not to speak of it out in the open, and there's been a hullabaloo going on with men and women coming and going all day."

"Because?" Shay asked, looking up at Drake.

"Security system the likes I can't imagine. Crews of technicians working around the clock and the scads of guards. The grounds are crawling with them. Take a look around and you'll see…if you look closely," Mrs. Wells winked. "I imagine that's the point though. They dress all in black. We also have a man from the Den here helping prepare food for the troops."

"Who is here?" Drake asked, his eyes glowing.

Shawn appeared at the end of the hall. "I checked everyone out so don't worry. But in case you're interested, you're back in our system and can login same as before."

She went to her brother. "Is Mom all right?"

"She's a little tired. Nothing to worry about. Mom's sitting by the fire and waiting to see you. She's asked about a dozen times where you were. Isn't that right, Mrs. Wells?"

"I dare say more like hundred. Dinner is almost ready. Come in and have a glass of wine or hot cider. I'll go see about dinner and let you know when it's ready to be served."

"Very good," Shawn said, sounding like the man of the house. They walked by a wall of photographs. Her eyes scanned them, remembering them all. Her gaze lingered on a black and white taken of her brother a few years back and her heart squeezed.

When she'd been in high school, her brother was a badass, just getting into the business scene but he'd been hurt when he'd gone that route, diving in deep and forming a mating bond with his business partner, a woman who'd royally screwed him over with their cousin. What a cluster of crap had gone down. So bad that Tristen and Fin had to get Shawn serious healer help, taking her brother all the way to Tibet, to a tiny village up in the Himalayas.

She'd be the first to be married and she glanced down at her engagement ring. "Look what I received tonight." She presented her hand up to Shawn and smiled at Drake. "Isn't it stunning?"

"Damn. Go big or don't go at all. Is that the Navy SEAL motto?" Shawn gazed down at her finger with a surprised glint in his eyes, and chuckled. "It's bigger than that ice rink we used to practice at downtown."

"Tiffany's. What'd you expect from a dragon," she replied. "He's a little over-the-top but definitely a keeper."

"Now who's calling the kettle on the carpet?" Drake retorted. "Baby, you created the term 'over-the-top.'"

"Frankly, you both rank high on everyone's chart so stop arguing," Shawn muttered. "You were made for one another."

She laughed and leaned into Drake. "He might have a point."

He put his arm over her shoulder and she nestled against him, walking into her old home, feeling a little more at ease—even under some very tense times. When they entered the living room, her attention immediately spiked with the scent of her mother nearby. She redirected her eyes from the twin sofas to the wing chair near the fireplace and would have missed her mother had Mom not yawned. Her eyes widened and Shay struggled to maintain a poised expression. Oh my dear God! Her mom stared at her with a blank expression, as if she didn't recognize her. A vague smile lifted the corners of her mouth, but Mom wasn't looking at her, she was focused on a woman…a nurse by the look of her starched uniform.

"Mom, look who's here," Shawn said as he approached their mother. "Shay and Drake just arrived."

Her mother's brow knitted. "Who?"

"Hello, Mom. I've missed you," Shay said haltingly as she continued to observe Mom and her lack of a reaction. Worried, she lowered to her mom's eye level and hugged her only to receive a vague pat on her arm.

Drake helped her rise with his curled fingers around her elbow. When he drew her upward, she turned and glanced at him, meeting his calm eyes. She latched onto his strength to buoy her flagging confidence at the state of her mom.

"Good evening, Amelia." Drake stepped forward and reached out his hand to her mom.

Slowly, her mom raised her hand and shook his hand, unblinking as she stared up at Drake with a 'who the heck is this' written all across her features. The very same look Mom had given her. The way Drake held the tips of her mom's hand, she could imagine his impression—unless she linked to him—she'd feel what he felt. But that would mean by-passing her own rule about mind linking. But this was important—crap, another rule broken! She focused on breaching his mind and instantly absorbed the sensation of him grasping her mom's hand. *What is going on— what the hell has happened to my mom?*

The nurse patted her mom's shoulder and said something but she linked back to Drake's mind.

*I'm so confused. This is worse than what I imagined!*

Kitten, take it easy. Remember, you haven't heard the real story. Your mom appears to be in some sort of shock…perhaps a loss of memory.

Shay returned. *You're right. We need to sit down with Shawn… and the doctors. I want some answers.*

The dinner bell rang from the dining room but it was the nearby commotion that caught her attention. The nurse lifted a wool throw, uncovering her mom's lap, cautioning Amelia to wait before getting up as she scooted to the edge of the chair.

Before Mom rose out of the chair with the help of her brother and the nurse alone, Shay stopped her mental whining. "Let me help," she said, coming to the other side of her mother. "Is it all right, Mom?"

Mom turned her golden gaze to her and nodded. "Thank you. My, you look lovely, dear."

She couldn't tell if her mom recognized her or was simply being polite. "So do you. You let your hair grow out."

"Hold on, Sis." Shawn waved his hands. "Let us do the lifting."

The nurse took one of Mom's arms and Shawn her other and before she could complain, they had Amelia out of the chair. Once out of the chair, her mom appeared less incapable. She actually appeared more stable on her feet, but then she bounded forward and almost tripped and she understood there was some motor issue also involved in her mom's concerning condition. Her stomach plummeted further as she took a seat at the table across from Drake. The table could have easily sat twenty-four people when all the leaves were inserted; still it was long and had been in their family for generations. She glanced down at her lap for a second, wondering about Dad. If Shawn pronounced that their mother was doing better, where did that place their father on the scale of health and well-being? She peered across the table and met her mom's unwavering stare.

"How long are you here for?" her mom asked.

"We aren't sure," she replied quizzically, unsure how it was possible that now Mom appeared more focused. Shay refrained from casting a concerned gaze down the table to her brother. Alrighty, definitely answers were in order on her mother's condition. "For a few weeks. At least."

Dinner proceeded with more questions but those were mostly tossed back and forth between Drake, Shawn and herself with her mom following along but for the most part, she said little. Ate little. She had a different meal prepared. A bowl of soup—or food pureed into a liquid form that she half-ate, and even that required prodding by Shawn. Shay could hardly swallow a morsel, as she sat there overwrought, battling with her feelings of guilt coupled with her growing outrage.

But she wasn't stupid, after meeting Drake's expression in which he leveled her with an arched brow and softly growled, "Watch it. Just simmer down."

*Fine*, she mouthed. Smiling across the table at him, she cleared her mind and nodded back to him. Oh she'd watch it all right. Come tomorrow, she fully intended on uncovering how big a part Dimitri Necrodemas played in this totally fucked up mess. Last summer, she'd run away from Denver, from her family like a scared little rabbit. She'd been a fool to hide from that jackwad. Not now!

When Drake went to his family, she wasn't about to sit around and knit a blanket or watch cable television. God, she'd done enough of that down in Harmony. If there was one thing she'd learned from Drake it was that a good plan involved several steps, so she carefully kept her thoughts on the down low, just in case he happened to slip into her mind. These weren't the type of thoughts he could hear and be pleased. Not her over the top fiancé. Hell no. He'd do something to limit her ability to run free like he'd done last summer in Lisbon. Carefully, she kept a seamless chatter of nonsense running through her mind. Each time she wanted to add something to her to-do list, she glanced around the dining room and focused on some object, recalling an event from her childhood that took place here, anything to keep rambling ideas at rest.

"Mom, do you still play bridge?" she asked.

Amelia's eyes widened and she smiled. "Sometimes. With Glenda."

Shawn interjected, "One of the nurses."

"And your hot house. The orchids?"

"There's one there that just came into bloom." Amelia pointed to the side table. "Cymbidium Kiwi Midnight. Popular name is Geyseyland."

"My goodness. It's jaw-dropping." And it was, with maroon-colored petals that ran so dark as to appear black. A memory jarred loose; one she'd forgotten about until this second. "It's one of your black orchids. I thought they all…" Her voice trailed off. Shay recalled a few black orchid species Mom had preened over when she was growing up, but they'd perished one summer. Didn't do well because of an intense heat wave or was it a cold snap?

"Mrs. Wells," Mom called. "Please bring the leopard orchid in from the den."

"Would you like to have coffee and brandy in the sitting room?" Mrs. Wells asked. "I could bring it there."

"No," Amelia spoke assuredly, sounding more like her old self. "Too much fuss in getting up and moving."

"Very well." Mrs. Wells nodded and disappeared.

Shawn had risen during the intersession. "Mom, I'm taking Drake outside for a cigar."

Mom smiled. "Your father has a secret stash of Cohibas in his desk."

Drake met her gaze and smiled, and she shrugged, more confused than ever. Mrs. Wells returned, carrying a small urn with a yellow dappled orchid that resembled leopard print. "Very delicate," Mrs. Wells murmured, setting the pot on the table.

"What's this one called?" Shay asked her mom.

"*Lophiaris silverarum.* Very, very rare. From Panama."

"Excuse me," Mrs. Wells interjected, "would you care for coffee? Or tea?"

"Please bring tea," Amelia said. For the next fifteen minutes, her mom talked about nothing but flowers, pouring and serving her a cup of tea. Then without warning and as if a switch had been turned off, she stared, unblinking, back at Shay, her face set in a glazed expression. "Are you here for the night shift?" Mom asked in a soft voice.

"It's time, Mrs. Barclay," the nurse announced, coming into the dining room.

"Mom?" Shay stood up from the table.

Her mother rose without a word, accompanied the nurse out of the dining room, and walked up to her room at the top of the stairs as Shay followed. "Mom, I'll help you get ready for bed. Okay?"

Mom didn't respond but kept her eyes lowered. *How is this fluctuation possible?* The nurse made no comment and Shay socked yet one more question into her bank of 'need to know.' Stat!

She helped the nurse settle her mother upstairs in her parents' bedroom. Changed Mom into a nightgown, brushed her hair, and watched her take a small medicine cup with different colored pills. After helping Mom into bed, she sat by her side, watching the nurse take her mother's vital signs. Even though this on again—off again switch randomly occurred, Amelia didn't appear in pain or in turmoil. Shay sat still and watched the steady rise and fall of her mother's chest and her relaxed expression as her eyes drifted closed. Things could be so much worse. At least, while she helped search for a solution—a cure—her mother wasn't tortured.

"Goodnight," Shay whispered to the nurse, not wanting to wake her mom.

When she turned around, Amelia was awake again and held open her arms. "It was so nice to see you, dear. When will I see you again?"

"I'd like to come back for a visit," Shay replied. "While Drake is…attending to business."

"Just set up an appointment," Amelia said. Shay glanced at her mother, unable to determine if Mom knew she was her daughter or not.

She walked out of the room and instead of going downstairs, she continued down the hall and paused in front of her old room. Opening the door, she stood at the threshold and peered inside. Her bedroom remained unchanged since she'd last been there. Same pale pastel mint walls, black lacquered furniture, and gauzy curtains. Only the light from the doorway cast any illumination into the room, but with her night vision, she scanned countless trinkets and keepsakes that littered the surfaces. The room was kept just as she'd left it and for an instant her heart thudded painfully against her ribs as she recalled all that had passed. Closing the door, she retraced her footsteps toward the stairs, meeting the nurse coming out of her mom's room.

"Oh goodnight, Miss Barclay," the nurse said again. "Your mother had a nice evening. Will we see you tomorrow night?"

"I'm hoping," she replied.

Shay returned downstairs to the library. It looked like Shawn had taken up residency within the room with folders strewn over the desk. Her father had always kept the place neat and tidy. Now a large computer had been set up with multiple screens. She sat down and typed 'Necrodemas' into the search engine. Page after page came back in her search, most of it PR propaganda. She needed real information, not this engineered bullshit.

Drake returned from smoking a cigar outside, and she jumped, her eyes going wide. "Sorry. I didn't hear you come in." Since the afternoon of sensually joining with Drake she felt as if she'd stepped onto a rollercoaster and had yet to disembark. She could have easily attributed the spikes and valleys of her feelings to hormones except what she felt wasn't simply emotional. There were haunting nuances of psychic, soul-deep feelings that were novel to her leopardess primal senses. Just like Drake had described, an itch she couldn't scratch, but this was more like a monsoon that had taken over her emotional horizon. She felt out of sorts and without solid ground to stand on, and she didn't entirely trust herself. Any second she felt ready for the mother of all emotional earthquakes to befall her and she was sure she'd burst apart. It felt like a fracture line ran the length of her being, and she waited, afraid to take a breath for fear she'd shatter into a gazillion pieces.

"Would you like something before we leave?" Drake asked, touching his fingers to her face.

"Yes." She trained her gaze on Drake and Shawn. "Real answers. I want to know everything about Dimitri Necrodemas. I have a right. Either you get the info or I'll go find it myself."

Shawn and Drake exchanged a slow look and they both gave a curt nod simultaneously as if in agreement. "I'll have a file box delivered," Shawn replied.

"That you're only to *read*," Drake replied forcefully.

"What else do you think I'll do? Pregnant and almost time to deliver? Your imagination is in overdrive." She shook her head and laughed, heading to go get her coat and trying to hide the heated blush creeping up her neck and over her cheeks.

On the front porch, she leaned into Drake's warmth, stifling a yawn of exhaustion. The babies must have felt the pressure of exhaustion as well, and hardly stirred by the time Fin had brought the car around. During the ride home, she and Drake didn't say much. She nestled under his arm while he traced her fingers, kissing the side of her head, and every so often murmured her name in his deep voice. By the time the car pulled up the Den, her eyes felt heavy and Drake shushed her as he lifted her and carried her upstairs.

After he removed her clothes, he took her face between his hands, kissing her firmly on the lips. "I'll be out in the living room."

"Don't leave," she said suddenly awake.

"You need your rest," he replied, brushing his fingers along the edge of her mouth.

"What I need is you." She held up the sheets and watched him slowly peel off his jacket and remove his tie. The sexiest striptease she'd had from him yet.

# CHAPTER 18

"You're certain your family isn't going to hold you there against your will?" she whispered to Drake in the doctor's waiting room as she flipped through a magazine.

He laughed with his arm flung over her shoulders, and hugged her tighter against him. "No. Not gonna happen. Ever."

She set the magazine down on her lap. "If they do, I'll come rescue you."

"No." Drake's expression turned serious. "If anything ever happens to me, you'll contact Noah. He'll help you with anything you need. Give me your phone."

"But you said nothing will," she replied, frowning from the prickling darts bombarding her senses. She riffled through her bag and dug out her cell. "Here."

"Just a precaution. The Cascade Mountains don't have the best cell phone reception. This bonding ceremony won't take long. I'm in. I'm out and back." He entered a series of numbers into her cell contact list. "Same as you last night."

"That was a little too slippery." She pressed her lips, contemplating her mom's unsteady psychological state.

Drake halted his rapid fire keystrokes. "It went fine."

"Fine if I was a dinner guest from Timbuktu. More like unnerving. I spoke with Shawn and we'll meet with the doctors later this afternoon. I'll get a handle on what exactly is being done for Mom. When is your flight tonight?"

He dropped his gaze and resumed keying information into her cell. "What do you mean?"

"Tickets have departure times. I'm not asking an overly difficult question."

"Uh…" He shrugged. "I'll fly out later today."

"Not tonight. So you changed your ticket." She tucked a strand of hair behind her ear and considered how to stretch their day as far as possible so she could deal with her mom's condition and spend a few hours of their afternoon doing more than chasing their proverbial tails.

"Guess so. It's open," he muttered, handing her phone back, and then pulling on his collar.

Her gaze sharpened and she felt her forehead crease. "Open? You must have a departure time, unless you're using the jet."

"Miss Barclay?" A nurse appeared, holding a clipboard.

"Shay, not exactly," he murmured, staring back at her. A muscle along his jaw flexed and he grimaced before he took a deep breath and helped her upward as he rose to stand. "Baby."

"Holy hell…don't you 'baby' me! You're flying in primal form. I should have known it."

"It's safer. Faster. And this isn't the time to talk about it." He cocked his head at the smiling nurse, who motioned for them to follow.

Shay smiled back at the nurse, who then turned and went into the inner offices, and she whispered sharply, "Unless someone is tracking you and takes a shot."

The nurse stopped in front of a doorway. "Right in here. And how are you feeling today?"

"Great," she said, glancing over to Drake and arching her brow.

"Is this your first pregnancy?"

"Yep. Our first," he replied before she could answer. "Got any advice?"

"About a ton!" The nurse took her vitals, all the while conversing in a lilting tone about giving birth—the ins and outs of myths versus fact. After a longwinded speech on diet, she suddenly asked, "So what birthing center are you at?"

"Um…center? None yet." Shay stiffened and patted her tummy. "We have time to decide."

"Says who? Oh my. You'd better hurry and pick one. You're almost due. Disrobe and put on this, opening at the front. Dr. Stiles will be right with you." The nurse held out a paper gown.

"Thank you." When the nurse left the room, Shay turned to Drake. "Nice try with the info dump. Stop waffling and answer me."

He scrubbed a hand down his face. "They could do the same if I was traveling by car into the Cascade Mountains, or by plane. The chances are better that I'll be a sitting duck if I have to take to the interstate and the tiny airport is no better. Necrodemas and his carnival companions aren't going to be huffing by foot or by cycle up those mountain trails. Where I hail from is well off the beaten path. If we went together, I'd fly you up to the top unless we went by chopper."

"Do you have a helicopter?"

Drake's eyes bored into her. "The last time I wanted to make tracks with you I bought one. So yeah. Just so happens, we do."

The door opened and a woman with bright red hair and thick glasses bounded inside. "Good morning. I'm Dr. Stiles. Mr. and Mrs. Barclay?"

"I'm Miss Barclay and—"

He rose in a blink. "I'm Drake O'Connor."

The doctor shook her hand, then reached for Drake's. "Pleasure. Well, let's examine you, Shay, and get a sonogram first thing. From what I can tell, you're pretty far along but the sonogram will verify just as far. Dragon twins. Wow! Bet you both are super excited."

• • •

Exiting the doctor's office, he placed his warm hand on the small of her back but switched to holding onto her arm. Good thing; she felt as if she were tottering with each step forward. Her head buzzed with the news: the doctor confirmed she would give birth next month. No wonder she was growing rounder and bigger as if by the minute since Drake had come back into her life. The doctor explained her sudden weight gain as the resulting effect of her being in her mate's presence—confirming that an alpha male dragon produced some off the charts hormonal surges within his pregnant female.

Shay glanced up a Drake, and felt the rapid pulse of a spark jetting across her skin when he returned her stare and smiled. "Baby, be careful," he said. "Or I'll carry you to the car."

Outside on the sidewalk, it had begun to snow. Fin pulled up to the curb farther down the block. "I can manage," she said, even though she clutched his arm closer to her side.

"Let's go," Drake murmured, steering her away from the building onto the sidewalk. He appeared unfazed by the honking horns, and the mad rush going on around them.

Someone laid on the horn making her cringe. Her claws sprung outwards and her canines erupted. She wasn't the only one on edge, so it seemed. Drake had his hand on his holster inside his jacket—the one she knew he carried even though he refused to discuss it—as he stopped and turned his attention to the blaring noise. From her peripheral vision, she caught sight of a Hummer wagon pulling up at the curb and her footsteps faltered. She recognized a disturbing scent as the skin over her body tightened and she felt the instinct to shift into primal form.

"Ugh!" She stumbled and if it hadn't been for Drake's unrelenting attention and his capable hands on her, she would have face planted on the slippery sidewalk.

"Shay," he exclaimed, preventing her from moving. "Are you all right?"

"It's one of those tanks…like Dimitri had." She swallowed, brushing back her bangs, and scanning the street. The memory of riding in Dimitri's Hummer flared vividly. God, she hated recalling that dismal experience minutes before she and Drake parted. No one exited the vehicle as it idled at the curb. The windows were blackened and she couldn't see inside. Dimitri could hide all he wanted—but she was aware that he lurked near.

Drake glanced over his shoulder toward the curb then back to her. He started to walk, guiding her forward. "Lots of people have them. Come on, baby." His stiff tone belied his usual circumspect attitude when it came to her. Was he also unnerved by the coincidence?

Apparently—he removed his cell phone, dialing either Tristen or Shawn. "Any sentinels around…us?" he bit out.

A reply bled from his phone: "Roger that. You're good."

She swung her attention to the sidewalk and, for ten o'clock in the morning, the street was pretty congested. Throngs of folks walked by. People in suits, people in jeans, even a few who appeared homeless shuffled along. The doctor's office was downtown, near to the city college, shops, and a slew of other office buildings.

As if on cue, a man and a woman fell in line, flanking and walking with her and Drake. "Time to move," one of them said.

"Oh. Question answered," she replied—really to herself—as they all moved in unison, walking down the block. They headed for their waiting car that began moving backwards in their direction.

"This way," Drake commanded, piloting her over the slick sidewalk and into the car. The sentinels climbed in—one in the front seat and the other, sat next to her in the back, his gun drawn.

"See what I mean," she huffed, her chest heaving and now more than ever convinced that Dimitri needed to be stopped. Drake was right. That worm of a shifter would definitely act in an underhanded manner. Now, more than ever they had to amass irrefutable evidence that would sway not only the council, but also the human justice system. With Dr. Stiles' assuring her that she'd delivered her twins in less than a month, little time remained to wait around for someone else to substantiate the truth: Dimitri Necrodemas was a pure slimeball.

News of her engagement to Drake might have made it back to Necrodemas, and maybe that was the reason he'd let her know he was close by. During the car ride back to the Den, Drake phoned the front desk, speaking in clipped tones about beefing up security. When they arrived at the circular driveway, Quinn and Sherry walked quickly past the doormen and in between the grounds crews without breaking stride. Dude didn't look a day over thirty-five, but from what she knew, he was a few thousand years old. Sherry, as a spell caster, was human and looked to be in her mid-twenties, with deep burgundy hair, and pale luminescent skin. Just a little older than Shay, but boy, she sure had a defining air about her.

Drake lifted her out of the backseat, growling. "Be careful. It's icy."

"Let me give you a hand," Sherry said, coming up next to her. "We girls need to stick together."

"You're a lifesaver." She smiled at Sherry. "I appreciate everything you've done. The clothes were delivered this morning."

"Drake gave me strict instructions to get whatever you required." Sherry's gaze traveled to her garnet-colored wool A-line dress and matching coat. "Love that set the moment I saw it. Thought you'd choose it on first sight, too. With the boots, it's perfect."

"You did an amazing job. They all were perfect. It almost came down to eeny meeny." She grinned and then said, "Thank you. Your taste is excellent."

"We'll do lunch and shopping. You still have lots to get. Call me. Soon." Sherry winked. "When you're feeling up to it."

Did she look as frazzled as she felt or was Sherry just super perceptive as a spell caster? The babies were as much on the move as her roiling concern about Drake's impending trip. Two pairs of feet kicked as if marching and, then one baby—or both—really did a number on her ribs. She gasped, clutching her belly but at the same time a thought crossed her mind about Sherry's spell casting abilities and potentially getting hold of a truth serum or spell, and she cleared it before Drake caught wind of that thought.

Drake wound his arm around her, shepherding her to the wall. He peered down into her face, concern piercing his eyes. "You all right? Quinn, slow it down some," he barked.

Quinn and Sherry flanked her and Drake. "Do we need to call the doctor?" Quinn asked.

"No. I'm fine." She realized all eyes were on her and she laughed. "Really. I could outrun any of you."

Drake held onto her and she followed along, ensconced in their own private huddle all the way inside the elevator. They rode upstairs in silence, but she and Drake exchanged several looks and smiles, and she felt she was about to start laughing, an uncontrollable fit of last minute nerves. He sidled closer and reached for her hand, grazing his lips along her jaw, all the way to her ear and whispered, "I can't wait to get you alone."

# CHAPTER 19

"Lay with me," Drake said once Quinn and Sherry departed. She'd see Sherry later but for now the pitter patter in her chest made her ache to tell him more than just her worry.

"Please be careful," she parroted the words he'd said to her downstairs. She led him into the bedroom and down onto the bed.

"Promise. You too." He laid his hand on her belly, and sternly reminded her to take it easy until a huge face splitting smile spread over his lips. "Our babies are beautiful." He pulled out the sonogram and fingered the edges. Their twins were brilliantly featured, complete with tiny little noses, their arms and legs entwined. Their daughter sucked on her thumb.

"We'll need names," she murmured.

"Most definitely. Any thoughts?"

"Nothing yet that sticks. You?"

"Mmm, I like your name." Drake lifted her dress up along her thighs. Higher and higher, as he separated her knees. "I like everything about you." He cast a searching dark look up to her.

"Everything?" she laughed.

"With one exception. These." With a snap of his wrist he removed her panties, the lace barrier between him and her. He unzipped his pants and freed his cock. "I'll be back before you know it. I like you so much…especially like this, I can't stay away."

Climbing between her legs, he positioned his crown at her opening. The glittery tingles of pleasure sank deep inside her. She arched her back, needing him to connect with her as something so deep inside her roared to life. "Please, don't stay away too long. I need you," she breathed out.

He caged her between his arms, staring down at her. "Shay, I love you." He didn't wait for her to respond but slid inside her, pumping his hips and pulling her near to him with one hand on her hip. He glided in and out of her pussy and unmercifully swiped his thumb across her clit as his body radiated intense dragon heat.

"Drake," she moaned, lifting up her knees, bracketing either side of his torso, trying to get as close as possible to him. The heavy ache built and built within her, leaving her hungry for all Drake offered as she melted faster, ready to fall farther.

Without stopping, he pumped his cock, using circular grinds punctuated by deep grunts. All the while he watched her behind his hooded green eyes. "Tell me, are you mine?"

"Yes. Yours."

"What do you want?"

"Make me come." So close to exploding, she shouted his name. Shouting…"Now, Drake. Now!"

"Baby, like this. Fuck!" he thundered, drawing her to him, sinking into her, and joining them together as a storming climax tore through her, and she clenched around his cock. His body went rigid, shuddering once, then again. Looking down and meeting her gaze, he whispered, "Shay. You are mine."

• • •

When it came time for Drake to depart, she accompanied him to the rooftop of the Den. Exiting the roof door, she had no idea what to expect but there were three shadowy figures that turned in unison toward them. Unfurling their wings, the beings perched on the ledge, and she gasped in seeing they weren't like any creatures she'd encountered before. As she and Drake approached, the creatures seemed to come fully alive. Burst in flame. Enormous, angry looking birds stared back at her, cawing in rapid clicks. One flapped a fiery wing, releasing wisps of spiraling smoke.

"What are they?" she asked, gripping his arm.

"Phoenixes. My crew."

• • •

She'd paced, sat, and paced some more. She tried to read but couldn't focus on the words of the page in her hand, her mind drifting to the clock and wondering about Drake's progress. Finally, her phone rang. "I'm here. Not a hitch," his deep voice washed over her along with a ton of relief.

"Oh thank God," she said. "How is your family?"

"Don't know. Literally. I just got here and wanted to call you."

"You made excellent time. I was worried, but…go. Please let your family know I'll come for a visit too." She wanted to speak coherently, tell him words that would assuage the ache in her chest, but none bubbled up. "I miss you."

"Me you. I'll phone later."

Shay sank down into the chair by the table, drumming her fingers, and felt a jolt. A tiny twinge between her eyes. Then again, but the twinge twisted into a driving lance of pain she'd never experienced before. The flare traveled up her forehead and spread out over her head, and she pressed her temples. She tried to focus on something other than what felt like the plates of her skull coming apart. She could make out the sound of Drake's voice and the voices of other men. Laughter. Oh shit. She needed to exit this channel where she'd accidentally tapped into Drake's mind.

"So are you ready for the Jinni's challenge?" a deep male voice posed the question.

"I'm here and will do what's asked of me," Drake replied.

"Word is you'll be given a whopper tomorrow night. Something to go down in the history of helping this family. You'd better check in and then get your team assembled."

"Any idea of what I'm being asked to do?" Drake asked.

"Only that if you fail, the repercussions will be astronomical. For this rage and others, especially your children."

Another lancing, knifelike pain tore across her head and she was near to crying out, but bit back any sound, unwilling to let Drake chance intercepting her muffled whimper. She exited Drake's mind and felt the burn of anger flare between her shoulder blades. Some team, she blustered mentally. While she was here warm and cozy at the Den, Drake was out doing more than male shifter bonding. Saving his children by the sounds of it. So rich and so Navy SEAL typical. Well this girl was going to be her own team of one and do something to help her family too. And if Drake had anything to say on the matter, she'd remind him of his dragon challenge. Come tomorrow, she'd begin her own leopardess challenge and Necrodemas was her target.

• • •

"Thanks for everything," she told Sherry when she dropped her at the front door of the Den.

Twin motorcycles rolled up behind Sherry's car as Shay checked out the parking lot, spotting her car parked in the overflow lot. Fin and another sentinel flipped up their visors and she flashed them peace signs. They waved back and she felt a twinge of guilt. All day they'd had the chore of following her. First up to her parents where she'd visited with Mom—who appeared better with less lapses into glazed stares. Dad came home in an ambulance and recognized her, but was weak and in need of recuperation. She'd helped out with her dad until the leopard shifter specialists arrived and kicked everyone out. Today the doctors were trying hypnosis and a deep brain wave therapy for both her parents.

Seeing Mom and Dad in this fragile state solidified Shay's desire to stop Necrodemas. She'd had quite the time losing her security team in the mall, but she'd done a little fancy footwork. She'd slipped out the rear exit from the lingerie store to her real destination, a spell caster, and away from the two wolf sentinels who'd opted to wait several feet from the entrance. She'd been smart enough to leave a piece of cardboard stuffed into the jamb so she could reenter an hour later, with her security squad none the wiser. Now, the expression on their faces was tense. Her brother would owe them big time she bet for doing mall duty, especially when she informed them she planned on doing more shopping… all week long.

"It was fun," Sher replied. "Hope you got everything you were looking for."

"I did, thanks to you." Shay was now the proud owner of a vial of truth serum and the incantation to say in order to get Necrodemas to spill his effing guts. Not that Sherry had given it to her, but she gave her the address to a reputable *botánica* shop in walking distance to the mall, where she conversed privately with the spell caster owner. The owner assured that what she'd shared was held in the highest confidence and Sher backed that up: what was disclosed between a caster and her client couldn't ever be relayed without strict and severe consequences from the Sisterhood Council. There were rules for spell casters. Lucky for Shay.

"How about a movie tomorrow night?" Sherry asked. "We'll gorge and cry. Best therapy."

Shay laughed. "Chick-flick and candy! Sure thing. My treat."

Striding back into the Den, she greeted the doormen with a wide smile and cheerfully declined their help with her shopping bags. Instead, she bolted up the stairs and nodded to the sentinels who stood outside the door to the suite with their serious falcon gazes. They weren't the most gregarious shifters, but then most birds of prey weren't much into talk. Those guys were going to be a slight problem in how they hovered while she was here, but she counted on telling them she was going down to the restaurant later for dinner. So far they seemed to use cell phones to convey her whereabouts. The only unknown was going out the door through the restaurant kitchen. Hopefully there wasn't a sentry posted at the back door, but if there was a guard, her newly acquired white chef's jacket, apron, and chef's hat from the uniform store at the mall would make her look like kitchen staff. No one would see that disguise coming.

She shut the door and immediately her gaze zoned in on the crystal vase of calla lilies that had been moved and the file box on the table. Shawn had stuck to his word and had the box of folders delivered. After dropping the shopping bags on the sofa, she snagged a bottle of water from the fridge and walked up to the table, pulled out a chair, and set the box on the floor.

One by freaking one, she removed each labeled file folder and read through the contents. The muscles along her neck and shoulders were pulled taut and she rotated her chin first to the left in a small circle, then to the right.

She tapped her fingers on top of the folder that pinned Dimitri to the bank account that had made a payment to Pestrolii's henchmen, a day before her parents were run off the road a few miles from their house. There was an encrypted message with the location and date, matching the horrific accident. Her parents' car along with the other car had careened off the road and down the side of the mountain, landing on a narrow cliff. Both cars were recovered and gone over with a fine tooth comb. The other car, a nondescript Buick, had been wiped clean, but not clean enough. It had been tracked back to a mechanic on the payroll of the Unruled.

After hours of leafing through pages and pages of information, some stamped as intel, she gathered that Shawn had acquired more than most of the documents from her very hardheaded and very closed mouth dragon fiancé. She wasn't surprised Drake was trying to keep her out of the loop. She couldn't be upset, given she wasn't exactly being upfront with him in her need to settle a score on her own.

But spending time reading wasn't the same as action. She wasn't a hundred percent sure about how much physical distance impacted mind linking after she sampled Drake's powerful ability to transverse realms. She couldn't expose opening a channel to him, or he might intercept her thoughts. Whenever they mind linked, she was well aware of when he tapped into her brain, just as he recognized when she linked with him. She'd have to be vigilant for any signs he might traverse the structure of her brain, and she could alter her thoughts. Give him the mental slip. He expected that she'd dive into these files. She smiled to herself, a little deviously. If he perceived her thoughts about Necrodemas, she'd play it off as stemming from these files. Priceless. She mentally slapped herself on the back. *Good one, Shay.*

Drake said he'd be in a meeting this afternoon—family business—and she bet that was code for his dragon challenge. Well, two could delve into important stealth business, she told herself. She'd camped out here, which meant she'd better get cracking on a to-do list for tonight. Luckily she'd had the foresight to ask Sherry where to pick up some dark clothing and Sherry had suggested an everyday maternity shop in the mall. Shay scored with two pairs of jeans—one dark and the other black—with expanding panels along the hips. A black silk turtleneck wasn't exactly sleuthing gear, but it would work. Unless she switched to primal form, then clothing became optional. But she'd have to have a place to stow her things or go streaking through Downtown Denver. Right now, she looked to be in her final month of pregnancy if she were carrying one baby, let alone twins, and if caught in the city limits as a leopardess, she'd be hauled away to a detainment center—a risk she didn't want to entertain.

Don't fret, Scarlett and Hunter, she mused. Since yesterday, she'd started to mull over baby names. She patted her expanding belly, convinced she couldn't wait. Not another day.

It felt oddly centering to walk across the room and sift through the clothing, deciding what to wear. Another step in the task of stalking Dimitri. She'd have to work fast if she was going to figure out a way inside Necrodemas's home with her only weapon being a dinner knife from the kitchenette. He lived in a posh neighborhood where upscale homes came with high tech security systems.

The simple approach suited her capabilities. She'd knock on his front door. He'd never suspect she had the capabilities of doing something gutsy in her condition. She could say she was there on Council business and excuse her rudeness in not phoning ahead.

And that's where her plan kinda petered. What was she going to do with him once she got hold of the jackass besides getting him to own up to being the scum of the earth? She wasn't a stone cold killer. Was she? Even as a leopard she'd never gone on a hunt. Never been allowed to, thanks to her parents. She studied her manicured nails, staring for a beat at her most wonderful engagement ring. But no, on the skin of her hands there wasn't a callus to speak of. Her hands didn't show signs of doing much manual labor at all. The closest she'd come was at the bar, lifting and toting the barrels of beer.

She might not be a hardcore kick-ass type, but she damn well knew if she got the goods on Necrodemas then she'd let the humans deal with him. It would be enough to get that moron to confess, then let justice be served by the officials who by rights should be doing this work. Not off to Vegas for a boys' night out. Her hands would remain clean and with that thought she smiled.

When her cell phone buzzed she flinched. Holy Moses, what if it were Drake and he'd caught her red-handed plotting the fall of Necrodemas? She glanced at her cell with Drake's number displayed. Not yet five in Oregon and hours before his final challenge according to the one she'd overheard.

"Hello!" she spat out nervously, answering her phone.

"Baby." Drake's deep voice evoked a rise in her heart rate and she gripped the phone, afraid she'd drop the darn thing. "What are you up to?"

Okay, take a deep breath. "Reading," she replied, attempting to control her voice from screeching and demanding to know what he was up to. "But now I'm so ready for a break. And you…how goes it? Still neck deep in family affairs? Nothing dangerous I hope." *Shay, shut up!*

"Missing you," he returned.

Her heart clenched and she whispered, "I can't wait for you to return."

He chuckled. "I'll be there but wish it was sooner than tomorrow. I'm harder than forged steel and titanium combined."

"I don't have anything to compare with that visual…other than I'm sitting here on my way to getting naked, my legs are spread, and I'm so, so wet and wishing you were here right now."

"Holy fuck! You win with the best visual."

"Don't know about that. Are you really hard?"

"So much, I'm on my way back to my room to take care of some *business*. We could both take care of some mutual business together…if you're game."

Shay rose from the table and moved into the bedroom, discarding her sweater and stepping out of her skirt. If he was game for some phone sex, that meant he was safe. Why not enjoy a sexy moment before tonight? She was on edge, adrenaline coursing through her veins, and she held the phone in a vise grip. "Sure. I am if you are."

"What are you wearing?"

"Umm…" She trailed her fingers down from her waist. "Panties, bra, and boots."

"Jesus. Shay, take off the bra and panties. Now. Then get on the bed, lay back, and open those beautiful thighs of yours."

"What about you?" she asked in a husky voice. She'd never had phone sex and this was so delectably hot.

"I'm standing inside my suite with my cock in hand."

She scrambled out of her lingerie and on to the bed. "I followed your directions. Now what?"

"Christ, I miss you so fucking much." His deep voice spread over her senses like warmed caramel. "Stroke your fingers once across your clit."

"Just once. I need more."

"Once Shay, and then stop."

She touched herself and melted. *Oh my God.*

From one stroke, she felt the pulsations inside her body… his body. They were linked. Twelve hundred miles of physical distance, but they were so very close—a heartbeat away from the arousal rippling under her skin. She could feel his pleasure twine with hers. "Again," he said in a gravelly voice. "Touch yourself baby, and make yourself come."

She arched upward, her body bowing as she stroked down her swollen and wet flesh. A moan burst from her, and she didn't hold back. "Drake, I'm about to shatter. Please."

"How wet are you?" he growled.

"Drenched," she panted, putting him on speakerphone and setting her cell on the bed. She plucked her nipples. This was maddening and she was ready to scream his name. How was this possible? Her body felt commanded, like he was thrusting into her—hard and steady with his dragon tempo and force.

"Come for me, baby. All over your fingers."

"And you?" she groaned

"I'm right there with you. God, Shay. It's like I'm fucking you with my mind."

"Oh Drake, I'm there!"

For seconds, she still felt him. Each stroke he delivered. She felt him handling his dick and the pleasure he derived, and then when he orgasmed, she climaxed again.

"Holy fuck!" he groaned. "Best phone sex."

She chuckled. "First time for me."

"It won't be the last, I can assure you," he rasped. "What are you up to tonight?"

Her eyes flashed open. "Err…I had a big day shopping."

"Then order in food and relax. How about the babies?"

She looked down at her abdomen and watched the rippling of her flesh as their children somersaulted. "Very, very active. I believe they are going to give us a run for our money when they finally get here. We'd better invest in sneakers. Lots of them."

"We'll be ready," he grunted, now sounding more relaxed albeit hoarse.

• • •

What was his little leopardess up to with that rise in the pitch of her voice that caught his attention when she'd answered the phone? He mused, walking toward his closet and unbuttoning his shirt. In an hour he'd be headed to the ring of fire within the magickal land in the Gifford Pinchot Forest, far inside the volcanic depths of Mount St. Helen's.

He'd traveled there as a sentry for his brothers, during their claiming challenge. This was the last step to accept and assert his rightful place in the universe as an eternal. Tonight, he'd breach the guarded citadel where his family kept their horde, leading a group of phoenix shifters, foul-mouthed and with even fouler moods. It had been a years at least since he'd last laid eyes on the keeper of their horde during his older brother's claiming, and now it was his turn to accept the challenge of the Hood Jinni, a genie who'd served his family and kept not only their horde safe, but was the keeper of the dragon flame, and his family's history records. Every male dragon had gone through the challenge, but not all had survived.

But if he did, his inheritance would be his to control and even more inviting was the fact that the Hood Jinni would serve to protect Shay and his children. That one factor was worth walking through the firestorms of hell to have the Jinni on board his team, a type of security no one would overcome—not even Dark Fae. According to his family's pledge, their Jinni could only be used to assist them for their personal protection, not used as a magickal pit bull. He couldn't sic the genie on anyone who made the dumbass decision to annoy him or his mate, but he and Shay would have their homes warded against any intruders—human or preternatural—as well as access to his family's riches as rightful heirs.

With that on his plate, Drake fought pushing aside his promise to remain on the periphery of Shay's thoughts, staying free from the deeper corridors of her mind and her inner most personal mental imagery. But he could, easily, when they were this enmeshed. During sex, she'd more than likely be unaware he'd crossed her intellectual boundaries—but that equated to breaking her trust. Fuck!

And what if she did the same to him and found out where he was headed? What he was up against. If he survived the Jinni, he'd have hell to pay to one leopardess dragon for all of eternity. That equation was all shades of fucked up.

He punched in Shawn's number. "Hey, what's up?" he barked. "Thought you were back at your parents'?"

"I am." He inhaled. "Need a favor."

"Boy, you're gonna owe me something terrible when this is all said and done. But hell, I guess you marrying my sister moves you into the category of family."

"It's about your lovely sister," he shot back, then scrubbed a hand over his face.

"We talked earlier and everything was fine. Did something happen?" Shawn's voice flared. "I should have known when she blew off my dinner invitation."

"Hold on. I just spoke with her and she said she's fine. So simmer the hell down and listen."

"Gotcha."

"Look," he began gruffly. "It's more like an itch I can't scratch. An instinct. Christ, this must sound like I'm whipped."

"Well past whipped," Shawn replied, snorting.

"Fuck, you sound like Noah."

"Bullshit. That'll be the day. How is that cynical fucker? He still working with you?"

He rolled his eyes. "We're tight, but that's beside the point. If you don't mind…can you check on her?"

"You're joking. Aren't you?"

"Naw. I'm up the side of a mountain and as you're aware Shay's at the Den. It's not that I don't trust your guys, but there are a few too many unknowns."

*Hell, maybe it's the wrong time to be in holed up here.* His family might not understand but wouldn't be the first time.

Shawn chortled loudly. "My guys are drawing straws on who gets *Shay duty*. It's what they call it. Don't get me wrong, I adore my sister, but she's putting it to them with shopping and not just a random run, but a full day."

"Shay's been hitting the stores for hours? Doesn't sound like her," he snarled, his muscles going rigid.

"She's a mother-to-be extraordinaire. Isn't that what pregnant women do? She had Fin and Slade waiting for over an hour outside a store in the mall today. Then she tried to give them the slip but they tailed her down the street to some spell caster's shop in Old Town. They didn't let on, but Fin questioned the shop owner who said it was some girly stuff. No biggie."

Drake stiffened completely; billowing puffs of smoke exited his mouth. *I need to calm the fuck down.* Just because Shay had him scurrying during the summer and she'd slipped his team, didn't mean she was doing the same now—well not exactly. She was up to her old tricks, but only to visit a spell caster. "Did she come out with any shopping bags?" he asked suddenly.

"Only about a dozen filled up Sherry's car."

Okay. Maybe she was shopping. He'd been gone for less than two days and besides visiting her parents, Shay had spent her time shopping. *It could happen.* "Can you check on her and keep a few tabs on her? She read through the information you delivered."

"Ah. And you think she might get an idea and act on it. Shay's always been rebellious, but to go looking for trouble when she's pregnant?"

"She's even more stubborn and easier to rile after seeing your mom. Wouldn't you after reading the intel?" He raked his fingers through his hair, walking into his closet and shrugging out of his shirt, and looking for something to throw on for the challenge.

"If I wasn't in charge of the justice council, I'd kick his teeth in," Shawn growled. "If something happens to my father, I honestly don't know if I can continue working for the council."

"Don't think along those lines. There are plenty of shifters who desperately need your help. Need I remind you without the council, the only redress shifters have is with gangs like the Unruled. You think humans would stand for that? We'd all be on the run and hunted or worse, there'd be a war and one I doubt shifters without real weaponry could wage and win." He closed his eyes.

"Easier said than done. This is my blood," Shawn growled.

"Bull-fucking-shit," he countered and flashed open his eyes. "My blood now, bro."

Shit, he needed to get this business with his family completed and return to Denver and deal with Necrodemas himself. Yeah, it was time to call his crew into action, even if it meant tapping into SEAL and family connections. With Shawn questioning his efficacy on the Council and his wife's predisposition to get into mischief if left unchecked, he'd cross the ring of fire tonight and be ready to deal with taking out the garbage as he should have done months ago.

# CHAPTER 20

Shay nodded to the sentinels, recognizing the guys on the night shift—Darwin and Peyton. "I'm going down to dinner," she announced, batting her lashes and keeping her eyes innocently wide. She couldn't tell if they were falling for it as their collective gazes dropped to the ungainly bag she lugged, pretending it weighed nothing.

"What's in there?" one of them inquired. "Need help?"

"Uhh," she began and smiled, dropping the cashmere wrap covering her shoulders and chest up to that point. Now, she revealed the cleavage she'd been hiding. Pregnant or not, she wasn't totally ignorant of the stares from the opposite sex that normally she choose to ignore. Now, she needed every advantage if she was going to give the Den security the slip, and damn, she used her curves like an assault weapon.

Darwin reached for the bag and she pulled back. *One whopper coming up.*

"Lingerie. I didn't like the color and I'm sending my exterior security team back to the mall to exchange these things. Unless you'd like to do that. Just some nightgowns, robes, and stuff." She patted the bright pink-striped shopping bag and peered up into the falcon shifter faces as they rapidly shook their heads.

"Better let your mall team handle that one. Right, Dar?" The one named Peyton elbowed the other sentinel.

"Yeah. Absolutely. I'm cool with that plan." Darwin knelt to pick up her wrap.

"Well, if you're sure. I love to escape to the mall. Bet you guys do too." She winked.

"Oh sure," Darwin said, shrugging and handing her back her shawl. "Like who doesn't want to go hang there?"

She did a rapid accounting. *Me, you, him.* "Thanks, guys. I won't be late." She walked to the elevator, biting the inside of her cheek, and pressed the call button. Shit, now they'd expect her back soon. She turned and added, "Unless the jazz trio is the same as last night."

"It is and they're good if you like that kind of music," Peyton confirmed.

She smiled and gave them a thumb up, turning as the ding of the elevator caught her attention. Step one. Check. Now, she just had to enter the restaurant and slip into a restroom, change and she'd be out the backdoor.

At the maître d's station, she waited to be seated and pushed aside a tightening of her chest, a pinching discomfort as though someone were staring daggers into her skin. Lifting her eyes, she met the seedy gaze of Dimitri followed by the immediate overarching instinct to shift into full leopardess form. She dropped the bag and grabbed onto the edge of the wooden counter. What was he doing here of all places?

Well so much for security! She watched, convinced her whole world had stopped spinning as he rose from his table, tucked in his tie, and buttoned his jacket. Please, she prayed. *Do not come over here!* She kept her face impassive but when it rained, it stormed. He must have excused himself from his dinner companions and waved in her direction. Exit. Abort. Leave the premises now! All good warnings and ones she should heed. Yeah, and run away with her tail between her legs. *Not this time, Shay.*

She flicked her attention to the other people at his table, and recognized two of them from the photographs in his home in Lisbon. Dimitri's daughter and his son along with two other men she didn't recognize. Thank God that slimeball Dark Fae Pestrolii wasn't here or it would go down as the night all hell broke loose. She curled her fingers and the two-inch long talons that had broken free at the tips of her fingers scraped the wood. Dammit!

Carefully she reached down, winding her fingers around the ribbon handles of the bag and pulled her parcel in front of her. These talons weren't feline claws but dragon—sharp, curved, and very deadly.

Surreptitiously she glanced around to see if she might spot anyone who worked security that she knew, but besides the elegant wait staff she didn't recognize a soul. "Shannon," Dimitri's raspy voice always made her name sound as if he was on the verge of a coughing fit.

"Good evening," she said, finding it difficult to look him in the eye without wanting to spit in his face.

"It's been months," Necrodemas replied, then his eyes widened as they fell to her neckline.

*Not long enough!* Christ, he still made her skin crawl the way he gaped at her cleavage, but if she adjusted her shawl, she'd expose her talons. That fun fact wasn't something she'd let him in on unless he tried something stupid.

"So you're here for dinner?" she asked, trying to find out if he was returning home afterward. She could hardly wait for their encore rendezvous where she'd settle this score.

"Ah yes. Campaign strategy. Do you follow the local political campaigns that are underway?"

"No. Never did," she returned.

"But you should. You're voting next week, are you not? Isn't that the reason you've returned? We had to delay the vote in order to convene a quorum and since Richard held half the voting firepower, we would be in the lurch had you stayed away. So glad you didn't. By the way, how is Richard's recovery?"

She flashed her gaze up to his face and noticed his eyes were narrowed, pulled tight, and gone was the charming veneer. He knew she'd have to come back to vote. What had lain in wait, now the older leopard revealed, and held her focus. In trying to set a trap, she became aware she may have stumbled into one—perhaps not all the way—that was invisible, but still it was out there waiting.

"Father is doing much better," she lied. "I don't know if I'll be needed to cast my vote at the rate he's improving."

Dimitri's brows shot up, and his eyes searched her face but she refused to drop her gaze. Steadily she stared back at him, notching up her chin a millimeter higher.

"That's good to hear. And you…where did you finally relocate to? You're not in Denver."

"Around. My business takes me all over." Oh brother, that sounded lame.

"Why don't you join us for dinner? Do you have a *date*?" He leaned over and whispered. "I know what happened. If you give me the slightest indication that fire breathing reptile forced himself on you, I can help. Deal with your litter and make arrangements for their adoption. We could still be friends…not mated mind you, but close. And I'll find O'Connor and make him pay."

She stared back at him and clamped her lips shut. Her heart pounded and she wondered how to respond that didn't involve her slapping Dimitri's face. She did what came natural and let her mouth get the better of her. "Actually, I seduced him. My fiancé is a complete gentleman."

The maître d' returned. "Miss Barclay," he said.

Dimitri's eyes glittered dangerously and she could kick herself for giving him a crumb of information except it felt so good to tell him to his face that she'd chosen Drake over him. "I'll inform Drake that you're looking for him. Better take care, Dimitri."

He bowed curtly. "I look forward to that moment. Until we meet again, Shannon."

If only she could fling in his face it'd be sooner than he presumed, but she'd said too much already. Christ, now what was she going to? Well, according to the spell, all she had to do was face him. Really, she could arrive on his doorstep and say anything—pretend anything. All she needed was five seconds to work the incantation. She arched her brow, confident she'd freaking prevail, and walked with the maître d' to the doorway, then stopped not wanting to push her luck. "Excuse me," she said. "I'd like to be seated in the other dining area."

"But of course," he said in a French accent and smiled at her. "We have the perfect place."

She glanced over her shoulder, taking note that Necrodemas had returned to his table. Her hands shook from the rush of adrenaline that had flooded her bloodstream. The maître d' led her to a corner table that truly was flawless—a stone's throw away from entrance into the kitchen. Bus boys entered and exited, and she wouldn't have a problem waltzing through to the back door and out to her car. No one would expect her to drive away.

As soon as the waiter came and took her order, she removed cash from her purse and placed it on the bread plate, more than enough to cover the meal. The other folks seated in the smaller dining area were couples who couldn't have cared less about anyone besides their immediate date. She could have done cartwheels down the aisle while on fire and they wouldn't have blinked.

She went into the bathroom and changed into her black garb and then put on her chef's costume. She stuffed her clothing into the bag and shoved it under the sink. Exiting the bathroom, one of the waiters glowered at her and whispered harshly, "That's not the staff bathroom. Marcel will have your hide."

"Emergency," she replied over her shoulder on her way to the kitchen entrance. She pushed on the swinging door, escaping inside. The place was buzzing with voices, shouted out orders, pots and pans clanging, and scads of people jostling at the stainless-steel tables, the stoves, and ovens. Off on the far side, there were the dishwashers in an alcove and busboys rushed back and forth with trays of dinnerware. But where was the back door?

No one really paid her much mind as she gingerly walked on the squishy black rubber matting and squeezed between the assistant chefs. Or so she believed until a firm grip encircled her arm. Oh dear God, she stopped and glanced back.

"Where are you going?" An older man asked her. "You that new sous-chef?"

"No. I'm just here to observe," she replied. "I spoke with Quinn."

"Quinn?" he replied like that was unimaginable.

"And Sherry," she said.

The chef frowned at her. "Oh. Well, okay just stay out of the way. Joe, man the sauté station. We're two down."

She spun around and headed in the opposite direction. A door flew open and a man walked inside adjusting a chef's paper hat on his head. "I'm here," he shouted.

Hunching up her shoulders, she sailed by him and made for the exit, not stopping until she was outside and only then did she slow to remove her keys from the pocket of the apron. No one was around and her breath came out in steamy puffs in front of her face. Her heart pumped overtime and she power walked her way to her car. At this time of night, the dinner crowd was arriving and keeping the doormen and valets busy. If they glanced up, they'd only see a kitchen worker walking and she doubted any of them recognized her car in the yellow sodium glowing streetlights.

Okay. So far, so good. Shay jiggled her keys, untangling them, and reached the driver side of her car when she felt the first sweep of his dank breath on her neck. Her heart lurched so hard it robbed her of her breath. Without turning or seeing him, Shay grasped that the gypsy Dark Fae had found her. Holy goddess, this bypassed suck ass and delved into the Richter scale of epic-fucking-horrible!

The sight of Pestrolii's eerie blue reflection in the glass of the driver's window, standing directly behind her convinced Shay there was no time like the present to shift. She had seconds to spin this impromptu meeting her way. Someone's posterior was gonna get kicked tonight. Not hers!

"Going somewhere, little leopardess?" Pestrolii snickered.

"I might not know karate, but, jackass, I got crazy down to a science!"

• • •

Noah flanked him as they descended into the forest, banking onto a ledge of the mountain. Drake landed and lifted his snout, sniffing the air and grunted to Noah, pointing his wing in the direction of a smoking vent. The phoenix swooped past him, leaving an aromatic trail reeking of frankincense and ginger. Christ, what a diet, Drake mused on what Noah and his crew consumed and kept boiling in the kitchen—a copper pot filled with a thick bubbling resin. They spooned it into glasses, added San Pellegrino and ice, then chugged the concoction down by the gallon.

As leader of his crew, Noah would announce him to the Jinni, a formality that he abhorred but was powerless to change. The Jinni had existed for as long as his family, faithfully serving the O'Connor rage, and these old formalities weren't his issue once he'd gotten what he came for.

Grant and Evan, the other two phoenixes stood guard outside the mouth of the ice cave, the hidden entrance into his family's horde. Noah turned back into human form and picked up a piece of wood.

"Mind? I need a light," Noah asked him.

Drake blew a gust of fire and the kindling caught, serving as a torch. Noah walked by him stark naked in the snow, following a path of glacial ice until he disappeared inside the cave, leaving a flickering shadow on the walls in his wake.

There were elements to watch for as well as preternatural thieves. With the tumultuous weather this week, they'd have to battle frozen mud slides and be alert to the cracking of the glaciers. The whole mountain was enfolded in a wall of ice that had recently begun to grow again. The environmentalists, geologists, and brainiacs all over the world were confounded, not that Drake gave a rat's ass. He'd witnessed weather conditions come and go and the nonsense associated with El Niño, La Niña, carbon dioxide, acid rain—in the scheme of living things, it was all irrelevant. Big picture folks: the sun was gonna burn out and sooner than the scientists anticipated. Then what?

But for now, this creeping wall of a glacier caused unrest in his family for the obvious reason that scientists nosing around might find their way inside the mountain. Problem in a nutshell: the Jinni didn't like surprise visitors and the shit would hit the fan.

Hence the reason he didn't put up a stink about this tradition of Noah announcing his arrival. The Jinni wielded a wicked saber and he for one enjoyed his head attached to his neck. He stood at the edge of the cliff and kicked a few stones with his paw, wondering what Shay was up to. Shit, she better be tucked into bed, enjoying something on television. He could even accept listening to music downstairs, not that he relished the idea of her sitting alone in a jazz club even if it was owned by Shawn. The place crawled with horny shifters. He clenched his jaw and leaned against the side of the mountain, staring up at the stars. A million twinkling lights all reminded him of where he'd traveled a few days ago as he'd made love to her. "Shay," he murmured, releasing a billowing flame.

"Impatient?" Grant ambled up to him.

"Yeah," he said. "I want to get this show on the road."

"Marriage. Honeymoon. Eh?"

Drake snorted a puff of dark smoke. "Dude, you can't imagine. How long have you been married?"

"Ten years and it feels like yesterday. Mind you, it takes fucking work. If it's not the kids, then Ellie wants something done around the place. Hell, I just want to get home and relax some nights. Kick back and down a beer."

They conversed in an ancient language that to the human ear sounded more like clicks than spoken words.

Noah's flickering torch appeared, illuminating the inside of the cave and Drake straightened. Noah flicked his wrist, waving an "all okay" sign.

"Good luck," Grant said.

Evan's glowing red eyes flashed in his direction and he caught his nod as well. "Here goes nothing," Drake muttered.

"Let's go," Noah said.

"What's his mood?" Drake inquired.

"His sense of humor is ripe. Shit-eating as usual." Noah changed back into his phoenix form.

"Great," Drake snarled and advanced toward the interior of the ice cave.

He and Noah flew, winding around the stalagmites and stalactites that jutted forth like sharpened teeth ready to eviscerate either of them if they didn't carefully navigate their flight pattern within the bowels of the mountain. The icy encrusted cave gave way to roughhewn walls, dripping with water that ran into steaming aqua-colored pools. The water reflected golden lighting from the stacks of shiny brick—pure twenty-four karat bars—that made up the outer chamber of Jinni's residence composed of his family's horde. If dragons were greedy, secretive, and very, very possessive creatures, then the Jinni was pathological in his desire to keep, count, and caress the vast riches that filled the cave. The quarterly inventory where dragon accountants entered to remove select items for trade was not a happy moment for his family or the Jinni. Much gnashing of teeth occurred on both sides of the table.

Drake flew past the huge piles of glittering gems, gold in all forms fashioned by mankind, and other treasures that included works of art believed lost. An exclusive assortment of plants and fungi were kept within a specially enclosed hot house where the Jinni worked to maintain precious botanical and fungal species that had gone extinct above ground and were priceless for their curative powers.

The Jinni bowed over a chessboard, holding onto his chin as if pondering his next move. He didn't acknowledge them even when one of his nude concubines leaned over and whispered in his ear.

Noah bowed, spreading his crimson and gold plumage upon the ground while the Jinni sat on a throne, pretending to be more interested in selecting a fig from a tray proffered by a concubine with snakes slithering through her hair. Drake gritted his teeth, waiting in silence until the Jinni got off his ass and got with the program.

Scratching a set of razor sharp talons down his neck, Drake curled the other talons on the tips of his hind paws into the ground, and produced a sound similar to human nails being scraped across a chalkboard.

The Jinni raised an inky eyebrow in question. "Am I boring you?"

"Of course not," Drake returned, attempting to flatten the sarcasm out of his voice. After all, the genie held his challenge and could, at the last moment, change it into something that would tax his abilities. He didn't fear failure, but he didn't want to walk away and require a period of recuperation. Not when Shay needed him full throttle.

"Leave us," the Jinni said to the female serving him.

"Your liege," his concubine replied.

Oh brother. Drake kept his eyes half-lidded, fighting a yawn.

"Get up, Noah," the Jinni commanded in an irked voice. "So the impossible has occurred. You've found a mate."

It was the signal that Drake was free to approach him. Hot damn. "Surprise."

"More like taken aback. What's she like?" the Jinni asked, tilting his head.

"You'd like her. She's full of spit and vinegar."

"She'd have to be to put up with you, but more than your union prompts you to return to us. Makes me wonder why the prodigal son has returned to the rage." The Jinni whipped the long braid he wore over his shoulder and picked up a pair of reading glasses. He dusted off a leather-covered volume that sat on a table beside his throne. Drake remembered the book. It contained the names of each of his family, his entire rage's history and now, his name and Shay's would be entered on a page, along with their children, and their children's children for as long as their line existed.

With his spectacles on, the Jinni appeared studious as he licked his finger and thumbed his way through the book. "Ah. Here we are," he said, peering over the rim of his glasses to Drake, and squinted. "Herensuge bloodline. Powerful. Loyal. But pigheaded as I've ever witnessed. Did you bring the seal?"

"Yes," he said curtly and removed the Herensuge seal. He handed it over to the Jinni and watched the genie study the inscription.

"*Family. Faith. Fire.*" The Jinni then murmured, "Paloma O'Connor de la casa Draco Herensuge. Eternal light. Your mother was a rare beauty in these parts." The genie clucked his tongue and shook his head, blinking his almond-shaped eyes, then exhaled so forcefully the flames from the torches on the wall flickered wildly. "She exists on other planes. Far, far away from here. Thank the goddesses."

He nodded, not sure what to make of the Jinni's words. Of course she existed in another plane, all dragons did whose life forms had been extinguished. Drake stood at attention, feeling more on edge and unsure what the Jinni might reveal next.

The Jinni fingered the book and crossed his legs, rubbing a hand over his face. "Drake, I won't lie. I've waited for this day for a long time. Your ego and your pride function as a double-edged sword at times in your life and the lives of others. You're aware of the rules of the game. Twenty-four hours. Not a second longer. If you fail, you will perish and your mate will go unclaimed. Dangerous for the mother of dragons. Are you prepared to receive your quest this day?"

"I am," he bowed, the over-indulged kind as was required, extending his foreleg with a flourish and deeply bending at the waist.

"Rise and receive your challenge Drake O'Connor *de la casa Draco Herensuge*."

Drake stood upright, his senses pulled taut, his muscles constricted into bands of steel. "Your grace," he replied.

"You are charged with bringing back the clutch of elemental eggs belonging to the flame throwing salamander."

"Hah, you almost had me." Drake cracked a smile. "Seriously, what's my quest?"

The Jinni turned his eyes to him, flashing rainbow colors outward. His steepled his tattooed fingers, flexing his arms in a gesture that made his bronze-colored skin ripple in response. "I'm very serious. Six eggs delivered to me by tomorrow. Free of the ranavirus. I want a pristine specimen. Get my drift?"

"Let me get this straight. I'm being asked to go on some sort of egg hunt." As Drake spoke, flames erupted from mouth and nostrils. "You're serious?"

"I'm not one to play games last time I checked," the Jinni replied, cocking his head.

Drake stood before the Jinni and growled, "My brother before me was sent out on a quest to bring back the treasure of the Voltan. He traveled to the Yucatan. And you send me out to go searching for the eggs…of a salamander?"

The genie nodded and dipped an elaborate candle into the flame of the eternal torch to his side, then he lit the wick of a stick of blood red wax, dripping several drops of magickal globules onto the page in Drake's family history book. On the page inscribed with his name and symbol, the Jinni wrote in an ancient scrolling text, signifying the quest had been given and received.

Closing his eyes, Drake clamped his jaws tight, unable to speak for a moment. Slowly, he peeled open his eyes, and forced himself to shut the fuck up.

The Jinni picked up and pressed the Herensuge seal into the wax. It effectively was a done deal.

Drake scrubbed his hand over his face, snagging his talons on his snout, uncaring that he scraped his chin. "Are we done?" he barked, baring his teeth, consumed by his foul mood.

The Jinni stood and held out the seal to him. When he reached for the seal, the Jinni pulled back and quickly changed hands and caught his foreleg. "This quest is very important to the survival of your family. Make no mistake: if I do not receive those eggs, your family will die out within a decade. The salamander is an elemental—keeper of the flame and only a handful exist. When they go extinct, so do you."

The Jinni whispered the last part and the entire cavern went dark. Mere seconds later, the wind howled and Drake felt a cold run through his bones, through his whole being, and he understood. Without the flame, the dragon lost his power. He had been charged with bringing back the fuel that kept his family alive.

*Fuck!* "Are we free to leave?"

"As you will," the Jinni's voice reverberated off the walls.

Noah nodded, his face hidden in shadows except for his feral red eyes. "Dude, let's make like the wind and book."

# CHAPTER 21

Gustov threw back his head and howled. Literally. "Funny. But I'm not afraid of you or that scaled mongrel fiancé of yours. He didn't do a thing back in Louisiana to me, now did he?"

This jerk didn't realize how close he'd come to being charred well-done by Drake. The irony that she'd begged Drake not to go after this idiot played upon her. She could barely contain the urge to kick him in the shin. Her canines sprung free and in seconds it would be this gypsy jerk's turn to run and hide. Did he really want to tango with a woman who'd spent the last five months reeling in her rage?

Glancing around, she needed to get her hands on something like a tire iron to smack him so hard, his Fae head would spin. In frustration she roared, hoping that someone from the Den would notice business as usual was not going down on this side of the parking lot. She waited, but the staff scurrying about didn't break stride. No one looked up or over. *A little help would be nice!*

"Gustov, don't touch her," a hoarse voice whispered.

Shay glanced around and saw no one, only a flicker. And then Dimitri materialized. "*Ta-dah,*" he jeered, snapping his fingers. His two children and the other men he'd had at his table materialized as well. "Now we're ready to roll, as you Americans like to say."

How did he shield himself as well as this tribe of morons? Had to be the gypsy's doing. Before she could shift into her primal form, Dimitri reached out and grabbed her hair, showing her the curved dagger before he pressed it into her neck. "I'll gut you without thinking twice. Those pups you're carrying are worth just as much dead as alive. Stem cell transplant mean anything to you? Because, to me, it's a highly lucrative endeavor."

She watched Pestrolii's hands, careful to avoid his touch and walked alongside Necrodemas, his hand digging into her shoulder. Out in public with cars coming and going, he didn't hide the knife he brandished. Duh! Now, she wanted to kick herself. There was some spell in play here where no one could see them. Crap, that's what she should have understood was in play earlier when Dimitri was in the Den. She whacked herself in the head with her mental palm. Dammit.

Really needed to bone up on spell options in the future. No time to feel guilty on that one. Hindsight—blah-blah. She imagined that no matter what Dimitri spouted off, live dragons were worth a helluva lot more than cells and she pressed her hand to her belly. Don't listen to this mean and nasty man, she mentally whispered to her sweet babies.

A valet walked right by her and nodded. "You out for a smoke?"

She had to try something and replied, "I'm being held against my will. Tell Drake—"

Dimitri yanked a handful of her hair and she screeched. "I'll kill the kid. His blood will be on your hands, bitch."

"You an actress?" the young man shot back. "That was pretty good. And funny." He must have thought her a nutcase, not an actress, and took off in a sprint towards a car.

Dammit. They approached a large black Hummer wagon. An unusual version. "You were downtown yesterday. Weren't you?"

Necrodemas laughed. "I wanted to see with my own eyes your betrayal."

"Dad, enough with the drama. She's nothing but a cash cow. Jeez," his daughter Morgan whined. The young woman trudged up to the side of the Hummer, rolling her eyes. "Someone unlock the doors already."

"Shut up, Morg," Dimitri's son replied in low voice. His golden eyes flickered over to her, lingering longer than necessary. She couldn't recall his name, but he had the same creeper qualities as his dad—especially with his gaze glued to her chest. He opened the back door to the Hummer and motioned to her.

"Deal with her, Duncan!" Dimitri shoved her in his son's direction.

For a second anger flared in Duncan's eyes but just quickly dissolved. Hmmm, maybe he could be used. He reached for her, clasping her by the elbow, and for a millisecond, their gazes fused, and he stared back at her. Assuredly she didn't find the anger he'd disclosed when looking at his father. Morgan and Duncan were probably offspring from Dimitri's mate number six or seven. She hadn't memorized any information on his wives other than he'd married a dozen—at least. Some of the marriages lasted for years, but the more recent ones lasted months and were a red flag to anyone with functioning brain cells. These Necrodemas offspring's mom had passed away and might be cause for Duncan to be willing to work against his father.

Pestrolii got in and took the wheel. Christ, this was going to be a wild and dangerous ride if the gypsy was driving. Necrodemas took shotgun and the other men climbed into the rear, taking the jump seat of the Hummer.

More eye rolling from Morgan who whined under her breath about being cramped but Shay would be damned if she'd get into a juvenile high school snipping match with this woman. She had to be older than Shay, but she acted insolently. No brainer—she was Necrodemas's kid.

Shay sat there, digesting the severity of the situation and made the decision to call on Drake. This was 9-1-1 material and he was the only one who could rescue her. Oh God! She'd have hell to pay for this fiasco she'd gotten herself into.

"What are you waiting for, Duncan?" The gypsy stared from the rearview mirror.

What the crap was he talking about? She peered over at Duncan and he grimaced, slipping his hand into his jacket pocket.

"You made this all too easy, Miss Barclay and for that I thank you," Pestrolii snarled.

Before she could reply or link minds with Drake, Duncan jabbed her with a syringe. "Holy hell! What's in…" She shivered at the sudden cloudy feeling of cold rolling over her body. Then everything went to black.

• • •

Drake landed outside the mouth of the ice cave and forcibly blew out a plume of fire, lighting up the sky. Not smart, but he couldn't help himself. He was two clicks past angry as the phoenixes gathered around him.

Noah touched down next to him, shaking his head. "Plan?"

He barked, "Hell if I know. I'm not a goddamn biologist!"

"No, you aren't but Evan's wife is," Noah replied, cocking his head toward his crewmate.

"Dude, what kind of challenge did you get?" Evan asked.

"Need to find half-dozen…eggs."

Grant whistled. "What kind requires a biologist?"

"Salamander. Not just any. Some virus is wiping them out. We need eggs from a healthy flamethrower that just happens to reside somewhere down there," Drake growled, straining to make out the valley below. With his dragon infrared sight, he zoned in on creatures and cold-blooded were harder to detect than mammals. Harder but not impossible.

"We're going to need nets, gloves, containers. That's what Fiona uses when she treks through the creeks and rivers. The forest has loads of critters."

"Even in January?" Drake asked, less confident as he turned back to Evan. "Not a lot of movement."

"'Cause dude, you gotta know where to look," Evan said with the utmost confidence. "I got this."

"Fly back to your place, load up, and meet us down off from Dead Man's Landing."

"You're going to be splashing around the Columbia River?"

"Ideas?" Noah snarled.

"Leaf litter. Think smaller bodies of water. Creeks or ponds."

"Where?" Drake asked.

"Spirit Lake. Panther Creek."

His ears pricked, and his heart squeezed. "Good idea. Meet us at Panther Creek," he murmured, thinking of his wayward feline mate. He hunched down without further address, and took to the night sky. Grant and Noah flew, drafting off him. They were fast, but he was much faster with a mission, less than a day to complete. *Eggs,* he muttered to himself. Yeah, he got their importance, but he'd never live this down. *Fucking Christ!*

* * *

By the first light of day, they'd scoured miles along the banks of Spirit Lake, and had followed the Lewis River into Panther Creek. They walked a grid, sweeping back the leaf litter, gingerly picking up rocks, and still every blasted salamander they'd encountered either tested positive for some fucking fungus or had signs of the ranavirus—missing limbs and red mouths.

A squiggly rust-spotted flamethrower ran over Drake's foot. He scooped up the bloated salamander in his fingers, and squinted. "Evan," he hollered.

"You got something?"

"Naw, I wanted to ask your opinion if my ass looks big."

Evan ambled over and peered down at his palm. "That one looks pregnant…like she's ready to lay her eggs. Man, don't drop her."

They were all out here, naked with the exception of wearing blue latex gloves. No place to tuck the plastic baggie except by holding it between his teeth. *Drake!*

He blew out a lungful of smoke at the sound of Shay's voice. He'd avoided mind linking with her, not wanting her to get wind of this snafu, and fully expected he'd have to explain why he'd gone mute from yesterday, but she sounded stressed.

*Baby! What's up?*

Mouthing to Evan, he said, "Test this one."

The phoenix pulled out a small field test kit from the pack his wife had loaded for them. Luckily for him, Evan's wife held a PhD in biology and was a professor at the University of Oregon—or maybe this was all feeding the Jinni's wry sense of humor. The genie had always enjoyed these types of chessboard moves, already had known Drake's personal phoenixes had the skill set to accomplish this task.

*Oh Drake, I've made a mess of things.*

His brows scrunched together.

*Shay, what are you talking about?*

She coughed. *Wait a second. I need to pretend that I'm still asleep. It's hard when I'm trying to mind link.*

"Good on this one. You found a healthy specimen," Evan stated, and whistled loud, waving his arms for the other phoenixes to group up.

"Whistle over there," Drake snarled, pressing his hands over his ears.

*Baby, what the hell is going on?*

Shit. He didn't have his cell phone and their only form of communication was a satellite phone that Evan had in his pack.

Nothing but static noise filled his mind. Shay, who had called out to him, had now gone silent!

"Let's get back to the Jinni, check in and I need to rock-n-roll back to Denver." During the flight to the ice cave, Shay moaned once and his patience eroded.

He bellowed molten flames at which Noah yelled. "Watch it, dude!"

Landing in the outer chambers of the Jinni, he clenched his jaw. That was it. No more Mr. Nice Guy. As he tore off his blue latex gloves, off came all the other proverbial gloves as well.

### SHAY, FUCKING TELL ME WHAT IS GOING DOWN!

He stormed into the Jinni's receiving room and signaled to Noah to go through the motions of bowing and scraping. "Your noble servant returns," Noah murmured.

"So soon. You've still hours before you were due back."

"We didn't kill the mother salamander," Drake said sharply, in need of dispensing this formality and getting his ass back to Denver. "My guard confirmed she's ready to lay her eggs."

"You brought me the mother as well as the eggs?" the Jinni looked over the top of his glasses as he sat by the fire, reading.

"Don't tell me that's a problem," he retorted, ready to blow his top.

"On the contrary," the Jinni said softly, laying down his book and rising. He came over to Drake and took the specimen box, observing the salamander that now glowed bright orange. "You've done very well for yourself."

The Jinni snapped his fingers and a woman fully clothed, wearing a lab coat and dark-framed glasses came forward. She looked around nervously and he nodded. "Dr. Matthew, your new project. This is the correct species, am I right?"

Lifting her glasses, Dr. Matthew peered closely at the box containing the salamander. "Yes. She's an excellent sample for our work in fire regeneration. You're correct, she's about to lay her eggs."

Dr. Matthew reached for the box and the Jinni didn't let it go initially, just held onto it as he stared at her unblinking.

Drake had the urge to hurl one of the boulders near the wall across the room. Oh fuck. Did that dude really think an educated human would find him amiable? When Dr. Matthew walked off down the corridor, and pulled open what looked to be the door to a newly fashioned lab, he swung back to the Jinni. "Really? Do ya think she'll ever give you the time of day? Right now I need you to focus on closing this ceremony ASAP!"

"It might happen, Mr. Know It All. You're proof that impossible things can occur," the Jinni snorted.

"So, we're square?"

"It appears to be that way."

"I hope you really needed that flamethrower, and this isn't some warped excuse for you to hook up with some highbrow researcher."

"Lower your voice," the Jinni snapped. "You can see as well as anyone the torches are dimmer than shit and if we don't get an elemental to harness the fire, they will go out completely. The fact that you succeeded on your challenge and are close to claiming a mate is very timely. I can't begin to explain, but the universe has its own rhythm."

"Destiny?"

"Precisely." The Jinni picked up a curved piece of metal from a table and tossed it high into the air. "Heads up."

Drake tracked the arcing metal and recognized it as a cuff to be worn if not cherished. He snatched it out of the air. "Ah, so this is mine."

"Don't lose it," the Jinni warned. "And don't rub too hard. I'm not deaf."

He slipped the polished gold cuff on to his wrist and nodded. "Where's the other one?"

The Jinni snapped his fingers and one of his concubines came forward with sterling tray that held a smaller version of the cuff he wore. The magickal jewelry would adjust to the wearer regardless of his or her form. But still Shay's wrist was tiny compared to his and he slipped the gold cuff over his talon, near to his knuckle for safekeeping.

He glanced upward, meeting the Jinni's frank appraising eyes. "Since you're right in front of me, I won't pretend that all is fine in Gotham. Truthfully, I need you help now."

"What can I do you for?" the Jinni asked, dropping his bored facade. "Are you referring to Denver?"

Nodding, he inhaled, flexing the muscles of his shoulders. "I need to get back there immediately and I want to take them," he motioned to the phoenixes.

"As you wish," the Jinni crossed his arms. "Stand over there, in the clearing."

Drake flapped his wings, landing next to the phoenixes, who'd momentarily stopped preening their feathers.

"Dudes," he shouted. "We're leaving so all three of you need to stop that."

Grant shot him the bird, but he quit and stared back at Drake. The Jinni walked forward, "When will I meet Lady Herensuge?"

Drake stiffened at the title, but it was true. When he wed Shay, she would be Lady Herensuge and he'd be known as Lord Herensuge to those of the dragon rages both here at home and all over the universe.

"I expect soon," he growled, locking onto the Jinni's gaze. "Catch you around. If I summon you, don't come to town thinking we're asking you over for tea. If I send word in the next day, it'll be serious shit that's going down as in Dark Fae. A fucking gypsy."

The Jinni faced him, taller than Drake in his human form. At least seven, closer to eight feet tall, and nearly every bare inch of skin had been inked from his neck down. "Have no fear, Lord Herensuge, I'll be ready when you call."

The genie touched his forehead in a display of allegiance. Gone was his jaded demeanor, and seeing this side of the Jinni made Drake that much more weary. What the hell was waiting for him back in Denver?

# CHAPTER 22



Drake's mind linked with hers and boy, he hollered, but she couldn't respond. She kept her eyes shut and focused on taking in shallow breaths, unable to mentally converse with Drake while pulling off this charade of still being unconscious, which wasn't as easy as it seemed. From underneath her lashes, she watched Morgan enter the room and harshly drop a tray on the nightstand. *God, I almost jumped a mile high.*

She'd wanted to leap off the bed and wrestle that idiot to the ground, but she shifted her focus toward a flickering shadow at the door. Duncan stood there, staring inside the room—especially at her.

Morgan stomped out and snarked to her brother, "Stop staring at her. She's not one of your bimbo tramps."

She bolted upright as soon as the door closed. *Oh Scarlett and Hunter.* One side of her mind cried out, afraid of whatever they'd injected her with might have a harmful effect on her babies.

Who are Scarlett and Hunter?, Drake demanded.

*Sorry, babe. I'm being held.*
Silence. That couldn't be good. Shit, Drake would have to leave his family's residence and whatever meetings he'd planned for tomorrow. What time was it?

I'm at the Den, he roared.

Now it was her turn. *YOU'RE WHERE?* Prickling sweat erupted from between her shoulder blades. Oh dear God! She must have been out for hours.

At the Den and you're not. Who has you? Tell me and I'll come get you.

Drake lowered his voice and sounded deadly calm.

She stammered, *I was outside taking a walk…to my car. And Pestrolii came up behind me.*

Shay for all that's holy, what the hell were you doing outside without an escort? I just spoke with the two sentinels upstairs and they alerted Shawn about an hour ago when you didn't come back. This place is crawling with security and no one knows what happened to you. Pieces of info but no dots to connect. You were dressed like a chef. A valet thinks he saw you, hollering in pain but no one was with you. Sherry's here but from all accounts, we need Kee and Carl to track you, unless you know the location of where you're being held.

So much for him being calm. When Drake stopped his rant, she interjected, *Can I talk now?*

Go ahead.

*At Dimitri's house. But I don't know the exact location. I'm in a room.*

I'll find the location and find you. Baby, give me a few minutes and I'll come for you, Drake growled.

*No one is here. They think I'm still unconscious.*

She heard Drake curse in his mind. A stream of not pretty or nice things about what he'd do to Dimitri and the gypsy. But she couldn't just sit here and wait for him; this had to be a trap. *Drake, don't you think they know you'll come here?*

Kitten, you'll let me worry about that. You sit tight.

Shay scooted over to the side of the bed and picked up the water bottle. Her throat was dry and she felt like whatever they'd given her had dehydrated her to the core. She downed the water, all of it and could have chugged two more bottles without a problem. The door eased open and she watched as Duncan glanced both ways in the hall before he entered and closed the door. In the dim light, his eyes glowed. Too late to lie back down and she sat, perched on the edge of bed.

"Shay," he whispered. "I've come to get you out of here."

"Why?" she asked, unwilling to trust him. He was a Necrodemas and she wasn't a fool.

"My father is disturbed. But he's also powerful. I'm not into rocking his boat, but I'm not down for this type of criminal crap he's got going on. He's basically sold his soul to that gypsy dude and I don't plan on going over to the dark side anytime soon."

She rose and teetered; the effects of the injection hadn't worn off completely. Duncan shot across the room and steadied her. He held her up by her elbows. Nothing creepy, but merely lending a hand. Okay, she was willing to hear him out. "Just how the heck are we getting out of here?"

"They've gone to bed. We could leave by the front door and they won't know you're gone until tomorrow."

"Stroll through the front door? Without a hitch?" she asked, unable to fathom her escape would be that easy.

"Not literally. We'll go down the back stairs into the basement. It's connected to the garage. This place isn't a fortress. Nothing like the Den with all those guards. But Pestrolii came through. It was a no-brainer in getting in and getting out using glamours. The only thing that idiot Fae was good for."

She drew her brows together. "But I need to get your father to admit to what he's done…"

"Why? Is that what you were planning on doing? Coming here and getting him to confess? You would have walked into a trap. He was there at the Den, has been for nights. This has all been carefully staged in getting you back. For months. Since they couldn't find you, he orchestrated this plot to get you to come out of hiding. Dad and that gypsy put this all into action to capture you and your mate, not to mention what he plans on doing with your children." Duncan glanced down to her belly, then up again at her face.

She exhaled. "I have a vial and a spell."

He squeezed her elbows and she flinched, but he quickly lessened the pressure. "Do you want to risk getting found out by Gustov? Do you realize what he'll do to you or your children? Better come with me while we still have time." He tugged her toward the door but stopped. "Not a peep. Just do as I say. You good with that?"

"Okay. I guess you're right," she muttered.

He let go of her arms and smiled. "Let's get you out of here and back to the Den. Sound like a plan?"

Well, considering she had no weapons and basically limited options, she decided she'd better get free of here and then Drake wouldn't be forced into a trap thanks to her.

"Lead the way," she replied, following in his footsteps.

Just as Duncan promised, the halls were free of anyone and as they walked down the backstairs, she couldn't make out any sounds other than the chiming of a clock on the ground floor. Five o'clock in the morning. It would be light soon and she felt edgy from being drugged and kidnapped. Down in the basement, Duncan walked ahead of her, punching the security code into a keypad at the doorway.

They entered the garage and there was the Hummer along with six other cars. He walked over to a two-seater which she thought was odd. "Isn't the Hummer safer, in case you have to outrun anyone?"

"I'm not driving," he said. "You are."

She tilted her head. "Me. Drive?"

"Makes sense in case someone follows us. I can deal with them. Unless you're willing to fire a gun."

"What kind of bullets?" she asked.

"The kind that gypsies don't do well with. Wood and mineral. Just one shot to the idiot gypsy's head and he'll be long gone." He smirked and she felt the creeping of her skin. Assuredly, this guy was pure creeper material.

She weighed the equation and in her condition, trying to turn and fire out the window of a sports car had stupid painted all over it. "Keys?"

"That's my girl," he said and held out the key fob.

That phrase coming from a Necrodemas sounded gross. Even if Duncan was helping her, she wasn't *his girl*. "Don't say that," she replied. "I appreciate you helping me, but you also injected me with a drug and that wasn't cool."

"We can assess blame and choices all night." Duncan held her gaze and instead of appearing sorry, he raised an eyebrow. "You do realize, yeah we both had choices. I could have refused, but then I'd be watched and you'd still be drugged. I made the best choice. But if you want to find fault, really, you were the one that exited the Den—that was your choice. Don't blame me for that mistake."

Guess he didn't like being called on the carpet. Note to self, get the hell out of here and away from these nutcases. Just agree with him. *Stop arguing, Shay!*

"We can agree to disagree," she said and grabbed the key. She didn't wait for him to get her door and as rapidly as she could, she climbed inside and started the car. So far, so good. The garage doors opened and the engine purred, but when she stepped on the gas and put it into the gear, she gripped the steering wheel as they jerked forward.

"Take it easy. This car handles better with a caress, not a kick. Suave, Shay." Duncan winked at her and she bit her lip, wondering if she'd made the right choice in getting into this car with him. Too late now, she eased out of the garage, and down the driveway, following Duncan's directions. Instead of getting on the Interstate, he directed her to a back road that snaked around the perimeter of Denver. Maybe he didn't trust her with his car after she'd given it too much gas.

Oh well, so what. Up ahead was Coleman Drive, a main road and the one that went directly back to the Den. "Keep going," he said and held onto the wheel, preventing her from turning.

• • •

Drake met Shawn and Quinn at the door to the suite. "I just spoke with Shay," he said. "Dimitri and Pestrolii have her."

"What the fuck happened?" Shawn snapped.

"Dimitri was having dinner here last night?" Drake retorted. "Is that true?"

"I have no idea how he got into the restaurant. Everyone is scanned who comes through that gate." Shawn was inches away from him.

"You two need to cool down," Quinn said and got in between them.

"I hear you." Drake raised his hands. Without a clear-cut direction, he couldn't summon the Jinni to a task. The genie had to have complete instructions; there was no grey when it came to a genie with a saber.

"Unless they're shielded," Shawn said. "Remember the building to the Den is warded, not the grounds. From what the valet said, it sounds like they had the gypsy cover their tracks."

"I don't understand why Shay left," he said. Jesus, he felt her essence move through him…like she was in the same room. Or nearby.

Sherry walked into the suite. "I'm a jackass," she announced. "I gave Shay the address to a *botánica* shop and the owner relayed she bought truth serum."

"How do you know the owner is telling the truth?" Drake demanded.

"She's from the Sisterhood Council and I had to get clearance to require that she divulge a confidence. It's pretty serious and spell casters take an oath, but this is more than grave."

"Where's Dimitri's house? I'll take my guards and go over there. We can get there faster by air and we'll let you know."

"Here." Quinn held out a piece of paper with the address.

*Babe…err. Help!* Shay's voice filled his mind.

Drake took the note. "Give me a second," he said to Quinn, turning on his heel. He strode over to the large windows overlooking the grounds and directed his entire focus to his mate.

Talk to me, Shay.

*I'm so sorry. I didn't listen. Again. I'm in a car. A silver 911 Porsche on North 104th Avenue. We just passed Brighton. He said he was bringing me back to the Den.*

He curled his fingers into fists. *Who Shay? Who has got you?*

*Duncan Necrodemas—Dimitri's son.*

Drake gripped the windowsill, delving into that mind-blistering feeling that tore through him when she was nearby.

Okay. Stay calm. I'm coming with help.

Shawn came up next to him and Drake exhaled sharply. "I gotta go. Now! Shay's been moved. She's in a car traveling away from Denver—not with Necrodemas senior. His fucking kid. I'm taking my guards and we'll find her. But be prepared, when I do I'll tear apart that cocksucker from limb to limb."

"I'll join you," Shawn said.

He stopped mid-stride. "You can't. Not as a council member. It'd be better if you and Quinn dealt with the authorities. Get them involved in arresting Necrodemas and whoever is involved in this shit and contain that gypsy Fae. Let me deal with the fucker who's got Shay."

"We'll go over to Necrodemas's and find out what the hell happened." Shawn clapped Drake's back. "Sorry for almost losing it back there."

"We're all in shock. I'll let you know as soon as I have Shay."

# CHAPTER 23

"Wait. Why'd you do that? Now, we've gone too far. That's the road that will take us back to the Den," she snarled, glancing over to Duncan.

"Shay, you made another shitty choice. You put your trust in the wrong man. Again." Duncan whispery voice coupled with his sinister snicker made her bite her lip.

*Need a solution and now!*

This section of 104th Avenue was on the periphery of the industrial section of Denver that had long ago been deserted. Factories and warehouses stood empty. The road widened, littered by debris…old newspapers, broken bottles, and rusted out cars lined the street. She let off the gas, and glanced from one side of the road to the other, seeking to find a place to do a U-turn. This was the section of town that no one crossed into during the day, even if it were early morning, and it still wasn't anywhere she wanted to be with or without Duncan. The sun was just starting to rise, evidenced by the silvery rays fanning upward at the horizon.

"Where are we headed?" she asked as snowflakes dusted the roadway and the glass.

From a dusting, more and more snow descended, falling in earnest but instead of blowing free, the flakes melted and clumped, so she turned on the windshield wipers.

"I've got a little hideaway, not far." Duncan displayed the handgun he had hidden. "Now, shut the fuck up and drive. I'm taking you to a special place where we can be alone. I'm going to enjoy getting to know you a whole lot better. Shit, I can't believe my father still wanted to marry you. You sure had him whipped. Here's a memo: I'm nothing like my old man."

Duncan dropped his other hand on her leg, digging his thumb and forefinger into her knee before he slowly stroked down her thigh as though he'd enjoy stringing out her torture.

Not on Duncan's best day. She elbowed him in his throat, then rapidly swung her arm again going for the bridge of nose. She would have jammed her elbow a third time, but he reached out, re-grabbing the wheel. *Son of a bitch!*

Shay didn't think twice as she slammed on the brakes and Duncan careened into the dashboard. The car started to slide on the icy roadway, fishtailed, and she fought to hold steady the wheel, letting off the brakes. It was too late. They headed for the sidewalk, then ate the curb, and sped forward, directly in line with the telephone pole.

The whole world dimmed as though she were watching a movie of her life that played in slow motion. She stared ahead, powerless to change the course of the car and when the hood hit the pole, she jerked from the airbag deploying. First she went forward, then she was hurled back into the seat. Oh my God. The seatbelt tightened way too much across her belly. *Scarlett and Hunter! My babies!*

The impact wasn't the worse, even with the cracking and falling of the pole onto the hood of the car. It was the explosive tightening of the seatbelt as it bit into her body that made her rear back in pain and cry out in agony.

Please, she moaned, trying to peel off the belt from her belly. *My babies.*

•••

Drake stormed outside followed by the phoenix guards. Each step across the blacktop echoed his rage. *Thunk. Thunk. Thunk.* His motorcycle booted feet thudded then stopped. Lifting his arms to the skies, he shifted into his dragon form. The ground shook and he bellowed, uncaring who or what saw him relay how fucked up this situation had turned. Curling flames leapt from his mouth with each breath he exhaled. Pure misery. More and more his blood flooded ripe in need of revenge—this fuckery tasted categorically bitter. From a mixture of frustration, anger, and anxiety that Shay his pregnant mate was kidnapped, he vowed he'd extract vengeance.

He took to the sky, rocketing upward for a count of ten before he arced, changing his trajectory toward the ground. A little velocity trick he'd learned by using gravity to improve his propulsion, racing toward 104th Avenue like a falling bullet. It didn't take long to locate the car in which Shay traveled.

*Fuck. No!* The Porsche abutted a downed telephone pole that lay cracked over the front of the car. He swooped to where the 911 had crashed and tore off the passenger door, pushing aside the fully inflated airbag splattered with blood. His heart pounded, but it was confusion that blanketed him when he encountered the bloody face of a man. Not his mate.

Drake grabbed the man, lancing him with his talons as the dude clutched his head, peering up at him with a look of horror spreading over his face as Drake roared, "Where is she?"

The man gaped at him, his lips working. He made no sound with a broken nose and crushed windpipe, but that wasn't was his problem.

He focused his energy on Shay. He could smell her scent. His heart thudded and for a millisecond Drake thought he'd gotten his signals crossed. He heard Shay moan and flashed his gaze to the driver's side where the ballooning bag hid the driver. In the light, he caught sight of dark fiery copper curls—familiar as his own hand. Bending down, he fingered the strands of copper hair that tormented his dreams. He pushed back the air bag.

*Holy shit.* "Baby," he groaned, skimming his knuckle along her cheek. Uncurling his girth from the passenger side, he roared for his guards who'd lifted the telephone pole off the hood of the car.

"She's on the driver's side," he thundered to his crew, glancing down at the fucker in the passenger seat.

Drake sliced his talons across that son of a bitch's jugular vein on his way to leaping over the roof of the car. He came down on the driver's side and tore off the door, hurling it away from him. The phoenixes landed next to him and he glared at them, snarling, "We need emergency rescue, and deal with that fucker for what's he's done to her."

They stared back, then Noah shifted into human form and raced around to the passenger side. "That jackass should have a cell phone. Don't worry, I'll take care of him and we'll get answers."

Drake shifted back into human form and unbuckled Shay's shoulder harness and whispered, "Kitten, can you hear me?"

Filigreed snowflakes floated in the air on his breath, and landed on his baby's face. Shay's eyes fluttered and she smiled weakly. The sight of her ashen lips curved was a caress across his ravaged senses and he was desperate for better signs that she wasn't badly injured.

"Yes," Shay whispered and winced, her skin blanched. "You came."

"I always will. You're part of my mind, heart, soul," he rumbled.

"Be careful of her neck and spine," Evan said thoughtfully.

His body tightened, and he wanted to howl in fear. Carefully, he slipped his hands under Shay's body.

"Babe," she murmured.

He lifted her from the car, his whole body growing cold and he fought the feeling. *No!* "Hold out your wings. One of you!" he barked at the phoenixes. With the utmost care, he laid her in Grant's embrace.

They needed more than a paramedic team who might not even show since this was a shifter accident. Drake rubbed his hand over the cuff and centered his thoughts. *Jinni. I need you now!*

He stared at his hands covered in blood. The scent was familiar and he grounded himself from all thoughts save one. Shay's life force must be maintained. "Give her to me," he said. "Fly back and find Sherry at the Den. Tell her we'll need a shifter doctor."

"Specializing in obstetrics," Evan commented as he glanced down at the street. "Drake, her water just broke."

"Drake." Shay reached up and lightly touched his face. "Please, our babies are coming."

"Shay, I swear on everything we both hold dear, that I'll keep you safe. Stay with me or I'll tear up this world and the outer realms to prove I mean it."

The Hood Jinni appeared next to him, bowing. When he rose, the genie asked, "How may I serve you, Lord Herensuge?"

Drake lifted his eyes. "Save her!" he commanded the Jinni. "Do whatever it takes."

"That is something I cannot do."

"I demand it of you!" Drake roared so loud the branches of the trees swayed as if a strong wind had blown through.

"You know it's impossible to alter lifelines in this realm. That is not of my power," the genie replied softly.

Fuck! It was true. If the Jinni could, surely he would have saved his mother. "What can you do? I won't accept that history is about to repeat itself."

"That isn't something I can determine. But there is something I can offer: modern medicine. If you agree, I'll deliver you both to the Greenleaf Clinic, experts in high risk deliveries. And clothe you so you aren't arrested."

He hadn't noticed those minor things, and probably would have barged into the hospital stark naked, breathing fire, and cursing…but he also would have gone down on his knees and begged, offered his life to save Shay's. Whatever it took, he'd agree to as long as she was saved. "Yes right away. Convey us to Greenleaf and get Shay admitted and treated. Please, do that. Now, Jinni."

"As you wish, so shall it be." The Jinni bowed.

# CHAPTER 24

Flames and shouting more like the roaring of a thousand angry men—or a terribly pissed off dragon filled her mind. The ground shook. She tried to escape but she was pinned in place. She pushed against a white sheet but it bounced back…it was soft like a balloon. Each time she slapped at it, her hand pressed forward and was swallowed within the confines of sheeting. But she couldn't keep her arm raised. The pain was too great. The balloon pressed against her face, no matter how she turned her head. With steely concentration, Shay lifted her left hand and pushed the balloon off her face, but when she suddenly coughed, her insides twisted. Jagged bolts of pain shot through her.

Her babies!

Scarlett and Hunter. Her mind raced. Oh my God! *I've been in accident.* Drake held her in his arms and then there was glaring light that made thinking next to impossible. *C'mon, someone turn out the light!* She kept asking or maybe it was only a thought that floated in her mind.

More pain lanced her body, razor sharp to the point of forcing cries of agony from her. She tried to link her mind to Drake's and beseech him to help Scarlett and Hunter, but the words remained glued on her tongue.

Green flaming swirls caught her, carried her. She blinked, staring up into Drake's distressed face. She'd never seen his eyes sorrowful and she wanted to reach up and brush away his sadness.

He kissed her and let go, infusing her with his fiery magick that wrapped around her, easing the pain from her being. "Whatever it takes, find her the best care!" His voice sounded like a sonic boom that echoed inside her brain.

She shivered as she was lifted away from him. Snow was falling in single flakes, then falling faster and heavier. She focused on the stranger who stood over her, a man covered in tattoos. He pressed his hand on her, wound a band of metal around her wrist. "Sleep," he whispered.

Sleep…that sounded good.

Then she floated into a void where no pain existed. Nothing existed. Afraid, she gasped, flashing open her eyes and meeting Drake's mesmerizing gaze.

"Baby, I've got you," he repeated over and over. He was with her.

She and Scarlett and Hunter were blanketed with Drake's dragon essence and she closed her eyes, reveling in his eternal magick. Her children were being taken from her and she cried out. Over and over, until her voice was hoarse, but she was too tired to fight the pain.

• • •

*Shay woke to the sound of beeping. Soft but constant. Something beep-beep-beeped. More glaring light surrounded her, so bright she shut her lids until a large palm—Drake's hand—curled around her arm. "Kitten," he said, tracing a slow circle with his finger on her skin.*

*"Where am I?" she whispered, her mouth too dry to even swallow. Her throat felt raw and she was so, so thirsty. She tried to lift her hand but her arm got snagged and she growled in frustration. She expected to hear him explain but he stopped touching her…he was gone.*

*She tried once more with greater force, using her other hand to untangle the vines holding her prisoner. She'd run a long way in her leopardess form to get to Drake. Maybe that's why she was so thirsty. She'd been hurled against a wall and had to reach the top to find her way out of a gully, toward the bright light. Surely, he'd be there waiting for her but she was so tired.*

"Sleep," a voice commanded and she shut her eyes. She wasn't alone anymore.

*Beep. Beep. Beep.*

"I'll be right here," Drake said in a voice that sounded as though he were far, faraway.

•••

Light streamed in from three large windows off to the side. At first when Shay woke, she clawed the sheets and tried to lift her head but was overcome by a cloud of dizziness. Nothing was about to happen fast in her condition as she struggled to sit up, clutching the bedrail. Curling forward, she fought the sorrow that lanced through her, bone deep. She brought both of her hands to her belly and cried out, terror gripping her to the core where her children no longer lay protected within her body. She hugged her arms to her middle, anguish filling her. Tears streamed down her cheeks and she rocked, wanting so much to have her children back. God! The images of the car crashing and fire wasn't some horrible nightmare. She was alone. So so so alone. Had she lost her children and Drake? Her world teetered, ready to come crashing down around her. She needed answers. Where on earth was this place?

The curtain slid open. "What are you doing?" Drake took a step inside the space and then rushed forward, a deep frown marring his handsome face. He stopped at the side of the bed, and she tried to inhale as if in preparation for what he was going to say. Up close, his face had shadows, darker under his unsmiling eyes, and his lips where stretched tight and pale. She gasped, pressing a hand to her chest as she slumped against the bed rail.

"Careful," Drake commanded, holding onto her by her shoulders and helping her back onto the pillows as he stared at her, eyes hard.

"What happened to our children?" she asked, searching his face as they both regarded each other in a heavy, drowning silence.

"You were in a car crash yesterday…what do you remember?"

"Don't hold back from me. Tell me. What happened?"

"You're in a hospital and you've been unconscious since yesterday. I've been waiting for you for to wake up…how do you feel?"

"Like I was hit by a train." She flashed her gaze over his shoulder at the pale yellow wall and the red numbers flashing non-stop on the machines. "Our children? Please, Drake—"

He caught her hands and lifted them to his mouth. Drake kissed her palms and her eyes widened as she watched him, reeling in pain and misery.

He lifted his head, meeting her stare and nodded. "Our babies are fine. Fighters, both of them. And as beautiful as you," he murmured.

"They're fine?"

"Fine and as equally stubborn as their mother."

"I—"

He cut her off and his features went steely. "You promised you wouldn't put yourself in danger and I believed you. You said we were a team. You endangered your *life* and the *lives of our children*!"

She swallowed, unable to find the words as her throat constricted. "I heard you talking about some covert mission you were on and I wanted to do something too. You were very much a team of one. Are you going to tell me I was wrong?"

"Wrong?" he echoed. "You can't imagine how wrong you got that one."

"What do you mean? Drake, I mind linked. I heard you talking to some man."

"*Covert* mission. I wasn't doing anything dangerous, unless looking for a salamander in a creek with a bunch of guys is edgy stuff. Not very exciting, but Christ, Shay, what you got involved in is mind-bending and has me seeing red. Your safety isn't a game and isn't open to interpretation. And if you don't respect me enough to be on a team with me, then just say so. Tell me you want to be alone, but don't go behind my back."

"I made a horrible mistake," she said. "But a mistake."

"A mistake of immense proportions. I would never do that to you."

"Are you saying you can't forgive me?"

"That's what makes this so hard. I can. I'm in love with you. But this goes to the heart of us staying together. Baby, have I ever lied to you?" Drake spoke in a low, low voice and she understood this was more than words and talk about love—this was being fully committed as mates and she'd hurt him deeply.

"No-o," she replied in shaky voice, so frightened he was going to level her entire world. Her heart boomed, ready to claw its way out of her chest.

"When *you* asked that I stand down, I did. I didn't let my pride get in the way of what was important to you. Did I?"

Anything she might have said evaporated. What he said was true. He didn't go out and seek revenge against the Dark Fae, which as a dragon must have required a helluva lot of self-control—for her, he'd kept his cool. She assumed he was out with his crew and family, doing something kickass and exciting when she should have waited for him to return. Talk about being the idiot of the century. "No. You're a straight shooter."

"Do you or do you not want to be my mate? I made a deal with myself to ask you without pressuring you into a reply. You don't need to answer me now, but I do expect an answer in the near future. I won't coerce you. No storming or yelling, and I won't take the kids. But I will go—"

"No!" Her heart hammered wildly beneath her ribcage. "Please don't. Drake, I was epically foolish and should have told you long before now. I love you."

He fused his gaze with hers. "Don't say those words because you feel obligated—"

Again, she cut him off. "I love you! I've loved you since the moment I bared myself on the terrace of the villa. Maybe before that. But you were so sure of yourself and you pissed me off. Yeah, I've got to work on my pride, but I do love you."

"Me? Piss you off? Damn woman, you totally own that one." Suddenly the sound of crying filled the air.

"Our babies. Where? " she blurted out.

"Right here." He stepped aside, tugging the curtain back, and she immediately focused on the two Plexiglas bassinets next to the bed.

"Please, let me see them." She gripped the bedrail, reading the cards on the front of each bassinet. "O'Connor Girl Baby and O'Connor Boy Baby."

*Scarlett and Hunter.*

Are those their names? Drake asked, mind linking with her.

*Oh my*, she gulped. "No. Not really. Not if you have another choice."

Lifting up their daughter, he came over to her, and lowered their sweet baby girl into her arms. "Paloma was my mom's name. I was wondering—"

She gazed down at their baby. Tiny little fingers and the sweetest little bow mouth. Her lashes were long and dark like Drake's and her skin was tinged golden like hers. She lifted her eyes to his, her heart thudding. "Oh yes. Yes, Paloma is perfect. I adore the name."

"And for our son?" he asked, caressing the tip of his finger along Paloma's cheek before he kissed the top of Shay's head. "Hunter is an excellent choice. Considering our family."

"Then it's settled. Paloma and Hunter."

"Paloma Scarlett and Hunter?" Drake looked at her and smiled his heart-melting grin. He arranged their son's blanket and picked him up, holding him snug in two burly arms. What a sight! Drake was already a pro at picking up their children.

"Hunter Drake O'Connor. You know you want to," she replied, smiling up at him.

He laughed, giving her a view of her son's face. A replica of Drake's. Both of them had a sleeping baby as he whispered, "I'm not going to deny it. I'm possessive and proud and I love you."

• • •

"Just sign here," the nurse said, handing Shay a clipboard with the doctor's discharge orders. The nurse cooed over the twins. "Your babies are so cute. And such good sleepers for being just a week old."

"Thanks for everything,,." Shay replied after signing the forms, and handing the copies to Drake.

When the nurse left them alone, Drake pulled her into his arms. "All set," he said. "Don't look so nervous. The pediatrician said the kids are fine."

"Oh, I'm not nervous about going home. This is the first time I've summoned a genie before."

"And he'll assist you through this. That's his job," he assured her.

"If you say so." Shay nodded and rubbed the solid gold cuff encircling her wrist. "Mr. Jinni, can you hear me?"

He held back from chuckling. "That was good. But he goes by just Jinni. No mister."

The lamplights flickered and the Jinni appeared inside the hospital room and bowed before Shay. The genie rose and lifted his mate's hand and kissed her knuckles. "Such a precious beauty. The pleasure to serve you is mine, Lady Herensuge. How may I be of assistance?"

"Laying it on thick?" Drake snorted.

"I try," the Jinni returned, and smiled broadly down at Shay. "Feeling better, my Lady?"

"Much. Thank you for your help." She lifted up onto her toes and pressed a kiss to the genie's cheek.

"You're making the old scallywag blush under his copper burnished hide," Drake said. Damn him, but the genie's face actually turned brighter red.

Shay flashed a warning to him, then smiled at the genie. "I know this is short notice, but by any chance do you do marriage ceremonies?"

"One of my specialties. Are we talking colossal or cozy?"

"Talking in the moment. As in right now?" Shay gazed at him, making his heart hammer against his ribs. "Marry me?" she asked in the softest voice that rippled through him.

He nodded, his mouth having gone dry, and his brain short-circuited. "Uh…"

"Well?" the Jinni arched a brow. "Obviously, my Lady just got one over on Lord Herensuge, and he needs a moment."

The genie's pointed commentary got him back on track and he nodded, throwing his arm possessively over Shay's shoulders. "We've got a roomful of witnesses. Let's do it."

"Here," the Jinni said, and snapped his fingers. "Sign the license, then take your places over there. The light is better. Noah, get your crew ready to take some pictures. Come on. I can't do everything."

While everyone in the small room moved toward the window, Drake captured her hands. "We can wait and you can have a fairy tale wedding. Grand enough for the front page of the Denver news."

"Nope. I'm not into fairy tales, just the happy endings."

He laughed, piloting her toward the window, and he nodded to the genie. "Please begin."

After reciting the traditional wedding vows, the Hood Jinni announced, "You may now kiss the bride."

Drake turned to Shay, hauling her closer within his arms, and kissed her deeply. Lifting his head, he uttered one word, "Wife."

"Husband," she returned. "May we please go home?"

"Ask away. The Jinni is waiting."

Shay turned and faced the genie. "Jinni, we'd like to go home now."

Drake cleared his throat, reminding her to be specific.

"Oh. The condo on 14th Street," she said, smiling widely.

Drake held out Hunter to Noah, and he picked up his little princess. Evan had two baby bags strapped across his shoulders and Grant stood there shrugging. "What can I get?"

"Keep your eyes open," Drake replied, lowering his voice.

Shay looked up at him and he felt the tender touch of her telepathic linking. *Is there a reason?*

We'll talk when we get home.

He nodded and with their daughter in his arm, he curled the other around Shay's shoulders.

The genie looked to Shay. "Ready, Lady Herensuge?"

"Very much."

He held onto his wife and daughter and glanced over at Noah, who was making funny faces at his son. In the next instant they were all standing in the middle of the spacious living room overlooking the river.

"Oh Drake," Shay commented. "This place is gorgeous."

"Provisional, pending your vote of approval."

"I vote yes." She held up her hand for a high five. "Where's the Jinni?"

"The Jinni delivers on his promise then that's that…unless you need him."

"But I didn't get to thank him," she said. "He'll think me terribly rude."

"The guys will let him know," he replied. "Won't you all?"

"Absolutely," Evan said. "Where should I put these?"

"Down that hall. Last door." Drake pointed in the direction of the master suite then he turned his attention on Shay. "We'll need to get furniture. So far there's this stuff which is from the staging company and the Jinni helped with the bedroom furniture, but the rest of the place needs your touch. If you want to we can hire a designer."

"Okay," Noah interrupted, coming up to them with their crying son. "This little man has got lots to say."

Shay sat down on the sofa, and held out her arms. "Please, I'll take Hunter."

His focus latched onto his wife and her fingers at the buttons of her top. She was about to nurse their son. Not a sight he was willing to share with anybody. "You guys, I'm going to ask you to take your leave. Thanks for all, but it's scram time."

"Later," Grant said, fist bumping him, and touching Shay on the shoulder. "Mrs. O and kids, glad to see you in your new digs. Call when you're ready for visitors."

"Stay cool," Evan said, leaning down and hugging Shay. "I'll bring Fiona. She loves kids."

Noah held open his arms to Drake. "Bro," he said. "Glad you found Shay and had the sense to not let her get away."

"Thanks for everything," Shay said, reaching up to Noah for a hug as well.

Drake walked them out to the terrace overlooking the city. "Funds are deposited in your accounts. Go enjoy. I'll be in touch when the next job comes up."

"You still in the game?" Noah asked, clearly surprised.

"After that fucker Pestrolii escaped…I'm not about to sit around and wait for the SOB to reappear. When I call you guys, be ready to saddle up. We'll track his ass."

"Sound the alarm and we'll be back."

He mock saluted them and waved, watching them shift and take to the clear skies in a V-formation. As he turned around, he paused, galvanized from taking in the sight of Shay holding their son up to her breast while Paloma lay sleeping on her legs. The sight solidified his vow, he'd find that Fae for them. With a deep breath, he banished all thoughts on retribution from his mind, and walked back inside, shutting the doors against the cool wind. "How are you feeling?"

"Time for some water." She smiled sweetly up at him, cradling their children.

"I'll get you a glass," he murmured, striding past her but stopped, planting a kiss on her neck. He reached over her and stroked his fingers down her arm, sucking in a groan at seeing her erect nipple, pink and glistening from nursing. Clenching his jaw, he reminded himself to get a flippin' grip. *Shay is a mother now, not at my beck and call as my sex kitten.*

"See something you like?" she asked, holding onto his hand. "And I am too your *sex kitten*."

"Sorry," he said sheepishly, meeting her gaze, and swallowed. "You're even more beautiful now."

"I'll feed Paloma, and then we can lie down for a *nap*."

"Baby, I don't want to act like a possessive dick," he ventured. Damn, if he straightened, she'd notice the hard-on in his pants.

"I have needs, too. It's been a week since I gave birth. Don't you want me?"

"Hell yeah, but it's too soon—"

"It's not too soon for my mouth," she whispered. "Now kiss me and prove to me you're still under my spell."

"Kitten, I'll always be under your volition."

• • •

Nothing compared with being a mother—except being the wife and lover to one over the top dragon. A dragon who had refused to do more than kiss her, groaning and hard, but he stopped. Didn't take their lust a step further. Her silly husband. What was going through his hard head?

Easy telepathically to find out.

*Shay is a mother now, not at my beck and call as my sex kitten.*

So that's what Drake thought over and over or some variation. She almost laughed, except gosh darn it—it had been a week. Besides a few bruises and scrapes which were mostly gone and giving birth—not a miracle considering how many babies were born every single second of every single day—she was on her *drapardess…leogon…*leopardess-dragon game. She wasn't exactly a leopardess and wasn't precisely a dragon. A mix of the two. Drake's dragon magick infused her and slightly altered her DNA, allowing her to carry their twins. Would she remain in this altered state? None of the doctors at the hospital knew for certain. The shifter specialists called in had never heard of such a thing as a dragon mating with a leopardess. Oh well. *First time for everything.*

Speaking of which…time to take other matters into her own hands and with his fingers on her arm, she did. Hunter stopped nursing and instead of covering up her bare breast, she gave Drake an eyeful. He nuzzled her neck, his breath hot on her skin, and then he stopped. "See something you like?" she whispered. No brainer. One bare boob and she got her husband's full attention. Better get this ball rolling or Mr. O'Connor would put her on a pedestal. A very lonely and sexless pedestal. Not gonna happen.

Even when she told him she most definitely was his *sex kitten,* she got the vibe something was running amok. "Okay, mind telling me what's got you going? And don't try and pull the wool over my eyes, cowboy."

"Hey, I only want to keep you safe," he said.

"Babe, I appreciate that," she replied, handing him Hunter. She undid the other side to her nursing bra, and lifted Paloma to her breast. Oh sweet relief to feel her milk let down. Thankfully, her daughter was a little tyrant when it came to nursing. Shay crossed her legs, and snuggled her daughter close to her chest. "But seriously, I'm not about to shatter. Unless it's from frustration. C'mere."

She patted the cushion next to her, tracking Drake with her gaze as he walked around the sofa. God knew how she adored him. Her husband and father to her children. But dammit, his head was as hard as a flipping rock. "Baby, I don't want to hurt you. Not after all you've been through," he said, worry creasing his brow.

"You couldn't if you wanted to," she began.

"Shay, I'm just a little on edge after the accident and everything."

"I guess the time has come to talk about it. I'm so sorry for everything that happened. I didn't want anyone to die."

"That wasn't your fault. A bunch of greedy people who got together. They got what they deserved."

"Not Morgan. She was spoiled, but she didn't deserve to be killed by her own brother. Or Dimitri. I can't believe Duncan killed his family and all the guards and house staff."

"But not Pestrolii," he said.

"Not Pestrolii," she echoed. "I've been thinking on him. We might not need to worry about him, am I right?"

"He wasn't there. He escaped and he's around. Maybe biding his time."

"You sure he wasn't killed? Duncan said he had mineral bullets. If he shot him, his physical form would have dissolved into thin air as a gypsy Fae."

"How do you know that jackwad son of Necrodemas had mineral bullets?"

"He told me," she answered. "Yeah, I know. I was too trusting, but why would he lie? He was bragging about it. If there were a set of motorcycle leathers lying around and a black leather jacket, it might mean that gypsy was sent back to the Dark Court."

"I'll get ahold of the accident report. I don't know if the authorities will let me waltz into the house now that it's cordoned off as a crime scene."

"Oh if I know you, you'll work your magick at getting past a little yellow tape."

He laughed, taking hold of her hand, and squeezing her fingers.

A knock on the door and their gazes snapped together. "Who could that be?" she asked.

"Your brother has been on me about when you and the kids were coming home. Hey, a lot of people are lined up, waiting to come over." He rose as she adjusted her bra and re-buttoned her shirt. When the door opened and her brother accompanied by her father and mother walked inside she stared, dumbfounded.

"Welcome home and surprise, Sis," Shawn said. "I brought a welcome home, house warming gift."

"You two are a sight for sore eyes." She glanced from Mom to Dad. Smiling, they strode toward her, holding several wrapped packages.

"Welcome back, honey," Dad said.

"And ditto to you. Dad, my God, I can't believe it." Shay scooted off the edge of the sofa and stood up with Paloma. "You're better?"

"All better," her mom replied, setting down the baby gifts. "It was like a veil lifted for both of us."

Shawn accompanied their folks and stood by the edge of the sofa. "Sherry explained that it sounded as if black magick was in play. A good chance whatever spell had been placed on Mom and Dad had gotten broken."

"But how?" she asked, hugging Paloma to her.

Her father responded, "Based on what was found in Necrodemas' house, it was him. When he died, as keeper of the spell, the effects were reversed. It's the only explanation any of the shifter and preternatural doctors agree upon. And heck. We're just happy to be well again."

Until today Drake had never told her all the details of the deaths and she'd not asked. And what the crap did Dimitri have in his home that made her brother blanch in just speaking about it.

"And you're sure this isn't going flip-flop back?" She glanced between her parents.

"Shannon, we don't know. This has been an awful experience this last year. We're thankful things worked out for you. A husband and two healthy children," Richard said. "Can you forgive us that we put you in a position of being a political pawn?"

"Dad, it wasn't you. It was that spell Dimitri had placed on you and Mom. It's over."

"We're so fortunate you were strong enough to follow your heart," Mom said.

"My destiny." She reached out to Drake, capturing his hand. "It led me right to this one and I'm not letting go anytime soon."

Another knock sounded at the door. "Ah, that's gotta be Mrs. Wells. If you'd like some help while you're settling in, she'd love to be of service," Dad said.

"I might take you up on that…for a day or so." She watched as her father walked across the living room, with the same bounce in his step that he'd had ever since she could remember—aside from the last week when he'd basically been catatonic. Shay turned to her mother. "How is Dad?"

"Much, much better. I promise, whatever we both had is gone. Like some horrible flu, and I hope it never returns." Mom smiled, holding out her hand for Paloma. Shay watched her daughter curl her tiny fingers around Mom's index finger and chuckled.

"Would you like to hold Paloma?" Shay asked.

"I thought you'd never ask." Her mother nodded and squeezed her arm. "I'm so excited to meet my grandchildren. Both your father and I have been since you gave birth. You were so lucky to get into the best hospital in the country."

"We had some help."

"Looks like that husband of yours is a pretty helpful guy," Mom said, her eyes shining bright.

"Roger that. He's amazing." Shay caught Drake's amused stare. Smiling, she whispered to their daughter, "Paloma, meet your grandmother. Mom, here's your first granddaughter."

Shawn stood by and grinned down at them. "How about a photograph?"

Drake came up beside her brother, and she bet he was asking about the accident report as her handsome husband tilted his head and spoke in a low voice. Her brother's eyes glowed, something that happened when his emotional state fired up. He shook his head, and Drake met her gaze.

Shawn said a whole inventory of the house was completed for an estate sale. He didn't remember seeing black motorcycle leathers or boots on the list, but he'll double check. Bullet hole riddled clothing would have gotten tagged as evidence.

# CHAPTER 25

*Two weeks later.*

There was still no evidence that conclusively supported or denied that the gypsy had bitten the Dark Fae dust. And Drake for one wasn't going to wait around for that motherfucker to materialize and wreak havoc on his world. Shay and he had gone slow and easy in decorating the condo and he didn't think that she'd miss this place terribly. What they needed was a spot where humans didn't overrun a city while simultaneously treating shifters like second-class citizens.

Harmony came to mind.

Shay climbed onto the bed next to him, wearing a silky short nightgown, and he couldn't help but reach out to her, rubbing his palm over the curve of her waist, down her hip until he had one of her firm ass cheeks in his hand. "Woman," he groaned as his cock stiffened.

"Babies are down for the count," she whispered. "And Mrs. Wells is here for the night. She thought it was best after we wrestled with the window treatments in the nursery and finally got the curtains all hung."

"There are such things as handymen," he murmured, bending his head down to capture her pillow-soft lips.

"Big talk," she moaned. "Not many workers are willing to submit to a background check that includes drug and Fae testing. The wallpaper hanger almost quit. Twice. He was sweating bullets as you watched him like a hawk, grumbling under your breath."

He flipped her over onto her back and moved his body over hers. "If a worker is innocent, then he has nothing to worry about. Does he?"

"Oh I beg to differ. No one wants to tangle with a dragon."

"Except you," he murmured. "Crazy girl."

She giggled. "Yeah, I guess I did the seducing in this relationship. Who knew this is where we'd end up?"

"Trust me, I had my suspicions all summer," he whispered, lifting up only to peel off his shirt before he recaptured her body. "You had me going for weeks when you were single and very much on the prowl."

"Only for you, Mr. Navy SEAL," she assured him, running her hands along his arms and wriggling her hips provocatively against him.

"Good answer," he replied, raising her arms above her head.

"What are you thinking, my love?"

"That I need to be inside you. Deep inside."

"Farther than my mind?" she whispered in a husky voice.

"Are you saying that you're ready?" He searched her eyes, feeling his cock turn harder than a steel pipe, and his chest constricted. Once he claimed her, she'd be his through eternity. Bonded souls until the end of time as eternals. He'd promised her three weeks of recuperation after giving birth, and even though she was the one that fought the timeline, he was the one who each night was exquisitely tortured. As he watched her bathe, her skin glowing in the heated bathwater, he'd almost shattered his back molars in wanting to sink his cock fully into her.

"I am—more than ready to take this final step. After all I'll be claiming you as well, Lord Herensuge," she returned, locking her gaze with his.

"Baby, I love you and now you'll find out how much." He used his knee to wedge open her legs until he was snugly between her beautiful thighs. "Ah. Feels so fucking good I might keep you busy for hours…days."

"It might feel better if you weren't wearing any pants," she snorted, tugging on her wrists. "You can't hold me in this position and undress yourself. So Mr. Navy SEAL, which is it going to be?"

Laughing, he kissed the tip of her nose. "Correct, almighty one. We'll both have to bend a little…if we want to achieve satisfaction in the end." He let that permeate her tumultuous little mind.

"I can smell a trap a mile away. Spill!"

Exhaling, he nodded. "What are your thoughts on relocating? And before you go ballistic—"

"Drake O'Connor Herensuge!" she roared. She sucked in her breath, shaking her head as her cheeks turned bright pink. "I just finished the nursery. All fire retardant materials. Do you realize how long that took?"

"One word," he whispered, skimming his mouth along her jaw as she twisted under him. "Harmony."

As if a switch had been flipped, she stopped struggling and relaxed. He picked his head up and their gazes fused. "You're serious," she said.

"Never been more," he assured her. "Without proof that Pestrolii has indeed been dealt with, Denver isn't a safe place. He or one like him could track you or our children, and in this city, who has your back? It's too large and too congested with humans and the borders can't be bonded. Your father and brother have contained the council and the vote to unite with Europe went smoothly."

"Babe, you don't have to tell me twice. Yes. I know Sol will let us crash at my old apartment until we find a place. The nursery is all set up."

"Yeah?"

"A little recounting. My love, I was the one who found Harmony and relocated there first. It's got friends, Cajun cooking, Wi-Fi, and I don't have to ride on a donkey up a mountain. Besides, I like Louisiana and so did you. Now let me go!"

"I'm letting your hands go, Lady Herensuge but only…" He slid his fingers down her arms and didn't stop until he cupped her tits, flicking his thumbs over her nipples, savoring the pert peaks pressing against his fingertips. "Because I've gotta get inside you. Now."

He rose up and away from her; it was excruciating to look down at Shay without touching her. She sat and removed her nightgown, every nuance a sensuous tease to him. Oh holy fuck! His cock jerked to full attention when she displayed her body—her naked, lovely and lush body—to his eyes.

"C'mere. Love when you go commando," she whispered, crooking her finger as he unzipped his pants and nearly tripped trying to walk, jump, and remove his feet from his pant legs.

He was beyond hard, skating the edge of sanity, ready to fully claim Shay as his mate. He stroked his fingers through her damp heat and gritted his teeth, hungry to follow suit with his crown.

"Baby," he groaned, swirling his finger around her clit in an arduous circle and relishing how she bit her lip and rolled her hips, widening her legs. She was as eager for him as he was for her. God, she did it for him.

Between her legs, he dipped his hips, lower until his crown was aligned with her pussy and he couldn't hold back. He drove his rod inside her, squeezing his ass cheeks and arching upward. Hot heaven wrapped around him, and he groaned so forcefully the walls shook as he worked his cock into her. "You feel so good," he growled, bowing forward and clamping his mouth down on her neck. No holding back when she moaned, arching her lovely neck for him, and he bit, piercing her skin and infusing her blood with dragon magick.

Their minds linked and he absorbed what she felt, tightening his hold on her as she was overcome with the feeling of falling through the air but he hauled her closer to him. "You're mine," he said against her ear. "Forever mine."

"Drake, yes!" she pleaded.

He bit her neck again and their minds cinched together entirely. Shay was filled with the rush of warmth—golden glowing fire—and she moaned his name.

"It's time, kitten," he prompted her, tipping up her face and nodding. "Your turn."

She bared her canines. They were sharper and longer than her leopardess teeth and he presented his neck to her. By instinct she'd know exactly what to do.

"This is the final step, baby," he murmured and she bit into him, lancing his skin and the erotic sensation gave way to hurling them through the ethereal. Never had he experienced the starry skies of the universe as he did when she sucked the skin at his neck, filling the void in his existence with her female part feline, part dragon magick, and from this moment forward, he was hers. Bonded as dragon mates, an unbreakable vow until the end of time.

Lifting her mouth, she said, "I love you. I so freaking love you!" She smiled at him, encircling his shoulders with her arms. "You're my mate." She rightly claimed him with all the aplomb of having walked through fire to find him and basically she had on many levels. He pumped his hips against her, their skin slapping together as waves of pleasure washed over him.

Together they wound their bodies around each other and they returned to the ethereal realm, existing in both dragon and human soul forms, pure energy that flickered with riveting ecstasy. Shay delivered into Drake's body her own magick now housed within her as his mate, Lady Herensuge, mistress of dragons in her own right, his lover, holder of his heart.

All at once, he roared his pleasure, releasing the erotically tempered red-black flame across her skin, and together they imploded into one another, their climax exploding like a supernova and reforming all at once. She clung to him as he slammed into her over and over, their bodies flickering between energy and shifter forms until finally they both clung to each other, panting in shuttered breaths, their heartbeats racing, and perspiration covering their skin.

She met his gaze and smiled, tracing her fingers over his face as shockwaves of their release rippled through their bodies. "Our connection is mind-blowing."

"And very much interwoven cogent bonds—locked in place." She'd felt what he felt, every shade and tone of ecstasy—their minds and souls were linked. That was what he'd tried to define for her—but what she now knew was beyond words and ideas.

He adjusted his hips, lifting her slender leg along his body, and didn't even try to hide the smug smile of satisfaction overtaking his lips. "Mine. Finally. All fucking mine."

"Yep. Hope you can handle me, my lord. I have no intention of being struck dumb by that display of astonishing lovemaking, even though it was stupefying." She laughed at the widening of his eyes.

"This calls for an encore…does it? Careful, kitten. It's been three weeks and I'm hungry. Wickedly hungry with only one dish on my menu." The piston motion of his hips sped up with each of her moans. She raked her fingernails down his back as he arched, driving his cock deeper into her. Shay teased his senses. She squeezed his dick with her muscles, milking him and he pumped harder, moving faster stroke by stroke. Reaching down between her legs, he pressed the pad of his thumb to her erect nubbin, toggling her clit, and pummeling her with his cock. He didn't stop until her eyes rolled upward in her beautiful head. "That's it. Let go and come. All over me. Again, baby."

He hoisted her hips, driving himself all the way home. At the point of no return, he roared her name. They both rode a wave into another eternal rush as he nuzzled and bit her neck, nestling his cock deep inside her where he'd found his comfort and his release. He was home in her. Didn't matter where they lived, not to him, as long as he could protect and provide for her and his children.

"I love you. Forever," he whispered against her mouth, relishing the intoxicated sounds she uttered in pleasure after they'd made love. Her whimpers of satisfaction brought him contentment, eased the flaming of his soul. Only with her could he be as fierce and predatory as he was a tender lover.

Only with her. Shay Barclay O'Connor. Lady Herensuge. With one hot kiss on a sultry summer night, his kitten had ensnared him and slain his dragon heart.

# More from This Author
## (From *Collared for a Night* by Susan Arden)

The immense grounds of the Downtown Den lay just beyond the trees. A private club for shifters located in the hip *LoDo* section of Denver just east of the river. The Den catered to all sorts of shifter appetites. From gourmet meals, a jazz club, and then upstairs to the individual rooms reserved for more private, sensual affairs.

Diana arrived at the Den shortly before nine for her appointment. Rolling up to the front of the guard tower, she was surprised at the change since her last visit. During the day, when she'd met with an intake counselor, she'd been ushered into the club by a side entrance and had seen virtually no one other than a few staff moving about the interior, tidying and getting ready for the evening events. The private club was gaining popularity due to its ability to cater to the exclusive, decadent proclivities of members and a few select guests as well as provide services for first timers in need of heat cycle sex. The Den maintained a highly-regarded reputation of anonymity for clients, assisted by a guardhouse stationed on the perimeter, admitting private members and permitted guests on the nightly admit list. The counselor assured Diana that tonight her name would appear on that list. Two guards with holstered weapons stepped up to the driver's window. "Your name?" the one with a buzz cut asked, briefly flashing a pair of amber irises in her direction. "Diana Hambre." She'd opted to use her own name. Either she trusted the Den completely to keep her safe or not.

Hell, she'd better be able to trust the Den, considering she was about to let an alpha male sexually service her out-of-control needs for the evening. The thought sent a shiver rocketing up her spine. A few more hours, and this yearning to grind her hips against something hard would lessen. She prayed it would, twisting the hem of her dress between her fingers.

Neither of the guards cracked a smile tonight, nor had they when she'd visited a day ago. Their clipped tones directing the driver to hand over her admission form pulled her already taut nerves further apart, and she fumbled in touching the fingerprint identification screen the silent guard offered to her through the lowered car window.

"Invalid. One more time, Ms. Hambre. Press firmly on the red circle." The guard handed her back the electronic scanner. Her finger trembled as she watched the blinking red light.

The guard nodded curtly at the change to a green flashing light. He stepped back, saying. "Thank you. You're all set."

Her heartbeat slowed once her admission to the Den had been settled, and she sniffed the air. These two guards with their golden eyes were shifters, beta wolves, and held no interest for her even though their muscular physiques might help assuage her cravings in a pinch. But they couldn't totally abate the mind-blowing urge for sex.

The driver grunted a response before starting through the gates that slowly swung open. A wrought iron fence surrounded the immaculately-kept grounds featuring yards upon yards of well-manicured grass rivaling a golf course. The Den was housed in the three-story brick and cement building up ahead, lit with flickering gas flames in ornate lanterns on massive columns. Two doormen decked in crimson-colored overcoats, dark hats and white gloves were at the front of the line, assisting clientele from their cars into the building. The doormen's movements were reminiscent of military precision in that no one actually milled about even though the parking lot was filling up fast.

Diana sat back against the leather seat, crossing and uncrossing her legs. She tapped her long manicured fingers against her knee, refusing to rearrange the hem of her dress for the fifteenth time.

She'd opted to wear a short little number, a black A-line dress and a laced up corset with garters to set the mood. Tonight required a little more motivation than signing forms and paying her bill.

A queue had formed in which shiny black cars similar to the one in which she rode were creeping toward the front entrance. She lowered the window a titch, glancing up at the overcast sky. Ribbons of clouds appeared to wrap around the sliver of a moon just visible and perilously perched overhead. Soon, the moon would fully rise and the heat within her would boil. The skin all over her body sweltered.

Diana jumped when the doorman opened her door, welcoming her into the club. After nodding, she moved past his gloved hand that held open one of the massive front doors. The heels of her strappy shoes announced her arrival within the entryway, tapping out of time to the music playing. She walked toward a woman whose inviting smile drew her across the polished floor.

Under a twinkling chandelier, the woman's copper-colored eyes mesmerized her. For a long moment, she forgot the lavish surroundings of the club and her reason for coming.

"Ms. Hambre, welcome to the Den. I'm Sherry. I'll escort you upstairs." The woman extended her hand. Sherry's tone and solid handshake calmed Diana's second thoughts.

Sherry started forward and continued speaking. "I hope our driver made the journey pleasant."

"Yes, he was more than hospitable." Diana's voice quivered. The trip pushed her buttons in all the right ways, and she arrived breathless from her journey in a privately-driven car by a tiger of a man. Sitting in the back seat, she'd nearly come undone from her level of arousal. Only her apprehension about making an unwelcome move on a club staff member had kept her sexual cravings in check. She couldn't…no, she wouldn't risk not having her needs dealt with as only the Downtown Den promised they would.

This heat cycle that leopard shifters experienced was common. Yet being without a partner, as she was, placed her in danger. Without question, she had to allow her sexual nature to be satisfied. Something she'd not done for nearly a year. So she'd silently drooled, observing the driver in his black leather pants, coupled with an inky shirt that seemed poured on, and accepted being reduced to a smoldering mess.

"Please come with me." Sherry's silky voice promised nothing but pleasure. "I'll show you to your room, unless you'd like to enjoy a cocktail in the lounge. There are several private members here this evening. Men and women who understand your predicament."

"No, I'd rather have a moment alone." Diana hugged her overnight bag to her side, unwilling to test her endurance one second longer than necessary.

"To unwind? You're smart. Fridays can be extremely stressful. Do you meditate?" Sherry asked, taking the lead.

"Not lately. My work schedule is so hectic. And now this…" Her voice trailed off. No need to mention the obvious.

Diana sniffed the air. An alpha scent lambasted her nervous system. She looked around, and there was no one else in the hallway. The scent was familiar. *Achingly familiar.*

"Christ," she swore, ever so softly. On top of everything else, her imagination was playing a mean-spirited game with her. She refused to give in to her warped olfactory ability even though she momentarily lost her concentration.

Sherry slowed her gait without warning. Diana had to swerve toward the wall in order to avoid bumping into her. She skimmed along the wooden panels for a few steps in order to avoid careening into several chuckling males who had just entered the corridor. Diana brushed back her bangs. Each of them nodded to her with garnet-eyed flashing interest, yet their scents were not the right shifter type to lure her. Only one shifter could ease her maddening carnal urge. Male. Alpha. Leopard.

"Sherry, a new member?" A man wearing an elegant black suit asked, hardly able to contain the wolf lick to his lips.

With one glance over to her, Sherry shook her head. "Gentlemen, we'll do introductions at a later time." A cast of hungry gazes erupted as pairs of glowing eyes traveled over her body; so sharp was their perusal it felt like having her dress torn from her body. Passing by, she had felt utterly naked in their midst.

Sherry stepped back, brushing against Diana, their shoulders coming into contact, and for a few seconds Diana's sensation of being hunted dissipated. The woman's skin was icy-hot, delivering a burn while at the same time cooling Diana's skin.

"You're not a shifter. Are you?" Diana said the first thing that came to mind. Sherry's eyes flickered, becoming obsidian black, then changing back to copper. "No. One reason I hold this position. If you're interested in venturing beyond your room, we have a sensational restaurant, or room service if you get hungry. I mean later, of course."

Diana nodded and waited. Nothing more was said. Obviously her hostess was not going to fully respond to her question.

She followed Sherry through a corridor lined with several doorways. All the while her escort explained the layout of the Den. They passed the restaurant where candlelight flickered over linen tablecloths. Diana sniffed the air, seeking the undercurrent of a hidden aroma that lay embedded within the gourmet-scented creations pouring from the restaurant.

Her skin tightened, and her nose twitched. "Tempting. I might come down later on." Diana pretended to admire the interior, clinging to the doorway of the restaurant. Her glance scoured the space, noting each of the inhabitants and wondering if, by chance, she was right in what she perceived. But no, she didn't recognize anyone present. For a second, the heavy feeling of disappointment sank into her limbs. A second whiff and her senses perked. Regardless of her inability to pick out the source of this alluring scent, someone was present who made the space between her legs grow moist. Her belly clenched, releasing a spasm downward. She pushed away from the doorway, confused, wondering how it was possible for duplicate scents to exist.

Diana trailed after Sherry, turning into another hallway at the rear of the club. Farther down, Sherry paused outside the club's main hub on the other side of the corridor.

The hostess pulled open one of the frosted glass doors. "We specialize in privacy. Our club prides itself on providing services in an unparalleled setting."

Diana observed several areas that were divided into a bar with an intimate dance floor off to one corner and what looked like cozy rooms. Some doors were opened, where couples sat eating, drinking, conversing. Everyone under control. Everyone rational.

Again she inhaled, and the pungent male scent saturated her lungs. She swallowed a jolt of concern over her flagging self-control and the need to unfurl her catlike claws and fangs.

The scent had to be one of the alphas, some imagining on her part. A growl twisted and turned in her breast. Her fingertips pulsed, with curved nails ready to spring outward. She longed to shift, so strong was this unbearable urge. If she didn't obtain relief soon, what would become of her…she groaned. There were places for wild shifters. None of those establishments were elegant or civilized.

No, the intake counselor had promised this was the place to find relief in the form of a shifter who'd service her for the night.

* * *

Diana pulled at the steel collar encircling her throat. The metal band weighted the top of her shoulders. She lifted the locked ring, moving the edge away from the base of her neck. For now, the collar rotated easily enough. She was unconcerned by the steel-gauged chain linking the band to an iron post. A necessary detail. The post was secured by four large bolts to the wall of the stark room. She tugged the chain with both hands and gritted her teeth.

"Ugh. Solid," she groaned, dropping the heavy links to the floor, convinced she wasn't going anywhere in the near future.

A wrought iron grate covered the outside of the only window on the opposite wall. *Good idea.* Diana crossed the room, kicking at the pallet on the floor. She stopped alongside the stainless steel sink. A matching industrial commode was housed in the corner, behind a Japanese screen.

Her whole body prickled with pinpoints of heat. So far, this irritating state had seared her body for two days too long. And now, inside the stark room, she forced her thoughts elsewhere. She studied a rectangular bin above the sink containing a rainbow assortment of condoms. The utilitarian vibe of the room was out of sorts with the sophisticated layout of the club downstairs. She vaguely recalled the aroma of roses, leather, and aged cognac from below. Her nipples tightened, remembering the scent of a man. One she recalled all too well amid a wave of lustful aching. She'd already agreed to stop compulsively reliving the delicious odor, licking her lips one last time. She shook her head, accepting it was some sort of sensory mirage.

Inside the room she smelled nothing but the sanitized floors and walls. No hot, dirty sex. Nothing of the sort…yet. Obviously, the room was scrubbed down to a hospital spic-and-span level of cleanliness. She gasped. *Just how out of control did other heat-frazzled shifters become in moonlight?* From what she knew personally, extreme recklessness occurred.

The gravitational pull assaulted her bloodstream in the same way the tides were pulled. Regular cycles each day, getting stronger and stronger. Hormones spiked in her tissues, running rampant during the rise of the full moon, and leaving her hunger to mate nearly uncontrollable.

If she wasn't careful, she'd lose all sense of decorum and any panther within twenty miles would know by her pheromones that she was hot and ready. To humans the scent would be unnoticeable, but every alpha male would perceive the patchouli rose essence emanating from her skin and sex; figuratively a bud in bloom during the apex of the full moon. The pull was too strong to resist.

She cautioned herself: Don't judge or guess your way into a further frenzied state. Her skin had begun to burn from a heat that boiled under her flesh. Soon, she'd have company.

Her belly lurched. She needed something to relieve the burning sensation of her skin. *Water.* She could cool her parched body with water. Diana untied her flimsy robe in front of the sink. She pressed the lever, releasing a stream of cold water over her hands. She ran a wet palm up her arm, then switched and repeated on the other side. The water droplets cooled her aching skin. Wetting her hands again, she rubbed her palms across her chest and over her breasts. Her nipples puckered into erect points. She pulled each pebbling areola, unleashing jolts of excruciating pleasure. She thumbed each tender nipple, again and again. Finally, panting, she cried out when no relief came. Her skin now sizzled as if sunburned. Blistering ripples of pain assaulted her every few minutes from the inside out.

Christ Almighty. They didn't call this a *heat* for nothing. She shuddered under the billowing fire spreading across her body and clenched her jaw, immediately catching the skin of her lower lip with two curved canines. She opened her mouth, swiping her tongue over dagger-pointed teeth.

Without gazing into a mirror, she could only imagine the changes taking place as her body shifted toward *panthera.* No longer would she peer out to the world through murky hazel irises, but through eyes flecked with emerald green sparks. At least that's what Cole had murmured each time she had shifted, and he had provided the heat cycle relief she craved.

Tears flooded her eyes, blurring the sight of the speckled rosettes forming over her skin. She blinked, noting the design had darkened remarkably in just seconds. Before long, a honey-colored coat spotted with smoky black designs would follow. She paced over the bare floor, coming up to a gouged, white wall. She turned and crossed back over the wooden planks, walking a grid in a search-and-rescue pattern.

Downstairs, laughter pealed. Voices erupted, followed by the crash of glass and applause. She prayed the loud occurrence was unusual for such an elegant club.

Out of nowhere, a devil-may-care attitude arose inside her. Her body shivered. Her sex throbbed. "Mmm," she moaned, crossing the boundary into believing a raucous evening would be exciting, in a club catering to solo shifters without mates.

That's what she was, and wasn't. At this moment she was sorely tempted to pound on the door and demand that an alpha-whatever be sent to her. This was the first heat in which she'd agreed to coupling without Cole by her side.

She closed her eyes, shutting out the unexpected raw vision of Cole's torn body. He had been the man she'd loved since high school. She fought against remembering him as she'd found at the bottom of a ravine. Cole was dead and here she was alive, throwing herself at a stranger. It should have been her at the bottom of the ravine. Not Cole, when he'd leapt to help her. *Cole — her mate — forever gone.*

Diana pulled the robe across her shoulders and cinched the sash around her waist. She turned away from the door, picking up the chain. She steered clear of the center of the room where a crimson column of heated light fell. Her eyes flattened and she could feel the elongation of her pupils, a physical sign of her leopardess cunning, prompted by the colored light which aided night vision. Unfortunately, it also fried her skin.

She peered up at the infrared light bulb within the ceiling fixture. Impossible to unscrew the darn thing. The ceilings were at least fifteen feet tall. Soon enough, she'd have no problem leaping up to punch out the light bulb, putting an end to the scorching red glare. Soon enough, it would be dark and she'd not need the light. Soon enough, she'd have company in the form of an alpha male who'd give her release from the torturous craving that rocked her mind and body.

A roar rumbled deep inside her, and if left unrestrained, she'd give in and let the vociferous sound tumble from her lips. And at this point, her cravings more than twisted her soul. One more night and she'd have sold her spirit to have one shifting male properly fuck her past this heat. The space between her legs spasmed. Her edgy condition, or the fact that she'd agreed to let a stranger fuck her into submission, no longer shocked or bothered her. She'd gotten past her morals, thrown aside her inhibitions, and overcome her loner tendencies when she'd almost pounced on Shawn, her boss, followed by a near streaking incident at home.

She shook her head. "Oh God, I've almost lost it." She continued pacing and swinging the chain.

After tonight's coupling, she prayed tomorrow would arrive with a hint of normalcy. Her current design project was running out of time with the deadline looming. She should have notified her boss and requested an extension.

Her whole body constricted when she thought of him and her near lip-lock fantasy. Shawn Barclay's muscular build and rugged good looks had sent her over the edge after a year of going it alone. Last Friday, before her heat cycle actually came on, she almost licked his face while they had stood shoulder to shoulder at her desk reviewing her work. Afterward she had left her office, telling the receptionist she'd be at home. She didn't understand why she had become out of control *before* her heat. It was no mystery that he was a shifter. Albeit just her luck, an alpha leopard. But not once had she sought any form of attention that wasn't strictly professional. Business all the way. That was, until recently — precisely, until this heat.

Once the cycle began, her cravings required she remove herself from temptation. So far, remaining inside her home and avoiding male shifters — all male shifters — had seemed to do the trick.

For the past year, contained within her house, she'd been able to weather the storm of monthly heat cycles while working flextime. A tremendous perk and the reason she'd accepted the position at Matrix Design. Shawn didn't care as long as her projects were completed on time. He was too good to be true. And what a body…she inhaled, closing her eyes.

*Shawn.* No wonder, she thought. Her boss waltzed around in sneakers and a pair of snug jeans that clung to his tight ass. He constantly complimented her work, to the point she hungered for him. Her one insurmountable problem boiled down to, Shawn didn't return her admiration. The man was all business, twenty-four seven. Shawn had this uncanny way of making her feel appreciated for her creative ability and work product. She would have sworn on a stack of Bibles an undercurrent existed between them, but not once did he reveal an ounce of carnal interest — which would have been tolerable had he not smelled good enough to lick. She sighed, wishing he admired her for something less ethical and more physical.

A pulsating spasm shot through her abdomen, forcing a caterwaul to expand within her chest, rising up her throat. Her eyes sprang open. She pulled at the collar in frustration, eyeing the door.

She drew in a breath to steady her racing mind. Hard fucking with a stranger no longer frightened her. Quite the reverse. She welcomed the moment a hard cock would save her. She was well inside her cycle of this body-wrenching heat when she'd made the mistake of thinking she could beat the odds. She had for twelve months.

Pride before the fall kept looping around her mind for the last month or two. Apparently, somehow her leopardess premonition had known she was close to breaking. She had already lived through one close call and feared she'd do something more than foolish without professional help. Last month, she'd lost it at the edge of the city's nature sanctuary and bordering private woods. She'd shifted without warning. She didn't remember much except running all night, for several nights in a row, and then waking up naked, dirty, and scratched.

Then, a day ago she hungered to run free again. Standing at her back door, shifting between her leopard and woman forms, she had sniffed the air. Thankfully, her neighbor's German shepherd had howled at a feline ear-piercing pitch. The sound snapped her back into human form long enough to close and bolt the door in lieu of running naked down the alley. With a brewing desire for her boss — and a newfound interest in streaking — she put her pride aside.

The Downtown Den had been a last resort yesterday. She'd requested an emergency intake. The cost of this stud service no longer mattered if she obtained relief.

Diana ran her hands through her hair. The chain rattled with each movement. Her choices were to sit or pace. She lowered herself onto the pallet covered by a clean, soft sheet. The cushion resembled a thick futon and was wide enough for two bodies. She crossed and uncrossed her legs, studying the shadows on the wall, letting her gaze wander out the window, up into the midnight blue sky. Hope mounted within her. Any second the door would open. She bobbed her head to the bass rhythm vibrating across the floor, wiggling her legs hard enough to make her breasts bounce.

She pressed her legs together, warding off the need to plunge her finger into her opening and satisfy her hunger. That hadn't worked since the time she almost bumped into her boss by accident, her hip grazing across his crotch. His scent continued to wrap her in cords of frustration. Now, she couldn't orgasm on her own. It was as though her body wanted one unattainable thing. Or shifter, really. This far into her heat, her appetite for sex had become unmanageable.

Without thinking, she rubbed her thighs together. Undulations swelled within her sex. She shivered as her unbearable longing awoke yet again. Any brushes against her slit exacerbated a hunger threatening to overtake her on the next breath. Diana nervously ran her fingertips along a row of scratch marks on the floor.

"Ouch," she cried.

A thick splinter stuck out from her skin. Without thinking twice, she used her teeth to extract the piece of wood. A droplet of blood formed on the tip of her finger. The pungent scent wasn't so much inhaled as the air was tasted. She sipped a wisp over her Jacobson's organ, perceiving her surroundings acutely. The smallest of bursts lit as she captured the tail end of an essence. She released a puff of air from her nostrils. A low, sawing growl escaped from her throat.

She sucked her finger, thinking she must avoid touching the deeply furrowed lines gouged in the wooden floor. For now she sat and waited, listening to the music from the dance floor downstairs pound a rhythm into her chest instead of focusing on her own racing pulse. She rued her decision to come up early into this reserved room, giving up the chance to enjoy a flute of champagne to blunt her needling anxiety.

Her blood raced, sensing it was almost time. The waxing moon would be overhead, creating an apex in her intolerable craving. She hissed in anticipation. Finally, she'd make her own scratch marks on this well-worn floor and upon the body of the alpha who'd agreed to take her on. She rocked back and forth, recalling the long questionnaire she'd filled out for the Den's intake counselor and then the photographs of countless men she'd been given to ponder. No one seemed better than the next, and she'd left the decision to the Den's counselor.

In Denver, there were several places where unmated shifters could go, including online coupling services. Daring shifters braved the underground clubs to seek fulfillment using kink and elaborate bondage gear, making this mere collar and chain appear very simplistic.

The Downtown Den was a highly regarded establishment known for confidential penchants, proclaiming experience in handling first timers in search of stud, and she'd sought services after learning about them as one of Matrix's clients. Here, the club provided a supervised face-to-face meeting where she could veto the chosen stud.

In truth, she needed a modicum of security, not for her but against her uncontrollable nature. In a BDSM club, she feared what would happen when her lustful nature let loose. She almost laughed at the thought of her needing assistance. What she required amounted to being leashed and unable to break free, but also protection against someone who'd take advantage of her. She wasn't up for a roomful of alphas who might tag-team a female. Some shifters mounted a female in heat simultaneously. Her pussy clenched and spasmed uncontrollably at the image of her body filled to the brim.

Diana stretched, arching upward, releasing pent-up energy. She had no doubt her own primal nature would get her into trouble if left unbridled. So she willingly sat with the steel collar locked around her neck.

When she shifted, she'd be almost six feet long and weigh in at more than a couple hundred pounds. Nothing dainty or fragile about her leopard body, and she wouldn't have to worry about splinters with a set of curved claws replacing her French manicure.

For more books by Susan Arden, check out

*Tempted by Trouble*

Praise for *Tempted by Trouble*:

"If you want a hot and sexy romance with a very sexy cowboy and a strong veterinarian that will not bend easily to the stronger body, whether animal or human, then you will definitely like *Tempted by Trouble* by Susan Arden."—Harlequin Junkie

"Ms. Aden penned a hot and sexy story for her readers to enjoy. Overall, this was a good book that helped me pass the time." —Night Owl Reviews